Review

Stefan Vučak is an exceptional writer. This book is classic, hard science fiction and will not be disappointing to any fan of this genre. The storyline is also classic science fiction; where an individual needs to make decisions regarding life and death, not only for himself, but for all of society. Some decisions are shocking, but all are made in the spirit of survival. Readers will find themselves wondering what they would do if placed in a similar circumstance.

Against the Gods of Shadow takes readers on a lightning fast adventure light-years away.

In the Library Reviews

I0592865

Books by Stefan Vučak

General Fiction:
Cry of Eagles
All the Evils
Towers of Darkness
Strike for Honor
Proportional Response
Legitimate Power
Autumn Leaves
All My Sunsets
F/X-26
28th Amendment
Night Sirens
Broken Rose

Shadow Gods Saga:
In the Shadow of Death
Against the Gods of Shadow
A Whisper from Shadow
Shadow Masters
Immortal in Shadow
With Shadow and Thunder
Through the Valley of Shadow
Guardians of Shadow

Science Fiction:
Fulfillment
Lifeliners

Non-Fiction:
Writing Tips for Authors

Contact at:
www.stefanvucak.com

AGAINST THE GODS OF SHADOW

By

Stefan Vučak

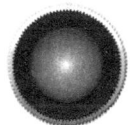

Dedication

To Ivanka … and her search for the far horizons

Acknowledgments

Eagle Nebula (M16) – Credit: NASA, ESA, and the Hubble Heritage Team (STSCeI/AURA).

Cover art by Laura Shinn.
http://laurashinn.yolasite.com

Map of the Serrll Combine

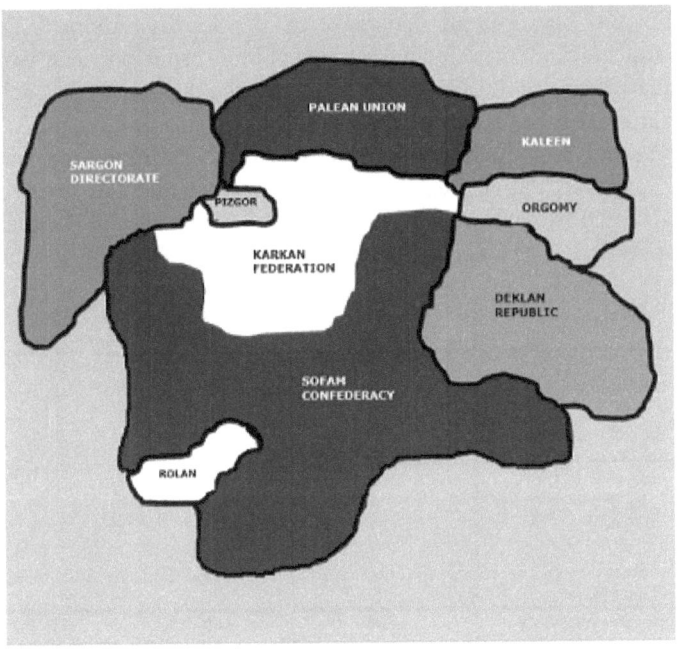

Composition of the Serrll Combine

The 247 star systems that make up the Serrll Combine is an association of six interstellar power blocks, split between two rival camps—the Servatory Party and the Revisionists. Each star system has a single representative in Captal's General Assembly from which members are elected to the ruling ten-seat Executive Council. Seats are based on a percentage of systems occupied by each power block in relation to the total number of systems in the Serrll Combine.

Name	No of Star Systems	Percentage of Total	Executive Council Seats
Sofam Confederacy	80	34	4
Deklan Republic	19	8	1
Palean Union	27	11	1
Karkan Federation	45	19	2
Sargon Directorate	30	13	1
Independents:		15	1
- Kaleen	8		
- Rolan	5		
- Orgomy	6		
- Pizgor	3		
- Other systems	15		
General Assembly	**238**	**100**	**10**
Outposts	44		
Protectorates	35		

Principal political blocks:

Revisionist Party:	Palean Union
	Deklan Republic
	Sofam Confederacy
Servatory Party:	Karkan Federation
	Sargon Directorate
	Nonaligned Independents

Composition of the Executive Council:

Security Council	Bureau of Colonial and Protectorate Affairs
	Bureau of Defense
	Bureau of Cultural Affairs
Administrative Council	Bureau of Administrative Affairs
	Bureau of Justice
Economics Council	Bureau of Economic Affairs
	Bureau of Technology and Development
Central Planning Council	Bureau of Central Planning and Development

Prologue

Against a backdrop of greens, yellows, and reds, lit from deep within by a trinary of furiously hot protostars, the nebula spread its fiery tentacles into the black deeps of space. Hidden in the stellar nursery a fourth protostar glowed a sullen orange. Thin lances of ejecta streamed out from its magnetic poles. Still young, its enriched core sustained by relatively cold fission elements. The reaction pressure kept gravity at bay until the moment when the star accreted sufficient material to trigger a collapse and induce fusion ignition.

Full of organics, heavy metals, and roiling plasma streams gathered from the ashes of long-extinct supernova sheddings, the nebula shone like a beacon; beautiful, but dangerous. Highly energetic particles sleeting outward from the core could tear apart the shield grid of any ship foolish enough to venture too close, destabilizing the distortion field matrix and dumping the unfortunate out of subspace to limp away at sub-light speed. Like a beacon, merchant ships and liners used the nebula as a waypoint when entering Pizgor space, or heading into Palean or Karkan deeps.

Three days out from planetfall, the crew of the Pizgor registered bulk carrier *Pagin* were irritable and weary. They wanted off the Sargon-made scow and taste open air again, uncontaminated by the accumulated scents of close living filters never seemed able to remove completely. On a last leg of a tortuous route picking up and delivering a variety of industrial stockfeeds, they wanted to see their families, old loves and perhaps make new ones. They wanted freedom to vent steam and lose sight of faces that had grown irksome and too familiar, if only for a while until the turnaround sent them out again. Pizgor offered a welcome layover where much needed

1

maintenance of ship and men could be made.

Gazing absently at the nebula displayed in the primary nav plot as it drifted by on their starboard quarter, the pilot allowed his thoughts to stray comfortably to his beloved partner waiting for him when they made planetfall. Quietly wise, she had grown philosophical about his need to wander the deeps and no longer tried to tame him. He didn't have to worry about his boys, both were grown men now and free to make their own lives.

He squinted when a white dot blinked into life on the big display plate. He glanced at his plot master and raised an eyebrow.

"Contact emerging out of Et-Aran Nebula's shadow. Indicating nav and primary screen only. Range, point-three-eight lights. That places them twelve minutes away at present closure rate."

"Mmm."

Chewing his lower lip the pilot watched with morbid interest as the computer rotated profile configurations of the unknown contact. His concern turned to relief when the final image stabilized.

"A picket M-3 sweeper," he mused and exhaled slowly.

"Contact has altered course and is heading for an intercept," the plot master announced.

The pilot nodded to himself. He expected that any prowling Fleet ship would want to check them out, but it could have been a different type of ship altogether. He sat back in his command couch, rotated it, and swept his eyes over his three watchstanders, seeing his thoughts reflected in their drawn faces.

Raiders…

Some of the raider scum were simple out-and-out marauders and freebooters preying on innocent commerce out of greed and easy profit. Others dished out mayhem and terror in the name of religious fervor. Of these, the Palean and

Against the Gods of Shadow

Deklan orders were the worst. The Almighty help those who fell into their clutches! They didn't satisfy themselves with simply taking cargo and ships. They took lives, and took them in the most grisly manner possible. In the vastness of Serrll space, there was a lot of room for misery.

"About time we had Fleet coverage. We pay 'em enough," the exec growled sourly and waved his hand at the main plot. "Not that the bastards are around when you need them the most anyway," he grumbled, his head bent over the engineering panel.

The pilot's thin mouth twitched. A year back, his exec lost a friend in a raider attack. The search never found anything, not even debris. The ship simply disappeared. Of late, lots of Pizgor merchant carriers were coming to grief, increasingly singled out by raiders. Judging by the results, or lack of them, the Fleet were doing precious little to root out the vermin. That left the risks and soaring insurance premiums squarely in the laps of ship owners and crews. With problems of his own, he happily left high finance to his owners. He had enough problems worrying about overdue maintenance. *Pagin* badly needed a thorough overhaul. Another run and they might as well scrap the scow. Everyone would relish a lengthy stopover on Pizgor.

"Raise them," the pilot ordered and nodded to his comms officer.

"There is heavy interference, sir. I'm not sure they have our ping."

Interference this far out from Et-Aran? Possible, but the pilot was not concerned. The whole region suffered from gravitational instability that induced localized subspace distortion.

"Give them a few minutes."

Three minutes later, the M-3 made contact. When the main plate cleared, the pilot looked at the stern features of a Palean Fleet officer. The image slightly snowy, broken from background interference, but clear enough. The Palean's thin hands twined in a characteristic nervous gesture and the long fingers twitched like coiling snakes. A delicate button nose glistened on a small triangular face above a pointed chin and high rectangular forehead. His enormous black eyes reflected no light. What struck the pilot were two purplish scars that angled from above the Palean's right eye and ran down across a pale cheek. One ended at the chin and the other cut across the neck and throat. They were striking disfigurations if it meant that modern genotherapy could not remove.

"Merchant vessel, this is First Scout Kai Tanard, M-3 picket SSF *Laverne*. Please identify yourself." The voice raspy, guttural and cold.

The pilot tore his eyes from the amazing scars. In a curious way, he felt reassured by Tanard's business-like approach. The underlying discipline meant efficiency and that meant no raiders, which made the pilot very happy.

"This is Pizgor registered bulk carrier *Pagin* on a return Deklan run from Pita. Ready to transmit ident dump. If I can add First Scout, you make a welcome sight."

The M-3 approached the carrier in a leisurely sweep. Its course would bring it close to the merchant vessel as it made a pass on its way out. The pilot thought nothing of it.

"You'll have a clear run home, Pilot," Tanard said with a thin smile that only touched the left side of his face. "Transmit ident."

The pilot glanced at his comms officer who touched a pad on his color-reactive console.

"Ident received. You're cleared for transit to Pizgor, Pilot," Tanard grated, nodded once, and cut contact.

"Bureaucratic crap!" the exec growled, shaking his head.

When *Laverne* got to within 28,000 talans, it raised its secondary shield grid. In the engineering spaces deep within the ship, almost directly above the phased array projector dome, the computer increased the level of energy management readiness. Stripped helium nuclei plasma powered the primary fusion chamber that fed the artificial antimatter convergence point and kept it from collapsing. The energy surge from particle annihilation channeled through the containment field into separation wave-guides. Most of the generated power surge directed into massive secondary bus nodes in the hull that formed the protective screens.

Laverne's secondary shield extended four talans beyond the primaries along almost spherical lines of force. With both shield grids in place, a cocoon of energy enclosed the M-3 that extended nine talans. The wave-guides allowed some of the energy to flow into a separate reaction chamber that flooded the single Koyami 2/F generator. Coils fully powered up, the computer waited for the command to synchronize the firing pulses with the shield management system and the ship would be ready to engage.

The pilot saw nothing unusual about the M-3 extending its shields, especially if it made ready to enter high boost, or checking out a strange contact. When the shields began to pulse, he felt his face drain and his mouth go dry.

"Sons of canal worms!" the exec snarled and lunged for the bright green flashing pad above the engineering panel. If nothing else, the emergency beacon pod would tell Pizgor SC&C they were gone. He never got the chance to launch the beacon.

Energy surged from the M-3's Koyami generator into the projector dome and formed an overload point. Slung beneath *Laverne*'s belly a track of dull yellow ionization lanced from the projector dome. It flashed between the two ships in a barely registered instant. A flare of secondary discharges ripped through the navigation deflector grid of the bulk carrier directly above the command bubble, the target carefully selected. The shield discharged around the impact point in a tangle of force lines that streamed around a yellow-green bubble of light. *Pagin's* nav deflector grid never designed to withstand impact from a warship immediately collapsed around the surge point.

A stream of eighty-two TeV sent in sixteen-millisecond pulses tore at the ablative hull material of the command bubble, forming an expanding cloud of metallic and ceramic debris. Under sustained bombardment the hull began to glow from dull red to searing white before it deformed and ruptured in a plume of molten spray from internal pressure.

When the M-3 opened fire, the merchant pilot knew he and his ship were doomed. That didn't stop him from feeling intense outrage at being betrayed by the very service meant to protect him. He saw death in the faces of his watchstanders and he could do nothing to save them. His nose crinkled at the strong smell of ozone as the air ionized from the near-field effect. Small blue sparks slithered across exposed surfaces, crackling eerily, jumping over naked hands and faces; a torment of a thousand insect bites. The three watchstanders plucked at their bodies, yelping and screaming in a frantic dance of contorted pain.

The pilot sat rooted, his face set in stony agony. *Pagin* gave a violent shudder when the screen collapsed and the internal temperature immediately soared. Audible computer warnings accompanied flickering alerts from the color-reactive display plates. The primary engineering panel glowed orange-white, indicating imminent power failure. Others pulsed brown in their demand for attention. The pilot felt his hair sear, the stink sharp, and looked up. The nav bubble heated bright white, spattering droplets of molten material on the crew below. The comms officer howled as fiery drops struck his face. He fell on the deck writhing, clawing at the burns. The hull creaked as frame plates deformed. The main plot display cracked with a snap that sent needle shards of polymer scything in all directions. The very air burned, cooking exposed skin, eyes, and lungs. The pilot managed a single anguished cry when the hull finally ruptured. Solid light tore through the command deck, vaporizing equipment and bodies, turning everything into glowing plasma.

Laverne shifted its fire to the carrier's drive spaces. The beam burned into the ship's hull and sliced through the antimatter reactor core. The screen collapsed entirely and *Pagin* immediately dropped out of subspace. Although no longer under direct fire, the reactor assembly breached. The containment field flickered and dissipated, setting off a runaway reaction. In a burst of white brilliance the reaction consumed the reactor core, blazing outward, turning the hull and the ship to vapor. As the expanding sphere cooled, it coalesced into an irregular cloud of sleeting particles and gas. The glow gradually died, leaving only a front of fading radiation.

Laverne powered down, dropped its secondary shield, and boosted back toward the glowing nebula.

Chapter One

Bulging and huge, Praxa dominated the sky and gave the impression it would fall and squash everything beneath it. An uncomfortable feeling and intellectually a baseless fear. Nonetheless, it took most people a while to make the emotional adjustment. So close to its primary, Lemos scooted in a tight thirty-nine-hour orbit around the gas giant to maintain its distance. In eons to come, it would be inexorably pulled into a tighter orbit and eventually torn into rubble by tidal forces.

Torn by violent storms, streaked with red, green, and muddy bands of nitrogen, ammonia, and organic contaminants, Praxa was a turbulent world. The different gas layers and the organics within them made it extraordinarily valuable as a cheap source of base chemical feedstocks. To Kai Tanard, hands clasped behind his back, fingers twining, Praxa was also a beautiful world to watch.

Praxa's sun hung low in the sky and dribbled out its yellow light with feeble enthusiasm. Outside, shadows were gathering, black and defiant. A thin wind chased a scrap of paper around the faintly glowing parking apron. His *Laverne* rested on the landing ring, connected to the ground by support umbilicals and an access tube. Two other M-3s lay parked beside it, legitimate Fleet units that belonged to Ril Seen, the base commander. He reminded himself he needed to call on Seen later.

Across the field, lights blazed from the open maw of a maintenance hangar. He could just make out *Zaradej's* stern, his specially modified cargo auxiliary, protruding from the edge of its holding cradle. The forced inactivity gave him a singular opportunity to refurbish the disguised carrier's single

Terrasec 8/B projector. Beside it, undergoing routine pre-flight checks, lay one of two haulers of his cover Tai-Mari Line.

"Well?" a softly modulated soprano inquired behind him.

He turned from the window screen and glanced sharply at the slim woman sitting casually on the corner of his desk. Tall for a Palean, gorgeous and deadly. Beneath a wide forehead, enormous black eyes, bold and provocative, silently mocked him, barely hiding her revulsion. Framed by a triangular face, her button nose accentuated a small, narrow mouth. Long flowing black hair hung straight to her waist.

"My intelligence shows an increased Fleet presence—"

"Not entirely unexpected," she said with a dismissive wave of her slim arm.

"You're missing the point, Re Nette. An increased Fleet presence implies that Captal may have gotten weary of Pizgor's complaints and finally decided to address the raider issue. I would start being very careful," he said affably, his voice harsh and heavy from his damaged throat.

"Oh, I'll be careful," she murmured with a seductive smile. Her single-piece light gray coverall clung without looking provocative, revealing a supple form. "You just keep giving me the targets."

"It might be prudent to cut back for a while."

She tossed back her hair. "I'll keep your suggestion under advisement."

He grunted and pursed his lips. *Have it your way.* He wouldn't be shedding any tears if she happened to run into an M-3.

"About your maintenance bill. You really should stop stressing that hull. This is your second major power plant overhaul in a year."

"I cannot catch them if I don't chase them. How much?"

"Four hundred thousand Serrlls," he said without a trace of emotion.

She winced at the scandalous price, much more than she expected. "With six fuel cells," she pointed out and her chin lifted in defiance.

"If you want the cells Re Nette, they're an extra three thousand each."

She pouted and turned her head slightly, which caused her finely shaped breasts to lift.

"That's plunder!"

"You want the cells, you pay the price. I don't dicker, you know that."

Re Nette climbed off the desk, shook her head, and placed her hands on nicely rounded hips.

"I'm good for it. In the two years we ran this venture, have I ever asked for anything? I even gave up good targets to make you happy. Palean targets!"

"I'm touched, really I am, but you weren't keeping me happy. It was your."

Her eyes blazed with fury, hating him. "You're worse than a thief, Tanard. A thief robs you once and you're rid of him. You, on the other hand, keep sucking without end."

"I run a business, not a charity. If you don't like the arrangement, you can always seek other opportunities," he said equitably. He could not forget even for a moment that behind Re Nette's beguiling eyes lay a cold, heartless killer. If he were to show weakness just once, she and her kind would pick him clean.

Raider scum!

He looked forward to the day when he would be able to take *Laverne* out and clean them all up. He savored the thought in a moment of pleasant anticipation.

"Urgh! The only opportunity I want right now is to slit your throat. My cashflow is rather tight right now and your maintenance bill hasn't helped. You know I'm good for it. Come on. I'll make it up to you on the next haul."

"I'm about to burst into tears, Re Nette. You know the

rules. No credit. You want the cells, I want to get paid."

She nodded slowly. "All right, but I'll remember this, and you better hope I don't meet one of your Tai-Mari ships out there."

Tanard walked to her and peered down into her eyes, the scars on his cheek suddenly brightening. He extended his arm and caressed her hair.

"If one of my crew develops even a sniff, darling, I'll be coming after you, and I won't be just taking your cash then."

She blanched at the naked threat in his deep black eyes, then smiled seductively and forced her slim fingers to run down his unmarked left cheek.

"Thief," she growled, backing down. His time would come, she'll see to it. "Two cells, that's all I can afford."

"And how were you intending to pay for them?"

"Lecher! I can give you some foodstuffs."

Tanard mulled it over. He can always resell foodstuffs and they both knew it.

"I'll notify Stores."

"You have a cushy operation here, Tanard. I wonder what the base commander would do if he knew—"

"Knew what? That this is a legitimate import/export business with its own repair facilities? Your complaint that I'm overcharging for my goods? Is that what you'd tell him?"

"I'd tell him a sight more, love."

Tanard laughed then, a horrible mangled sound. A bright red spot appeared on her cheeks and her tiny fists clenched in fury. He reached with his fingers and lifted her chin, his eyes boring into hers.

"Nothing personal in this, Re Nette. It took all of us a long time to get this going. So far, it's been profitable, very profitable. You wouldn't want to spoil it now…for the others. Would you…love?"

One of the major problems the raiders faced was lack of secure maintenance and logistics resources to service their ships. The other, shipping intelligence. The whole covert operation revolved around those needs, and Tanard provided both. For the privilege, he took a cut off the top. Early on, one enterprising individual thought to beat the game and refused to pay the squeeze. Tanard went out with his M-3 and personally took care of business. There were also a few untimely deaths in the families of the luckless raider crew. The other raiders didn't know how one of theirs vanished, but he had not been required to repeat the demonstration.

"I can't see how you manage to sleep at night," she snarled and walked out, the sliding door panels barely getting out of her way.

"I sleep just fine," he said softly to the retreating back and shook his head.

For some, it took a bit longer to get the message. What did she expect? That he would fall swooning at the sight of her enticing figure and beguiling smile? Stupid female! If she only knew what was at stake here. The bitter irony of the whole setup, he really didn't need raiders anyway. The AUP Provisional Committee in its infinite wisdom thought otherwise. To him, they were a major security risk, one that might compromise them all, but the operation had grown too deep and intricate to start changing the organizational structure now.

The comms alert beeped. He turned and tapped a pad on the inlaid console in his desk. The Wall cleared and he resigned himself to another dull pep talk.

"Friend Maran, a pleasure as always," he said formally as custom dictated. "And my apologies for keeping you waiting."

The Palean in the Wall frowned as his eyes flickered involuntarily across Tanard's scars. "Business?"

"An enterprising, ah, partner," Tanard rasped wryly to his boss and Le Maran nodded.

"You've kept up with the latest developments?"

"I understand Prime Director Kernami Asai Tainam received permission to address the General Assembly," Tanard said heavily and bobbed his head. "The Executive Council would not have done that unless they intend to take action."

Le Maran hooked a finger at him. "They already deployed additional Fleet units. The extra patrols have captured three raiders and destroyed another."

"You won't see me mourning."

Le Maran tilted his head slightly. "Not even for your own?"

"My own? Very amusing."

"If Kernami's petition is approved, our operation could become untenable, friend Tanard, and I don't mean because of an increased Fleet presence. We could become subject to a Bureau of Cultural Affairs intelligence penetration."

"Irrelevant. Lemos is secure and deniable," Tanard pointed out with a tight smile and Le Maran shot him a cold look.

"Nothing is totally secure or deniable. Especially where our raider partners are concerned. However, Fleet presence or not, the Provisional Committee wants you to intensify your operations. We must show Pizgor that even with Fleet support, they're still vulnerable. If we hurt them enough economically, the Triumvirate will fold."

"The Committee is wrong," Tanard said bluntly. "Instead of being aggressive, we should rein in our activities, at least until the situation stabilizes and the pattern of Fleet unit movements becomes more predictable."

"Your activities will be curtailed in any case. The raiders will know what is going on, if not from their own sources, then from yours. They'll be cutting back their raids through sheer self-preservation. At least the smart ones will. We must counter that. To continue pursuing our objectives, you will need to use your own assets."

"Isn't that defeating the very reason why we got raiders

involved in the first place?"

"The reason why we got them involved in the first place, friend Tanard, is that we couldn't achieve the level of penetration into Pizgor's commerce using our ships alone. I know you deplore the tactic, but the results have more than overcome your moral squeamishness. If we back off now the last three years of effort will be for nothing."

"So far," Tanard murmured absently and touched the scar on his throat. "It's not the Fleet we need to worry about, friend Maran. Like you said, it's BueCult. If they become involved, it means penetration in depth. Even if the Fleet units are eventually pulled out—CAPFLTCOM cannot keep them around Pizgor forever—BueCult will keep digging, and they don't give up. The Committee must know that."

"I will try and get you more information regarding the BueCult side of the penetration if it eventuates."

"Should they ever suspect we're using active Fleet units—"

"They suspect that already," Le Maran piped irritably and pursed his thin lips, hands working in characteristic agitation. "They just cannot prove it."

"You know, of course, the Fleet will start escorting commercial shipping."

"Then you eliminate the escorts," Le Maran said harshly and Tanard stared at him in disbelief.

"You can't be serious?"

"I'm perfectly serious."

"The Fleet will—"

"I know the implication, friend Tanard. Do you?"

Tanard bristled. *Oh, you little shit!* Le Maran could not mean what he just said. As a Fleet officer, Tanard knew more than anyone the presumption of this stupidity. Hadn't Le Maran learned anything from his last attempt to mess with the Fleet? Apparently not. Well, Tanard would not take the fall for this one.

"I need to have these orders on formal record, friend Maran." He smiled oily, hands twining. "Including my strongest protest at this action. I suggest this is inviting disaster."

Le Maran studied his protégé and gave his famous imitation smile.

"You don't want to be playing this game with me, *friend* Tanard."

"Oh? And what would that game be?"

"Careful you don't overreach yourself." Le Maran bit his lip, then nodded with a jerk. "If that is what you really want…"

"It is."

"You'll get it, then, but I must express my severe disappointment at your attitude."

"I regret that, and I am only pointing out a possible scenario, in case of any, ah, misunderstanding later," Tanard said sweetly, his mangled throat turning his voice into a rasping growl. "When I get your confirmation, you can inform the Provisional Committee that I will maintain the raids using my assets. Including action against Fleet escorts. One other thing. I want to renew my application to be relieved."

"When we're possibly facing a major disruption? Out of the question!" *Got you, you sly bastard*, Le Maran gloated. "You have a duty, First Scout, that outweighs any personal consideration. Carry it out," he piped and cut contact.

The Wall resumed its cycle of random color whorls, not dissimilar to Praxa's own display.

First Scout…It sounded more like hollow mockery than an honor, and Tanard felt sure Le Maran knew it. To the pits with him. Tanard grunted in disappointment and strode back to face the window screen. His application to return to normal Fleet duty had been a long shot at best, and playing this charade had grown tiresome. The Committee must know that the longer he stayed locked in this post, the chances grew proportionally that his cover with COMPALOPS, Commander

Palean Operations, would be penetrated. With the BueCult machinery likely to turn its attention on his activities, it would only be a matter of time before they caught up with him. He has already pushed the security limits now. Well, if he couldn't be relived, he would simply have to make sure Lemos could not be compromised and he didn't get caught. Executed as a traitor wasn't part of his game plan.

To date, the operation turned out stunningly successful, vindicating the Committee's bold strategy and the staggering investment. Three years ago when a senior Palean Congress representative approached him and the plan laid at his feet, he goggled with incredulity. His widely known dissenting views cost him promotion to Master Scout and made him even more determined to voice his dissatisfaction with the Palean's submissive role within the Revisionist coalition. His was not a lone voice. A fervent supporter of the Alikan Union Party, others also saw Palean interests coincide with Sargon's. In the end, he agreed to head the Pizgor project. What price patriotism?

Setting up the legitimate side of the business operation on Lemos turned out to be complicated, but uneventful. They picked a civilian to run the ground operation, and the humorous irony of the whole thing, Tai-Mari Line turned out to be very profitable and helped offset some of the running costs of his cover. The covert side took two long years of threatening and sucking up to raider pilots trying to convince them of the overwhelming advantages in joining the cooperative, constantly having to allay mutual suspicion and mistrust. In the end, ship by ship, they came. Despite the travails, they were also years of duty and opportunity undreamed of. To actually help shape the future course of his people! His part would be recognized eventually, he knew that.

If he could only shake off the growing feeling of foreboding.

Dismissing the thought, he turned his attention to more

immediate matters. Some of the raiders would undoubtedly be nervous or skittish. Le Maran was right about that. Still, the lure of easy profits would keep most of them in line, provided he did his part. Le Maran's easy dismissal of the Fleet as an operational threat represented a major concern. He considered Le Maran a fool if he did not see the danger. Captal's political machinery might be ponderous and slow to move, but it did move. Once started, it was equally difficult to stop.

No, Le Maran knew the implication, all right, he decided. The cold reality, Le Maran and the organization that stood behind him could not afford to be swayed by these developments. Too much lay at stake in time, resources, and expected results to be sidetracked now. In the larger scheme of things, the faceless men behind Le Maran considered Lemos expendable. An untarnished, if unpalatable truth, one Tanard had momentarily forgotten.

Still, attack Fleet units? He considered it a rash action borne of expediency.

All right, he would continue to raid, but the missions would need careful planning and organization if he were to take out his ships. He didn't relish getting caught by a passing M-4.

Out on the open apron hovered Re Nette's ugly ship. He stared at it for a while. Boxy, utilitarian, and deadly, a predator. A flicker of light caught his eye and he looked up. A large bulk carrier, its pale crimson nav grid pulsing, came down under SC&C guidance. It could be making a delivery or picking up, no way of telling. He watched as it settled smoothly, leaving it hovering two or three katalans above the apron. Flat cargo pads rushed toward it from the storage tank farm. Two slabs of the apron dropped away and from the holes emerged enormous hose couplings. They attached themselves to the carrier's hull and the flexible pipes twitched as liquids gushed through them.

So, the ship appeared to be making a delivery as well as

picking up, Tanard mused and swept his eyes across the sky. The atmosphere on Lemos thin and frigid, but at least it had one, and the moon's principal point of attraction, representing an incalculable saving in infrastructure investment that would otherwise have been necessary in a vacuum environment. He liked the night skies the best. Barely eighteen light-years away the Et-Aran Nebula provided a spectacular and free display. What entertainment Lemos otherwise provided verged on considerably more earthy and expensive attractions.

Hands twining, Tanard felt the fates suddenly crowding him, and not bearing gifts either.

* * *

Still early in the morning, beneath the white sun's relentless glare, the pale amber sky already swam and shimmered, turning the flowing sands into a silver sea that chased away the shadows. A thin wind, hot and parched, stirred the sharp dune crests and drove whispering sand into ribbed ridges along the sweeping dune slopes. A band of brown haze from a distant dust storm hugged the eastern horizon. The rolling dunes fell away and blended into beds of yellow sands and pea-gravel flats. Low in the sky, Aribus a dull gray crescent, waited to sink into oblivion after a tiring night.

With the wind tugging at his cape, Terr pushed back his hood and squinted. Against the shimmering horizon, the pale sands merged into browns and reds as they piled against the Katai Than escarpment heaving itself out of the desert. The cleaved buttresses separated the highland plateau beyond from the lowland plains behind him. A solidity and permanence about the towering, jagged cliffs brought from him a quiet nod of satisfaction. It also brought back mixed memories of his crash four years ago up on the plateau beyond. The burning sands failed to claim his life then, but they managed to take his soul, perhaps a crueler fate.

A shadow merged with his and he looked up at the tall hooded figure beside him.

"We should pitch camp," Terr muttered wearily and dropped his pack. He sat cross-legged on the cool sand and sighed, his leg muscles protesting at this unaccustomed abuse.

Dharaklin stood still, his sinewy two-point-three katalan frame a column of rock. The shadow he cast sharp and black. In a fluid economical move, he lowered his pack and pulled back the yellow hood of his brown surtaf robe. The vertical red slits of his large orange eyes betrayed nothing. The thin membranes designed to protect the eyes from fine sand slowly lifted, revealing an inner fire. His dark yellow skin dry, drawn tight over the bony ridges of his long face. His broad flat nose, nostrils flared, added to his skeletal appearance.

"We had a good walk, Sankri," Dhar said heavily, his deep voice lingering in the air like a ripple of dying thunder. Alien he might be, but as a Saddish-aa Wanderer, his brother deserved to be called by his warrior name.

Terr grunted and wiped oily sweat off his face. He unclipped the water bottle from his belt, bit into the spigot and took a long mouthful of deliciously cool liquid. He dropped the container into his lap and exhaled loudly, content.

"It will be a good walk once we reach the base of the escarpment tomorrow." He stretched his arms and swung them back until the joints creaked. "Right now, my legs are killing me and I need sleep."

Dhar chuckled, his narrow dry lips pulled back in a thin smile that revealed even brown teeth.

They found a little hollow where two low dunes merged. On the lee side, the morning breeze only a dying whisper. Its attraction lay in its shaded position as the sun burned across the northern sky. It would provide some protection during the day.

They scooped away the soft loose sand to enlarge the hollow, revealing a pea-gravel base. Two telescoping poles were driven into the sand face some one-and-a-half katalans above the ground, leaving them protruding about a katalan. The elbow joints folded down and the ends were driven into the gravel. They dropped an insulation sheet over the poles and secured it on the outside with piled-up sand. The spread surtaf robes made a soft ground sheet. It might have been crude, but nevertheless an effective shelter against the fierce day sun.

Sitting cross-legged, humming to himself, Terr rummaged through his pack. He didn't mind the rustic Wanderer existence, but insisted on a few simple modern conveniences, and rations were one of them. Munching on a bar concentrate, he looked up at his frowning gangly brother and grinned.

"What's the matter? Lost something?"

"I thought I had a jar of berry paste in here somewhere…" Dhar mumbled absently, pawing through his pack. His face lit up as he triumphantly held up a white ceramic container.

Terr grimaced at what was about to come. "Must you?"

Dhar frowned and shook his head in admonition. "This is the ultimate in culinary delight, you heathen."

"It's the ultimate in sensory assault, that's what it is."

Scowling in disapproval, Dhar unscrewed the jar and took a long sniff of the contents. Wearing a beatific smile, he waved the open jar at Terr with a flourish. A sharp pungent aroma immediately filled the shelter and Terr fell into a fit of feigned coughing while he wiped his eyes. The smell not really bad, a mixture of lube oil and rotting wood, a ritual they played every time Dhar unveiled the foul substance.

Terr stuck to munching his bar, occasionally shaking his head at Dhar's obvious relish at consuming the sticky reddish paste. He did try the stuff himself once. In fact, the delicious mixture, a leftover from the prana water-making process, was highly nutritious. Perfect desert food, but he had to get past the awful smell first.

As an all-purpose insect repellent, the paste had few equals.

Later, stretched out, hands behind his head and his pack for a pillow, Terr allowed the dry heat to suffuse through him. The scent of burned rock, sand, and dried tarad grass strong in the air, his spirit soared. Right now, without cares or responsibilities, there was no tomorrow, he felt happy. Next to him, Dhar already asleep, face relaxed and peaceful, the stern features now soft and vulnerable. A side of a Saffal Wanderer few ever came close enough to see.

Terr dozed off to the soft whisper of the sands.

* * *

Already dusk and cooler when they stirred out of their shelter, the crispness tempered the oppressive heat, heralding the creeping night. Overhead, blotched by winking stars, purple streaks smeared the sky. Low in the north the bent pattern of stars that made up Amulran the Damned burned bright, waiting for the Stalker to loose his arrow of revenge at his enemy. Those stars always came out first. A warning from the gods, perhaps? A message?

Feeling drowsy and lethargic, they took their meal in silence, each still living among the thoughts of his dreams. They collapsed the shelter and packed up. With darkness settling around them, they silently headed toward the stars of the Stalker and the dark escarpment.

It became easier once they hit the long stretches of rocky flats, leaving the rolling dunes far behind. They didn't talk much and there was no need for words. Each content to bask in the warmth of being together, sharing an intimacy in this reality far removed from the discipline and demands of shipboard life. Words would only limit and confine the bond they had.

Total silence ruled the desert. Only the soft crunch of gravel from their footfalls and even breathing made a hesitant intrusion. As night consumed them and it got colder, the sky assumed a bright, crystal clarity, and the stars burned steady. Terr reveled in the quiet satisfaction of reuniting with this land of wonder and magic that once tried to claim his life, and which he now came to love. Love also brings with it uncertainty, rejection, and pain.

The gods who ruled the Saffal deeps wanted nothing, and everything. The shadow of Death within which he now walked a heavy burden sometimes. He hadn't flaunted his power or used it to dominate another even when tempted. The mere fact that he could unleash untold destruction at a whim transformed him. Feeling invulnerable, cloaked with immortality, it was inevitable that sooner or later arrogance and pride would rear their ugly heads. Dhar understood him better than he thought, and his quiet, simple words of warning left Terr deeply disturbed. A sobering revelation that led to much soul-searching. Tomorrow, beneath the shadow of Katai Than, he hoped to find some of the answers.

'The mere presence of power is an influence', straight out of the *Saftara* chronicles…and he allowed himself to forget.

Deep into the night, Aribus lifted itself out of the desert; the fat crescent all golden and bright, and the sands came alive. The shadows gathered and hid the dips between the dunes, while the sand glittered and sparkled like fields of new snow. Terr paused, rested his left leg on a small boulder, elbows on his knees, and looked around in wonder. Seeing this, no one could fail to feel the pull of this land. Rima peeked over the horizon, still wearing a cloak of blood, but the moon would soon catch up with its larger companion and chase the shadows away.

Dhar met his eye, sharing the magic, and they continued their march toward the growing blackness of the escarpment that loomed before them.

Dawn broke out of a dark red sky and the stars fled. Towering over the landscape the orange and brown granite buttresses of Katai Than almost glowed beneath the sun's cool light, and the desert transformed. Dark shadows still lurked among the smooth cliff faces, and the sand pools took on the soft yellows and whites. With sunlight warming his left cheek, Terr gazed with satisfaction at the welcoming wall of rock that stood before him. To his right, not more than 120 katalans away, the cliffs opened to reveal a dark, forbidding gorge. Pointing at the opening, he turned triumphantly to Dhar and grinned.

"Hit it right on!"

Dhar frowned and chewed his lower lip. "Not *quite* on."

"Picky."

Pleased with himself, Terr rubbed his hands to kill the chill. Renewed with energy, they headed for the opening.

Shrouded in gloom and shadow the sheer cliffs stood protectively over a world remade. Stands of tall tarad grass crowded the mute canyon walls. Their broad spiky leaves were still curled until the sun coaxed them to open when it broke over the cliffs. Spare thorny brush poked timidly through the grass. An occasional solitary peelath, its wide leaves heavy and limp, leaned away from the rocks. Stillness and peace permeated the harsh landscape that went beyond mere tranquility and rustic beauty. Even the cold air held its breath, heavy with the sharp smell of rock and sand, of burned tarad and oily peelath.

Between the cliffs, the twisting dry watercourse worn smooth by ancient rains, making it for easy walking. The wild beauty and serenity of the rough backdrop tugged at Terr's heart. Since his crash, he walked these sands but once, fulfilling Sidhara's demand that he confront his demons. It took him another two long years, troubled years, to be here again, but why was he here? Did he seek to restore himself, to replenish some emptiness that had started to grow inside him? Instinctively, he knew he needed this moment to still, if for a while, the turmoil raging within him; a legacy left him by the gods of the Saffal.

Dhar, sensitive to his alien brother's mood, did not intrude. As a Saddish-aa Wanderer, he more than anyone understood Terr's ordeal. Intially, Terr had not wanted to come to Anar'on, preferring to spend their leave somewhere more boisterous. Dhar watched Terr's inner struggle with his terrible heritage, able to help in the only way possible—by just being there for him. In the end, still uncertain, Terr finally agreed, silently contemplating what awaited him in the desert keep. With quiet satisfaction, Dhar watched as his brother's spirit cleansed itself among the whispering sands.

They walked on in silence, aware of each other, alone with their thoughts.

After a time the dark cliffs opened to reveal a grassed valley floor and a still pond surrounded by a wooded glade of gently swaying peelath. Taklan moss palms leaned over dark, still waters. Long strands of moss hung limp from the branches and nodded at their reflection. The soft white sand of the small beach merged with the glassy brown pool without a ripple.

Arms hanging at his side, Terr pushed back the emotions that crowded him and turned to face Dhar.

"Nightwings," he whispered. "We're home."

* * *

"It's a conspiracy!" Kernami Asai Tainam thundered, his fist raised, and the Assembly floor erupted with a collective roar of thousands.

Standing tall and regal, his dark ebony eyes burned with scornful intelligence. His face narrow and gaunt, belittling his powerful frame, his skin almost black. He surveyed the chaos before him with quiet satisfaction.

The two visitor gallery levels that ran above the General Assembly floor were packed with Captal citizenry. A more than usual mixture of dignitaries from around the Serrll added flavor. Assembly sessions didn't normally attract a full house, but this one far from usual. An almost palpable undercurrent of excitement and expectation ran through the galley. Everyone wanted to see the Sargon and Palean representatives roasted. The session also held particular significance for the independent nonaligned systems, and the visitors didn't want the proceedings sanitized by government propaganda.

The din of rousing voices drifted and rolled through the chamber like booming surf. Raised above the main floor at the back of the chamber stood a three-tiered platform. On the second platform, arranged behind a horn table were twelve seats, now filled by nine somber-faced Executive Council directors and the Moderator. The upper platform held a longer crescent table for the senior commissioners, themselves engaged in huddled discussions. On the lower platform, four exquisitely upholstered formchairs were laid out for visiting dignitaries. Kernami stood there alone, grasping the sides of a transparent lectern. Above the platforms a giant Wall switched from the solemn faces of the directors to the uproar on the floor.

They built the General Assembly chamber to house nine hundred delegate seats, each seat holding a representative of one-star system. It would be a long time before they were all filled. An ancient building, round with a high domed roof, classical Sofam cursive adorned the rim between the dome and the ornate walls. Every few years some Assembly rep would motion the floor to tear down the structure, replaced with more modern architecture. Modern being so subjective, the various committees made it impossible to agree on a new design. So the building stood, patiently enduring.

"Order. Order!" Tari-Lama roared, enjoying himself hugely, and banged his gavel against the desk. "These proceedings shall come to order or I will clear the floor!"

The announcement generated gleeful hooting from the chamber and calls of derision from the visitor gallery. Any attempt to suspend the session would cause a riot and Tari-Lama knew it. Despite the seriousness of the proceedings, this was obviously not the time to stand on official protocol. He meant to give Kernami wide latitude to present his case, but that didn't mean giving him leave to flaunt all the conventions.

"I caution you, Prime Director, the Assembly will not tolerate flights of colorful rhetoric as a substitute for facts," he said, staring at Kernami with a distinct lack of approval.

Kernami raised an eyebrow at the ponderous form of the Moderator outlined in the lectern display plate.

"He cautions me!" He sneered at the floor and pointed an accusing arm behind him. "Pizgor is locked in a struggle for its economic survival and he cautions me! Palean and Sargon raiders are plundering our commerce and he cautions me."

This sparked a howl of indignant protest from Palean and Sargon representatives, as Kernami intended. Tari-Lama loved it, relishing the undisguised political process, away from the silent and deadly counterthrusts played within the Executive Council chamber. He banged his gavel furiously in a vain attempt to restore a semblance of control over what threatened to become a spectacle. Pleased with himself that he resisted giving into pressure from Palean and Sargon directors to grant Kernami a closed session, some laundry had to be aired in the open.

"Order! Order! I will have order or this session will be ended right now!"

The remark only served to trigger another round of applause and cheering as delegates jumped out of their seats, arms waving wildly. It took a while to restore a semblance of propriety, and only after the marshals bodily ejected some of the more vocal gallery visitors. Even after everyone had settled down, there remained an undercurrent of seething, hissing voices.

His patience strained, Tari-Lama rose to his full one-point-seven katalan height and glowered darkly at Kernami.

"And you, sir. If you persist at inciting the floor, I'll have you thrown out!"

Kernami gave a grim smile and swept his arm at Tari-Lama and the other executive directors.

"And I submit that this august body has already thrown me and my cause out," he said with dignity, then turned to survey the Assembly floor. A dangerous gamble, but sometimes one had to gamble to win. The prize this time, Pizgor's very survival. He nodded to himself at the ensuing silence and grasped the sides of the lectern. "I'm charged with making wild accusations. I in turn charge the Assembly with dereliction of duty and failure to uphold the Constitution and the Articles of Association. I charge the Executive Council for its complicity!"

That almost ended it. Even some of the commissioners were making protesting noises. If Kernami sought, his approach would not get him any. The media thrived on it. Assembly sessions were usually dull and stuffy affairs. This one shaped to be a ratings buster.

Ed-Kani Takao rose and locked eyes with Kernami, his quiet dignity radiating a frosty hostility. His icy blue-white eyes were blank windows set wide on a narrow, bony face. Completely hairless, it offset the deep character lines around the eyes and mouth. He pulled back his lips into a toothy smile.

"Mr. Director, you were given a singular opportunity to present your case to the Assembly. If you have evidence supporting your charges against the Sargon Directorate, I would urge you to present it. Emotional outbursts are a futile gesture, wasting everyone's valuable time." The last delivered with an almost silent hiss as he snapped his delicate jaws several times. Without taking his eyes off Kernami, he settled himself back into his seat.

No one could mistake Ed-Kani's warning or enmity. The considerable power wielded by the Sargon Executive Director should not to be forgotten or underestimated. Sargon could make life much more difficult for Pizgor in many more subtle ways. Kernami acknowledged the warning with a barely perceptible nod.

Tari-Lama banged his gavel and shot Ed-Kani a look of clear displeasure.

"The Chair has not recognized you, sir!"

Ed-Kani shrugged stiffly, unconcerned. He might have failed in preventing Kernami from having his moment of glory before the Assembly, but that did not mean he or Sargon had to take cheap tirades from the provincial. Utter nonsense anyway. All this fuss over three lousy systems. It is not as though Sargon would plunder and sack them if Pizgor ceded. Couldn't Kernami see that? Sargon would not interfere with Pizgor's internal machinery. It was simple politics and numbers.

Tari-Lama fumed. Damnation, this was getting completely out of hand. He allowed a trace of pique to creep into his voice as he pointed his gavel at Kernami.

"I will not tolerate this kind of behavior from you any longer, Prime Director. This is your last warning."

Kernami heard the words and sensed the Moderator's growing frustration. What can the old fool do to him anyway? He checked that thought. Needlessly antagonizing the Executive would not be prudent. In the end, the Assembly would give him what he wanted. The evidence he intended to present irrefutable, but their memory and mood a fickle and transitory thing. He cannot afford to forget the Executive Directors ruled here, and there was nothing wrong with their collective memory. To them, Pizgor represented a minor irritant, which they could go on ignoring if he pushed them too far.

With evident reluctance, he swept his gaze over the nine directors and commissioners seated behind them, and gave a curt bow. Bitter as the taste might be, these men controlled the Serrll, and he needed their help.

"My apologies, Mr. Moderator. It shall not happen again."

Tari-Lama nodded stiffly. "Then proceed, if you please."

Damned provincial!

Kernami had turned the Assembly session into a personal performance, and well done, he admitted grudgingly. It's not as though the wily devil didn't have a case, and he played the emotional card to the extreme.

Facing the floor, Kernami clasped his hands behind his back and thrust out his powerful chin.

"Pizgor is not a major power; three systems and two outposts. That's all. By virtue of our location, we turned Pizgor into an important commercial hub. We happen to be at a nexus through which several vital trade corridors intersect; routes between Sargon, the Palean Union, and to a lesser degree, the Karkan Federation. In the past, this position generated considerable commercial benefit for our systems. Benefit that enabled us to maintain our independent nonaligned status." He paused, allowing the audience a moment of anticipation.

"That was in the past. Now, dreams of an empire are threatening to end our very existence!" he thundered and chopped with an open hand before him. "An empire that's even now swallowing individual independents in order to bolster its percentage of held systems. Kirkov and Tolan 2FB, gone in the two years since the last general electoral session. Now, those forces are eyeing Pizgor! Having failed to seduce

29

us with hollow diplomatic platitudes and empty economic inducements, they now seek to force our cooperation by blatant disruption of our commerce." Kernami brought himself up to his full height and pointed an accusing finger at the Assembly.

"I accuse the Sargon Directorate and the Palean Union of orchestrating a policy of active destabilization of an independent group in blatant violation of the Articles, and I seek your help to stop them!"

Beautiful to watch, the floor on their feet, applauded, jeered or protested. The visitor's gallery loved it. Waves of noise swept through the chamber while Tari-Lama, enraged, ineffectively pounded his gavel. Order finally restored, the air tingled with tense anticipation of more to come.

Tari-Lama gave a final bang with his gavel and stared fixedly at Kernami.

"Mr. Director, I hope you're able to substantiate those allegations. The Assembly takes a dim view of any breach of the Articles or the sovereignty of its members. However, it takes an equally dim view of attempts to subvert the due process using hollow histrionics."

Since the Revisionists controlled the government, it was a foregone conclusion the Executive Council would authorize action to investigate Kernami's claims. However, more lay at stake here than Pizgor's immediate problem, and the Revisionists were looking at other issues. Any Sargon/Palean merger would relegate the Karkans to bit player status and destabilize the Servatory Party. The Revisionists wouldn't mind seeing that at all. Unfortunately, such a merger would also plunge the Serrll Combine into political and economic turmoil, and perhaps general warfare. That could not be tolerated. Even if it meant indirectly bolstering the Karkans—what a thought! The Executive could not afford to forget that the Captal government ruled for all.

Against the Gods of Shadow

Kernami knew he had Tari-Lama's support and the support of the Revisionist Party directors, regardless of the fact that they were using Pizgor for their own agenda. It wasn't over yet. He tapped a pad on the lectern's control panel and the giant Wall behind him cleared to show a holoview schematic of Pizgor, Sargon, and Palean borders. Deep orange lines traced the major trade corridors, all converging and crossing through Pizgor space. A network of bright blue dots surrounded the five systems. Many clustered around the Et-Aran Nebula in Palean space, twenty-eight light-years from Pizgor.

"There you have it, and it's not histrionics," Kernami said with a sweep of his arm and waited for the Assembly to digest the information. "That chart represents two years of raider activity on our commerce." The view expanded to include a substantial portion of space around Pizgor. The incidence of blue dots displayed an all too clear correlation with trade routes that wound their way deep into Palean, Karkan, and Sargon space. However, the density profile in striking contrast to the evident abnormality that surrounded Pizgor. The rising murmur from the floor showed the point had not been lost on them.

Kernami tapped another pad and the Wall began a regression sequence.

"A year ago," he said quietly, the force of his words unmistakable.

Everyone could see a clear reduction in the density of dots surrounding Pizgor and the intersecting shipping lanes. The other routes maintained their random distribution profile. After all, raiding *was* profitable anywhere, however abhorrent to the victims.

Kernami did not bother watching the repeater plate set into the lectern, concentrating instead on gauging the mood of the floor.

"Two years ago."

The density reduced even further.

"Three years ago."

The buzz from the floor now pronounced. The distribution of raider events around Pizgor and its approaches assumed the same random pattern as for incidents elsewhere in the Serrll. It was a devastating demonstration.

Tari-Lama had seen the figures and the graphics as part of Kernami's submission to address the Assembly, as did the other Executive Directors. Most of them conceded that Pizgor had a legitimate grievance, to the fulminating protests from Ed-Kani Takao and Tao Karam, Palean's senior representatives. They were voted down and Kernami received his hearing. No one could have predicted, though, the effectiveness of Kernami's performance or the impact of his charges. Could those charges be really true? On the surface, the statistics were damning and were even now being checked by the Bureau of Economic Affairs. Tari-Lama had to keep in mind that Ed-Kani Takao ran the Economics Bureau. Would the senior Sargon representative attempt to thwart the investigation in the pursuit of his merger policy with the Paleans? For the stakes they played here? Something to watch, but if Ed-Kani sought to manipulate the due process, he ran a fearful personal risk, as was Sargon.

He banged his gavel, deep in thought.

"A very effective display, Mr. Director. On the basis of your presentation the Executive Council is inclined to acknowledge abnormal levels of anomalous raider activity around the Pizgor group. Can you now demonstrate how this implicates the Palean Union and the Sargon Directorate?"

The wave of murmuring from the floor and the gallery indicated a tense expectation of another fiery outburst. Kernami bowed to Tari-Lama and faced the floor.

"Under the umbrella of the Alikan Union Party, our two giant neighbors flanking us seek to establish themselves as the power in the Servatory Party opposition. It's no secret they see themselves supplanting the Karkan Federation as the senior coalition partner in opposition to the Revisionists. Before they can aspire to realizing this lofty goal, they need a third seat in the Executive Council. Everyone here knows what that means. They need to boost their quota of held systems to at least twenty-five percent of all member systems. Ordinarily, Pizgor would not care what they do among themselves, but when they seek to achieve their ends by swallowing isolated independents, we take notice. If through inaction, this Assembly allows Pizgor to be swallowed by one of our neighbors, Sargon will win and the Serrll Combine will be wreaked from within."

Elderly, still vigorous, Tao Karam stood up. "If the Moderator will allow a question?"

Tari-Lama turned toward the Palean. "The Chair recognizes the senior Palean Union representative."

Tao Karam nodded and twined his hands. "The Assembly has been presented with entertaining speculation mixed with questionable statistics. As a recognized nexus of trade corridors, everyone would expect Pizgor to come in for more than its share of raider attention. I now ask Prime Director Kernami to tell us how this translates, as he so colorfully puts it, into a conspiracy."

Kernami smiled at the wily old Palean. *This will be sweet.*

"I will be glad to," he breathed. "Director Tao Karam is correct when he asserts that Pizgor's trade nexus is a natural magnet for raiders, and it is, but it's not that simple. Analysis of raider activity on our commerce, attack profiles and location densities, clearly show that this level of penetration is beyond anything even groups of raiders could sustain, let alone mount. Such protracted effort requires coordination, logistical support and control. As everybody knows, raiders are loners, opportunists who shun any cooperation or control, unless the profits are so overwhelming as to outweigh the risks. I submit to this Assembly, only sophisticated organization and

a communication infrastructure can execute the demonstrated and sustained level of raids perpetrated against us. I
also submit this infrastructure can only be supported from a
central base of operations. A base provided by, supplied and
protected by Sargon and the Paleans to further their merger!"

* * *

"Prime Director, do you realize the magnitude of your
demand? Ach!" Sill-Anais retorted incredulously, trying hard
to keep amusement out of his voice.

The man was indeed provincial if he could not see past
parochial delusions. As a main trade nexus, shipping corridors
around Pizgor presented an almost irresistible target for raider
attention. But a campaign by Sargon and the Paleans to stifle
the three core systems as a preliminary to a takeover? It
seemed incredible. Still…Sill acknowledged the *possibility*,
however outrageous. Despite Kernami's assertion, there had
to be a more innocuous explanation. The alternative could
plunge the whole Serrll into open warfare. Sargon wouldn't
dare!

Standing beside the floor-to-ceiling window screen, Kernami watched streams of communals, combies, and private
sled-pads wind their way through Captal's darkening sky. In
the distance, murky haze swallowed the city. What did people
down there know of Pizgor's struggle, or care about it? If Sargon did swallow Pizgor, would it even be noticed? Probably
not, he mused. The loss of his five systems would not be
newsworthy enough to warrant a mention. He knew he was
being cynical, but whether the comfortable masses below
knew it or not, the status of every nonaligned independent
system might be threatened, and it was his job to make them
aware of that. If Pizgor fell, the Paleans would openly move
on Kaleen. Sofam stopped them doing that once, but would
they care to do so again if the merger succeeded? The Deklans

would carve up Orgomy, and years of work to make the Unified Independent Front a political reality would be destroyed. With it would also be destroyed the moderating influence the independents wielded within the Executive Council with their single seat. The Captal government could become an autocratic bureaucracy, severely limiting individual freedoms.

It simply made it all the more imperative his efforts did not fail.

The political road he trod a rocky and tortuous trail. Twelve years in the Triumvirate Assembly have prepared him well to deal with external and internal obstacles. Wresting control of the Triumvirate was only a stepping stone. One more year and he would complete his first eight-year term as Prime Director of the Pizgor group. Behind him lay achievements to be proud of. Surrounded by Sargon and Palean systems, Pizgor could not expand. It could grow in other ways, and under his leadership, it had. He invested heavily in infrastructure of the two outposts, to the maligning of his opponents and doubts within the Triumvirate. In the end, the gamble paid off. The young and the vigorous took up the challenge to mold what they saw were better worlds, certainly different.

Still to be completed, his greatest satisfaction lay in the expansion and integration of cargo receiving and handling facilities on the three principal worlds. The offshoot had been steady growth in Pizgor's shipping ventures that brought in valuable revenue and helped finance local public infrastructure and facilities, while raising everyone's standard of living. Would the people continue to accept his policies and the frenetic pace of change by his administration? Although he expected a comfortable nomination to a second term in the next year's Triumvirate elections, he could not afford to stumble. Supported by Sargon and Palean funding the conservative factions would instantly pounce and drag the populace into ignorance and blind servitude. He cannot allow even the possibility of that happening.

He swayed the Assembly with his flamboyance, but he needed to know if Captal was serious in its commitment or merely sought to brush him off with bureaucratic maneuvering. His gamble fraught with its own dangers, he felt irritated that Tari-Lama chose to handle the issue by two commissioners rather than at the Executive Council level. Perhaps that was simply his ignorance of the due process. Whatever the reason, he wouldn't leave Captal until he got what he wanted.

He half turned and swept his hand at the somber order of the Center and the sprawl of Captal beyond.

"What do you see out there, Mr. Commissioner?"

Sill glanced at Enllss, who didn't even twitch an eyebrow while maintaining diplomatic inscrutability.

"Stability," Kernami said firmly. "A certainty in your future, gentlemen. For the people out there, even a measure of contentment. The only thing concerning them is satisfying their drives and ambitions. Anything else is completely incomprehensible or irrelevant. Even the naked political struggle between the Revisionists and the Servatory Party is merely a diversion to be debated as an intellectual preoccupation, not something to be fought over."

Sill sat back into the yielding couch and pulled at his chin. Lines of responsibility etched their marks on his dry, pinched face. His brow may be knitted in concentration, but his wide-set green eyes were alive with interest. Kernami had shown a level of innate skill on the Assembly floor, but he lacked experience dealing with Captal's political machinery. His frontal assault on the Assembly effective only because of its novelty. Still, if Kernami thought the Executive was moved by Pizgor's plight, he would be disabused. His presence merely a fortuitous coincidence of events that allowed the Executive to address two problems within a single objective. Gazing at the grim determination of the towering alien, Sill reminded himself that this meeting was a culmination of almost two years of relentless lobbying by the Pizgor Triumvirate, and its leader in particular. He admired his persistence.

"You can save your sales rhetoric, sir. The Executive has agreed to review Pizgor's situation and I am tasked with executing it. Ach! But what you're demanding is extreme."

"Extreme? Abolition of raiders is extreme? Stopping political bullying is extreme?" Kernami raised his eyebrows and gave a rueful smile. "Given Captal's predilection for inaction, perhaps my expectations are extreme and my trust in the due process misplaced, seeing how Deklan itself has in the past used those same tools in the execution of its expansionist policies."

Sill bridled, stung by the half-truth of the remark. Impatiently, he ran his fingers through the two bands of gray in his otherwise white hair, and his eyes clouded. This infidel would lecture him on political correctness or observance of the Path? Sill took a deep breath.

"The qualitative difference in the pursuit of our policies, sir, the Deklan Republic uses the rule of law to achieve its objectives. We don't stoop to using raiders."

Kernami raised open palms before him. "Forgive me. That was unconscionable, Mr. Commissioner," he said in contrition and bowed. "You have my unreserved apology for that thoughtless remark."

Sill nodded stiffly. Still smarting, he nevertheless respected Kernami's tactics. The apology undoubtedly sincere, as was the reminder of Deklan's less than glorious past. If he were honest with himself, that past also reflected the Synod's present misguided policies as well. It would be useless to deny that Deklan lusted after the nonaligned Kaleen and Orgomy worlds. With the pending merger of those two groups into what would become the Unified Independent Front, that longing was destined to become an unrealized one. Thwarted from the Path by heathen infidels. An insufferable situation and a sin against the Path! He checked the unworthiness of his thoughts and muttered the words of the second litany of subservience, praying for forgiveness and enlightenment.

"I shall consider it but an aberration in the context of wider issues at hand here," Sill said, still slightly miffed.

Enllss-rr propped his chin with the palm of his hand, thoughtfully studying the imposing figure of the tall Pizgor leader. He had never seen Kernami before, but he recognized a competent politician at work. Kernami played Sill beautifully, histrionics and all. This might give him momentary satisfaction, but he skirted danger with his provocative tactics. No one takes kindly being held up to ridicule, and Deklan was particularly prickly where Orgomy was concerned. Sill was also a priest of the Path and a real power in the Ecumenical Synod on Deklan. During his twelve years in the Assembly, Sill nurtured a reputation as a careful and decisive decision-maker. His elevation to Commissioner for the Bureau of Cultural Affairs two years ago, all too clearly demonstrated the care with which he took in shaping his political career. The very Bureau Enllss used to head and Sill used to be one of his Branch directors. From their early clashes on the Assembly floor, he came to respect Sill's enormous abilities. Kernami had to know Sill was nobody's fool. So why goad him?

Strictly speaking, as Commissioner for the Bureau of Colonial and Protectorate Affairs, Enllss had no business sticking his nose into the Pizgor affair. When Sill asked him to attend, he accepted readily, with Tari-Lama's unreserved approval, probably because Enllss was a Sofam Confederacy Assembly rep and Sofam wanted to keep an eye on the proceedings.

He cleared his throat and reached for the still-steaming pot of special herbal tea. His powerful and muscular body alert to the underplay of nuances around him. He filled everyone's cup and leaned back into the folds of the formchair, savoring the redolent aroma permeating the room, his dark gray eyes noting everything.

Unabashed, Kernami walked to the low table and lowered himself into a formchair. He picked up his cup and sniffed appreciatively.

Enllss knew Sill detested the brew and served it only to humor him. Outside, dusk stole over Captal, tingeing the sky with streaks of red. The city already ablaze with light and color. Unobtrusively, the services management system increased the brightness of the walls and the ceiling, lighting the open office spaces.

"You're quite correct, Mr. Director, when you say that what you see out there represents stability," Enllss mused and sipped at his tea. A smile lifted a corner of his mouth as he scrutinized Kernami over the rim of his cup. "Despite your highly effective eloquence on the Assembly floor, sir, Pizgor cannot say that it isn't enjoying the same level of stability."

Kernami lowered his cup and looked at Enllss in astonishment. Could Enllss have penetrated his objective already?

"You cannot mean that."

"I do mean it. Consider. Is your populace oppressed? Is there warfare? Is there persecution or denial of personal liberty?"

"The political and economic cost—"

"Exactly, sir," Enllss said quietly and thrust out his square jaw. "Only Pizgor's political sovereignty is threatened—"

"Only? I suggest that much more than our sovereignty is threatened, Mr. Commissioner. The whole foundation underpinning the right of independent systems everywhere to exist is threatened. The tenets of the Serrll Constitution are now undermined by Sargon's aggression!"

"Perhaps. How does that impact on the quality of life of your citizens?"

"Without freedom and the right to self-determination—"

"Hypothetically speaking only, would the Triumvirate disappear if Sargon or the Paleans absorbed Pizgor?"

Kernami's internal struggle evident, his dark ebony eyes burned bright. "The threat to Serrll stability—"

"Is purely a political dimension." Enllss smiled with grim satisfaction.

"*Purely* a political dimension? Hardly that. The trade network supporting the prosperity of all is attacked here."

"Which is an economic threat only, is it not? The populace tends to rise up and swallow governments only when their basic material needs fail to be met. Consider Sargon. Despite their martial and authoritarian regime, their rule is generally a peaceful one. To ensure they remain in power, the ruling elite gives the people what they want. I would suggest, Mr. Director, by threatening your commerce the raiders are undermining only your economic policies, which I suggest is Pizgor's principal concern," Enllss said, forcing Kernami to acknowledge the blunt reality of his position.

Kernami pursed his lips in frustration, then smiled ruefully.

"You would know a lot about that, Mr. Commissioner. Economic warfare is Sofam's principal weapon of choice."

Enllss chuckled without taking offense and placed his cup down with a soft click. He would have been keenly disappointed if Kernami failed to recognize *all* aspects of Pizgor's predicament.

"And we have achieved much with it. Not least securing the senior position in the Revisionist Party coalition and a government majority on Captal. With the history lesson cleared up, let's move on. Despite what you profess to believe or say, Mr. Director, the Captal government views the level of raider activity on your commerce with gravity."

"You mean, the Paravan Trading Association does." Kernami did not want to annoy the commissioner unnecessarily, but he needed to be convinced.

"They may be only shipping and trading conglomerates, insurance underwriters and financiers," Enllss said casually, his eyes sparkling. "In your view, bottom crawling, scum-sucking profiteers. Not at all worthy to be associated in the same breath with lofty ideals such as political self-determination, or a lone cry for freedom about to be stifled by an insensitive empire, right? Before we all get swept away with patriotic fervor, it would be prudent to remember that those same scum also enables the Serrll to enjoy a remarkable period of stability you admire so much. I would therefore table my pretensions and cheap shots in the interest of achieving my objective. That's to facilitate Pizgor's traders to operate without hindrance or threat in the pursuit of *their* profitable interests. Does that sound about right?"

His cup poised before him, Kernami looked thoughtfully at Enllss. "While Sargon and the Paleans are set to annex us?"

"Please! That one made good copy for the late news, Mr. Director, but you cannot be so naive to think Sargon or the Paleans would do anything so foolish—"

"I don't know anything of the kind! Their raids—"

"Are crude instruments of persuasion, not an invasion force. Contrary to popular folklore, political objectives are *always* subservient to economic ones. You must know that, otherwise, you would not be here pleading your cause."

Kernami nodded with a gleam of open admiration in his eyes. Enllss was wily and he should not seek to deceive him.

Sill watched the exchange, comfortable with Enllss dominating the dialogue. Although his operation, he didn't mind. On the Assembly floor, Enllss had been a skilled debater and a formidable opponent. Their clashes were classics of partisan ideologies, but Sill knew when he was outmatched. Enllss didn't hesitate to field a razor tongue as a foil to his keen intellect to totally destroy an opponent. Kernami might be good in his own environment, but he had never been tested in the crucible of the Assembly floor, as many a shattered career testified.

"Mr. Commissioner," Kernami said, "although I agree with you in principle, Sargon's tactics against us demonstrate that in our case, their objective is hardly an economic one."

Enllss grinned, his smile now predatory. "That's why they will fail. If they'd been prepared to simply attack you economically in any serious way, you would be part of a Sargon Prefecture even now."

Kernami chuckled and nodded. He could work with these two.

"I apologize if I appeared to be provoking you. I needed to know if Captal is serious about helping us. Since we're to talk about objectives, I may look it, but I am not *that* naive to believe Captal's resolution to help us is prompted by a sudden gush of concern for Pizgor's economic or political plight. I suspect you just happened to see both of these interests coincide with yours."

Enllss smiled. "My dear, Mr. Director, please understand. Raider activity has a social impact and the government was compelled to act. You merely accelerated the process. Whereas what Sargon and the Paleans are doing is personal, revolving as it does around individual political power."

"You're right to remind me of the distinction. However, the results for Pizgor are equally unpleasant, regardless of the motivation. Since the political dimension of Pizgor's plight has already been addressed, what's Captal going to do about our economic one?"

Sill leaned forward. "Ach! That, sir, is what I want to talk to you about."

Chapter Two

"Why am I not surprised you called?" Anabb growled at the Wall, his chiseled narrow features set in a heavy scowl.

Hidden beneath ridges of thin white eyebrows, his close-set brown eyes drooped in resignation, the amber flecks in them hardly showing. His olive skin a wrinkled parchment marred by a ragged blue-veined burn on his left cheek—a reminder of past action. He could have the burn removed, but he found it too valuable as an intimidation tool.

Sill-Anais was still getting used to his straight-shooting Diplomatic Branch director, but he found the former Prima Scout's unmistakable competence and revulsion of any subterfuge and all things bureaucratic refreshing. He suspected, though, to simply survive, Anabb probably developed a veneer of obfuscation. It was in the nature of the job, but he hoped it wouldn't happen. He had not pushed the Branch or its new director too hard while Anabb relocated to Taltair. Time now for Anabb to do some real work. Time to test the unbeliever in the crucible of the Path.

"You followed Kernami's performance on the Assembly floor?"

"Thunderation! And what a performance. Let me guess. You've cooked up a deal and plunged me into the mess."

"Hardly the words I would use. Ach!"

"I am keen to hear your version."

"This is an easy one," Sill said comfortably and smiled as Anabb rolled his eyes, seeking inspiration from above.

"Relocation to Taltair was easy. Dealing with Captal's dark schemes, on the other hand, isn't fun at all."

"You should have stayed in the Fleet, then."

"Don't tempt me! Okay, Sill. Lay it out for me."

"You'll be getting all this through official channels, but the bottom line is, we want you to find the raider base—"

"If one exists."

"One exists, and perhaps more than one."

"Perhaps. Did you consider that raiding Pizgor commerce is simply lucrative? Pizgor draws in ships, and ships draw raiders. Despite Director Kernami's fulminating, the scenario doesn't necessarily need to have a political overtone."

"Ach! You're contradicting your own reports, Anabb," Sill chided him, but happy to see his director prepared to argue a valid option.

"Contradicting nothing! Logistical, service, and tactical support isn't free, you know. By definition, those raider scum would shun any cooperation such a support infrastructure would demand. Kernami was right about that."

"This has nothing to do with commerce and you know it. Ach! The political indicators are simply too overwhelming. This is intimidation, plain and simple."

"And I suppose you want to lay this at Palean feet?"

"Or Sargon's. It is always a pleasure to deal with a professional who understands the broader implication of his position," Sill said with obvious approval and ran a hand through his hair. "The Executive Council wouldn't mind seeing either one of them squirm a bit. They wouldn't mind that at all. It won't do the government's image any harm either if something visible is seen to be done about Pizgor's problem."

Anabb snorted. "Ignoring your cynicism, you must realize the magnitude of your demand."

Sill grinned and pointed a long finger at Anabb. "You know, that is exactly what I said. Ach!"

"Mmm. What are my constraints?"

"Don't fail."

"Thunderation!"

"This shouldn't be too difficult. Katan at the Bureau of

Defense has already instructed CAPFLTCOM to move additional Fleet assets to cover Pizgor's commercial corridors."

"Obviously not enough or you wouldn't be calling me now."

"Prepare your proposal and we'll go over it. A lot is riding on this one, Anabb. For both of us."

Anabb looked thoughtfully at Sill. "Looking beyond Pizgor, you know, of course, raider activity across the Serrll cannot be dismissed as pure material opportunism or religious extremism. It's a social mollification index, reflecting unrest and protest against the very structure of the various power blocks and the Combine itself. Albeit it's an extreme example of such protest."

"Ach! Very perceptive." Impressed, Sill wondered how Anabb worked that out. "Why do you think Capital hasn't moved against them before? Government is more than just legislation and revenue collection, my heretical friend."

Anabb frowned deeply as he thought that one over.

"I'll need tactical oversight over COMPIZOPS and Sector TACOPSCOM. A liaison on Pizgor would be good to have."

"Anything else?"

"I'll let you know."

"Humph! Sounds like you intend sending the whole Fleet out there."

"It'll make a start by curbing raids and bring Pizgor onside. The government will also get a pat on the back for quick action."

Sill grinned. "Your grasp of hard realities is comforting, Anabb. Contact me when you formulate a penetration plan."

The Wall cleared and Anabb groaned. Politicians! Bovine Captal idolaters, all of them. Throwing crumbs to the populace and begrudging them even as interference from their main pursuit of personal power and party byplays. To the pits with all of them. He wondered again whether leaving the Fleet had been such a great idea.

He tapped the comms pad and stood up. "No interruptions, Ariane," he growled and strode to the wide window screen.

Dusk painted the sky gray, shrouding a sultry autumn day. The towers of the Center crowded the city skyline already smeared with light. It had been a tough fight moving the Diplomatic Branch from Captal's stifling bureaucracy, not least within the Bureau of Cultural Affairs. He argued passionately with Sill the advantages of divorcing Serrll's principal intelligence organ from Captal's political machinery. The Branch was losing its perspective, servicing the whimsical interests of the various Bureaus and executive directors, instead of focusing on issues affecting the Serrll as a whole. Sill accused him of naiveté and idealism, but in the end, he gave his reluctant approval and the Executive Council unexpectedly ratified the decision.

In hindsight, had he known the enormity of relocating the Branch all the way to Taltair, he would probably have shied away from doing it. After a year of cajoling, bullying, and threatening physical violence, he got his way. Not everyone in the Branch was happy at the prospect of leaving the intensity of Captal's lifestyle. Anabb did not mind. The relocation served as a natural and necessary winnowing process that resulted in a smaller organization, but those who remained were focused professionals all of them, and Anabb liked it that way.

Leaving the Fleet, after what some saw as an enviable career, was one of the most personally turbulent decisions he ever had to make. It also earned him the enmity of some high-ranking flag staffers at CAPFLTCOM, Captal Fleet Command. He achieved significant rank and influence, and his reputation ensured promotion to major commands. Had he stayed in, it would have been a dubious honor, his position ensuring the assignments would be desk jobs. Fighting the various Fleet factions and Captal's multifarious self-absorbed machinery had grown predictable and weary. He wanted to shape policy, not merely execute it.

His chance came unexpectedly during the last general elections campaign. Enllss-rr, himself slated for the post of Commissioner for the Bureau of Colonial and Protectorate Affairs, approached him on behalf of the Revisionist Conservative Party. The offer simple as it was complex. Leave the Fleet and head up the Diplomatic Branch. If he refused, he knew the offer would never be renewed. Other talent waited in the wings for their chance. He would end his career embittered and crabby, the very image of a bureaucrat he had grown to despise.

In the end, the decision made itself. It took him over a year to clear his backlog and delegate the various projects he'd been running. When the moment came, Sofam arranged a by-election on his home world and Anabb found himself a brand-new member of the General Assembly.

Staring at the gathering darkness and growing blaze of the city, he searched for any nagging traces of uncertainty or doubt. There were none, of course. What he needed to master was the necessary cunning and skill needed to deal with some of the same Captal bureaucrats that plagued his Fleet career. The difference this time? He now piled on the heat. He allowed himself a quiet nod of satisfaction. He regretted his decision many times, and probably would again, but it felt good to have the shoe on the other foot. Captal canal worms!

All he needed to do now was prove his ability and the capability of his Branch. By damn, what a task! The issue of raiders marauding through Serrll commerce was nothing new. There was always an enterprising individual or splinter group, operating under the umbrella of some agenda or other, who were not above a little profiteering and wealth distribution on the side. Good healthy fun that exercised everyone's initiative. The Paleans, on the other hand, were a singularly unique breed. Discounting the religious overtones that surrounded raids on ecoforming planets and their penchant for savage assaults, the raids on Pizgor commercial lanes smacked too much of organization, elaborate communication, and tight control. The results to date pointed too strongly at a planned and sustained execution of a program with a definite objective in mind. He had been involved in too many military campaigns not to recognize one.

Could Sargon be really masterminding this? He could not deny Kernami's damning statistics. Something clearly irrefutable was happening, and he had an obligation to look at all options. As a military strategist and tactician, he also knew when to abandon procedural dogma and cut to the chase. Paleans tended to be shifty and manipulative in the pursuit of their objectives—and very, very good at grinding down their opponents with unyielding deliberation. They didn't mind if a plan took a decade or two to mature.

Sargon's martial background, however, shunned such subterfuge, preferring a frontal assault that decided the issue quickly one way or another. Using raiders to plunder Pizgor commerce was a perfect example of such direct action. The only thing bothering him was whether Sargon or the Paleans had come up with the scheme. If he had to bet, he would pick the Paleans. This was something they were familiar with. The raids also clearly illustrated Sargon's lack of patience. There were many subtle ways to apply pressure on an intransigent system to make it toe the line without resorting to a direct onslaught—if one was prepared to wait it out. Obviously, Sargon wasn't.

He did not kid himself when he told Sill that Captal did not appreciate the magnitude of this task. Or maybe they did and saw an opportunity to properly tackle a problem that festered for centuries. To get this done would require a multifaceted operation no one individual would or could crack. He would need intelligence gathering on a vast scale. He had that.

Surveillance capability he had, and resources in depth he had. Adding it all up, he realized the ops was going to be expensive, very expensive. He would let Sill handle that one. The other dark cloud, the process could take a long time to yield tangible results, something he did not have. Then again, there was always a chance of a lucky break, a random element. Anabb never relied on luck as a substitute for thorough, painstaking preparation, but a dash of luck at the right moment had won empires. A factor not to be discounted. As an impartial participant, luck could favor either side, something always worth remembering.

Given Kernami's bulldozer tactics on the Assembly floor, direct and visible action definitely in order, or there would be a public howl of protest. Kernami must have taken that factor into consideration when he made his presentation to the Assembly. An increased Fleet presence in the area an obvious first step. It might be obvious, but it would still be effective. He hadn't seen a raider yet who would care to match itself against an M-3 sweeper, and M-3s he had in plenty, or the Fleet had. Which was the same thing, really. How long he would be able to keep them there before Captal tired of the game was something else.

Finding a base represented an altogether different proposition. There were too many ways to hide such an operation and too few means of unearthing it. Would he be able to maintain the Fleet pressure long enough to uncover it? Another issue for Sill to tackle. Projecting power into the area would be a major pain. Pizgor's five systems occupied a very small and lonely patch of space, squeezed between Sargon, the Karkans, and the Paleans. Militarily, it was on the ass end of nowhere, far from Fleet supply bases. Logistics would become a scramble in any extended stay. Well, that's why they had COMPIZOPS, Anabb thought comfortably. They can worry about the details.

He remembered fondly young Terr's unorthodox involvement with the Four Suns mission and the way he managed to disrupt Kapel Pen's plot to cede the system to the Karkans. Pursued all the way to Anar'on, two M-3s shot down Terr's ship. Against all odds, the boy survived under the ministration of the tribal Wanderers and became a Discipline adept. Finding a raider base seemed the ideal type of assignment the boy's irreverent attitude toward authority and due process called for. Cloaked as he was in the shadow of the Wanderer Discipline might be the very random element Anabb looked for.

He walked to his desk and tapped the comms pad.

"Ariane, find Second Scout Terrllss-rr for me, will you?"

* * *

"This sucks," Terr complained feebly, looking glum.

Dhar listened to this tirade ever since they left Anar'on and paid no attention. As Terr's brother and friend, *and* first officer, Dhar did not mind acting as a wall against which Terr bounced his frustrations. He checked their position and automatically scanned the status displays. Satisfied, he leaned back into the couch, enjoying the silence and the small ship noises. A pad on one of the color-reactive panels blinked occasionally, causing shadows to shift around the otherwise dark command deck.

Above him, Cordia-Prime bulged as a distended blue-green crescent, slipped visibly down their starboard quarter. The gas giant only eleven light-minutes from its bloated orange primary. The system's four rocky planets were strung farther out, a common arrangement among this group of stars. Talon itself was one of nine C-Prime's moons.

A brief flicker as several reactive pads changed in a cascade of color.

Against the Gods of Shadow

"Approaching Talon Surface Command and Control insertion point," the computer announced flatly. "Initial interrogative verified. All systems nominal for orbital approach."

"IP approved," Dhar said softly after glancing briefly at Terr.

"Landing configuration procedure nominal. Entering IP."

The M-1 immediately dropped below lightspeed into normal space. Talon still some six hundred and eighty thousand talans off, but SC&C didn't like ships emerging too close to Deklan's premier Fleet base. Almost occulted in C-Prime's shadow, Talon itself barely visible, Dhar imagined he could see whorls of light from surface installations.

SC&C brought them down directly on one of the landing rings. C-Prime crowded the sky above them. The open apron glowed off-white, surrounded by a complex of brightly lit terminals, hangars, and maintenance facilities. An access tube slid swiftly toward them and connected with a clang.

An M-3 hovered on the landing ring bay beside them, connected to the ground by umbilicals and power extensions. Terr could just make out the opaque nav bubble over the curve of the hull looming beside him. He frowned, stopped before the cable-tube hatch and squinted hard.

"That's my ship!" he declared in outrage and scowled at Dhar. "What's it doing sitting out there, eh? Tell me that?"

Dhar checked the markings: *Ramora*, all right.

"I am sure the base commander will have a perfectly plausible explanation, Sankri."

"This sucks," Terr muttered again and stepped into the tube.

A very young Base Scout ambushed them as they entered the departure lounge. The Karkan walked briskly to Terr and knuckled his forehead in a salute.

"You must be—"

"Yeah, yeah. We know who we are."

51

"Sir, if you will permit me to escort you. The base commander will see you immediately."

"The base commander…"

Terr looked at Dhar who wore a what-did-I-tell-you expression. He shook his head and waved at the young Karkan.

The ride to the administration center mercifully brief and spent in silence. Curious stares followed them as they cleared the floor's buffer zones and the atmosphere became more subdued when they neared the commander's office. Terr found the reception area gloomy, humid and depressing, reflecting his mood. Their escort invited them to make themselves comfortable in the luxurious formchairs set against one corner, then padded away through thick violet pile.

Terr slumped into the yielding couch and locked his hands behind his head. Dhar took a more dignified posture and Terr grinned at his brother's look of mock disapproval. Getting pleasantly relaxed and drowsy, he saw a large heavy door slide back with a hiss.

The Karkan who filled the doorway was a senior master scout. His flattened head, covered by broad green scales, tilted slightly. Small fishy black eyes locked on the two figures before him. He didn't say anything, allowing himself a hiss of impatience.

Terr got up, not hurrying, and stood to.

"Second Scout Terrlss-rr reporting as per orders, sir."

"I expected you eighteen hours ago, Mister! Joyriding were you?" the Karkan hissed, his eyes unblinking from horizontal slits.

Terr didn't say anything. What the hell was the old fish head pissed off for, anyway?

"No matter. Come with me, you two."

He led them through the foyer of his office and into one of the meeting rooms. High-backed wood-framed formchairs surrounded a narrow sickle-shaped table. A floor-to-ceiling window screen occupied one entire wall, showing the Center and the surrounding buildings. The far end of the room held a full-dimensional Wall station pooling through thick swirls of color.

"Sit," he commanded and strode to the end of the table. He placed open palms on the reflective surface and leaned forward. He waited until Terr and Dhar finished pushing chairs around. The Karkan's expression suggested he wasn't all that excited by their presence.

"No commander likes to have undue political influence put on him and I am no exception. I don't know what you two did to merit this attention, but I intend to find out. You will give me a detailed briefing before you get out of here. Is that clear?" The fishy eyes glittered.

"Copy that, sir," Terr said evenly.

Scowling, the Karkan tapped commands into the inlaid control panel. Without a word or a backward glance, he stomped out. The door closed after him with a loud click. Terr and Dhar exchanged glances.

"Warm personality," Terr muttered.

Just as he began to wonder what was going on, the Wall cleared and he groaned.

"I am glad to see you again, Second Scout," Anabb said gruffly, his voice hard and gravelly. The ragged blue-veined burn on his left cheek turned pink with restrained emotion.

Terr didn't share his enthusiasm. The last time he tangled with the crusty prima scout almost cost him his life. Mixing it up with the Four Suns brand of family politics had been a revelation—one that resulted in him crashing on Anar'on. He walked away from it, only to find himself in the hands of Wanderer nomads. His trek through the desert left him half mad and Dharaklin reached into his mind and lifted him out of insanity. The process enabled him to stand in the shadow of Death through circumstances he even now had not come to terms with.

He wasn't ready for a repeat performance. The sight of

Anabb's olive features did nothing to fill him with a warm fuzzy.

"I suppose, sir, you're the reason why our leave was so abruptly terminated?"

"You're aware of Pizgor's General Assembly petition?" Anabb demanded, ignoring Terr's implied impertinence.

"We managed to catch up on the latest events on our way here," Terr said cautiously, trying to work out what that had to do with him. Getting involved in high politics made him nervous. Getting involved with raiders, especially if they were organized, made him apprehensive. The fact that Anabb chose to talk to him probably meant he would be risking his ship and skin in some mad scheme, which made him anxious.

"Good, good. Then this should be simple. As of now, you're detached to the Diplomatic Branch. All this is in your ship's computer, but circumstances dictate that I give you a personal briefing. Everything discussed here is subject to the Nondisclosure Act, which means you don't discuss this...with anyone. Clear?"

"Sir, if—"

"Is that clear, Second Scout?" Anabb rasped and glared through the Wall.

Rit!

"Copy that, sir!"

"What I want you to do is find the raider base that's supporting the disruption of Pizgor shipping commerce."

Terr blinked as he digested the words, then smiled and stood up. "No big deal, sir. It'll only take a day or two."

Anabb grinned and the amber flecks in his eyes glittered. "I see you haven't lost your sense of humor. You'll need it where you're going," he said, pleased to see the boy still paraded his aggressive independence. After four years, he needed to see it for himself.

Terr sat down, his face hanging in resignation. "With respect, sir, what you're asking me to do is likely to take the combined resources of the Bureau of Cultural Affairs and the whole Scout Fleet—"

"It will."

"What am I expected to achieve with a lousy M-3?"

"Your mission! But don't worry, you won't be alone. The resources you mentioned? They'll be at your disposal."

"Great. Alone or not, this is hardly an operation where any single individual or ship can hope to undertake a task of this magnitude."

"I know all that. You should credit me with the ability to do my job, Second Scout."

"I did not mean to imply—"

"You did, and your attitude is understandable. Son, what I need is a random element. Operating independently, unencumbered by procedural overheads, you'll have a free hand to pursue some of the more unorthodox avenues."

"Which are likely to end up with my ship blasted in a well-orchestrated maneuver for poking around where I'm not wanted."

The burn on Anabb's cheek began to color. "You could also end up herding an oiler on the Orgomy run!"

Terr didn't need it spelled out. He suspected this job would have more than Sargon and the Paleans keenly scrutinizing the developments; and helping to derail them, no doubt. If Anabb failed to produce results, both of them would probably end up herding a cargo tramp on the Orgomy run, no matter whose fault. With Captal's own machinery ready to stab him, Anabb didn't need to look for new enemies.

His problem. Terr simply felt uncomfortable sticking his butt out inviting it to be kicked, especially when the kick would most likely be a terminal one. Glory and promotion didn't count for much when lying cold on a slab.

"I understand your questions," Anabb went on, "but study your brief first. I want you on your way to Pizgor without delay. That'll give you plenty of time to formulate an action plan."

Terr's shoulders sagged. What action plan? There had to be a way to get under this.

"Sir, I left *Ramora* undergoing extensive maintenance and upgrade of the main drive power reactor," Terr pointed out in a last-ditch defense.

"I know that and I've taken appropriate steps. Maintenance has completed the task list and your ship is fully provisioned. You'll need to conduct your trials while underway. As far as the base commander is concerned, you're detached with other Fleet units to patrol duty around Pizgor. Which is true in a way. You don't want to draw attention to your activities."

"He wants a debrief—"

"Then he'll be disappointed, clear?"

Rit!

* * *

"And that's the program, people," Terr said and swept his eyes confidently around the briefing table. To his senior staff, this must appear like any other ops, no matter how hopeless. "To cut it, we must have the ship ready and have the crew ready. Shan…"

A sparse stick of a man with a perpetually dour and unhappy demeanor, the chief engineer bit his lower lip, scratched the back of his knobby head, and gave a heavy sigh.

"It's nineteen days at max boost to Pizgor." He shook his head in protest. "Longer, as we won't be able to boost max for that long anyway. If you want to do all the fancy trials with the reactor—"

"The works."

Shan-arin took his duty as an engineer very seriously. He had to, or his fire-eating young commander would turn the ship into a cut-down M-4! His beady yellow eyes blinked at

Terr in alarm.

"Then there are all the system checks—"

"Once we start active operations, there won't be time to fool around," Terr said.

Shan pulled at his long chin, stretching it even longer. "I don't know—"

"Handle it. Kieran, you'll have to be on your toes with weapons on this one."

Naturally plump, skin pale gray and hanging in folds down his round face, his button blue eyes were expressionless. His large flap ears pricked, that being the extent of his emotional response.

"When you say fire, sir, they'll fire," he said softly and Terr grinned.

New to the ship, Kieran still explored the limits of his authority. In the natural order of things, a grade one Base Scout was everyone's ground mat, even on an M-3 where there weren't that many people. After two mild chewing-out sessions, he learned early that his commander didn't believe in delegating responsibility. Kieran managed the weapons station, and Terr expected him to handle it, all of it, from fire control to weapons engineering. It took some getting used to.

"Senior Chief, I'll need your marauders sharpening up their close-quarter tactics," Terr said.

Razzo glowered. His bald head shone a mottled pink, all scarred and patched. He obviously liked a bit of fun as much as the next guy. Short, powerful and mean, he ruled his small assault team with an iron fist.

"I'll get 'em wrung out and nasty again, sir," he growled with a heavy scowl.

Terr nodded, satisfied. He didn't much care for the strict interpretation of regulations and allowed the crew more latitude than normally customary in other ships. To keep that privilege, they needed to work at it. Those who mistakenly sought to take advantage of his easy ways were weeded out, their careers permanently blighted. Terr didn't care whether the miscreant happened to be an officer or a rating.

"Tighten things up and get everybody frosty. For sure as hell, once the worm shit starts curling, we'll want to be heaving it out as quickly as it piles up. Right, that's it, everybody!" He nodded and clapped his hands. "Get it unwrapped and put them to work."

When the others stood up to leave, Terr glanced briefly at Dhar to stay. As the last of them filed out of the lounge, he leaned back, clasped his hands behind his head, and stuck his legs out on the table. Lousy mission or not, it felt good to be back in his ship.

Dhar raised an eyebrow. He had a lot to do if the crew and the ship were to achieve the demanded level of readiness. Not that Sankri was a stern commander or a martinet. His easy and sometimes casual approach to discipline contrasted sharply with Dhar's more formal methods. On reflection, the differences seemed to complement each other surprisingly well. The crew were fiercely loyal to their quirky master and nothing else mattered. Dhar accepted that as a Wanderer, they respected and even feared. He yielded long ago to the realization. They all knew he and Terr walked in the shadow of the god of Death, but the crew did not see Sankri as a monster.

Terr momentarily gazed through the transparent section of the lounge hull, almost totally black out there. A star here and there glittered in the deeps. Brown lines of gravity waves coiled around them, long and flat now that they left the influence of C-Prime's sun. Opposite him, Dhar discreetly cleared his throat. Terr brought his legs down with a crash.

"Thinking about our orders. What would the *Saftara* say about them?" He grinned and raised a quizzical eyebrow.

Dhar did not smile. He frowned as he searched for a suitable phrase from the wealth of teachings that comprised the Discipline.

"In the waiting, even the muddy waters eventually clear."

"Mmm. Haven't got time to wait for them to clear. Did you ever hear the like? A Pizgor Trade Commissioner and an Executive Council Ambassador at our disposal. Just for us! It's ridiculous. Anabb's cracked if he thinks this is going to work."

"It's always nice to have high-level patronage, my brother. We don't want to get caught up in Fleet protocol on this one."

"Right. Because we'll be too busy untangling ourselves from local protocol."

"Like it or not, we will need Pizgor's support."

"That kind of support I can do without," Terr muttered.

"So tell me your plan, Sankri."

Terr grinned and rubbed his hands. "You'll like this. A bulk carrier loaded with cargo attractive enough to tempt a raider into an attack. We then trace it back to its base."

"And that's your plan?"

"Okay, so we need to work out a few details—"

"A few details…"

"All right, there might be a slight difficulty inducing a raider to target a specific carrier—"

"And even more difficult to follow it back to its base," Dhar said heavily and shook his head, his features stern and uncompromising. As first officer, he sometimes had to dampen his brother's enthusiasm. "In any event, it's highly unlikely the raider would scoot directly back to its base. Especially if the base is a secure location, as it's likely to be in this case, this will be a certainty. Another thing; if the bait is made attractive, they could smell a trap and we'd have wasted our time."

"Not if we change the manifest of an already scheduled transit."

"You're basing this scheme on a questionable assumption that all raiders operating around Pizgor are in fact using a single base. Why not several scattered support installations?"

Terr shook a finger. "No way! Scattered installations only increase logistical and security problems for you. Command and control grows in direct proportion to the number of such installations. No, whoever is running this thing will want the operation to be small and tight."

"Something else to consider, then. I would imagine it would be singularly difficult to induce any commercial crew to man your bulk carrier. If attacked, they know they would face almost certain death."

"*We'll* crew the damned thing!"

"Mmm."

"Let's forget the crew for a moment. The tricky bit, as we both know, is shadowing the thing after it makes its haul. No matter what we do, we're bound to get detected at some stage of the game and that'll be it."

"Trace the cargo?"

"Right! Something indirect and foolproof, otherwise our friends will get suspicious. Can you think of anything a raider would keep for its own consumption rather than sell?"

"Fuel cells!"

"Tempting, eh?"

"Oh, that's good." Dhar smiled in admiration, then frowned. "Wait. Sure, each cell has a registration signature, but unless the trace is recorded..."

"SC&C takes in a whole bunch of ship stats on approach and departure."

"Which the raiders are bound to know."

"Maybe. We exchange fuel cells all the time. I'm sure merchant pilots do same thing. Nobody thinks about it. If someone were to seriously crosscheck all the crap the Serrll bureaucratic machinery hoards away, the system would grind to a slow death. I'm betting no one else has thought of using the data in this way before."

"If the data exists, my brother."

"Let's find out." Terre tapped contact pads on the inlaid

console set into the table and turned to the Wall. "Computer, state if SC&C interrogative captures fuel cell signatures from transition data pack dumps."

"All engineering logs are routinely downloaded on entry and departure from SC&C."

"State access level requirements."

"Source data is restricted to the Bureau of Economic Affairs. Statistical derivatives are unrestricted."

"Not good." Terr frowned and scratched the scar on his left temple. "We need source data on individual ship movements, not some correlated preprocessed mush."

"The volume of data will be considerable, Sankri."

Terr gave a dismissive wave of his hand. "Not my problem. Anyway, that's not necessarily true. If we restrict our search to commercial traffic only, excluding military and passenger hulls—"

"It would still leave us with an impossible load."

"If we were processing it, yes."

"Anabb?"

"Put all that AI hardware and brainpower he's got stashed away on Taltair to some use, I say. Computer, connect personal with Diplomatic Branch Director Anabb Karr."

It took a while for the connection to be established. Terr wasn't surprised. He figured Anabb would not be chewing his fingers waiting for him to call. When the Wall cleared, the Prima Scout's stern expression did not exude happiness.

"Hardly cleared the system and you're already in trouble?"

"I need access to some restricted information, sir. Access that will not be linked back to my activities, in case anyone is curious."

"If you're going to be bothering me like this, talk to the head of my internal team. It's spelled out in your orders."

Rit!

"Ah, sorry, sir. Must have missed that part."

"Humph! Okay, my boy. Talk to me."

"It is likely that Captal has carried out previous studies into raider activities. If they have any specifics on Pizgor, I would like to see them, but this is only background. It would be interesting to know if any new shipping-related ventures were started around Pizgor within the last five years or so in a say, fifteen-light-year radius. If we're talking about a support base, it's got to be operating behind a cover screen."

"That's all you want?"

"Well, sir, it would also be useful to check out the hull types preferred by raiders. The manufacturers, registrations, movements—"

"I see the pattern, Second Scout," Anabb growled, glaring through the Wall. "However, you're not crediting me and my Branch with competence. Never mind. You're thinking and that's good. When the correlations come through, if they do, you'll be informed. Now, if you're finished wasting my time…"

Surly old bastard.

"Sir, raider ships are not self-sufficient. It takes a lot to maintain a hull, especially a fighting one."

"Your point being?"

"Spares. Where are the raiders getting theirs? If you're correlating facts, sir, check up on local suppliers. Maybe we can track an item taken in a raid and dumped on the used parts market. Look into inventory and movement records. After all, if a raider cannot sell his cargo, he's out of business. The stuff has got to go somewhere."

Impressed, albeit grudgingly, the boy showed fine judgment and discrimination of relevant issues. What Anabb wanted, though, might very well be impossible to get. The Serrll wasn't that rigidly run to allow capture of such low-level data. Individual systems would resist such imposition anyway. Even if the data did exist, was it stored in a readily accessible format? The boy simply didn't appreciate the tangle his request implied, or didn't care. Still, he had the right approach: stick to the objective and let the bureaucrats take care of the details. The wry realization that he could be counted as one of those bureaucrats not lost on him.

"Got anything else?"

"Yes, sir. Perhaps our best shot."

"Spill it."

"Fuel cells, sir. All SC&C dumps are sent to Captal where the data is sanitized. I cannot get at the stuff. At least not at the level of detail to do me any good."

Anabb blinked. Unorthodox, but a brilliant idea. His staff missed that one.

"I'll put someone on it. Well done, my boy," he said gruffly and cut contact.

Terr slapped the table and grinned broadly. "See why I love the guy?"

Dhar did not listen, already thinking of changes needed to get the crew and ship into shape.

Chapter Three

Sprawled in the comforting looseness of the command couch, Re Nette tried to relax, but found the task impossible. Her long slender fingers drummed restlessly against the armrest, betraying her agitation. Mouth set in a thin line, she dared anyone to try and make something of it. What fueled her fury, the crew didn't even seem to care about her problems. Nibbling her lower lip, she nodded wryly to herself. What did she expect, a shoulder to cry on?

Without breaking her train of thought, she swept a critical gaze around the command deck. There were only two other watchstanders on duty, both engaged in casual conversation. She didn't mind. Contact with the ore bulk carrier not due for another two hours. Display plates lined a quarter of the rounded deck, merging into sloping color-reactive control consoles. Above her, the nav bubble transparent, polarized to keep out the harsh glare of the nearby yellow star.

Moodily, she slumped back into the yielding couch. *Oh, that infuriating man!* To treat her with such disdain and indifference, making her crawl to him, begging. It was insufferable. Six lousy fuel cells. Not too much to ask for, was it? What really galled, he dismissed her casually with only two cells to show for her efforts. She'll show him, the high and mighty Tanard. By the time she landed on Mitlan, her holds would not be exactly bulging, but she would earn enough to turn her bottom line well into the black. More importantly, proceeds from her previous raid should have come through. She needed those proceeds as badly as she needed the cells. Not that any of her crew were grumbling, a firm believer in a simple philosophy that the best way to keep a ship humming was to pay everyone's share promptly. Still, ship needs came first, and the four hundred thousand Serrlls maintenance bill came as an unexpected and unwelcome development. What would *this* run cost her? She hoped her two silent partners back on Askaran would be as understanding.

Suddenly, she grinned, the prospect of a raid evaporating her tension. With an increased Fleet presence along the trade corridors, a risky move, but an acceptable one. Her prey only a marginal proposition, hauling preprocessed metal halides from the Four Suns. Second in a convoy of four ships, the run made every two months, supplying raw industrial feed-stocks to Pizgor and Sargon refineries. Ordinarily, she wouldn't attack Sofam vessels, more so if they were on a Sargon run. She certainly wouldn't bother with an ore carrier. An almost useless cargo to her and difficult to get rid of. Her need for fuel cells overrode all other considerations. To the pits with them anyway. She was in business for herself and didn't owe Sargon or anyone else anything. Unlike some of her brother raiders who plundered in the name of religious conviction, Re Nette and her crew craved simple profit. She learned very young that a muscular bank account represented independence and power, and she craved both. If that meant taking lives, she could live with it.

The nav plot watchstander cocked his head at her from his workstation.

"We have contact. Distance, one-point-three lights."

"They're early," she mused, studying the repeater plot before her. She'd had *Drakin* sitting in the lee of that infernal sun for the past nineteen hours, waiting at the transition zone, eleven million talans out. Her weariness lifted, welcoming getting into action. "It's not an escort, is it?" It would be more than a little embarrassing if they came out charging, only to find an M-3 on the other side waiting for them instead of a hapless carrier.

Taplan shook his head. "Profile signatures match. It's *Rakish*. No other contacts within scan range."

"Attack plot?"

"Closest approach will be point-seven-five lights. He'll reach IP in sixty-four minutes. At max boost, we'll intercept in fifty-eight minutes. Recommend we run in four minutes, allowing one minute to clear the transit distortion zone."

"Mmm. Get everyone hot, but keep an eye open for a screen." Always possible that an escort could be shadowing outside the effective acquisition envelope. She had fallen for that gag once before and didn't relish a repeat encounter. If the escort hadn't stopped its pursuit to pick up survival blisters, she and her crew would be pounding rocks on Cantor now, Serrll's penal planet, or worse. Thought made her skin crawl.

The hatch opened behind her and two more watchstanders took up their stations.

"Tay-nee?"

Built like an earthmover, the weapons operator studied his board and his fingers danced over the touch-sensitive pads. No one would dream of suggesting there was anything amusing about his name. He turned his two-katalan-frame and scowled at her.

"The projector is online, unmasked, and we're running ready," he rasped from a battered mouth.

She nodded. "Power?"

"Power management all okay," Tay-nee added heavily. "Ready for max boost."

"Are we still clear?"

"No contacts," Taplan said without looking up from his board.

"Profile?"

"Target maintaining profile. Three minutes to commencing run."

Re Nette pressed a pad on the small armrest console. "Chad?"

"Boarders ready," came the response from the hold.

"Stand by."

The minutes ticked down and Taplan nodded to her.

"Okay everyone," she declared. "Let's do this like a drill. Tay-nee? Move us out, nav shield only." Extending their primary grid would be like sending out a beacon burst, asking to be detected.

A flattened boxy oval, the four hundred and forty katalan-long raider shifted attitude and began to move. Within seconds, *Drakin* boosted at better than one percent of lightspeed. Keeping the yellow sun behind it, masking itself in the outflowing plasma stream, the raider boosted to clear the ferocious magnetic and gravitational space distortion, enabling it to transit into subspace.

Forty seconds later and over eleven million talans from the sun's photosphere, *Drakin's* distortion field torus charged fully and the ship transited in a discharging flash of white light. It boosted to under point-nine of a light-year per hour, but at a prodigious consumption of its fuel, strain on the drive systems and structural integrity. The hull manufacturer would have paled at the sight.

For Re Nette, these speed runs accounted for the bulk of her maintenance expenses. A raid that didn't pay a net profit was a bad miscalculation. Several such runs and she'd be out of business, permanently if the crew decided to throw her out the lock in protest. They were loyal only as long as she kept filling their pockets. What she planned now was marginal in the extreme. She could only hope that picking over the carrier would turn out to be worth the effort. She'd be happy if she broke even.

Nine minutes from the target, *Rakish* stirred into life and sent out a nav interrogative ping. Re Nette waited two minutes, then nodded to Taplan. He casually tapped the comms pad.

"Bulk carrier, bulk carrier. You are about to be boarded. Drop normal and take to your survival blisters immediately.

If you attempt to launch an emergency beacon or activate your transponders, you will all be killed." A far more personal and effective than saying 'destroyed'.

Taplan immediately pressed a pad to activate a powerful multi-spectrum interference pattern, effectively jamming all short-range subspace comms. They won't be able to keep this up for long, but if everything went well, they wouldn't need to.

A few seconds later, *Rakish* shifted attitude, changed course, and accelerated. Its attempt to run a futile gesture. Re Nette's anticipation turned to rage as a repeated sharp *blurr-reep* on the emergency band shattered the silence of the command deck.

"Stupid!"

Two puffs of ejecta cleared the ponderous hull and small lights streaked away. Immediately, two more *blurr-reeps* joined the clamor. She jumped out of her command couch and whirled at Tay-nee.

"Silence them!"

Drakin easily matched the hulk's slower speed and extended its primary shield. The Palean-built Terrasec 14/E phased array projector synchronized its pulse frequency with the shield grid and the extended dome beneath the ship glowed dull orange. Even from 18,000 talans, *Rakish* loomed enormous: a fat cylinder twelve hundred katalans long and four hundred wide. At the projector's maximum range, twin pulsed beams of fifty-six TeV bracketed the speeding beacons. In an eye blink the searing lines of orange light shifted and stabbed again. Two smudges of white gas marked the destruction of the beacons, cutting off their panicked signals.

Drakin moved closer and a single powerful beam fanned at the ore carrier's primary screen. The grid flared, collapsing and reforming around the central drive spaces. Another burst and the whole grid destabilized, fluctuating wildly. As it collapsed in an arcing discharge, the distortion field precursor failed and the emergency signal died with it. *Rakish* promptly dropped out of subspace. Ready, Re Nette dropped normal with it, managing to maintain a fair relative position. *Drakin* closed with the carrier.

"Have they gotten through?" she demanded and glared at Taplan. He made a face and shrugged.

"I doubt it, but it's possible."

"Of all the…"

Just then five survival blisters launched from the stricken hulk and boosted briefly to clear the vast mass in case of a catastrophic power core disassembly; an annihilation explosion.

"Take them out. I want them obliterated!" she hissed, glaring through the transparent nav bubble. Nothing would deny her this prize.

Taplan half rose out of his seat, but her eyes pinned him in place. "Don't say it," she grated in warning.

He shrugged and sat back. Not his ass, but it could very well be if those two transponders managed to punch through his interference. The consequences were simple to work out. The emergency band signal carried for eight light-years. An M-4 boosting at one-point-six lights per hour, it didn't take much to figure they wouldn't want to linger, no matter what the haul.

The projector dome glowed and a single beam leaped into blackness. The blister's hull barely one tetalan thick and unprotected by any ablative shielding. It had a basic navigation screen grid that gave it minimal ship-to-ship and subspace comms capability, not designed for combat cruising. The beam tore through the nav screen and the grid collapsed at once in a discharge of blue and white arcs. The hull material barely registered the energy impact as its molecular structure broke down. The beam vaporized the hull and the fragile contents inside. The containment cell around the power coil failed at this abuse and the blister exploded into an expanding cloud of cooling debris.

Drakin fired again and the second blister vanished. It kept firing...

"Serves the bastards right," someone muttered.

Re Nette nodded and lowered herself into the command couch. "Tay-nee, move us in and check if they've shut down the reactors."

"Main reactor is dampened. Secondary systems are still online."

It happened to another raider, the intended victim managing to outwit its tormentor by setting off a delayed runaway reaction in the antimatter cores of both reactors. The resultant plasma cloud consumed the stricken carrier and took the moored raider with it. An act of sheer desperation, but one that worked. Re Nette always wary falling for the same trick. She didn't have the luxury of time to stand off and check out the hull. Get in, get what they came for, and get out.

"Right, get us docked. Chad, take whatever seems useful, the fuel cells first, then rig her to blow."

Slowly, the raider began to drift toward the enormous bulk of the carrier. It maneuvered to within sixty katalans off one of the huge cargo hatches and extended docking hooks, ready to clamp itself into place.

* * *

Pizgor stood an azure beacon, a dazzling lone jewel against the backdrop of night. Ragged tentacles of white marred the pristine green of the southern polar cap. A single ocean stretched from the high southern latitudes to flare out along the equator, cutting across bands of yellow and orange deserts before it faded into the terminator.

SC&C swung them past a cluster of orbiting commercial carriers and Terr appreciated why traders considered Pizgor a waypoint. There must have been over three hundred hulls in that swarm., one of only a number of clusters stacked in various holding orbits. This represented wealth, wealth on a staggering scale. No wonder such traffic attracted more than its share of raider attention. They didn't need a political reason, he thought.

Their massive triangular bows angled down, two M-6s flashed by them. Terr glanced at Dhar. Apparently, Anabb wasn't kidding when he said there would be an increased Fleet presence. *Ramora* followed the ships down.

Suratan's Katar Field quite an operation, stretched for several talans into a sprawling complex of civilian terminals, military installations, and vast repair and maintenance yards. Even so, it looked crowded with dozens of ships squatting on landing rings or parked on the outer aprons. Polarized nav bubbles stared up like cataract eyes. The M-3 settled on its landing ring with barely a tremor. As they were shutting down, an access tube slid toward them from the terminal and connected with a hesitant bump. The nav bubble polarized, cutting off the glare from the sun clearing the distant city spires. Even from this far out, visible lines of private and commercial traffic crowded Suratan's skyline.

Terr pried himself out of the command couch and stretched his arms. A joint popped here and there, and he grunted with satisfaction. He gathered Dhar with his eyes and strode toward the cable-tube. Before stepping in, he turned, placed his hands on his hips and frowned at the deck watchstanders. He shook his head in disgust.

"Maybe on the next hop, they'll give me a decent crew. Mr. Mati, don't bend her while I'm away. I don't know how long we'll be tied down here, but—"

"I know," the second officer said mischievously. "Get her resupplied and topped up."

"Right. When I get back, I don't want to hear that one of my clowns caused trouble dirtside. If I hear that, I won't be happy, but the luckless individual will be even more unhappy."

"Got it."

Dhar hid a smile as they entered the tube.

The hatch clicked shut and they were going down. On the main deck, hands were already organizing the loading of extra consumables. At the tube exit, Shan held court over an animated discussion with two locals who had that something indefinable about them that said dirt huggers. Probably engineers arranged to assist with final tuning of the various systems that hadn't quite stood up to some of Shan's trials. Terr considered Shan depressing and constipated, but as an engineer, he wouldn't have any other.

The tube dumped them at the main military terminus complex. There were lots of different uniforms on display. Dress blacks and dark green of the assault forces added color to the mainly plain working grays worn by most. The terminal echoed to hollow footsteps, a background of voices, and the blare of public announcements. Giant Wall displays projected streams of flight and berthing data, mixed with flashes of Suratan's various attractions. An impressive place with a high, brightly lit flat ceiling. Tall transparent wall panels gave an unobstructed view of lush park-like greenery outside. Attractive, but it looked and smelled enough like a civilian terminus that Terr felt eager to get out of there.

A discreet cough brought him back to reality. He turned and tilted back his head to see the dark ebony features of a young Pizgor native. The boy touched his chest with an open hand.

"Second Scout Terrllss-rr? It will be my pleasure to transport you and Mr. Dharaklin to the Center."

Terr didn't know why he merited such preferential treatment, but he wasn't about to question the fates. If someone thought this appropriate, who was he to say otherwise?

"After you," he said and extended his hand.

Against the Gods of Shadow

The youngster nodded and strode toward the exit panels. Cool outside, the slightly musty air held a hint of rising humidity. Their escort walked briskly to a row of parked combies. Terr scrambled to keep up with him. They piled in and with a surge that pressed them into the yielding seats, the combie cleared the Field and entered one of the controlled lines of traffic that threaded its way toward the city.

Suratan spanned a narrow delta mouth that pushed its way between towering snow-capped peaks. Bulging white storm clouds hugged the steep slopes. A humidity heat haze softened distant outlines, merging everything into a blue gauze. Overflying the city, tropical greenery an explosion of vegetation crowding wide boulevards filled with strolling or hurrying locals and offworlders. Suratan a checkered pattern of order and evident material prosperity.

Terr found it hard to see how issues played out light-years away could impact this tranquil setting. He reminded himself that a lot of detail remained fuzzy flying this high up. The scene below might be idyllic, but it did not necessarily diminish the passion of the struggle waged elsewhere.

In a gentle turn, the combie angled down out of the controlled traffic stream and headed for a narrow cylindrical tower that stood guard over its lesser rivals. Gray, with bronze stripes running down its length, the color-reactive panels glittered in dawn's light, energizing the internal environmental management system. Near its top, two narrow landing rings encircled the tower. A regular pattern of sled-pads, combies, and communals were taking off and coming down on the rings.

The tower loomed large as they approached, obscuring the city. The combie hovered for a moment, then squatted, and they were down. As the bubble lifted, their lanky young escort scrambled from the front and waited until Terr and Dhar alighted. With a nod, he strode toward the open foyer and stepped into one of the waiting cable-tubes. The doors hissed shut and a moment later retracted. Transparent window screens surrounded an open floor and presented a stunning view of the city. Their young guide gave them a moment to gather it all in. A profusion of plants and blooms sheltered secluded desks and people brooding behind them. Curious faces looked up. The party stopped before a floor-to-ceiling sky-blue partition and a panel slid away.

Two men stood waiting for them, surrounded by sprawling formchairs. The black Pizgor native stood out as a towering, imposing figure, dwarfing his companion. A low table between them contained a tray of edibles, a carafe and glasses. Behind them, facing the windows, a higher than normal desk lay surrounded by potted plants. Against the partition wall, ceiling-high open shelves were cluttered with odd memorabilia, data cubes, and what looked like rolls of parchment. Their guide turned to Terr.

"Sir, may I present Commissioner Hiraki from the Ministry of Trade and Shipping," he said respectfully and nodded to the towering individual. "If I may…" With a glance at the other figure, he withdrew. The panel clicked shut after him.

"Welcome to Pizgor, Second Scout," the Commissioner said pleasantly, his voice deep and throaty. He smiled broadly and turned to the small individual beside him. "I gather introductions are not required here?"

"Indeed not, sir," Terr said beaming and looked at Dhar. "My brother, I want you to meet Rayon Tantour, special Executive Council Ambassador, and our mentor for this mission."

Dark red, Rayon's large egg-shaped head hairless. He had no ears, just little black holes. His nose broad and flat above fat purple lips. A striking combination. Judging by the pronounced rolls around his belly, life on Captal could not have been all bad. A career diplomat, he spent most of his time in the General Assembly honing his troubleshooting skills, shunning line responsibilities. From what Terr knew, Rayon's reputation for settling difficult interstellar problems justly deserved. In his third and last ten-year term, it looked like the reputation-building program was to continue; Terr hoped successfully, for all of them.

Four years ago, Rayon acted as a special General Assembly Envoy to the Four Suns system, investigating allegations of slavery on the capital world Elexi. Rayon needed a replacement military aide and Anabb had picked Terr. Supposedly a milk run job, the assignment went sour from the onset. Terr intensely disliked his first encounter with interstellar politics, whose taste still lingered unpleasantly in his mouth.

Dhar nodded once. "I am honored, sir. Terr has spoken often of you."

"The shadow who walks at night," Rayon said indulgently and his slanting dull-brown eyes crinkled. "A pleasure to meet you at last, young man. Pleasure."

"If you please…" Hiraki swept his hand at the formchairs and sat down. "Do try the keneeps. You'll find the fillings delightful."

Terr allowed the formchair to mold itself around him, then reached to take one of the finger-long golden pastries, firm and warm with a mild spicy aroma. He popped the whole thing into his mouth and chewed. The pastry crackled and released a savory sour paste that tasted of meat, vegetables, and something tantalizingly familiar. Dhar bit into his piece, grinned, and Terr knew: peelath berry paste. He could only wonder how Hiraki managed to get his hands on a supply. As far as he knew, no market existed for the stuff.

"An extraordinary mixture, sir," Terr said. "I never saw it used like this before."

"I thought you would find it different. A gift from Controller Marrakan on Director Kernami's last visit to Anar'on. Now, to our mutual problem," he said briskly, a busy executive giving his valuable time to a very junior Fleet officer. "I understand Field engineers are aboard your ship assisting with some outstanding maintenance."

Terr studied his host, as much as necessary for the mission. Hiraki led a powerful progressive faction in the Triumvirate and acted as Kernami's deputy and Controller of Pizgor while the Prime Director was off-planet. His presence here demonstrated far better Pizgor's determination to stamp out raiders than any battery of bureaucratic underlings. Known to be ruthless and ambitious, he relished being seen as a policy and decision-maker. Opposed, they said he made an unforgiving enemy.

"The help is appreciated, sir," Terr said honestly. "If this mission takes us into prolonged action, there might not be another opportunity to get my systems sorted out."

Hiraki glanced at Rayon, his dark features furrowed with concern.

"There is something you should know. The bulk ore carrier *Rakish* from the Four Suns is overdue. There are no comms to indicate what might have happened, but we suspect the worst."

"Isn't that somewhat unusual?" Terr ventured. "A bulk carrier doesn't appear to be the kind of target to attract a raider."

"Ordinarily, I would agree with you. Agree," Rayon said calmly and crossed his legs. "It's a target of low profitability with a high risk of detection if they took the hull in tow. High risk. Where would they sell the cargo?"

"Unless, of course, the attack wasn't motivated by profit," Hiraki declared in disgust.

"Or motivated by a different need," Terr mused thoughtfully.

Rayon nodded and smiled. "Anabb told me of your fuel cells theory. A sneaky idea, by the way. Sneaky. Never would have thought of it. A radical approach, but plausible."

"If the raider desperately needed fuel, it could explain the attack."

"Without corroborating evidence, that must remain simply another supposition. Yes, supposition."

"Has a search been mounted for the carrier and its crew, sir?"

"An M-2 will be in the general area within a day."

"Well, if they do find debris, we'll know what happened. Either way, we'll know from any projector emission residuals." Terr frowned and bit his lip. "Sir, have any escorted transports ever been attacked?"

"Strange you should ask. Strange. A while ago, we lost two hulls and the M-2s that were with them. Two. Why do you ask?"

"They were either caught by a pair of raiders working in tandem, or…" Terr chuckled and shrugged. "Just a wild idea, sir."

"Indeed? Hiraki and I went over your proposal to, ah, attract a raider. Transfer your crew to one of the already scheduled transports and wait to be jumped, then overpower the raider? Overpower?" Rayon shook his head and Terr felt his cheeks grow warm. "Ingenious, but you failed to take into account one glaring fact. Failed. With the exception of that missing ore carrier, over the past fifteen days, there have been no raider attacks of any sort. None. Increased Fleet activity has already netted us several raiders caught or destroyed."

"Something Pizgor finds gratifying, sir, I'm sure. An expected and predictable outcome, as your tactical models must have already told you," Terr said without irony and glanced at Hiraki.

The Trade Commissioner smiled faintly, aware of the duality of early success. Killing raiders would provide undeniable relief to the shipping companies, but that would also make finding their base much more difficult; a far more important objective in the scheme of things. If only he could get his hands on a raider crew, he would get the information they needed.

Rayon faced Hiraki and chuckled. "I told you." He peered fondly at Terr and leaned back into his formchair. "What else have our models shown? What?"

"Although the incidence of raider activity will fall off in direct proportion to the intensity of Fleet presence, it will be a transitory outcome only."

Hiraki leaned forward and peered closely at Terr. "Oh?"

"Mr. Commissioner, the blunt reality is that Captal Fleet Command cannot maintain a saturated presence around Pizgor indefinitely. The operation would involve too many assets for too long and—"

"Is politically questionable?" Hiraki's black eyes glittered dangerously.

"You can best judge that, sir. I only carry out orders. However, *should* there be a political dimension to this, the current effort *has* to produce quick results before the majority of Fleet units are pulled out. Short of setting up a convoy system, a solution that would create more problems than it solves, resumption of raider activity is a certainty."

"You, a Scout Fleet officer, are telling me Prime Director Kernami's petition to the Assembly was a waste of time?"

"Sir, the Fleet netted several raiders caught or destroyed," Terr reminded him and Rayon grinned.

"My boy, you mentioned that any Fleet effect would only be transitory. Mentioned."

"If the density of raids begins to show a dispersal pattern away from your shipping lanes, and that trend is maintained over the next six months or so, in the short term, Pizgor will have achieved its economic objective."

"Indeed?"

"I am certain you appreciate, sir, the more successful the Fleet is in its immediate effort, the less likely it will be that Captal would be predisposed to sustain its search for any raider base."

"What of the Bureau of Cultural Affairs investigation?"

Hiraki demanded.

"What steps Captal may take to uncover a political connection between the Palean and Sargon merger and raids on Pizgor commerce, I cannot say. I submit, Ambassador Rayon may be in a better position to answer that one. Then again, the whole problem might go away on its own. If enough raiders get nervous and head for more profitable or less hazardous pickings, their support base will have to shut down for lack of customers, no matter who is running it."

"What you're really saying is, if our commerce picks up again, the political dimension underlying our cause will be quietly buried, only to resurface in a more insidious form," Hiraki murmured ruefully. "You paint a disheartening scenario, Second Scout."

"Unless Captal is serious about maintaining Pizgor's sovereignty—"

"All this is merely a public relations exercise, right? An exercise," Rayon finished for Terr. "I can say, however, it's not. You still haven't said why you think raider activity will resume despite the Fleet's effort to curb them. Despite."

"Because, sir, if raids on Pizgor commerce are politically motivated, they will continue...even if not executed by raider ships."

His comment echoed in the stunned silence.

"Humph!" Hiraki cleared his throat and glared at Rayon. "You leaked this!"

"Me? I told you he was smart. Told you."

"To have months of strategic thinking exposed so casually," Hiraki complained bitterly and frowned at Terr. "Explain yourself, Second Scout!"

Terr found it only mildly incongruent that, as a lowly Second Scout, he discussed Serrll strategy with a planetary minister and a Captal ambassador. Then again, the whole mission bordered on the discordant.

"With respect, I would have thought the point obvious.

For Pizgor to make its accusation, you must believe Sargon and the Paleans have ships outfitted as raiders to prey on your commerce. They probably used them as a nucleus to attract real raiders into the scheme, then pulled them back once the operation gained momentum, allowing real raiders to assume all the risk."

"Bah!" Hiraki snorted and slapped his thigh, much to Rayon's evident amusement.

"Exceptional reasoning, my boy. Exceptional," Rayon said with an approving nod. "You understand then why we're keen to have this scheme uncovered quickly. It would be a political disaster for the Paleans. Disaster."

Terr shrugged. "Worth the gains if they pulled it off."

"Unlikely, my boy. Now, your plan and that cargo vessel you intend to take over. It wouldn't be one of the Devon 3-VL4 supply trains due to transit in four days, would it? Like the *Hronin* being prepared now?"

"It's perfect, sir. As an ecoforming operation, Devon shipments have a regular known schedule and route. To any raider, these trains represent a priceless haul and are—"

"Attractive in themselves not to arouse suspicion," Rayon said comfortably. "A raider would also expect to see a valuable hull like that escorted. Expect."

"An escort that could experience a sudden problem that would regretfully compel its return to Pizgor."

"Leaving *Hronin* an easy and tempting target. Neat, and the escort? Holding back, perhaps?" Rayon said, grinning broadly.

"Well, sir, the problem wouldn't need to be *that* serious," Terr said dryly.

Hiraki chuckled. "An impudent move. With increased Fleet activity, why do you think a raider would care to take the bait, no matter how attractive the cargo?"

"I don't. Since *Hronin* is going anyway, let's see what happens. The raiders must continue doing business around here or be forced to hunt elsewhere."

"How would you make the crew transfer, Second Scout?"

"I wouldn't, Mr. Commissioner. The civilian crew would remain in place. While in transit, I will pull up alongside and simply transfer some of my men to the ship. Anything that might look suddenly unusual and we face a serious security risk. The whole operation must, for all intents and purposes, be a genuine run as advertised. No one must know of our plans. No one."

"Mr. Dharaklin, what are *your* thoughts on these flights of fancy?"

Dhar looked down at Rayon. "Terr and I worked on this together, Mr. Ambassador. Like any plan that has not been executed, it has its strengths and weaknesses."

"And one that needs a large measure of luck," Hiraki added pointedly. "But no one expected this to be easy."

"Sir, has any useful information been gained from captured raider crews or their ships' computers?"

"Nothing. At least nothing that makes sense to us," Hiraki amended. "Maybe it's time we considered more vigorous interrogation techniques."

Rayon cleared his throat and forced a smile. "The Commissioner is only jesting, of course. Only jesting."

Hiraki shot Rayon a deadly look and Terr wondered what Pizgor would do if they landed themselves a raider. There were many ways to extract information from an unwilling subject, not all of them pleasant or consistent with the Serrll Constitution. It wasn't always convenient being the good guy.

"Mr. Ambassador, there is one other thing, if I may. I would like you to instruct all Fleet units within thirty light-years around Pizgor to suspend transmission of their IFF. They should also maintain a level two comms protocol." That meant not responding to identification and position requests by other Fleet units. "For the duration of my escort, I'll be sending you a regular single status ping on a secure, but random frequency channel to which only you will have the key."

Rayon looked thoughtful as he studied Terr, then nodded slowly. "Reasonable."

Hiraki stood up and the interview ended. "Second Scout, your plan will be taken under advisement. Until then—"

"I know, sir. We'll be working on your models," Terr said with evident lack of enthusiasm.

* * *

Rubbing his scar, Terr crossed his legs and leaned back into the command couch. The deck dim and quiet, just the way he liked it. Dhar preferred it brighter, but he would have to put up with Terr's quirks until he got his own command. One of the watchstanders shifted in her seat and whispered to the computer. A display pad flickered on a console and the shadows shifted before settling down again.

The nav bubble transparent, stars crowded the black deeps. Faint brown lines of gravity waves twitched and contorted as *Ramora* plunged through them, distorting the space fabric around it. Low on the port quarter, the Et-Aran Nebula a smudge of yellow, red and green tentacles. A day out of Pizgor at forty percent boost, the crew were starting to look crisp again as the after-effects of leave's excesses were purged.

He didn't begrudge them that, or the odd altercation with dirtside authorities. Dhar drove them hard, but in a quirky way the novelty of their assignment acted as a stimulant and they didn't resent the effort needed to make sure the ship was ready. Only after they took off, Terr revealed to them the full scope of their escort duty. The off-duty attractions in Suratan were compensation enough and Razzo's heavy hand kept the more spirited in check. Terr didn't want to contemplate what or who kept Razzo in check. Some things a commander didn't need to know.

Against the Gods of Shadow

There were also the mandatory exchanges of complementary visits with *Hronin's* merchant pilot and his ship. The pilot faced a long voyage to Devon 3-VL4, grateful to have a Fleet escort well into the Palean Union. His gratitude even extended to a dinner invitation for Terr and his senior officers. As a social and culinary experiment, the evening had been a hit. Terr wondered whether the pilot would be as grateful when he finds what lay in store for him. Grateful or not, it needed to be done. The M-2 surveying the action area failed to locate any sign of the Four Suns ore carrier. What it did find only confirmed what they already suspected—debris and high-energy particle decay of the type generated by a weapons burst. They found no trace of survival blisters.

He glanced at Dhar sitting behind the main tactical console and nodded. Dhar immediately tapped pads and the deck brightened.

"Chief?"

"Told off and ready, sir," Razzo's voice rasped from the maintenance hold of Hangar One below.

"Base Scout Osinara?"

"Crew ready, sir!"

"Very well," Dhar said and looked at Terr. "Sir, boarding party ready."

"Thank you, Mr. Dharaklin," Terr said formally and tapped a pad on his armrest. "Shan?"

"Random power fluctuations still running as ordered," Shan-arin's tired voice came from below and Terr nodded wryly. The engineer obviously disliked stating the obvious.

"Plot? Are we clear?"

"No vessels within detection range," Dhar said.

"Right. Move us in."

Ramora surged, rapidly closing the eighty-four thousand talans between the two ships.

"Comms?"

As the second officer, Mati was responsible for comms,

maneuvering, and engineering. He enjoyed his duty, in awe of the first officer. He heard stories about Wanderers and the powers they supposedly wielded. The one about being able to kill someone by wishing it took a bit of swallowing, but he was not about to ask Mr. Dharaklin for a demonstration. Not that Dhar wouldn't help, but his intimidating presence gave the impression of holding back an explosion. What a contrast with the commander! Mati was prepared to follow Terr anywhere. He sort of knew Terr also followed the Wanderer Discipline, although he didn't know all the details, the commander did not project the level of threat that seemed to surround the forbidding first officer. That didn't mean he would test the commander's geniality either.

Would they see action this time around? The commander certainly seemed to expect it, almost as though he looked forward to it. Mati wasn't sure of his own feelings about that. Not afraid exactly, he had a realistic enough outlook to understand that in an action, someone could always die. That it could be him lay as a remote and theoretical possibility. Young, he still felt immortal.

He glanced at the rating beside him and nodded. The operator leaned forward slightly and thumbed a pad.

"*Hronin* transport, this is SSF M-3 escort *Ramora*," she said and nodded to Terr.

The main plate cleared and the pilot's round features settled into a quizzical, but friendly stare. "Is there a problem, Second Scout?"

"No problem, Pilot," Terr told him. "Request you drop normal and prepare to receive a boarding party."

"A boarding party?" the pilot deadpanned and his mouth lifted in a wry smile. "You aren't about to hijack us, are you?"

Terr grinned. The civilian master had taken it well. "Not quite, sir. You have a coded message in your computer from the Pizgor Commissioner of Trade and Shipping."

"I wondered what that thing was, especially as I couldn't

open it."

"Access enable is bravo, indigo, echo, niner, two zero. I will answer any of your questions when I board."

The pilot appeared understandably curious, and apart from harboring mild contempt for all things military, he remained unconcerned. It wasn't hard to guess the young man's mission, but a boarding party? That sounded dangerous. After all, that's what he had the M-3 for.

"This is highly irregular Second Scout, but I don't mind a diversion along the way."

If Terr's plan worked out, the pilot would get more diversion than he bargained for.

"Docking instructions?"

"Use the number two access hatch. Dropping normal."

A few seconds later the transport's distortion field precursor changed polarity and began to collapse. Terr dropped the M-3 out of subspace almost as soon as the transport's field flickered, overshooting *Hronin* by a mere thirty-six thousand talans. Not too bad, given the relative insertion velocities. Docking with another vessel while in subspace could be done, but a highly tricky maneuver. Close proximity tended to disrupt the delicate geometry contours of the distortion fields of both ships, sometimes with less than desirable results. The effect induced by gravitational distortion caused by the two masses. If one of the ships refused to cooperate, the effort turned into a futile gesture.

Ramora slowly moved into the looming shadow of the transport. Velocity matched, it extended an access tube toward a large cargo hatch and mated with a silent clang of clamps.

"Mr. Dharaklin, you have the deck," Terr said and strode to the cable-tube. The tube took him down to Hangar One. Two looming ABPs lay parked side by side, their hatches open. Angular pebble shapes, the twenty-two-katalan-long

Stefan Vučak

platforms were designed to carry a six-man assault team, attach itself against a target ship, burn its way through the hull, and board it. Heavily armored to withstand limited bursts from an M-4, the little ships could penetrate a vessel's secondary and primary shield grids, making them particularly deadly in any close-quarter encounter.

Osinara swept a critical eye over his men and Razzo smiled. The boy had a lot to learn about men and command, but if he lasted, he would one day make a fine officer—despite current evidence to the contrary. Razzo didn't mind playing the nursemaid, and only time and experience would tell whether Osinara had what it took to make a line officer. Well, this action would give the boy experience, one way or another.

"Boarding party ready, sir," Osinara said, sucking in his stomach.

"Very well," Terr said sternly and nodded. The boy still all thumbs and insecure at discharging his authority. He was trying, perhaps a bit too hard. "Status of your ABPs, Mr. Osinara?"

"On the ready deck being preflighted for transfer to the transport, sir."

"Pressurization sequence completed. Egress enabled," the computer announced flatly as the amber pad above the hatchway turned yellow.

Trying to ignore the intimidating presence of his commanding officer, Osinara poked the hatch control pad. With barely a strained hiss the double hatch snicked into the bulkhead, revealing the beige-lit interior of the tube. Terr strode through with the rest of the boarding party in tow. Twenty paces and they were hard against the drab gray hull of the transport. Osinara pressed the yellow hatch pad and waited for the square lock to cycle. On the other side, two merchant pukes and a Second Pilot were slightly taken aback at the sight of Razzo's assault team, decked out in full combat gear with phase rifles held casually at port arms. Osinara glowered at them as they filed into the hold, followed by his twelve ratings.

"Stand them to, Chief," he said gruffly, the image of a seasoned officer, and stood silently by as the men formed two neat lines, their boots echoing in the cavernous hold. With a heavy clang, the airlock hatch banged shut. Razzo glanced at his men and nodded to Osinara.

The diminutive merchant officer watched the proceedings with amusement. With a shake of his head, he tugged down his dark blue zip-jacket and looked at Terr.

"Sir, the Master Pilot will see you on the command deck."

"Very well. Mr. Osinara, get the two ABPs on board and the men squared away."

"Sir!"

"ABPs?" the merchant officer queried.

"Assault Battle Penetrators, Pilot, for close-in work," Terr said comfortably. "Just in case."

In case of what, the merchant officer thought and blanched. Combat units in his ship?

"I'll need roughly five hundred cubic katalans to stow them. They don't need to be in the same hold."

Five hundred cubic katalans? With every cubic tetalan worth its space in kerner stones? The Scout officer was nuts! And where in the pits was he supposed to bunk fourteen men? Sixteen, if he counted the two ABP drivers. Despite its enormous size the transport itself carried a crew of only eighteen.

"Ah, I must clear this with the Pilot, sir," he mumbled uneasily.

"Right, let's go and see him," Terr said and extended his arm in invitation. With a last look at the Fleet invaders, the merchant officer nodded to his two men and walked briskly toward the cable-tube hatch.

The fully lit command deck instantly familiar, the nav

bubble opaque. The two watchstanders looked at Terr with undisguised curiosity and some amusement. It wasn't often they had a chance to watch the military in action. The Master Pilot swiveled his couch and stood up. Bemused, his small eyes crinkled in a smile, he gazed keenly at Terr and shook his balloon head.

"Second Scout, after reading the message, I don't know whether I should applaud your initiative or have you thrown off my ship."

"It wouldn't be the first time."

"Well, Pizgor is underwriting this wild scheme of yours. That's something. At least the owners will be compensated if this thing goes sour."

"About your owners, sir—"

The pilot raised his hand. "Don't worry. I understand your need for security and I will not be contacting them." He shook his head again and glanced at the Second Pilot standing beside Terr.

"Number four and six holds have sufficient space for the Scout's ABPs. I'll leave it up to you to arrange berthing for his men." An easy order to make, but judging from the young officer's glum expression, less than easy to implement. "Mind you, Second Scout, even using passenger quarters, there won't be enough bunks for all your men."

"I understand. They will try not to get in your way."

"I can see now why I was told to refuse supercargo," the pilot muttered. Passengers would have been underfoot and also at considerable risk.

One of the watchstanders turned and cleared his throat. "Sir, two ABPs have cleared *Ramora*. They're holding position and requesting docking instructions."

The Second Pilot immediately strode toward the watchstander's station and issued orders. In the main display plate, split images showed huge hold hatches opening on the opposite sides of *Hronin's* hull. One of the ABPs broke formation and slowly maneuvered over the looming hull. Close to the open port hold, the other ABP moved toward it, hesitated, and then drifted in. The hold hatch closed silently behind it.

Terr admitted grudgingly Osinara executed the evolution well. He looked at the pilot and returned his quizzical smile.

"Satisfied?" the pilot asked.

"Yes, sir."

"When will you initiate your part of the scheme?"

"In six hours. If there is a raider out there and they're watching—"

"Beyond the detection range of your M-3?"

"Unlikely, I admit, but it isn't uncommon for a raider to mount some pretty enhanced sensor packages. You can understand why. When I drop normal again, and if someone is watching, I want them to interpret this little stop as unsuccessful repairs."

The pilot pulled on his chin, suddenly serious. "You realize, even with your men and the ABPs, there could still be casualties if I am attacked. You won't be able to bring your ship in quickly enough to stop a strike."

"You don't understand, Pilot. I don't *want* to stop a strike."

"What's that?"

"I want to capture their ship. That's why I have the ABPs. They will attach themselves to their hull and board it. This will prevent the raider from detaching, standing off and pounding you."

"While their boarding party massacres my crew," the pilot said bitterly.

"No one will get massacred if you don't let them board. That's what the ABPs and the marines are for," Terr said patiently, letting the older man think it through, suddenly aware he had a silent, but attentive audience in the two watchstanders. As soon as he left, this would spread like wildfire among *Hronin's* crew.

"Preventing them from boarding isn't always possible, my boy," the pilot grunted, then patted Terr on the shoulder. "It's risky, but workable. I don't like the idea of you shadowing me two lights off."

"Squirt a signal if you think you're being intercepted. I'll be able to close within two hours."

"A lot can happen in two hours, Second Scout."

"I need to play like I'm having drive problems, and I don't expect anything until we reach Banard. By then, I'll close with you. If we're separated, obey whatever instructions they give you and my men will take care of the rest. Remember, they'll be after your cargo, Pilot."

"You hope! Why not simply skirt Banard?" the pilot grumbled sourly, having second thoughts about the whole mad scheme. Terr sympathized with him.

"Because it's the best place along our course line for anyone to jump us, and I want to give them that opportunity. It's all in my contingency orders."

"Sir," the comms operator looked up. "*Ramora* is requesting that Second Scout Terr return immediately."

"That was all?" the pilot queried.

"Nothing else."

"Well, I guess I better get back," Terr said. "Once underway, maintain three-quarter boost. I'll hold normal separation." Less than half boost for *Ramora*, but fast enough.

The Second Pilot deep in thought as he accompanied Terr down to the hold. Osinara and Razzo were waiting for him. The rest of the men were deployed unloading the ABPs. The young pilot nodded to them and looked questioningly at Terr.

"We really won't be going into action, will we?"

"Why? You nervous?"

"Frankly, yes."

Terr chuckled. "Don't be. Another thing. If any of my men give you trouble, throw them out the lock. Okay? Hear that Razzo?" he demanded without taking his eyes off the young pilot.

"Aye, sir."

Terr turned to Osinara. "Just like a drill, Mister!"

"Yes, sir," Osinara said crisply and stood to.

He yearned for a chance to show his commander he could handle himself. Now that he had command, he couldn't hide a little disquiet and the fluttering in his stomach, or the sudden dampness in his armpits. Just like a drill...

Terr grunted and glanced at Razzo, who nodded briefly. Osinara needed to exercise command and the crusty chief would see to it the boy did not do anything dumb. Without looking back, he strode toward the open hatchway and the access tube.

The lock cycled shut behind him and he let out a loud breath.

"Tah, the gods will tell," he muttered and walked purposefully toward his ship.

He took the tube to the command deck. When the hatch opened, he automatically glanced around out of habit. Dhar and Mati were bent over the engineering panel, deep in discussion. Someone gave a discrete cough and Dhar quickly looked up.

"Mr. Dharaklin, get us underway," Terr ordered and flopped into the command couch as Dhar nodded.

"Mr. Mati, disengage from *Hronin* and retract the tube. Comms, advise the transport that we have detached and he should prepare to transit."

"Access tube clear and retracting."

"*Hronin* has acknowledged, sir."

In the main plate, *Hronin's* huge bulk already receding quickly before it vanished into darkness.

"Engineering?"

"Cleared distortion limit and ready to transit."

"Sir," the comms operator looked up. "*Hronin* has transited."

Mati glanced from tactical at Terr. "Ship is ready to maneuver at your command, sir."

"Very well. Get us into flight mode and transit."

The deck darkened and the nav bubble cleared. Stars shifted as *Ramora* adjusted its position to the murmur of computer status reports. In a brief flash of blue-white light the M-3 slipped smoothly into subspace. Brown and yellow gravity waves coiled around it, writhing at the intruding distortion. Terr swept his eyes over the displays and stood up.

"Mr. Mati, you've got the deck. Keep an extended sensor watch and call me if anyone comes looking."

"Aye, sir."

"Dhar, come with me."

In his quarters, Terr eased himself into a formchair and extended his legs before him. On his left, a section of transparent polymer hull peeked into blackness. He swept a hand at a seat.

"Is everything well, my brother?" Dhar asked gravely as he sat down.

Terr buried his face between his hands and rubbed his eyes. "*Hronin's* pilot is nervous and having second thoughts," he mumbled between his fingers.

"I've been having second thoughts ever since we started this," Dhar said dryly, his face expressionless.

Amused, Terr looked at him. "Your declaration of support is appreciated. Anyway, why the recall?"

"Message from Ambassador Rayon. *Rakish*, the Four Suns bulk carrier? They matched two of its fuel cells with a ship that landed on Mitlan two days ago." Mitlan lay on the ragged edge of Karkan space, a minor trade waypoint.

"Yes!" Terr grinned and pumped his fist.

Against the Gods of Shadow

Dhar smiled indulgently. He realized the whole mission was an impossible task. He also knew his brother would do everything possible to fulfill his orders. Tracking the raider to Mitlan came as their first real break.

"Unfortunately, by the time they confirmed the match, the raider had already unloaded its cargo. Diplomatic Branch operatives are working to penetrate the ground organization."

"They haven't taken any action against the raider?"

"Keeping an eye on it and its crew for now."

"Good, good. Two days." Terr tapped his teeth with a finger. "You know what I would like to do, don't you?"

Unhappily, Dhar did. He had been with his brother long enough to recognize the gleam of unorthodox tactics. Always in the extreme.

"Take over that ship?" He frowned and shook his head. "Sankri, that is insanity."

"Yeah, but what a thought, eh?"

"I get nervous when you start getting such thoughts. In this case, don't! Suppose you did take the ship. The first time another raider asked you to ID yourself, the plot would be up. We would not only compromise ourselves, but more importantly, the raiders would be alerted."

"Okay, Mr. First Officer, what *do* we do then?"

"Well, *sir*, I don't see there is much we *can* do. We cannot abandon the Devon transport."

"I wonder. What's our mission objective?"

Dhar peered closely at his alien brother. "To locate the raider base."

"Go on."

"We must take any and all action to achieve that objective."

"Based on that startling insight, what is your recommendation, Mr. First Officer?"

"Change course for Mitlan," Dhar said in disgust. "I hate it when you do that. Still, we cannot simply discard a plan of action that might yet work, and Anabb's operatives will not lose that raider."

Terr grinned, reached between them, and patted Dhar fondly on the arm. "I agree. I don't exactly relish herding *Hronin*. With the raider tagged, SC&C will be able to keep an eye on it. Still, let's look at the possibilities." He leaned across the desk and tapped a pad on the inlaid console. The Wall display station came alive in a swirl of color. "Computer, display present position in relation to Mitlan. Project position after four days using current ops parameters and state flight time at max boost."

From the softly glowing blue dot, a thin orange line pierced deep into the Palean Union. Far on the right, a yellow circle tagged Mitlan, and a pulsing orange line connected the circle from the projected endpoint. Terr read off the flight time and hissed.

"Four days before we can leave *Hronin*. That's eight days before we'd get to Mitlan. Not good. They'd be gone before we got there. We would need to intercept sooner. Computer, show all Fleet units within fifteen light-years of our projected course."

"Unable to comply. IFF restrictions and level two communications protocol in place."

"Rit! I forgot about that. Never mind; it was only a passing thought."

"Sankri, this level two comms protocol, are you expecting to encounter a Fleet vessel?"

"Why do you ask?"

"The meeting with Commissioner Hiraki. I saw that faraway look when you mentioned a wild idea. The Paleans may be pushing the envelope on what is acceptable behavior, but to use a Fleet unit…"

Terr stood up and gazed at the gravity waves coiling around the ship. When he turned, his eyes were icy.

"I wasn't kidding when I said Sargon and the Paleans are

probably using their own ships to conduct raids. It's a logical necessity. What I haven't said, this might be deeper than anyone realizes, or is willing to admit, at least openly."

Dhar helped plan their strategy and tactics, but the possibility that Fleet units were subverted shook him. When he considered the stakes, it was a plausible and even expected conclusion, however unpalatable. To have to fight one of their own seemed inconceivable, but would it be one of their own? Would the people behind the raids see it as treason against the Serrll or a fight for independence? Dhar did not need to think too long about that. What Sargon and the Paleans were doing, if they were behind this, could in no way be compared with the struggle by Kaleen and Orgomy to achieve political independence. Murdering innocent merchant crews to engender political change went plain piracy and any redemption.

"What if we do meet another Fleet ship?"

Terr grinned. "We give the son of a canal worm a ping with our projector and watch him roast!"

Chapter Four

Side by side, the two ships waited.

With no sense of motion, they drifted at sublight speed. Pale yellow light permeated the subdued atmosphere of the command deck. Beyond the transparent nav bubble, even the stars seemed frozen in place. One of the watchstanders looked up and met Tanard's eye.

"*Hronin* has transited."

"Escort?"

"Moving, but continues to show power fluctuations."

"Mmm." Tanard pulled at his collar and frowned, his finger momentarily lingering on the scar at his throat.

Instead of charging in and disposing of the escort, then pick over the Devon transport's rich haul at his leisure, he decided to shadow them when the power fluctuations were detected from the M-3's drive. There were any number of possible explanations for the fluctuations, all of them plausible. When both ships dropped normal, that decided him. If the escort did have drive problems and unable to continue, all the better. He fully intended to destroy the M-3 in order to accomplish his mission, but preferred not having to fight. He had no qualms about attacking the transport, it being merely a target. The M-3 sweeper, on the other hand, was a fellow Fleet unit manned by colleagues, even if they shared different political convictions. It was also a sound tactical decision. His augmented projector gave him a distinct power advantage over the other M-3, but he knew random variables present in any battle did not always make the encounter a certainty. A lucky shot, failure of a vital system, and the confrontation would suddenly take on a different and an altogether unwelcome dimension, and not only for himself.

Against the Gods of Shadow

He knew what an M-3 could do. Built by Sofam Industries as a medium interceptor, it had the speed of an M-4 cruiser, matching its profile as a general-purpose patrol craft. The M-3 had a particularly well-armored hull that could withstand several seconds of direct unshielded fire. In its standard configuration, armed with a single Koyami 9A phased array projector, it could unleash almost continuous traversing bursts of seventy-two TeV. With a standard complement of fifty-eight officers and crew, it formed the mainstay of all Fleet activities. A formidable vessel under any circumstances.

"Closure rate?"

"At present divergence, four hours will make them three point-eight lights from our position."

That would take them well out of his detection range, but the target wasn't maneuvering, and he knew where they were going. He would find it when he wanted it.

"We'll wait here for a while," he rasped quietly and leaned back into his couch, the material squirmed as it molded itself to him.

Standing off some forty talans, *Zaradej* looked like any medium-sized bulk carrier, as indeed it basically was, but its ordinary lines hid the sinister nature of the predator. He would need its firepower in any encounter with the M-3 escort. A quick kill and get the job done. Others can worry about honor, or lack of it.

Moody, he took a break and went below to his quarters. Lying on his bunk, hands clasped behind his head, he ran through the possible scenarios that could unfold over the coming hours. If the M-3 could not complete its repairs and withdrew, he had a clear run at the transport. Even if it called for support, with level two comms protocol restrictions in place, another Fleet unit would not be in a position to respond in time to help the Devon transport. If one did show up on the scene, the tactical situation would essentially remain the same. He would simply shift his focus on the new arrival. Provided the new arrival wasn't an M-4, of course.

Frowning, he shook his head in rueful admiration. Whoever dreamed up the IFF restriction was strikingly smart. In a single stroke the move denied him a real-time disposition picture of Fleet units in the area, and this time, Le Maran could not help him. Without knowing where they were or what they were doing, he ran a real risk blundering into another ship, possibly a more powerful one. Admittedly a minimal risk. However, disentangling himself from an M-4 would take more than just fancy talk.

Well, when he took on the job, they didn't tell him it would be easy. He tried to sleep, tossed, then fell into its dark embrace.

The comms alert beeped. He opened his eyes instantly as if someone had switched on a piece of machinery, swung his legs down and padded to the desk. The years of watchkeeping were too deeply ingrained. Momentarily staring at his reflection on the polished surface, he jabbed a pad.

"Yes?"

"It's four hours, sir."

"What's the escort doing, Mr. Winn?"

"Just before we lost track, it was still there and showing power surges. They have slowed to one-third boost."

"Anything between us I need to worry about?"

"We're clear for Banard."

"Perfect," he said and pictured Winn's crafty smile.

Banard's Star hung as a bloated K2 puffing itself into a red primary. If it ever possessed any inner planets, they were consumed long ago, leaving behind two gas giants, dozens of moons, and a junkyard of assorted rubble between them. What made the system interesting, both giants were powerful radio emitters, which created a tangle of electric current flux lines and gravitational interference fields. A bad place to get stuck in, but that blanket of interference would also keep him out of the M-3's detection envelope, until too late to escape.

Random factors appeared to have worked in his favor. In other words, he may have gotten lucky.

"Get us moving. In three hours, I want to be at extreme detection range of the target. We will commence our run when they get to within half a light from Banard. I'll be up in a minute."

He pulled on his zip-jacket and strode out. Now that action had started, he pushed aside his misgivings and the political dimension of this strike. There would be time enough to pick over the bones later. The cable-tube took him to the command deck. When the hatch slid away, he walked to his seat and automatically looked around, checking the displays. Satisfied, he settled down and stretched his legs. Winn swiveled, bobbed his head, and pointed at the main plot display plate.

"Our course will effectively keep us in Banard's shadow. It will also lose us sight of the target."

Tanard rubbed his hands and grinned at him with the left side of his mouth. Winn was very capable, but tended to be somewhat nervous and uncertain. In many ways, a perfect subordinate.

"So?"

Thoughtful for a moment, Winn's face cleared. "It doesn't really matter, does it? If the target changes course, we'll know it as he gets out of Banard's signal cone shadow. If it doesn't, by the time we make our run, he'll be coming straight at us."

"We'll make a commander out of you yet," Tanard said comfortably.

The comms watchstander smiled. Winn grinned and shook his head.

"You can keep it!"

"When do we occult?"

"Two hours eleven minutes."

At less than one-third boost, *Laverne* and *Zaradej* were coasting. Tanard could easily close the distance with *Hronin* and its ailing escort, but he refrained. He required the tactical advantage Banard's interference blanket offered, should the target attempt subspace comms or launch beacons. He only needed to wait some two hours. No need to be impatient.

"Perfect. Go to secondary alert and warn Val Keen. Tell him to maintain port station at one hundred thousand talans and to run a target contact analysis after one-point-eight hours."

Winn issued orders and an additional watchstander came up. Railee took up the weapons station and started his checklist. Running his long fingers over the color-reactive panel, he quickly scanned the display plate readouts. Only his second raid with his sometimes irascible commander, Railee wasn't worried; at least not about the Devon transport. The escorting M-3 was something else, a fellow warship, almost identical to theirs. Even with a power curve advantage, he wasn't too keen to put it to a test in an actual exchange. He had seen Tanard work and knew his commanding officer to be an excellent tactician, but they never fought another M-3. Not for real.

He glanced briefly at Tanard and no longer felt a moment of disquiet and revulsion that used to grip him at the sight of that scarred face. The right side a mask and covered whatever turmoil lurked behind those enormous black eyes. Tanard more than compensated for that lack of expression through his left side. Now, Railee almost ignored the terrible wounds and only saw a stern, but fair commander.

In the engineering spaces below, readiness levels were increased, the power management system tested, and the powerful Koyami 2/F projector run through a status check. Standing beside the giant primary system display plate with its intricate energy pathways that traced power feeds to every part of the ship, broad hands on generous hips, Vukhan scowled. He always scowled.

Against the Gods of Shadow

Short, round, shoulders stooping from a lifetime of crawling around access ducts and cramped drive spaces, he stared critically at the slight fluctuation in the power feed loop from the projector interface assembly. About to make one of his standard stock caustic remarks, the flow stabilized. The power management system had not raised a fault alert. Still scowling, he stared at the display a while longer. Ever since they'd had the perishing projector augmented, the bitch had acted twitchy. His fingers drummed against his hips, tying themselves into a knot.

The alert order had hit every individual differently. Some were glad to get into action. For others, it was only a message, their duties unchanged. A few were uncertain about fighting another Fleet vessel, not sure how that reconciled with raiding Pizgor commerce. Outwardly at least, the informality dropped away and they became cold professionals.

Taller and lanky than usual in a Palean, Winn settled back into his couch. The status displays in the main repeater plate before him showed the ship waking up, getting ready. Everything moved with smooth, quiet precision. The endless drills and tactical simulations honed the crew into a single coordinated unit. It hadn't been easy. Selected for their professional ability—Tanard had no use for political zealots—as new arrivals, many of the crew anticipated a soft assignment picking over hapless merchant vessels. The Lemos facility shook their complacency, as had the sight of their commander.

He remembered fondly when he and Tanard received their first all-Palean rotation crew. Tanard looked them over and shook his head in disgust. He turned to Winn and with his broken voice, simply said, "Get them into shape before I burst into tears." Winn took him at his word with relish and evil anticipation. The result generated predictable: resentment, hate, grudging acceptance, and finally, loyalty and pride.

They were a bunch of pirates, all of them, Winn decided wryly.

He knew Tanard thought him sometimes indecisive. However, he saw it as his duty to point out unpleasant options and be a tempering influence on his commander. He took comfort from that, the alternative being his caution masked cowardice. Not in his nature to charge in like Tanard, he preferred to calculate all the odds and variables before committing himself. Was that cowardice? Certainly, the crew never hinted they considered him less than capable. Different styles. Yes, that was it.

Loyalty to the cause above everything else, even if it meant he would one day have to betray Tanard.

The minutes ticked away slowly while the orange star grew in the nav bubble before them. On the dot, Winn made a slight course adjustment to bring them out of Banard's shadow cone, and immediately searched for the transport and its escort. Nothing, but it would not be long now. They continued their watch in deathly silence.

Short of two hours into the run and on the extreme limits of detection, the main plate showed a yellow blip.

"Anomaly track identified as a type four bulk transport hull," the computer announced. "Range, two point-two light-years."

"Devon transport detected, sir," Winn said comfortably as another blip appeared. Seconds later, it flared in an energy spike.

"Detecting a transit discharge from a K/11 type M-3 picket sweeper," the computer declared flatly.

Winn's face creased. "The M-3 has dropped normal."

"Occult time?" Tanard said softly.

"Fourteen minutes."

"What's *Hronin* doing?"

"Maintaining course and speed, sir."

"Mmm. The M-3's power curve?"

"Down by eighteen percent."

Tanard scratched the scar on his chin. Even at reduced

speed, it appeared the escort had not been able to affect sufficient repairs to continue its mission. He liked it, but not completely happy. Why did it decide to drop out now, just as its charge entered a known navigational hazard? Coincidence, or forced into it? Tanard was wary of coincidences.

"Can the transport detect us?" he asked suddenly.

Winn frowned and shook his head. "Not unless they boosted their sensor suite. Intelligence didn't indicate that any such retrofit took place. By the time we get into the M-3's acquisition envelope, we'll be occulted."

And blind, Tanard added to himself. Trying to put himself into the other M-3 commander's mind, a most curious feeling, he had the oddest urge to flee. His fingers twined in agitation. What the pits was the matter with him? He commanded two powerful ships, more than a match for any single M-3. This one also happened to be sick. Yet his sense of unease would not leave him.

"Occulting in three minutes," Winn said quietly, noting Tanard's preoccupation. Did they have a problem?

"Computer, intercept time from start of run?" Tanard demanded harshly.

"At maximum closure rate, thirty-eight minutes."

"Very well. Comms, alert the auxiliary to get into position. As soon as we're occulted, go to primary alert and commence run."

Winn nodded and waited. On the three-minute mark, he immediately turned to Railee. "Get us hot, but don't raise the secondary grid."

"Charging weapons array, sir," Railee acknowledged and his fingers danced over the console. Head bobbing, happy doing what he was trained to do, and killing lumbering transports simple target practice.

"Vukhan? Stand by all energy demand systems," Winn advised.

"Engineering ready," Vukhan growled from below and

103

Winn grinned.

"Comms? Order the auxiliary to go to four-fifths boost as planned."

"Val Keen has acknowledged." Winn turned to Tanard. "Ship ready to maneuver, sir."

"Very well. Two-thirds boost."

"Two-thirds boost."

Both ships accelerated, *Laverne* drawing slightly ahead. Winn checked the repeater readouts on his plate and turned to Tanard.

"Sir, ship is at primary alert and running."

Tanard merely nodded, his fingers working.

In the tactical plot, Banard's Star rapidly grew into a blue ring. The outer gas giant showed as a smaller ring with a cluster of surrounding dots of its moons. Overlaying the plot, a faint yellow cloud of interference blanketed the system. Brighter orange smears denoted areas of especially heavy gravitational turbulence. At closest approach, they would be more than fourteen light-days from the massive yellow-green giant. At that distance, it wouldn't even show up as a point of light.

Thirty-two minutes into the run, Winn looked up from his tactical station.

"Detected navigational interrogative from the transport," the computer announced. "Designating target one. Range, point-three-six light-years. Distance from Banard, nineteen light-days."

"Contact made with *Hronin*, sir," Winn said comfortably. "He's alone."

Tanard nodded. Nineteen light-days was only three-and-a-half minutes at maximum boost for an M-3; not much time if he wanted to maneuver toward Banard. The red target blip firmed up on the edge of the interference cloud. Seconds later, a smaller blip materialized behind the transport.

"K-band interrogative scans detected from a K/11 type

M-3 sweeper. Designating target two. Same range," the computer said without inflection.

"Holy crap!" Winn whispered in a strangled voice. His large black eyes widened and his long finger fluttered in agitation.

"It's the escort," Railee murmured bleakly and stole a glance at his commander. Tanard didn't move, his stony features fixed on the plot. Wordlessly, his eyes locked with Winn's.

"Any power fluctuations?" he asked quietly.

"Showing normal, but his power curve is still down." Winn frowned heavily. "He *can't* know! So what the pits is he doing there?"

The left side of Tanard's mouth twitched. "No, he cannot know. Like us, if anyone planned to jump the transport, it would be here. Not altogether surprising that the escort would make an effort to see the transport safely past this point."

Despite what he said to Winn, the totally unexpected appearance of the escorting M-3 placed him in a dilemma. Was it simply a logical tactical maneuver to cover the transport? Something he would have done himself. To be here the M-3 must have transited within minutes of Tanard being occulted. Damned quick repairs, that's for certain. What if there weren't any repairs? He didn't much care where that train of thought took him. Curiously, his inner tactical sense warned him to break off the engagement. Why this sudden skittishness? His long fingers drummed on the armrest.

Maybe he should force the issue.

"Give the M-3 an IFF ping and transmit *Zaradej's* ident dump, then take us down to half boost," he ordered gruffly.

"Sir, there are IFF restrictions—"

"Just send the damn ping, Mr. Winn."

The escort closed the separation with the transport before answering the ping. Nothing unusual in any of that. What *was* unusual, the escort commander chose to answer his ping. Now, what did that tell him? Patiently, he waited for the escort to open a channel. After a minute of silence, he grinned ruefully and nodded to Winn.

"Open a channel."

* * *

The envelope of Banard's interference field obscured the starboard side of the nav bubble plot. Surrounded by its clutch of scattered moons and assorted rubble, the gas giant had a cloud of debris designed to snare anyone foolish enough to venture within its grasp. Its ferocious magnetic flux generated vicious current flows between its moons. A brooding god throwing lightnings. Within the trailing edge of the field a red blip blinked into life and firmed, encircled by a faint ring of its primary shield. A larger and fainter blip lumbered behind it. The computer quietly reported tactical details about the two contacts.

"An M-3 shepherding what looks like a medium bulk carrier," Dhar rumbled, studying the main repeater plot. "Course track shows them heading for Karkan space. The course is a little abnormal, though. They also seem to be in a bit of a hurry."

"Would you want to linger around here? Designate as targets one and two. Go to initial alert, but hold secondary shield grid," Terr ordered, sitting unmoving in his command couch.

Tempted to alert Osinara, but the boy would know from the transport's sensors, and Razzo would keep him steady. The appearance of the M-3 and its charge was unusual, but not *that* unusual. Before leaving Pizgor, he closely studied all scheduled commercial departures and arrivals from every nearby system that had a legitimate reason for crossing his course. He also knew that any number of unscheduled flights could explain the two visitors.

Against the Gods of Shadow

"Sir, we have an incoming from *Hronin*," Mati announced without looking up from his station. The contact stirred the watch crew and the deck became awash with quick glances and eyebrows raised in questioning speculation. Mati felt an undercurrent of anticipation at the prospect of possible action. Within that excitement also lurked a suggestion of fear. *Please, don't let me screw up…*

"Put him through," Terr said, slightly irritated at the interruption. He didn't have time to nursemaid the merchant now.

The display plate cleared, revealing the *Hronin* pilot's round features, now creased in a deep frown.

"Second Scout, I presume you're tracking the two contacts?"

"I am. Until we clear the datum point, please keep this channel open for my tactical commands."

"I thought you *wanted* an attack?"

"I do, but I don't want my moves debated. Just execute my orders."

"Now, see here—"

Terr turned to Mati, nodded and the display returned to its tactical mode.

"We have an IFF ping from the M-3. His aspect shows him slowing to half boost," the comms operator reported and Terr exchanged a quick glance with Dhar. The driver of that heap either hadn't received the comms restrictions notice, possible but unlikely, or he deliberately ignored the order.

"Mr. Mati, close to fifty-five thousand talans off *Hronin*. Computer, give me target one's IFF ident dump."

"SSF *Laverne* IFF valid, First Scout Kai Tanard commanding. Detached duty to Sector TACOPSCOM."

"Very well. Comms, return the ping."

"Sir? There is a level—"

"Just return the ping."

Dhar got up from his tactical station and stood beside

Terr's command couch.

"What are your thoughts, Sankri?"

Terr scratched the scar on his left temple. "It could be a chance passing."

"I meant the IFF violation."

"I know what you meant."

"If we close, our course will take us well within Banard's interference zone. We will lose our subspace comms capability."

"I know."

Dhar stared hard at his brother, then nodded. Terr had no choice. He would allow the situation to develop, even if it meant an encounter with a warship and a disguised raider, even if it meant their lives. Achieving their mission objective only required they communicate their findings to Ambassador Rayon. The mission did not require them to survive. He swept his eyes around the deck and heads hurriedly turned back to their stations.

Kieran waited for the first officer to settle himself into his seat before glancing casually at Mati, who shook his head. He often saw the commander and first officer discuss tactics, but violating a comms protocol? In the end, it didn't much matter. The decision way above his pay grade. If it came to a fight, all he had to make sure the projector kept firing. His large flap ears pricked a bit as he started doing status checks, just in case.

"Sir, *Laverne* has opened a channel. Signal strength is degrading rapidly."

"Very well. Put him through."

Even at point-three lights the main plate cleared into a burst of white interference and scanning lines, the subspace signals distorted by Banard's complex gravitational fields. Tanard's narrow features firmed and his enormous black eyes glinted.

"Second Scout Terrllss-rr, a chance but wary meeting,"

he rasped heavily, head bobbing.

Terr blinked at the scars as he considered the Palean's words. They could have been his. He genuinely hadn't contemplated the possibility that Tanard may be seeing *him* as a potential raider to be avoided. An ironic reversal of roles and a valuable lesson.

"A wary meeting indeed, First Scout. I'm herding a Devon 3 VL-4 resupply transport, *Hronin*. It seems your course may be paralleling ours for a while."

A burst of interference snowed the plate with crackles and pops.

"Only for a while," Tanard said affably. "My base course is taking me and *Zaradej* into Karkan space. Should you wish to close with us, you have my permission. We can keep each other company for a while. Any lurking raider will think twice before chancing himself against the two of us."

Exactly what Terr might have said. "Thanks, I'll do that. I'll form up on you at forty thousand talans."

Static drowned out Tanard's waved acknowledgment as he cut contact. Terr pulled at his chin. Tanard hadn't asked him for *Hronin's* ping. Now, why would that be? Unless he already knew?

"Mr. Dharaklin. Go to primary alert and hold primary shield grid. Notify *Hronin* of my intentions and have Mr. Osinara stand by to launch the ABPs on command."

"Primary alert engaged."

Terr punched a pad on his armrest. "Shan? Give me a power fluctuation and maintain a reduced energy profile, but I'll want everything online on order."

"No problems. Just give the word."

"Right. Mr. Mati, shift starboard and maintain one-third boost. Match and bring us to forty thousand talans separation from *Laverne*."

* * *

At a combined closure rate of two-thirds boost, Tanard watched *Ramora* and *Hronin* change their aspects in the tactical plot. Too easy, and why wouldn't it be? Why should Terr think this was anything but a chance encounter? They were two Fleet units doing boring escort duty. As the range closed between them, even fleeing no longer an option for Terr. The Devon transport could not hope to outrun Tanard's ship.

The young commander returned his ping, and even accepted direct communication against standing orders. What did that tell him? Terr could be brash, contemptuous of silly orders, or simply confident in his ability? It didn't matter. Once Terr closed, Tanard would destroy him.

"Warning, detected increased power level emissions from target two," the computer stated. "Augmentation in primary shield grid energy status." Tanard nodded. Only to be expected when maneuvering with an unknown contact. "Closure rate is one-point-nine-three billion talans per second. Contact in twenty-nine minutes."

"Comms? Advise Val Keen to engage *Hronin* as soon as I open fire on *Ramora*."

"Auxiliary acknowledges."

"Very well. Mr. Railee, stand by secondary shield and weapons synchronization."

"Weapons are online and synchronization with the primary grid is complete. Ship is ready to synchronize with the secondaries."

They waited.

"Detected K-band nav scans from target two," the computer said. "Primary shield configuration only. Detecting increased power core emissions. Maintaining closure rate."

Tanard frowned. Increased power core emissions? *Ramora* supposedly had power problems.

"Initial firing point?"

"Two point-six minutes to IP."

Railee nodded, confirming the computer's report. Allowing for maneuvering, reaching the optimum firing point
would take a bit longer.

But it didn't take longer. *Ramora* slowed quickly to match
speed and slid smoothly into position portside, at exactly forty
thousand talans separation. Tanard pursed his lips and nodded approvingly. Young Terr certainly seemed to know his
business. A shame to kill him. *Hronin* fell back and more or
less matched with *Zaradej*.

"Optimum firing solution," the computer said coldly.

Tanard felt the skin at the back of his neck crawl and he
suddenly felt cold. The irrational urge to flee came back to
haunt him.

"Mr. Winn, order Val Keen to commence firing. Raise
our secondary grid, synchronize, and fire."

On receiving the firing order, Val Keen retracted the double hatch in *Zaradej's* underbelly to uncover the energized Terrasec 8/B projector dome, now glowing dull orange. The ship
rolled slightly to starboard to bring *Hronin* into optimum firing position.

Laverne raised its secondary shield grid and automatically
sent a ranging ping. Shields pulsing in synchronization phase,
energy streamed along the projector flux lines as the computer established targeting lock. It swooped in for the kill.

* * *

"L-band lock established by target one in preparatory firing
phase," the computer announced suddenly and Terr's heart
beat faster. "Target has raised secondary shield grid and is
synchronizing. Target two has established lock on *Hronin*."

He had been right about a trap, he thought savagely and
jabbed a pad on the armrest console. This was no longer a
case of simple raider piracy. Using a clandestine Fleet unit

provided proof that Sargon or the Palean Union were engaged in political intimidation. Rayon needed to know about this at all costs.

"Pilot! Drop normal now…now!" He jerked his head at Kieran. "Lock on *Laverne's* projector and fire as soon as you get the secondaries up and synchronized. Don't wait for my order. Just keep firing at him. Mr. Mati, maneuver us behind *Laverne* and head for *Hronin*." *If you can*, he added to himself. Tanard executed a textbook pincer engagement. Caught between two ships, Terr needed to neutralize his weakest opponent before Tanard's fire distracted him too much.

He was also relieved that action had started. He hated the waiting part and the thinking, the worrying, and anxiety that went with it. Once everyone started shooting, there wouldn't be time for second thoughts or being afraid. They were committed. Death could come with a swipe of an energy beam, but different to staring it down. His senses came alive and his body tingled. He hardly glanced at the displays, the tactical situational awareness burned bright in his mind. His eyes lit in anticipation of a hunt.

At forty thousand talans, Tanard could hardly miss. A track of yellow ionization flashed between the two M-3s and traversed *Ramora's* port side, sending the delicate geometry lines of the distortion field torus into purple scintillation. Hit part way through the synchronization cycle, the ship staggered and the shields flared with blue-green discharges. In an overload surge the power management system sullenly recycled the sequence, preventing Kieran from firing. *Ramora* checked its tumble and rushed toward *Zaradej*. Tanard fired again and his eighty-two TeV beam rippled along the whole length of *Ramora's* side. Shield grid arcing, holding synchronized, Kieran able to at last return fire. He focused on *Laverne's* projector dome and struck with a sustained burst. *Laverne* slued, its shields discharging in a lightning display, but otherwise, they showed no sign of damage.

Against the Gods of Shadow

Hronin simply wanted to get out of everybody's damned way. As her distortion field precursor depolarized in a preparatory to dropping normal, *Zaradej* fired a long burst directly at *Hronin's* drive spaces. Its shield collapsed immediately in a cascading shower of bright flares and the ship lurched beneath the crippling blow. Where the beam struck, the hull glowed blue-white as the plating material ablated. *Hronin* vanished as it dropped below lightspeed.

Val Keen could see *Ramora* bearing down on him and blanched. Although armed with an equivalent of an M-2 type projector and equipped with an enhanced shield grid, he could not hope to match himself against the more powerful vessel in any direct exchange. That was supposed to be Tanard's job and he could have it. Intending to follow the crippled *Hronin*, leaving the two M-3s to sort it out between them, Keen started to depolarize his distortion field.

Before *Zaradej* could drop normal, Kieran fired. With his slightly starboard up attitude, *Zaradej's* projector dome became almost fully exposed. The incoming beam flowed along the shield flux lines, probing for a weakness. Momentarily, the primary shield held, then the beam ripped through and struck the hull beside the dome housing. A converted carrier, *Zaradej* did not have armor like a warship, and the hull breached almost at once, allowing a massive energy surge to tear at the projector assembly. The system designed to take combat damage, but not designed to take it from within. Its containment lining penetrated, the complex energy interface circuits vaporized. All this happened in less than a second. Reeling, *Zaradej* dropped normal, having lost its main offensive capability. With the ship shuddering around him, Keen saw *Ramora's* shields flare under Tanard's sustained fire. The sight didn't make him any happier.

Tanard's eighty-two TeV fire came as a rude shock. Facing an adversary who delivered almost fourteen percent more firepower into his bursts than Terr could, his situation was grim. If he elected to hold position and slugged it out, unless he got in a disabling shot, he would likely be overwhelmed and ground down. He must keep the broader objectives of his mission in mind, even if it meant abandoning the Devon transport and part of his crew. At least he eliminated one variable from the encounter. The auxiliary raider wouldn't be firing at anyone anytime soon. If it attempted to close with the transport, Razzo's ABPs should be able to board and overpower it, unless Tanard chose to pursue. Terr thought it unlikely. He contemplated finishing off the auxiliary, but if he dropped normal, Tanard would be obliged to follow. By destroying the raider, Terr could also be inviting *Hronin's* destruction and death to a third of his crew. *Hronin* might be in trouble, but as long as it survived, it could exploit the situation as it developed, and no tactical advantage existed in pursuing the auxiliary.

Reduce the problem! Do not add variables to a situation already saturated.

Straight out of the Fleet Strategy and Tactics manual.

All right, that left *Laverne* to deal with.

"Computer, range to Banard-two?"

"Fourteen point-three light-days."

Almost three minutes at maximum boost. *Ramora* shuddered beneath him from another impact and the air smelled of ozone. Everyone tense, but steady, doing their job. They might have been concerned and even afraid, something normal. Training kept them functioning. Terr made his decision.

"Mr. Mati, break off and make for Banard-two. Full boost."

In the nav dome, the stars wheeled as the M-3 swung to its new course. A raking burst traversed along *Ramora's* starboard side and the ship lurched, its shields flickering in point collapses. Another burst hit the same spot and penetrated. The hull plating ablated and distorted as it softened. A small breach opened and a white jet of venting atmosphere shot out before the hull material sealed itself. As *Ramora* rolled from the impact, another beam played the length of its underbelly, burned through the secondary shield force lines, and brushed the primary grid opposite the projector dome and its housing. A backsurge of energy arced against the housing.

The dome not holed, but the structure took a heavy dose of high-energy particle decay. On the command deck, the re-straining field largely negated the sudden shift in internal grav-ity. The effect like being squeezed and twisted at the same time, the sensation extremely unpleasant. For some of the crew, more than unpleasant. Thrown against bulkheads, the deck or various fittings, broken limbs, ribs, and bad sprains disabled several.

Terr held tight to the armrests and waited for his body and the ship to settle down. The pounding of his heart sounded unnaturally loud. The comms operator held her right wrist and blood trickled down her temple from a gash on her head. Kieran didn't need orders to continue firing at Tanard's ship. Although able to track, his hits were not causing any ap-parent damage. Worse, his projector power seemed to be down.

Ramora steadied and accelerated toward a distant invisible point, taking them in an instant beyond Tanard's firing range. Thick coils of distorted brown gravity waves snaked around them. The strain on the drive would increase as the gravita-tional distortion grew around Banard-two.

"Command deck, Engineering. Whatever just happened damaged our shield sync assembly," Shan protested in out-rage. Terr could picture the engineer scowling in disapproval. "We're also down eighteen percent on our firing capability."

"Noted," Terr said and glanced at Dhar. "Get a status update." Dhar immediately began calling the decks for dam-age reports. "Mati, what do you have for me?"

"Target one is following, sir."

As Terr knew *Laverne* would. Tanard compelled to follow.

As the primary threat, Tanard could not allow him to get away with knowledge of his identity, or that an M-3 actively supported raiders. Previously, this may have been only a supposition. Actual proof would have enormous and very unpleasant repercussions for whoever ran the operation. Using disguised raiders was one thing. To use an active Fleet unit meant that elements of the Palean Scout Fleet command were implicated. Rayon would strip down every M-3 in the Palean Union to find a match with Tanard's ID dump. It would be a public relations disaster with very disagreeable consequences for the Paleans.

"Mr. Mati, can we transmit?"

"Subspace comms range is now less than six light-days, sir, and getting worse."

It would get worse still the closer they got to Banard.

"Time elapsed of our last status ping?"

"One hour eleven minutes."

Terr nodded. Rayon wouldn't be expecting another one for almost three hours, then. Even if he acted immediately when the next ping didn't arrive, no way to tell how long it would take a relief vessel to get to the datum point. If one did, how would Terr make contact? Once within Banard's system, even ship-to-ship would have limited range or reduced to line-of-sight. The effects of Banard's unhealthy environment were at last making themselves painfully felt, something he could also turn into a tactical advantage.

"Can we ping *Hronin*?"

"Barely within range. With his gear, there is no telling if he would pick it up."

Well, that wasn't all bad. If he couldn't contact the transport, then Tanard wouldn't be able to reach his auxiliary either. That left Terr with a set-piece confrontation in two dimensions: space and time, where he had freedom to wrest any advantage from the available variables. He could deal with that, *Laverne's* greater firepower notwithstanding..

He glanced at the comms operator. "Get below," he told her and jerked his head at the cable-tube hatch. About to protest, but with a broken wrist, she realized she would only be a liability.

Dhar watched the comms operator leave, then stepped to Terr, his features grim.

"There are two killed on deck four. Explosive decompression. Another survived, but suffered serious blood vessel ruptures. Medical has a line of people waiting to be treated for sprains and fractures. So far, we have five unfit for duty. With sixteen in the Devon transport, it leaves us critically undermanned."

Two killed and five seriously injured, Terr mused. Six, if he counted the comms operator. Almost as if his own body felt their pain. He barely nodded, blocking out images of death and wreckage. Time to deal with that later.

"Ship damage?"

"A few things shaken loose, but otherwise we're secure. Repairs are underway. Tactically, our reduced projector yield is of major concern."

"Especially when Tanard can squirt eighty-two TeV at us. Weapons and maneuvering, that's all I need to have working right now. I cannot fight him one-on-one, not with his firepower. We'll be sliced up. If we cannot kill him or disable him, we must get away from him somehow."

"And *Hronin*?"

Terr paused. "I cannot do anything for it now. Once we transmit our logs to Rayon. Only then."

The transport and his crew could be dead by then and they both knew it. Dhar searched Terr's clear eyes, noting their hardness and wondered why he wanted command. Faced with real death, shattered bones, twisted bodies and minds, command was more than running simulations, but he knew if command were ever offered him, he would take it.

"Navigational warning," the computer announced coldly.

"Banard-two on collision course. Impact in seventy seconds. Target one is closing."

Terr had one minute in which to shake off or evade the pursuing M-3. Dhar touched his arm in support and resumed his station.

"Mr. Mati, take us into B-2's atmosphere, edge on."

"Sir?

"The atmosphere envelope will hide us."

At maximum boost, they were traveling at over 8,300 times the speed of light; a frightening velocity this close to the approaching gas giant. If there were any debris along their track large enough to disrupt the nav deflector grid and they hit something, they'd never know it. The only thing left of *Ramora* would be an incandescent plasma trail. They wouldn't actually *hit* anything, not while in subspace, but slamming into a gravitational protuberance induced by a free mass in normal space, it might as well be the same thing.

"Sir, we should be dropping normal now," Mati pointed out, more than a little concerned. Gravitational twisting induced by close proximity to a free mass would disrupt the delicate geometry contours of the distortion field and dump them into normal space with an effect of slamming into the neck of a three dimensional funnel. It would induce a forced collapse of the distortion field and do dreadful damage to their main drive. "For B-2 the distortion limit is two point-six million talans. Any closer and we risk going critical and scrapping our drive. I won't be able to time it that close." Terr risked ramming *Ramora* right into the massive planet, but he wasn't about to say that aloud. They had another problem. "With all the debris and junk in there, we could also induce a forced collapse long before we reach B-2."

Banard grew perceptibly on their port quarter, and the gas giant wasn't even a point of light yet. At their speed it wouldn't be, not until they were right on top of it.

"I know," Terr said quietly. "Tell the computer to take us

into the atmosphere. It will drop us normal automatically before the distortion field goes critical and ruptures." He hoped. Two point-six million talans gave them no time at all to do anything if things went wrong. A split-second maneuver only a computer could manage. "I want a full stop at twenty talans inside the atmosphere. We'll be leaving a plasma bloom in our wake, but that cannot be helped." Terr searched Mati's worried face. "If we reach criticality, dump normal and repolarize immediately. Whatever happens, we've got to get into B-2."

Mati didn't like it, but he nodded. Even if they survived the approach turbulence and transition, the shock of hitting the atmosphere envelope would be horrendous. The shields would either hold or they would all get smeared. He glanced briefly at Kieran and read his fear in the blue eyes. Well, he wanted action. He turned to his console and issued instructions.

"Set," he said and leaned back. Whatever happened now was out of his hands.

"Emergency override active," the computer said. "Impact imminent. Recommend immediate change in course."

"Maintain course," Mati ordered and felt sweat bead on his forehead as the ship quivered from increasingly steep gravitational turbulence.

"Target one has established an L-band acquisition lock."

"Sir, he'll be in firing range before we can drop normal," Dhar announced.

"Impact in four seconds," the computer said. "Target one in preparatory firing phase."

Tanard fired, but Terr was still outside his acquisition envelope. He fired again and *Ramora* trembled beneath Terr as the shields channeled the burst into space. Then he saw *Laverne's* distortion field fluctuate and the ship vanished as it dropped normal, braking its headlong run.

Less than a second from impact the restraining field gripped hard and Terr grunted painfully as *Ramora* shuddered and bucked beneath him, literally being pulled apart by gravity distortions induced by B-2's system of moons and orbiting junk. The gas giant became a sliver of orange-green and suddenly flared into a huge full crescent in the nav bubble, its starboard half in darkness. Terr flinched as *Ramora* skidded and began to rotate. A sudden jarring wrench as they broke into normal space, the computer desperately overstrained the secondary drive to keep the ship from plunging into the planet. The image filled the nav bubble and they hit.

* * *

Coiled and twisting, the massed orange-brown gravity waves whipped around *Laverne*, making the ship quiver and jump in the roiling turbulence. Buffeted by growing gravitational instability as they penetrated deeper into the system, the ship strained to maintain subspace flight. Within two minutes, Tanard received two bitter outbursts from Vukhan about damage to the engineer's precious drive.

Eyes fixed on the pulsing blue dot in the plot, he wondered if his nerve would hold. His instincts screamed at him to break off before he killed them all.

"We must sheer off!" Winn urged fiercely beside him, pointing nervously at the tactical plot and the growing accumulation of debris in their path—and Banard's second gas giant.

"A few more seconds and he'll be in range," Tanard said comfortably, his voice tight and thin. Terr had to veer off. He *had* to!

"A few more seconds and we'll be plastered against one of those rocks out there. We *have* to slow down!"

"If there is anything in our way, *Ramora* will hit it first," he rasped, irritated at Winn's tentative attitude when he rightly pointed out the nav perils of their headlong rush. Tanard couldn't break off, not now. The problem with Winn, he realized in a flash, his first officer was not a combat commander. Different type of reactions were required in action and Winn didn't have it. Steps would need to be taken, if they survived.

The fleeing M-3 showed no sign of its previous drive fluctuation problems and its power curve looked normal. The whole thing a trap, then, and he had been suckered into it royally. How much did BueCult know, or was this merely a random fishing expedition? Random or not, he couldn't allow *Ramora* or *Hronin* to live. The ship shuddered beneath him and the restraining field squeezed his insides. He grunted at the pressure, keeping his eyes on the plot and the M-3 ahead of him. If he were lucky the detritus cluttering the system would do the job for him, but he didn't believe in the fickle whim of fate. He had to silence Terr one way or another. No one must learn that a Palean Fleet unit conducted raids on Pizgor commerce, and no one could learn it attacked *Ramora*. He imagined Le Maran's reaction and shuddered at the thought. It just wouldn't do.

Le Maran and his idiotic orders! If Maran had ever sat in a command couch, he would never have issued such an asinine order. He might be a fine tactician, but it wasn't his butt on the line. Tanard rubbed the scar along his throat. He should not be blaming Le Maran really. His instincts did warn him, but he had grown too confident and ignored them. Mistake or not, he was committed now and he could not go back.

Tanard cast a quick glance around the deck. Everyone understandably looked tense. He also felt an undercurrent of something else almost palpable. He commanded ships and men too long not to recognize the rank smell of fear. Did they misinterpret his tactic to close with the escort as something other than professional? The problem, he decided savagely, the crew enjoyed the fleshpots of Lemos too much, used to easy kills against lumbering transports that didn't fight back.

They had lost the edge. Something would have to be done about that as well.

"L-band acquisition lock achieved. Range, sixty-nine thousand talans. Firing point in four seconds," the computer announced flatly. "Warning, distortion field critical. Precursor failure imminent. Warning, collision with Banard-two in eleven seconds. Immediate transition recommended. Emergency course override will be initiated in eight seconds."

"Commence firing," Tanard ordered. "Maximum yield!"

Fingers fluttering, Railee didn't need to check his console to know that *Ramora* was still out of range. He didn't exactly have to hit it. A near miss would be enough to disrupt and collapse its already unstable distortion field and plunge the ship into normal space. Once normal and with all the gravitational turbulence and energy flux walls around it, *Ramora* may not even be able to repolarize, let alone transit; if lucky enough to have escaped critical damage to its drive. Helpless, it would make for easy picking.

He realized bleakly that *Ramora* could do the very same thing to him, but why didn't it return fire? Did one of his hits damage their projector?

"Engaging," he acknowledged and sent a lance of yellow death at the fleeing, skidding M-3. The beam dissipated, still out of effective range. He kept firing. The range closed rapidly. Disregarding the collision alarm, he had four seconds within which to kill or cripple *Ramora*. He sent a long traversing burst across the escort's stern, only to have it miss as *Laverne* shook beneath him, throwing off the guidance system. Savagely, he stabbed the commit pad again and smiled with grim satisfaction as *Ramora's* shields flared under the impact. In the targeting plot, he could also see B-2 rushing at them.

"Initiating emergency—"

"Cancel!" Tanard snarled. "Keep firing!" Two extra seconds...

Winn stood up and gripped Tanard's shoulder. "Sir! This

is madness!"

Tanard shook him off. What did Terr intend? He could not believe the young commander would slam his ship into the gas giant at 8,300 times the speed of light even if the ship's safety systems allowed him to do so, but he didn't have time to puzzle it out now. If not careful, his ship could meet the same fate. To pits and perdition with him.

"Computer, drop normal!" he snarled, his frustration clear in his mangled voice.

The restraining field gripped them hard and *Laverne* sagged as the tortured distortion field depolarized. It took less than a second, but at his speed, he almost left it too late. With *Laverne* still shedding residual velocity the tactical plot suddenly filled with the onrushing shape of the gas giant. Then the plot jarringly froze as the ship lay suspended and still. The orange-green crescent blotted out the sky less than four-and-a-half million talans ahead of them.

It was a close-run thing.

Winn glanced at the plot, then gave Tanard a hard stare and shook his head. He heard a nervous shuffling of feet and clearing of throats, the command deck thick with relieved tension. His hand poised stiff over the console, Railee gave a weak smile when he realized he was still alive.

Tanard swept his eyes around the deck and snorted. "Pits! We aren't even close," he chided them and frowned at the tactical plot. Someone chuckled and the tension oozed away. "What's happened to *Ramora*," he demanded.

Winn cleared the nav bubble and the stars crowded the half-lit ponderous majesty of the gas giant with brittle points of white. So close, despite what Tanard might have said. He thought his commander reckless to endanger the ship like that, except they were still alive. Others may call it fine judgment, but he saw the look of cold determination in Tanard's rigid face as he stared at the fleeing escort. They wouldn't be helping anyone if they were dead. He then heard Vukhan scream over the comms.

"—drive is screwed! I won't guarantee—"

"Are we disabled?" Tanard demanded harshly, his fingers twining in a moment of stunned silence.

"Well, not exactly—"

"Then why don't you stop wasting my time. Start work on it and call me when you're finished."

Down in the engineering spaces, Vukhan spluttered with indignant outrage at being spoken to like that, Tanard notwithstanding. Scowling mightily, he glared around the deck, daring anyone to say something, anything. Still scowling, his mood foul, he started checking through the intricate drive stats displays.

Tanard swiveled in his command couch. "Mr. Winn?"

"He's not dead," Winn said ruefully, head bobbing, his voice slightly unsteady. "There is a clear energy discharge from a depolarizing field, probably a forced collapse. That would not have done his main drive much good. It could also be a deciding tactical factor. He has entered the planet's atmosphere. The plasma trail is still visible, but he's gone. There is nothing to indicate he came out. If he hasn't smeared himself, he's still somewhere under that envelope."

"He is in that goo, all right," Tanard mused darkly, the two purple lines of his scars betraying his agitation. "I'm certain of it. He did that maneuver deliberately. Emissions? Anything?"

"Sensor distortion is heavy this close," Winn said defensively, his body still trembling from nervous tension. "If he is moving, we would be able to pick up his energy signature. That means he probably shut down his systems and is carried along by a jet stream."

"Cute," Tanard murmured and smiled in approval.

Well done, friend Terr, but it's not going to be this easy. You must come out sometime, and I'll be waiting.

Chapter Five

Under the relentless surge of the energy beam, *Hronin's* hull temperature soared until the plating glowed white, ablating, then vaporized, instantly venting jets of atmosphere that turned into a cloud of glittering crystals. The melted plating edges promptly froze into razor scimitars as the beam traversed along the hull, leaving behind a gaping eighty-katalan wound. Three bodies slammed through the gap, carried by the hurricane of escaping air. Their mouths were open in a contorted scream as blood gushed from every opening. The jagged hull plating caught them like shredding knives that sliced through cloth, flesh, and bone. No one heard their mercifully short shrieks.

Staggering under the impact of *Zaradej's* projector, *Hronin* vanished as its distortion field dropped. On the command deck, hull breach alarms shrilled as watchstanders gazed stupidly at one another in shock. The alarms suddenly cut off, the silence still ringing with the memory of the clamor.

Base Scout Osinara sat dazed in his formchair, too numb to do anything but gape at the savagery of the attack. When he realized he still lived and the ship had stopped twisting beneath him, he started to shiver violently. This was nothing like the simulations and the exercises. This was…death waiting! He hugged himself trying to still the shivering. He didn't want to die.

When *Hronin* steadied, the Master Pilot exhaled slowly and looked around the deck. Shaken, but he'd lived through worse. Everyone started to focus again, turning to check the systems. In the transparent nav bubble, the stars were frozen. That meant they had dropped normal and were at rest.

"The damned raider! Where is it?" he growled and pried

himself out of his seat. The Second Pilot took a deep breath and quickly turned to check the nav plot.

"We're alone, sir. The three ships are still engaged."

"What's our damage?" the pilot demanded and stepped next to his diminutive officer scanning the displays.

"Looks like we took a heavy hit in the support machinery spaces," the Second Pilot ventured. "We seem to be all right otherwise."

The pilot pressed his lips and nodded. "All right? We were lucky! Go aft and give me a report, including casualties. The Exec is somewhere in Engineering. Tell him to come up here."

The Second Pilot paused, his eyes on the displays, his mind still full of violent memories. Then he gathered himself and stood up, steadied his wobbly legs, and hurried to the ca-ble-tube hatch. The pilot glanced at his two watchstanders running through diagnostic checks and nodded approvingly. He then turned to the ashen-faced Osinara.

"Your commander wanted an attack, and by thunder, he got one!"

Osinara jerked his head and stared at him. The pilot saw the dead vacant eyes, snarled and turned away in disgust. Sending a child into combat! It had been a foolhardy plan from the onset.

The tube hatch opened and Razzo hurried through. One glance about the deck seemed to satisfy the seasoned assault chief until he saw the young base scout. His mouth tightened. He had seen this before and didn't like it. *Don't give up on me now, kid.*

With barely a nod to the pilot, he walked briskly to Osi-nara.

"Sir... Mr. Osinara!" he hissed fiercely.

Osinara's eyes focused on him. "Chief..."

"The men are all right, no casualties. What do you want us to do now?"

126

"Casualties?" Osinara hugged himself and pushed back into the seat.

Razzo grabbed his shoulders and shook him. "Damn it. Snap out of it!"

Osinara jerked as though electrocuted. His eyes cleared and Razzo waited to see which way the boy would go—slide back into his shell or face reality and deal with it. Razzo didn't have time to nursemaid the kid. They could be attacked again at any moment and he needed to get back to the ABPs. Color returned to the boy's face and Osinara let out a forced breath.

"Sorry, Chief," he mumbled sheepishly and Razzo smiled. For a minute there...

"Not to worry, sir. After you've been through one of these three or four times, you won't even notice it."

Osinara felt overwhelming shame at his moment of weakness. He had been terrified. The thought of death had frozen him. He failed himself and he failed his men. Chagrined, he realized that most of all, he failed his commander. If no one said anything, perhaps it would still be all right. He took a deep breath, gave Razzo a weak smile, and tried to stand.

"If you say so, Chief. The men?"

"Ready to kick ass."

Osinara's smile widened. He looked at the pilot and tried to still the wobble in his legs.

"Sir, any sign of pursuit?"

The pilot gave him a measured stare and relaxed. Probably the boy's first action. There was no easy way to introduce one to death, pain, and blood.

"Nobody here but us, son."

Osinara nodded. "Chief? The ABPs?"

"Ready to launch, but not manned."

"Good. Then we wait," he said more confidently and turned. The pilot reached for his arm and spun him around.

"What are you talking about?" The pilot pointed at the

transparent nav bubble. "We could be under attack at any moment." The two watchstanders sat back warily, unsure of what happened.

"True, sir," Osinara said equitably, more sure of himself. After what he went through, what could be worse? "If that M-3 comes after us, running won't do us any good. He'll pick us off at his leisure. As for the auxiliary, we'll face him with our ABPs."

"While he slices us up? Great, sonny! Well, I don't need to wait. We're clearing out right now."

"After four hours, sir," Osinara said calmly, amazed at his control. He glanced at Razzo and the chief gave him a minute nod.

The pilot snorted. "We could be dead in four hours."

"Yes, sir. You haven't forgotten Second Scout Terrllss-rr's instructions, have you?"

"Those orders were never intended to cover this situation. We're transiting now!" He turned to the engineering panel and reached for the touch-sensitive pads.

"Please step away from the console, sir," Razzo rasped, his needler pointed unwaveringly at the pilot's chest. The pilot gaped and color rushed to his face. His eyes were filled with fury.

"You dare…"

The two watchstanders made to stand up. Razzo didn't even look at them and shook his head. They glanced at the pilot and eased back.

"Put it away, Chief," Osinara said testily. Razzo hesitated, then slipped the weapon into his tunic holster.

"My apologies, Master Pilot," Osinara said harshly. "We move in four hours unless Second Scout Terr orders me to stand down before then. You would run out on him when he may be needing our help?"

The pilot, old and wizened, recognized steely determination in the young man's voice. He could not possibly resist armed marines. Truthfully, he allowed himself to get carried away, completely forgetting Terr's carefully thought-out instructions. His shoulders relaxed and he grinned.

"He could be dead already, Mister, and you know it. All we're doing is presenting a fat target to that bloody M-3 and its auxiliary."

"We don't know that, sir."

"No, we don't." The pilot stared at the boy, then nodded. "All right, Mister. We wait."

"Now, sir, can we get a plot update?"

The pilot nodded briskly and turned to the nav plot display plate. "The two M-3s have broken off the fight. Track shows them going full boost toward Banard-two." He stared at the plate and shook his head. "Mad. The raider has dropped normal. It's about nine billion talans ahead of us and it looks like he's just sitting there. Unbelievable."

"Damaged, or cannot boost," Osinara mused.

"Or he's lost his weapons pod," Razzo added slowly and a lazy grin cracked his face.

Osinara and the pilot exchanged glances. They both grinned and the tension lifted. The pilot suddenly remembered that his ship was also in trouble and his face hardened.

"Mr. Osinara, I may need some of your men."

"At your disposal, sir," Osinara said crisply and stood to.

Razzo looked from one to the other and sighed with tolerant amusement.

* * *

Thirty-two talans beneath the roiling atmosphere envelope, *Ramora* hurtled in the grip of an eighteen hundred talans per hour jet stream. The internal gravity field compensated for the wild bucking and swooping of the ship, but for the two watchstanders, with the nav bubble cleared, it made for an exceedingly uncomfortable ride. Kieran polarized the bubble, the alternative being to bring up buckets.

The ship survived transition and the fiery plunge into B-2's atmosphere, but at a terrible tactical price. Abused far beyond its operating tolerance the primary drive now a lump of fused circuitry. Terr stood beside Shan as the engineer glared at a huge main status display plate that covered most of the bulkhead. The automatic repair system hadn't even bothered to initiate a diagnostic cycle. Shan chewed his lip, turned to Terr, and shook his head.

"It's a pile of junk...sir," he added tersely, indicating his extreme displeasure with his reckless commander. "Even if I had all the parts, which I don't, this is a full base refit job. A brand-new unit, too," he muttered in disgust and shook his head again.

Terr let out a sigh and bit his lower lip. To him, the drive was a box of machinery that worked or it didn't. The fact that this box didn't work right now keenly regrettable. His options have suddenly become very limited, but he was more worried about the crew. With two more cases of broken arms, those who could drag themselves around were forced to do double duty. To keep them all alive, he must have a ship that can fight until this ended. He still found it hard to believe only eighteen minutes had passed since they went into action. An eternity.

"Is there *nothing* you can do?" he demanded, ignoring Shan's insubordination.

Shan scratched his head. "I can replace some of the fused modules and see if the diagnostics can at least come up."

"Do it. Can we maneuver?"

Shan sniffed. "The secondary drive is fine—"

"Projector?"

"The reaction chamber is undamaged, but you won't get maximum yield flooding. One of the hits we took must have caused a backsurge. It has taken out some of the focusing modules and I cannot replace them underway. It requires access into the dome itself. Getting in without breaking the containment seals would be tricky. I have the shield sync assembly repaired, but seventy, seventy-five percent is all you'll get."

"Not enough. Work on it," Terr ordered and strode to the cable-tube without looking back. He didn't care for any more of Shan's litanies, afraid of what he might hear.

Shan stared after him in disbelief. The man was impossible! He placed his fists on his hips and turned to his two assistants.

"You heard the order. Let's get it unwrapped!"

Terr went around *Ramora* inspecting damage and checking running repairs. He had time and no immediate rush to confront an enemy waiting for him above this soup. Bruised and shaken the crew were nevertheless in high spirits and joked with him as he did his rounds. The hull breach in one of the compartments almost patched. Terr stared in fascination at the distorted plating, marveling at the unleashed energies that caused the incredibly tough polymer construct to soften and flow like toffee. This one also cost him two lives, clearest proof that only death would allow him or Tanard to walk away.

It was worse in Medical. Sprains and bruises were treated easily enough and the discharged were eager to get back to work, even if only on limited duty. For those with more serious injuries, no reprieve. They had to endure the enforced confinement and the depressing atmosphere that surrounds every clinic. Terr found Dhar talking to a Second Powerman who fractured his leg after being thrown against unyielding equipment during one of Tanard's strikes. A clean break, but the man could not carry out his duties. He gathered Dhar with his eyes and waited for him to come over.

"Mr. Dharaklin!" he whispered fiercely, loud enough for heads to turn. "I'll not have the crew malingering like this!

From now on, anyone who dies or is injured without permission is on report. Is that clear?"

"I will pass the word, sir," Dhar said sternly.

"See to it!"

The exchange generated smiles and a few chuckles that lifted the atmosphere, if but for a moment. Terr glowered at the filled bunks and stalked toward the cable-tube hatch with Dhar in tow. Inside, he sagged against the bulkhead. The short engagement had drained him and left him wondering how he would pull himself out of this one. The loss of the main drive a cruel body blow…but he saved the ship, he told himself.

"Command deck," he said and the tube hummed as it surged up. "How bad?" he asked as he rubbed his eyes.

Dhar had seen Death and felt the finality of its touch. He hadn't experienced before the brush that left its victim alive, but nonetheless affected in some profound way by the experience. He looked deep into his brother's eyes.

"We were lucky, Sankri," he ventured. Terr's smile was grim.

"Yeah."

"I do not mean to add to your concern—"

"Spill it."

"We were in action before—"

"Against raiders, but not like this. Then, I always knew I controlled the situation, that I dictated the end game. With an M-3 around me, who could stand against me? There is a qualitative difference here. I'm the one being hunted and it's an interesting reversal of roles."

"The intensity of the exchange…" Dhar began and faltered, unsure how to express his reaction to the encounter. "When we dropped normal and B-2 rushed at us—"

"The shadow of the god of Death within which we walk looked pretty thin right then, eh?" Terr finished for him and chuckled. "Despite the power we wield, our mortality felt awfully close. Still, the maneuver worked and that's all that matters."

Dhar peered at him. "A command decision?"

The tube stopped and Terr said 'Hold' before the hatch could open. He looked hard at Dhar, his face stone.

"It cost us our subspace capability, yes, but we lived through it. To survive, you sometimes must take desperate measures. That's why you get to sit in that formchair. Above everything else, you need to keep focused on your mission objective. Forget that once and you're dead."

"Even if it means the lives of your crew?" Dhar looked shocked.

"At times you have to treat them as just another piece of equipment."

"It is…such a cold attitude, my brother."

"Better cold, Nightwings, than dead."

"I wonder, Sankri. I saw your eyes when you were with the injured—"

"I cannot afford to think like that. Not now. Once we're out of here—"

"Not an 'if'?"

"Why? You doubt my command ability?" Terr demanded with a grin and ordered the hatch to open.

Dhar stared at his back. His brother may joke about it, but he had seen the hurt in his eyes, as though he felt the pain of his men and the ship itself. Dhar realized Sankri was right. They could not afford to lapse into morbid sentiment, not now, but such a callous outlook, and clashed with so many precepts of the *Saftara* and the Discipline. Perhaps he did not have the right to wear his uniform. Easy to moralize as long as he wasn't the one giving the order to kill. His master warned him he would face such moments, and Dhar suspected that pride may have clouded his uncertainty. He would need to think about that, if they lived.

Kieran looked relaxed as he swiveled the command couch.

"Good fit, Mr. Kieran?" Terr asked with a smile.

"I could get used to it, sir," Kieran said easily and climbed out.

"Very well, *commander*! What do you recommend we do now?"

Kieran did not expect this and his button nose flared. He minded the watch when nothing was happening, but this...his thoughts suddenly turned to mush and his ears sagged. Dhar gave him a nod of encouragement.

"Well, sir...we can maneuver. Our shield grids are fully online and our projector is up. We can still fight, but we lost situational awareness. We need to know what our enemy is up to..." With both of his superiors staring at him, he trailed off.

"Not bad," Terr said. "However, you gave me a sitrep. What I'm looking for is a recommendation, Mister."

Kieran cleared his throat. "I would lift and take a quick scan around."

"That would expose us to detection," Terr said and watched Kieran struggle with the obvious. The boy squared his shoulders and his mouth firmed.

"Yes, sir. It's a risk, but it's also the only way we can orient ourselves to the tactical situation."

Terr smiled and patted him on the shoulder. "Very well, give the order."

"Sir?"

"Get us moving, Mister."

Kieran looked helplessly at Dhar, who stood rigid, a faint smile of amusement teasing his hard features.

"Here." Terr grabbed him and shoved him into the command couch. "Since you find it such a good fit." He stood back, clasped his hands behind his back, and waited.

Kieran gulped and turned pale. Terr couldn't really mean what he said. This wasn't an exercise. One mistake and they could all pay the ultimate price for his moment of ego-tripping.

He squirmed as the formchair molded itself to him, the armrest control pads and the main color-reactive panels around the inward-sloping circular bulkhead suddenly took on an altogether different perspective. The crushing load of responsibility, having to decide, seemed to press him deeper into the couch. It all looked very easy a few minutes ago. Painfully aware of Terr standing beside him, he settled himself firmly into the seat and exhaled. He knew what he needed to do. Only... *Please gods, let me get through this in one piece.*

"Computer. Initiate primary alert. All shields at maximum. Tactical display." The nav bubble changed from its opaque gray to a grid showing B-2's surface more than forty thousand talans below them and the thin layer of atmosphere above. The blue blip of their ship still in the grip of a hurtling jet stream. A uniform black blocked their view out, interference from the energy flux coursing from the atmosphere envelope.

The tube hatch opened and Mati hurried out, followed by another watchstander. He gave Kieran a startled look as he took up his station. Dhar had already started the tactical scans.

"Mr. Mati? Are we ready to maneuver?" Kieran barked.

"Ready to maneuver on secondary drive, sir," Mati answered automatically, then glanced curiously at Terr standing silent beside the command couch.

"Tactical?"

"No anomalous contacts within detection range," Dhar said solemnly.

"Mr. Mati, take us to within two talans of the atmosphere envelope and hold."

Ramora pushed herself out of the jet stream with barely an occasional tremor. Kieran watched the main plot and felt sweat bead his forehead. A wet trickle ran down between his shoulder blades. Was it getting hot?

Tactical cleared slightly as they ascended, showing one of a handful of low orbit moons, B-2 Three, 320,000 talans off, high on their port quarter. The display plate cluttered with large hunks of odd rock. A nasty piece of space to be flying in. Twisted lines of force streamed from the gas giant and coiled around the moon like some massive dynamo winding. This represented an almost limitless supply of current, free for the taking. The ship fast approached the terminator without sighting *Laverne*.

"Two talans and holding," Mati said quietly.

Kieran almost jumped when Terr touched him.

"Well done. Still feel it's a good fit?"

Kieran climbed out shakily and let out a long breath. "Sir, I won't even *look* at it again!"

Terr smiled and indicated with his eyes at the weapons station.

His feet a bit unsteady, Kieran walked to his seat and lowered himself, grateful it was over. His flap ears drooped with nervous exhaustion. He clenched his fists to stop his hands from shaking as he checked the board. Mati's long black face split into a huge grin, showing brilliant yellow teeth.

Command? No way!

Terr settled himself down and studied the main tactical plot. He glanced at Kieran and stifled a grin. The boy had done very well considering the circumstances. His other officers could benefit from a similar exercise. He pursed his lips and concentrated on the task at hand. No sign of Tanard. He would have been very surprised to see *Laverne*. B-2 was an enormous planet with plenty of room to lose oneself in. Even if *Laverne* did suddenly appear, he still felt fairly safe. Two talans down, he could see out far better than Tanard could see in, and he needed room to maneuver should Tanard show up.

"Mr. Mati, let's head for B-2 Three. Three-quarter standard boost. Hold one talan above the terminator."

"Port or starboard side of the satellite, sir?"

"Tactical?" Terr looked at Dhar.

"The moon's orbital motion is from our relative starboard to port. I would recommend port. That way, the whole mass of the moon will be between us, irrespective of whether he comes in high or low."

"Provided Tanard is moving with B-2's rotation," Terr said. "Still, port it is, Mr. Mati. Transit time?"

"Approximately sixty-one seconds once we clear the atmosphere envelope, sir," Mati said and faced Terr. "At three-quarter boost, we'll be leaving a signature trail. Even with all the ionizing radiation—"

"And all those electric current lines streaming between them?" Terr added quietly.

Mati blinked, chagrined at making such a basic blooper. "Three-quarter boost, sir."

The whole space around the violently emitting gas giant would be like the inside of a huge energy coil with low orbiting junk acting as polarizing nodes. A good reminder why subspace comms were ineffective here. A signature trail or an organized energy stream, even one traveling thousands of times faster than light, would be instantly shredded in this environment.

Ramora eased through the two talans of atmosphere to avoid creating a telltale plasma trail and streaked toward the fast-moving moon. During those sixty seconds they were naked and vulnerable. Terr locked his fingers to keep them from drumming on the armrest with anxiety. Everybody had enough tension already without adding his own.

It is vital that in moments of crisis the commanding officer projects a calming and steadying influence, the Tactics Manual stated. He allowed his mouth to twitch briefly.

The seconds dragged, almost stopping, deliberately taunting him, while his imagination ran riot with worst-case scenarios. He didn't feel happy until the yellow-orange sulfur surface of the moon loomed large before them. The ship slowed as they approached the day-night terminator line. It stopped, hovered, and slowly dropped, then stopped again.

Terr glanced at the nav bubble. *Ramora's* attitude had the ship vertical to the surface, exactly on the terminator line.

An excellent example of precision flying and he said so. Banard shone orange and huge at them, with B-2 a glowing outline, its interior a black hole carving a passage into another eternity.

"You're two katalans out of position, Mr. Mati," Terr growled sternly.

Mati grinned and nudged the ship down a tad. "Sorry, sir," he said, still grinning.

"Mmm." Terr settled back to wait. An interesting tactical scenario.

Without his main drive, he cannot run, and with reduced offensive capability, not an ideal position to engage either. Yet, he must evade or somehow cripple Tanard. He *could* hole up somewhere and simply wait it out and hope Rayon would act quickly. The idea didn't hold much attraction for him and he covered this ground before. He discarded the option now for the same reasons.

What if Rayon sent in another M-3? Tanard would jump it and carve it up. No, no, it simply wouldn't do. He *could* attempt to hop between the moons and the surrounding rocky rubble, drawing farther from B-2 and into open space. Then what? Squirt an emergency signal and limp off at sublight speed? This close to B-2 any signal would be swallowed by the interference field and only serve as a short-range locator for Tanard to home in on. He would be a nice slow target out in the open, ready for picking.

So, if the easy options won't work, he would have to take the hard ones.

"Detected emissions from an S/14 monitoring unit," the computer announced dispassionately and Terr squinted. "Range, one hundred and fifteen thousand talans. Closure rate is nine hundred and sixty talans per second."

Rit!

Tanard had evidently sown sensor pods, and this one was going against the rotation of B-2, and coming directly at him. If he were Tanard, this would be a time to be clever. Had Tanard scooted along with the planet's spin and released the pods to go the other way, or had he released them to go both ways? Terr knew what he would do.

"Closest approach?" Terr demanded.

"Seventy-four thousand talans. Time to contact, forty-two seconds."

"Probability of acquisition?"

"Thirty-four percent at closest approach."

Not good. Hanging one talan above B-2 Three, *Ramora* lay surrounded by streaming current flux lines that distorted any return signals to the sensor pod. Sensor pings worked at subspace speeds—a return *could* get through the interference and paint him if the probe got close enough. It would only take one ping to unmask him. He could also destroy the probe in place. Unless Tanard hung above B-2's horizon, Terr would remain undetected. However, once Tanard *did* come up, he'd be screwed. Tanard would detect the absence of the pod and know Terr was alive, close and prowling. Worse, the residuals from projector fire would clearly show Terr's hiding place. Even if the flux lines did disperse the residuals, B-2 Three would be a glaring 'I am here' beacon.

Definitely not good.

"Mr. Mati, take us down real slow," Terr ordered quietly. "Minimal drive emissions. Also, nudge us beyond the terminator into the night side."

"Descending at fifty katalans per second. Surface hover in twenty seconds," Mati replied and the ship nosed down.

He knew what Terr hoped for; lose himself in surface clutter until the probe went past them. The S/14 relied mainly on energy emissions and motion differentials for detection.

Shut down and lying still represented their best chance. What if there were more of those infernal things out there in a higher orbit? Getting caught in a bistatic grid search would be bad news, glad it wasn't his problem.

The ship maintained its vertical attitude as it went down and frozen sulfur mountains rose to meet it, clad in orange, yellow, purple, and red. There were minimal signs of cratering. Tidal forces exerted by B-2 must cause the moon to regularly flood its surface with magma, erasing its past.

The ship stopped.

"Hovering at five katalans," Mati announced.

"Computer, report any aspect change from the S/14. Report detection of other units." Probably superfluous. Terr didn't care. How many of those horrid things did Tanard sow? He turned his seat and jerked his head at Dhar.

"I have an idea," he said when Dhar stood beside him. "I want you to program two survival blisters for terminal ejection. When we engage, launch them at *Laverne*. You'll have to use your judgment on the timing."

Dhar gaped at him, the red slits in his eyes mere lines. "You want to use them as missiles?"

"That's right. We'll ram him!"

"We will need to be really close, or he will simply evade," Dhar mused uncertainly.

"We'll be close."

"Not good, my brother. Even at 800 talans per second terminal velocity, an M-3's shield grid will easily handle the impact, even if the nav deflector screen doesn't push the blister aside. We would shake him up, but that's about it."

"Not if we set the containment field to shut down on impact. The resulting explosion will do more than shake him up. I know what a cooking blister can do," Terr said dryly, remembering his crash on Anar'on. When his blister blew, nothing remained but twisted hull frames and a fused hole in the sand.

"If his secondary shield is extended more than nine talans, it'll handle a blister blast," Dhar pointed out.

"I know, but he's a Fleet officer and will follow—should follow—standard close-quarter tactics. He'll have his shields pulled in tight, say five talans." Terr's face hardened with determination. "I've *got* to cripple him somehow. We sure as hell can't sit here waiting to be picked up by one of his probes."

"I will get it done right away," Dhar said heavily and resumed his station.

Missiles against energy weapons? It had never been done. Then again, crazy as it sounded, it could work. After all, a blister was an energy delivery device, and warfare was controlled application of energy, but missiles? He would never have thought of it.

"Detecting secondary drive emissions from target one," the computer said suddenly. "Nav scans only. Target is at primary alert configuration and synchronized. Range, eighty-two thousand talans. Closure rate is 1,740 talans per second. Optimum firing point in ten point-three seconds." Assuming a standard firing point of 64,000 talans maximum separation.

Tanard came in high over B-2 Three at quarter boost and obviously prepared for business. Terr expected nothing less. If Tanard had come a few minutes earlier, he would have detected Terr's exit from B-2. Terr's luck still held. Nav scans also meant they were undetected. Hugging the sulfurous surface with hardly any emissions had worked in his favor, but that wasn't going to last long. Any second now, he expected an acquisition lock on him.

"Mr. Kieran, ready maximum yield fire," Terr ordered and turned to Mati. "When he's overhead, come up underneath him as close as you can, one thousand talans, and match his speed. Mr. Dhar…"

"Blisters armed and ready, sir."

"Optimum firing range in four seconds," the computer stated. "Warning, L-band acquisition lock established."

141

Terr had two seconds at most before Tanard could lock and fire. Time to go.

"Dhar! Maximum on all shields. Mr. Mati, now! Half boost."

Ramora stirred and swooped on the approaching M-3.

Tanard's secondary shield pulsed and the projector dome cycled in preparatory firing sequence. At three-quarter boost combined closure rate, it took only a second to close the distance between the two ships. A searing slash of yellow light swept past *Ramora* in a near miss and the ship shuddered.

Kieran kept his eyes glued on his board, then jabbed a finger on the commit pad as the ships matched speeds, eleven hundred talans separation. This close, his reduced projector output more than compensated for. Tanard's shields flared under point collapses and *Laverne* staggered as though hitting a wall. Kieran fired for almost two seconds at the wallowing M-3 without any return fire. One of his long bursts tore through a point shield collapse and worried the hull, making the ablative material boil off. Another burst targeted the projector dome. Although the shields held, backsurges arced around the housing.

Dhar did not wait for Terr's order and committed the computer to launch the blisters. In the ejection tubes the holding clamps retracted and the hatches snapped open. The two blisters streaked toward *Laverne*.

Seconds later, one of them detonated. Then Tanard fired and an eighty-two TeV full yield burst crashed against *Ramora's* secondary shield grid, which discharged in a cascade of wild arcing along the force lines. The shield resisted momentarily, then point collapsed, exposing the weaker primary grid and the vulnerable hull beneath. Terr lurched in his seat as the ship slued and flipped over under the massive impact. The air thick with the smell of ozone, his hair started to rise. Little blue sparks slithered and danced over panels from the near-field effect of the beam. Where the sparks touched exposed flesh, they left little brown burn marks. Exquisite agony and everyone yelped and cursed from the tiny bites.

Momentarily held immobile by the restraining field, they could do nothing but endure the torture. The tactical panel flashed orange-white, indicating system failure. Others flashed pale green in overload. The computer calmly announced hull damage reports. The weapons panel crackled with discharges and Kieran grunted as a jolt rushed through his arm, throwing him back. He fell heavily against the deck, momentarily dazed.

Tanard's single burst was brutal. The drive spaces took the full force of the strike. The hull wasn't penetrated, but backsurge discharges collapsed the drive's containment field, inducing automatic shutdown of the secondary reaction chamber. The ship without mains power and drifting. The primary and secondary shield grids failed and collapsed.

Stunned by the suddenness of the onslaught, Terr slowly looked around the deck. Kieran picked himself up, one hand reaching for the back of his formchair. Mati stared vacantly at his dead board. Dhar looked calm enough, trying to coax information out of partially active systems. He did not see the second blister explode. Terr looked up through the transparent nav bubble, expecting to see *Laverne* swooping in, but there was only blackness. At over one thousand talans separation the other ship was invisible. He wondered why Tanard didn't finish him. Without power or shields, *Ramora* wallowed helplessly. It wouldn't even take a full burst.

Waiting for Death, he felt mild regret that he failed his mission. Dying wasn't a problem. He did not fear Death. He felt its touch before and knew if for what it was. He feared life, mutilation, and suffering. Dying came easy.

He turned his head and gazed into Dhar's orange eyes. *Ramora* drifted silently.

* * *

"Warning!" the computer blared. "Target two detected on Banard-two Three's surface. Range, 70,960 talans. Optimum firing point in four seconds. Engaging L-band acquisition lock."

Young Terr!

"He's coming up, half boost!" Winn warned and his large black eyes grew round as he looked at Tanard.

"Rake him!" Tanard shouted, his damaged voice thin and shrill.

Pits!

Railee frantically engaged the target tracking system and got the projector online. It took less than a second to get the systems fully active and ready. He fired a long burst, only to have it slide past the twisting escort as it returned fire. *Laverne* staggered and reared and the bulkhead frames groaned in protest. Despite the restraining field, the comms watchstander was wrenched back and flung out of his seat. He crashed heavily against the tube hatch and lay still. The air smelled of ozone and his skin crawled with static charges. Another sweeping burst savaged the shields and *Laverne* wallowed.

"Inbound!" Winn screamed and pointed at the main tactical plate. "Survival blisters..." he muttered incredulously in total disbelief.

About to order Winn to evade, Tanard saw the first blister impact the secondary shield. *Laverne* barely trembled. Then incredibly, the blister brewed up in a blinding flash of blue light. The force of the explosion ripped through the shield grid and sent molten fragments scything into the hull a mere five talans away. The polymer construct never designed to withstand explosive force, the material buckled and deformed under the pressure. Where the shower of fragments struck, they penetrated. Internal atmosphere vented through the rents. *Laverne* shook like a toy on a string.

Dazed, Railee stabbed the commit pad and watched with satisfaction as a full yield burst traversed along *Ramora's* hull.

Against the Gods of Shadow

Amazingly, the force of the impact flipped the escort over. Before he could fire again the second blister impacted against the shields and detonated, sending *Laverne* skidding from the shock. The restraining field held momentarily, then failed. That one moment enough to save the fragile flesh inside. The whole port side of the hull peppered with fragment holes. Some of the ruptures were small enough to allow the hull to seal itself. Others remained torn and gaping, like the crew trapped in those compartments. One rupture lay in the projector dome.

Battered, torn and bleeding, *Laverne* had enough. The computer initiated emergency shutdown of all secondary systems to prevent the reaction chamber going critical. Power suddenly reduced to minimal life support only. The shields dropped and the ship drifted, dead in space.

Shaken and bruised, Tanard climbed unsteadily out of his command couch and gripped Winn's formchair. Winn groaned and sat back. A line of blood oozed down his left temple. In shock, everyone stared at each other with bewildered relief they were still alive. Railee climbed out of his seat and knelt beside the still comms operator. He looked up and shook his head. Tanard grunted and tapped pads on Winn's tactical board, looking hungrily at the display plate. Terr's ship nav bubble down drifted toward the moon. Its shields were down and there were minimal power emissions. It must be running on emergency power only; proof it too appeared mortally struck. Unless it recovered, it would crash. One burst, that's all he needed. He ground his teeth in frustration.

"Computer, project target two's orbit."

"Target two will impact Banard-two Three in forty-eight minutes and twenty-six seconds."

I've got you at last!

"Can we maneuver?"

"Negative. Secondary drive diagnostics currently underway. Autonomous repair procedures have been initiated."

"Offensive capability?"

"Damage beyond repair capability while in flight."

Pits!

Watching the tactical plate, it looked like B-2 Three would finish the job for him. Survival blisters...*a brilliant move, friend Terr*. Tanard shook his head and smiled. *All honor to you.*

Now, to clean up the transport, but without a working projector, that might be a tad difficult. Difficult or not, he would first have to claw out of this orbit or he would be smearing himself next to Terr.

* * *

Terr found himself amazed he was still alive.

In the deathly quiet the indirect milky bulkhead lighting faded, then steadied, but dimmer. Glances of relief were exchanged and status boards were checked. Dhar cleared his throat and pointed at B-2 Three.

"I think we are in a decaying orbit," he growled.

The moon almost as large as some planets, its gravitational pull correspondingly powerful.

Terr shrugged. "We could be going the other way," he said and pointed at B-2.

"Both are unpalatable choices, my brother." Their eyes held momentarily, grateful that Death had not claimed them yet.

Terr tapped a pad on the armrest console. "Shan...Shan?"

"Engineering."

"Talk to me."

"Nothing to talk about, sir. I cannot bring up the secondary reactor containment field. With our primary down as well, our energy reserves won't last two hours."

"We don't have two hours. We're in a decaying orbit. I need power now."

There was a moment of silence. "How long?"

"Forty-eight minutes," Dhar said when Terr looked at him.

"I recommend we abandon," Shan said at length.

"And get picked off one by one?" Terr demanded, clearly seeing Tanard maneuvering lazily beside each survival blister and blasting it to atoms. "Wait, I'll be right down," he snapped, annoyed at his engineer's fatalism. He turned to Dhar. "Get a status check and see to the crew."

"Do we prepare to abandon ship, sir?" Dhar asked formally and watched Terr struggle with inner pain. The commander part of him won.

"If I'm not back at minus fifteen minutes, everyone is to be in a blister. Distribute them evenly over the remaining seven units. If Tanard attacks, some might get away."

"What if we used two of them to haul her into a more stable orbit?" Dhar said.

Terr immediately shook his head. "Think of the mass differential. At best, it would only buy us a bit of extra time, but it wouldn't be enough. Once ejected, it's a friggin' job to attach them to the emergency hatch. We certainly could not get them back into the launch tubes. We would also be down two more blisters. No, if we're going to lose her, we need to make sure the crew gets the best chance possible of making it."

"What about the ABPs?"

Terr stared at him in surprise. The assault craft were powerful, more so than the survival blisters. It was possible.

"How do we launch them?" he said and Dhar grimaced. Without mains power, they had no way to initiate the depressurization sequence or open the hangar hatches. "Good idea, though." Terr got up and strode to the cable-tube hatch. It sighed open and he stepped inside.

The engineering spaces brightly lit with little sign of damage. Some equipment lay torn loose, and containers littered the deck, but everything seemed normal, until he looked at the flickering status display boards. Shan noticed him and walked over.

"Anybody hurt down here?" Terr asked gently, noting the strain on the engineer's face. He hated to think what it was like down here, not able to see anything and the ship tumbling around him.

"A couple of bruises, that's all."

"Reactor containment, show me."

"Well…" Shan placed his hands on his hips and leaned toward the main display plate. "The interlink fuel feed coupling is stuck. Shock most likely. The automatic systems cannot retract it and it's blocking the fuel regulator. There is no way to restart the injection sequence and the thing's got two backups!" he said in disgust.

"Can't you clear it manually?"

"Manually?" Shan stared at him. "Don't even think about it…sir. The radiation—"

"Start the mains. I know we cannot transition into subspace, but—"

"No good. It would take too long to disable the safeties. The whole power reticulation system is designed around the intent that mains are used to power the distortion field. With the drive trashed from the forced collapse the computer will not allow the reactor to be engaged. I could program overrides, but not in forty-eight minutes."

Terr scowled. He had to have power!

"The blocked feed, if you used a containment suit…"

Shan shook his head. "I know what you're thinking, but it's too bulky. There isn't any space in there to get a glove through. Even if you could, you won't have the sensitivity. The damned thing is not *supposed* to jam!"

Terr slammed his fist against the display plate and closed his eyes, his thoughts a whirlpool of ideas. Without power they would be forced to abandon ship and take to survival blisters. Tanard hadn't looked so hot back there. That could also be only a temporary state of affairs. He could not gamble that *Laverne* was disabled. He would be condemning everyone to certain death, but if he didn't break orbit soon, it would be death either way.

He needed power!

There was a way…He looked at Shan and his heart hammered.

"And if you didn't use gloves?" he said slowly and the words echoed loudly in the sudden silence. Shan frowned, then his eyes widened. He licked his lips.

"You can't be serious! Even with a containment suit, without gloves, I'll probably lose both hands."

"Could it be done?"

"It…wouldn't be hard."

Terr gazed into his chief engineer's eyes, his mouth suddenly dry. No, this was madness. What was he thinking! Get everyone into survival blisters and take their chances. He had enough blood on his hands to contemplate mutilating a man. Like Shan said, he would likely lose his hands, but amputated stumps could be made to regenerate.

"Can you do it?" he heard himself say, startled that his voice could remain so steady.

Shan gaped at him, swallowed, and nodded once. "I can do it," he growled and cleared his throat.

"I want you…" Terr faltered and the lump in his throat choked the rest of it.

"You always wanted to get rid of me and I guess this is it." Shan chuckled. "Never thought I'd go like this, though," he muttered gruffly and turned to one of his watchstanders. "Mannick! Over here."

The First Powerman walked briskly toward them and stood to. The crewman gave Terr a curious glance and turned to Shan.

"Sir?"

"Get ready to start the injection sequence. As soon as the

block is cleared, you start her up."

"But I thought—"

"Just do it!" Shan snarled and stomped off. Terr hurried after him.

They walked through an archway into the secondary power room. Shan pulled down an orange containment suit from the wall bracket and climbed into it. He glanced at the gloves, smirked, dropped them to the deck, and clipped on the helmet. Striding to a narrow hatch painted bright yellow, he pressed his palm against the entry pad.

"Warning!" the computer blared immediately. "Radiation hazard. Unauthorized entry. Access denied."

"Computer, override code beta, santo, data, three, one, one, enable."

The hatch pulsed darker yellow and retracted to reveal a containment lock. Shan picked up a small toolbox off a shelf and was about to step in when Terr touched his arm and stopped him.

"Shan, I…" Terr whispered brokenly, the words of a lifetime eluding him. What could he say to someone he just condemned to possible death. Without power, though, everyone was dead.

Shan pursed his lips and stood to. "I am privileged and honored to have served with you, sir," he snapped and walked into the chamber. The hatch closed behind him.

Terr stood still and stared at the hatch for one eternal minute. He slowly turned to see a powerman watchstander look at him in total shock.

"Get into a containment suit right away."

The crewman gaped.

"Move!" Terr barked, and without another glance at the man, hurried into the control room.

Clenching and unclenching his fists, he hovered beside the main status plate. The First Powerman didn't look at him. For three long minutes nothing happened. Then a ripple of colored lines snaked along suddenly open circuits.

"The interlink is clear," Mannick's voice came from the speaker and Terr nodded to Mannick.

"I will start the injection sequence, sir."

"Control?" Shan's strained voice came through.

"I'm here, Shan," Terr said gently.

"Have you started the ejection sequence?"

"It's underway, Shan."

"Then get her home safe."

"I'll do that."

Nothing else after that. A few moments later, he didn't know how long, the display rippled again. The reaction chamber slowly heated up to its pre-ignition temperature. With power restored, the antimatter containment field could be energized and the secondary reactor started. Terr glanced at Mannick working on the main control board. He walked silently to him, paused, and continued into the power room. He looked at the suited crewman waiting beside the hatch and hooked a thumb.

"Get Mr. Shan-arin out of there and call Medical," he said, his voice cold and unwavering. He spun around and hurried back to the cable-tube.

Only when the hatch clicked shut that his body convulsed and he gasped at the pain gripping his chest. He buried his face between his hands and exhaled loudly. Eyes burning, he moaned and leaned against the bulkhead. After a while, he straightened, his eyes cold. Tanard's scarred face clear in his mind and he felt his body shiver as Death stirred within him. If he only knew how to reach out for *Laverne*...

When the hatch opened to the command deck, he was back in control. However, nothing could relieve the lead weight in his chest from what he had done. Devoid of expression, he strode to his seat, stopped, and sank onto it with unutterable weariness.

"Sir, Engineering reports secondary mains will be online

in eleven minutes," Mati reported and trailed off when he saw Terr's face.

Eleven minutes, not much of a margin. Dhar stepped beside him.

"I thought—"

"Cancel abandon ship routine, Mr. Dharaklin. Make preparation for landing and get me a tactical sweep as soon as you're able," Terr ordered, his voice crisp and hard.

Dhar did not press him. He simply nodded and resumed his station. What happened in Engineering? The look of tortured hurt in Terr's eyes pierced his soul. What happened down there?

The minutes dragged and B-2 Three loomed large in the nav bubble. The surface looked awfully close. What if he miscalculated, Terr wondered. What if power wasn't restored in time? It would be cutting it fine to get everyone into blisters now if this didn't work. He clenched his fists and clamped his mouth. It *had* to work or Shan's sacrifice would have been for nothing.

On the tick, the deck brightened as the mains came on and the color-reactive panels flickered into life. For some, only a partial activation. They still had damage to contend with.

"Command deck, Engineering. Secondary mains now available at your discretion, sir."

"Thank you…Mannick, isn't it?" Terr ventured.

"Yes, sir," came a guarded reply.

"Well done. Mr. Mati, nav shield only and set her down."

From a dead, falling mass the ship became alive and responsive. The difference subtle, but unmistakable. *Ramora* rotated slowly, presented its belly to the ground, and slowed its fall. At two hundred katalans above the surface, Mati allowed the ship to drift as he searched for a flat, solid place to squat. Accompanied by ongoing computer prompts the M-3 extended its shock pads and gingerly settled. The pads sank almost half a katalan into the sulfur powder before the nine-and-a-half thousand mikans dead weight came to rest.

Nothing much to see: sulfur flats, gently rounded hills, what passed for mountain peaks in the distance, stars and impenetrable blackness overhead…and the overpowering view of B-2 that hung above them, dark and brooding—like Terr, listless and weary.

"Mr. Dharaklin, status of enemy vessel." This was the second time he actually thought of Tanard as an enemy rather than merely as target one. Perhaps the Palean officer not directly an enemy, but certainly everything he and his backers stood for were. He felt a familiar tingle course through his body as Death threatened to rear itself. He forced it back. His power cannot help him now and he couldn't afford to make this personal. *Focus!*

"Target showing uncorrelated movement, sir. Altitude, eighty-two hundred talans. No shields. Power levels showing secondary mains only. His track will take him below our horizon in nine minutes. He's in a decaying orbit, insertion in nineteen hours."

"When will he emerge above the horizon?"

"Six hours, forty-one minutes and twelve seconds if he maintains current profile."

Six hours…

* * *

Tanard's long fingers fluttered behind his back in a characteristic gesture, reflecting the turmoil of his thoughts. He stopped himself, then unconsciously, his fingers started working again. Helpless, on minimal power, he watched Terr's ship angle belly up toward B-2 Three. He regretted seeing the death throes of any ship and Terr had been a good opponent, very good. He no longer wondered how a mere Second Scout came to command an M-3, normally a First Scout billet. What he could have done with the two of them working together! That, of course, could never be. Too bad they had to meet on the opposite sides of a political divide.

The victors write the rules.

His own predicament was nothing to be envied either, the weapons pod a fused shambles courtesy of a backsurge discharge and a debris strike. Vukhan doubted it would be coming up anytime soon. That wasn't great news, but it looked like he wouldn't be needing the projector anyway. His entire port side peppered like a sieve. Fortunately, none of the structural frames were hit and hull integrity wasn't totally compromised. Holes can always be patched. What could not be patched as easily were holes in his crew. He lost eight to explosive decompression and eleven more to various degrees of immobilizing injury. He did not count sprains and strains and minor contusions. The encounter with those infernal survival blisters bruising and brutal. It also cost him maneuvering power. The engineering spaces were holed, but nothing vital damaged—if he didn't count two of his powermen. Vukhan and his gang were working on the secondary drive and believed full power could be restored within four to six hours. Plenty of time to drag themselves out of B-2 Three's deadly grip. The primary drive shaken up a bit and the autonomous repair systems were on top of it. It was likely he wouldn't be getting full boost, but that wasn't even on his worry list.

Get power, then find out what happened to Val Keen and the Devon transport. He cannot afford to leave any evidence behind.

"Mr. Winn? Status on *Ramora's* orbit?"

"Twenty-two minutes to impact."

"Any aspect change?"

"Negative, sir. The M-3 is in terminal descent."

Their own orbit would soon take them below the impact zone's horizon, but not before he would see Terr's ship crash.

Tanard wondered why Terr hadn't taken to survival blisters. He was bound to go after them, but he didn't relish the prospect of destroying a helpless enemy. Without a projector, destroying the pods presented a problem, but there were other ways. Take each blister's crew on board and execute them? An even less palatable option. Some lines could not be crossed, no matter what.

"Target two is energizing secondary drive," the computer announced suddenly. "Predict maneuvering capability in eleven minutes."

So, not as dead as it would seem, Tanard mused. *You are stubbornly hard to kill, friend Terr.* His admiration tempered by the suddenly grim nature of his tactical position. Without a weapons pod, the tactical advantage lay firmly with Terr. One thing he learned about his tenacious adversary, as soon as he was able, Terr would come boiling over the horizon, projector blazing and anything else he could throw at him. Tanard didn't particularly savor being around when that happened.

No longer a case of destroying Terr and the Devon transport, but one of basic survival. Strategically, his operation compromised, but not irretrievably. All Terr knew is that a Fleet unit was involved with raids on Pizgor commerce. Although not good, the information did not in itself threaten Lemos or its cover. It would be uncomfortable for the AUP Provisional Committee and the Palean Union, though. In time, the issue would blow over and it would be business as usual. The Bureau of Cultural Affairs can investigate and make searches, but they'd walk away empty-handed. He had Lemos far too well camouflaged. His own cover? Almost certainly blown, and that had always been a risk factor. One thing was clear. He no longer had a Fleet career. What price patriotism?

Tanard's fingers twined. Was he being overly hasty here? Okay, Terr may be alive and anxious to hunt, but did he have the capability? Did he have a functional weapons pod? If he didn't…but what if he did? Tanard needed to take steps to protect himself.

He tapped a pad on the armrest.

"Engineering," Vukhan growled and Tanard pictured a scowling face.

"Vukhan, can you give me one or two seconds of power from the main drive?"

"Why? You planning to transit somewhere in a hurry?" came the perceptive reply and Tanard smiled.

"A few seconds…"

"No good, sir. With B-2 over the horizon and its steep gravity well, not counting this piece of slag we're hugging now, we would never be able to polarize the distortion field precursor."

"What if we positioned ourselves at a gravitational neutral point?" The point where B-2 and the moon's gravitational pulls exactly matched would be a zone of stability, albeit a precarious one.

After a few seconds of silence, Vukhan sighed audibly. "I suppose theoretically it *could* be done, although I've never heard the like before. Even if we managed to polarize, the field would collapse almost instantly when we engage the drive."

"A few seconds, enough to shift us out of here."

"Even if we engaged the drive, you would only get a few *microseconds* of boost at best."

"It will be enough."

"Keep in mind, as soon as we clear the neutral point, we'll be in a forced collapse mode. There is going to be some damage and I don't relish being stranded here. Before you can try this stunt, we first need to *get* to a neutral point. No secondaries remember, and you're looking at four hours minimum before I can get them back online."

"We may not have four hours," Tanard pointed out, trying to soften the harshness in his voice. "I only need enough power to get us to that point and hold it. Quarter boost, anything!"

Vukhan hissed. "If you want to go out and push?"

Tanard stiffened. "I've put up with your crap, Vukhan, because of a misguided impression you were an engineer. When you have to deliver, you're full of shit." He cut contact and smirked.

Winn blanched and glanced at Tanard. "Ah, sir, wasn't that a bit extreme?" he ventured and Tanard grinned, making the two lines of his scars stand out.

"You sometimes have to stick a spike up Vukhan's butt to get him activated, but he'll deliver."

Then the tactical plot cleared and a thin ring sprang around *Ramora*.

"Target two shows nav screen enabled," the computer said. "Target is in controlled descent."

Eleven minutes exactly. Tanard watched as *Ramora* righted itself and slowly sank. Almost at the surface, it drifted and then settled. Probably to carry out repairs, or it would have come after him. Tempted to start chewing his fingers, he refrained. That, of course, would not have been appropriate. Right now, he would be happy just to walk out of this alive, and the mission be damned.

* * *

Quiet around the briefing table, the silence caught everyone in a mood of grim contemplation. Terr looked at each of his officers in turn.

"We took a lot of damage. The ship is hurt and so is the crew, but we survived and I aim to keep it that way. The loss of the main drive makes our position slightly difficult. However, we can maneuver and we can still fight. We don't know the extent of Tanard's damage, despite his apparently helpless attitude as he went below our horizon. He has partial second-aries and you can bet he's working to restore full power. He could come hurtling in at any moment, and that would spoil the day for us. Or he's dead and will crack in."

Terr paused, giving them an opportunity to say some-thing, anything. They looked tired, but ready to keep going. It was hard to imagine that only three hours ago, Tanard had just been a blip in their plot. Modern warfare exacted a heavy psychological price.

"Mr. Mannick has joined us as temporary chief engineer," Terr said softly, his throat suddenly tight. "Mr. Shan-arin is seriously injured in the performance of his duty, but is ex-pected to live. Mr. Mannick? What's our power status?"

Surrounded by commissioned officers and haunted by the nature of Shan's injuries, Mannick looked uncomfortable, unwilling to meet Terr's eyes. He didn't exactly blame his commander. Well, he did, but what choice was there? Shocked by the suddenness of it all, and still not really sure it was necessary. He took a deep breath and leaned forward slightly.

"You have three-quarter boost available on the secondary drive, sir. The weapons pod is carrying damage, but it will de-liver up to seventy percent. Both shield grids are fully charged. We're not so good on some internal power reticulation—"

"Anything critical?"

"No, sir. Inconvenience mostly."

"Just being here is an inconvenience," Mati muttered, raising smiles and chuckles.

"Mr. Dharaklin?"

"Ship is tactical ready in all respects, sir. Medical is a bit crowded and there is a raft of waiting repairs. I stopped work on everything except environmental support and the projec-tor. System checks are underway right now."

Terr nodded. "Good. We've been sitting here for over an hour, licking our wounds and feeling sorry for ourselves.

We're in an end run and it's time to go hunting. Those who haven't finished feeling sorry for themselves will have to save it up until we're back on Pizgor." That brought more grins. "If Tanard is waiting for us, then we've had it, and he won't be gentlemanly about it, either. The fact that he *hasn't* attacked tells us something. Either way, we need to find out. We *must* communicate with Ambassador Rayon."

"Sir?" Kieran looked around the table, his button eyes expressionless as always. "The Devon transport and Mr. Osinara, is it possible they managed to contact the Ambassador? We could hole up somewhere…"

"It's possible, Mr. Kieran, and I could be placing us at unnecessary risk, but we don't know Osinara made contact."

"I understand, sir."

"We don't have any options. Tanard must be eliminated as a threat. I'll throw formchairs at him if that's what it will take. When you get back to your sections, keep your people informed. Tell them what's going on." Terr gave each of them a glance and looked at Dhar.

"Primary alert, Mr. Dharaklin. Back to command deck and let's get underway."

For some the prospect of action meant a break from arduous repair duties. For others, it meant doing what they trained for. The likelihood of dying had crossed their minds and they have seen two of their comrades on a slab in Medical, but dying was part of the job description.

"Tactical on nav," Terr ordered. The nav bubble momentarily went gray, then reconfigured to show their position on B-2 Three relative to B-2. "Computer, include orbital track of target one." Tanard's projected position showed up as a pulsing red dot. An amber line indicated his insertion orbit, while a fainter dotted line showed his anticipated track if he maintained his previous flight profile.

"Mr. Mati, take us up to eighty-two hundred talans and hold."

The M-3 rose a few katalans and paused while the shock pads retracted, trailing sulfurous dust, then surged straight up. At their holding position, Dhar did a quick scan. No sign of *Laverne*. With his quarry gone, Terr ordered the ship to follow Tanard's course at a bare four hundred tps. No use rushing into trouble.

Nine minutes later...

"Target one detected eleven hundred point-two talans above our orbit and climbing," the computer announced. "Range, seventy-six thousand talans. Target showing navigational deflector grid only. Velocity, one hundred and four talans per second. No belligerency indicated. Optimum firing point in forty point-five seconds if target maintains current flight parameters."

"He's under power, sir," Dhar commented slowly.

"Not so wounded after all," Terr mused icily and cupped his chin. "But where is he going?"

"Target is at relative rest. Optimum firing point is now thirty seconds," the computer said.

In the tactical plot, *Laverne* did not show raised shields or that its projector was powered up. The ship's power curve way down, which accounted for its crawling speed.

"Target's power profile showing activation of primary drive systems. Detecting distortion field precursor modulation," the computer said.

"Is he trying to transit?" Dhar looked surprised. "He will never be able to polarize."

"Mr. Mati! Close on him. Mr. Kieran..."

"Ready to engage, sir." The last encounter damaged some of the control systems, but he could still fire. That was all that mattered.

Dhar looked at Terr, his eyes bright with amusement. "He is holding at a gravitational neutral point!"

It took a second to bring Tanard into effective firing range. Kieran stabbed at the commit pad and yellow fire raced toward Tanard's ship. Just then, a blue-white corona of light enveloped *Laverne* and the ship vanished. An instant later, the yellow beam slashed through the empty spot.

For a few fleeting moments, Terr stared vacantly at the tactical plot and the point where Tanard had disappeared. Absently, he rubbed the scar above his left eyebrow.

"Relative stop, Mr. Mati," he said quietly.

"Relative stop, sir."

Terr nodded slowly and pursed his lips. The deck around him quiet and expectant.

"Mr. Dharaklin?"

"No sign of him, I'm afraid. Residuals show a track, but—"

"How far can you track him?"

"Track distorts beyond effective resolution after eleven light-minutes."

"Computer, time to cover eleven light-minutes at maximum secondary boost?"

"Fifty minutes."

Good enough. "Mr. Mati, distance to B-2 Eleven?"

"Almost twelve million talans, sir."

"Get us moving, then. Maximum available boost and stand down to initial alert. Dhar, you're with me. Mr. Mati, you have the deck."

In the briefing lounge, Terr flopped into a formchair and stretched back his arms until the joints creaked. He nodded at one of the chairs and his brother settled down in a more dignified position.

Dhar waited patiently for Terr to work through his thoughts. He could well imagine what thought ran through Terr's mind right now. By fleeing, Tanard could have broken off action completely due to damage he is carrying, or he may have merely postponed the final encounter. Dhar did not believe it, though.

"What do you think?" Terr asked him, hands folded

161

across his chest, his deep gray eyes shrouded in shadow.

"If he were able to press an attack, he would have done so," Dhar said thoughtfully.

Terr smiled grimly and nodded, but the smile didn't touch his eyes.

"Indeed."

"We could pursue him—"

"No. Remember our objective. Tanard's move doesn't change the tactical situation in any way. Without a main drive, we're still vulnerable. By departing the engagement area, we merely bought us some time. Time we'll use profitably once we reach B-2 Eleven."

"How?"

"The only way we can contact Rayon, or any other Fleet unit, for that matter, is if we're outside Banard's interference field. Since *we* are not subspace capable..."

"You bring the capability here," Dhar said and grinned. "*Hronin.*"

"*Hronin.* Once the four hours are up, his orders are to follow us in. Even if Tanard decides to backtrack, and I'm not sure he will, he has to find us first. The transport should get to us in time."

"If he can," Dhar said dryly. "They took a pretty solid hit in the drive spaces before dropping normal, you know."

"Hopefully not a disabling one. At least Tanard's auxiliary is out of it. If he tries to board, Razzo's ABPs should be able to change his mind. If *Hronin does* come for us—"

"We need to attract her attention. *If* she comes."

"There is that. Once we get to B-2 Eleven, we'll send a survival blister down our insertion course with its emergency beacon pinging for all it's worth. Even with all the interference, *Hronin* should be able to pick it up once it gets close enough and home in. An encrypted pad message will tell them where we are. Then we wait and see what happens."

Dhar looked thoughtful. "You know, of course, by bringing *Hronin* here, you may also be giving Tanard the very opportunity he needs to clean us all up."

"Life is full of crap, I know."

"But the blister—"

"Think it through."

In a moment of silence, Dhar's forehead creased in concentration.

"We are tactical," he began slowly, "but we are still carrying a lot of damage. The crew needs a break, and since time is not a factor, we can afford to sit it out. As for Tanard, the risk is there, and he may have problems of his own." Dhar shook his head. "And you figured all this out when Tanard transited?"

Terr laughed, but it was strained and hollow. "Once I'm finished with you, Nightwings, you'll be able to do this in your sleep. When I was a greasy Third Scout, my commander took sardonic delight in my torture by making me his tactical officer. Of course, he had a *real* tactical officer. He would dream up these scenarios and expected me to solve them there and then, on the command deck, on watch."

Dhar chuckled and Terr shuddered.

"I used to stand watch-and-watch. He made my life hell. I would go off watch soaking wet, shaking with tension. The only thing that kept me from murdering him, he harassed everyone else with equal impartiality." Terr paused and smiled at the memories, then his face went cold. "The first time we went into action, I almost crapped myself, but I didn't. I was too busy doing it right to screw up. He did the same to me with weapons, engineering, everything. On an M-4, that asked for a lot. I learned to hate him real bad. Only later, once I was given command responsibilities, I realized what he had done for me and I could thank him. Albeit grudgingly," he added with a lazy smile.

"It shows," Dhar said with a grin. "Young Kieran…"

Terr's eyes had an evil gleam. "Put him in charge of the repair parties. Let him ask for advice. Don't guide him. Let him figure it out."

"Sankri, that might not be such a good idea right now."

"I don't know a better time to do it. Put Mati in Engineering and see if he can do something with the main drive. There won't be anything else for him to do until we land. Who knows, he might come up with something. As for you, I want options," Terr said and waited.

Dhar instantly became serious. "Everything Tanard can do alone or in tandem with his auxiliary, either before or after we link up with the Devon transport?"

"You go it."

"What if the transport never shows up?" Dhar said carefully and Terr winced.

"I don't want to think about that right now and spoil what has been such a good day so far."

Silence slithered around them.

"Sankri, my brother, what happened to Shan?" he asked softly.

Pain clouded Terr's eyes. He swiveled the formchair until he faced the transparent section of hull. "Go away now. I want to watch the scenery for a while."

Dhar sat there feeling his brother's hurt, then rose slowly and quietly walked out.

Chapter Six

"Do you know the gross mikans that's on-forwarded by Pizgor every day?" Ed-Kani Takao remarked casually, tapping the glossy black surface of his huge desk with a bony finger. "One-point-eight billion. At roughly five hundred mikans per container, that's 360,000 containers—day in and day out. You know how much they charge to on-forward? Four Serrlls per mikan," he said with raised fingers. "Four Serrlls. Think of it, four crummy Serrlls. Even at that price the annual revenue stream is preposterous."

"So are their running expenses. Your point being?" Ti Inai ventured with an oily smile as though this came as startling new information, his large black eyes devoid of expression as he studied the Executive Director. Ed-Kani's skin shone with a faint sheen beneath the indirect ceiling lighting. Deep character lines marked his mouth.

Ed-Kani hissed impatiently at the Palean. Surviving twenty-two years in Captal's boilermaker environment, it was a wonder he remained sane. Within his party, though, that was a matter of some dispute. What drove him to thoughts of murder were the machinations of his would-be partners. The Paleans were such a moody and shifty lot. If it were not for the fact that Sargon needed them so badly, his preference would be to annex them, rather than coddle to them. Ti Inai was as bad as they came: sly, manipulative and predatory, an ideal Assembly representative.

"Don't you see? Paravan's own shipping lines charge twice as much to haul one mikan of cargo point-to-point anywhere in the Serrll, and they're the best, even if they are Sofam scum," he added pensively and snapped his delicate jaws. "When a hauler can ship his freight at half his normal cost by

165

letting Pizgor's carrier lines do it for him, what would you do?"

"Pizgor carriers charge just as much as anybody," Ti Inai piped and bobbed his head.

"Because they're subsidized, and the outside carriers don't deal with them directly. They contract through the Pizgor government to get these low rates. Sure, Pizgor is making a loss on its own lines, but the policy ensures they have a healthy commerce and shipping base. Ordinarily, any government doing this would go broke. Where Pizgor manages to keep ahead of the curve is by offering an array of support facilities to the carrier lines, including their own. It cost them a fortune to set up, but their ground and orbital cargo handling terminals are the best anywhere. Something that hasn't been lost on the competition, by the way."

"Friend Ed-Kani, you're not suggesting we compromise Pizgor's infrastructure, are you?" Ti Inai mused, his fingers twining.

Ed-Kani blinked, then chuckled. He reached for the slim carafe of amber ice wine and refilled their crystal balloons.

"A charming notion," he murmured and sipped, pausing to savor the rich bouquet and the subtle honey flavors of the delicate, thick dessert wine. "However, it would make a hollow political prize if we destroyed their economy. We don't want that." His fingers tapped sharply against the desk and his eyes were raptorial. "No, we need them just the way they are, rich and fat."

Ti Inai pursed his small mouth. "You must pardon me, but why are you telling me all this?"

"Subsidizing your own lines is not a new idea," Ed-Kani said, ignoring him. "We're all doing it in one form or other. What *is* new is the way Pizgor has implemented it. They underwrite a percentage of all cargo and hulls of any line that buys into their on-forwarding scheme. The carriers love it and the insurers love it. Who wouldn't? The Pizgor government is carrying all the risk, but our raids have driven up premiums to a point where the local underwriters picking up the margin are starting to have second thoughts. More importantly, it's beginning to have a real effect on Pizgor's cashflow, and that's got to hurt. Kernami and the Triumvirate Council may have the political will to stand up to us, but economic rationalism and jittery Triumvirate Assembly seat holders will eventually force their hand," he said comfortably.

"What's your point? We know Pizgor will fold if we keep up the pressure."

"The point, my misguided friend, is *how* we're applying that pressure."

"The Provisional Committee has instructed Lemos to maintain the raids—"

"Not by attacking Fleet units!" Ed-Kani roared and slammed his fist against the desk with a crack that made Ti Inai flinch.

The atmosphere became suddenly electric and tense. Ed-Kani never forgave, something the Paleans may have forgotten when dealing with their aggressive and martial partner.

"Le Maran—"

"Was misguided at best and a fool at worst!" Ed-Kani snarled, snapped his jaws shut, and glared at the Palean. "We warned him twice for his importune and excessive zeal. In both cases, the incidents involved an altercation with Fleet units. Only sheer luck avoided bringing the whole Serrll Scout Fleet on our heads. If that hadn't been enough, what does he do now? With the Fleet and BueCult on the prowl, he orders Kai Tanard to attack escorts!"

"He gave no such order!" Ti Inai spluttered in outrage. Surely Maran *couldn't* have been so stupid to take a passing idea they discussed literally.

Ed-Kani bared his needle teeth and tapped a pad on the inlaid desk console. The Wall display at the end of the room cleared.

Stefan Vučak

"Tanard's report says different," Ed-Kani growled and Ti Inai's face flushed as he read the damning words. Ed-Kani tapped a pad and the Wall faded into whorls of random color patterns. "Obviously, you haven't seen his report," he said flatly.

Ti Inai squirmed. "No, I haven't."

"As a key Committee member, it is your responsibility, just as it is mine, to see to it that our policies don't get derailed. This time, Le Maran made a bad call, one that could come back to haunt us. That's not the reason why you wanted to see me, is it?"

Ti Inai slumped into his formchair and grunted with weariness. Turning Pizgor was always going to be a problematic proposition and this development hadn't helped any. Short of outright annexation by Sargon or the Paleans, something that would never be tolerated by Captal, other means must be found to convince Pizgor of the merits to voluntarily join one of the two political blocks. He dealt with domestic raiders and knew the disruption they caused to Palean commercial shipping. He thought he was being clever when he unveiled his plan to use them against Pizgor. Inevitable and expected resistance came from some in the Provisional Committee, but when Ed-Kani brought the weight of Sargon behind him, Lemos became a reality. A reality that could now be undone by an act of misguided patriotic zeal, especially after things were going so well.

"No, it's not," he said at length. "It's possible that some in the Committee know this already. Before we convened, I wanted to brief you personally, friend Ed-Kani."

"Not on the fact that Kai Tanard attacked a Devon 3-VL4 transport escort, but that he failed to destroy it?"

Ti Inai smiled thinly, and there was nothing oily about it. "There is no faulting your intelligence apparatus."

"What I fault is Le Maran's lack of judgment and his incompetence as a tactical commander," Ed-Kani hissed sarcastically. "He has become a serious liability and I will be asking the Committee to have him moved into the planning group where his demonstrated skills can be more profitably engaged. As a commander, he is a walking disaster, and he's too useful to be eliminated, otherwise, I would be calling for it."

Ti Inai's glum expression only confirmed the validity of Ed-Kani's assessment.

"I suppose it is necessary," he piped and bobbed his head. It was clear now that Le Maran should never have been placed into an operational position, factional payoffs or not. Simply political reality despite the stakes they played for. Grease that made the wheels of bureaucracy turn. Surely Ed-Kani had to know that.

"You have considered options, of course, to mitigate the damage?" Ed-Kani said flatly and Ti Inai bobbed his head.

"There is no question about keeping Lemos operational, friend Ed-Kani, otherwise we might as well pack up and shut down. Some, ah, oversight reorganization will be required in the interim and Kai Tanard will have to be replaced."

"Ah, Tanard, our erstwhile raid commander," Ed-Kani said with satisfaction and tapped his teeth with a finger. "Singularly difficult to eliminate."

"He was lucky."

"Indeed. Pity he couldn't finish the job. It would have saved all of us a lot of sleepless nights."

"If not for his auxiliary, he would still be out there, stranded."

"Mmm. This Second Scout Terrllss-rr, what do we know about him? The name sounds familiar."

"Not much," Ti Inai admitted, hands wringing. "It's being looked into."

"Whoever he is, he has effectively shredded Tanard's cover and any hopes of a career in the Fleet, and maybe his usefulness to the Committee as well. Regardless of Le Maran's orders, Tanard should have known better. Dumb!"

"Friend Tanard is a patriot who risked everything for the cause!" Ti Inai piped in outrage. "I deeply resent your casual dismissal of someone who made this whole operation possible. Tanard *created* Lemos! His efforts were unstinting and I will see to it the Committee recognizes—"

Ed-Kani raised his palm and laughed. "Peace! It's obvious that such sterling qualities should not be wasted." He paused and his eyes grew round. "Got it! Four years ago, the aborted Four Suns secession to the Karkans, remember?"

Ti Inai's mouth opened, then he smiled slowly. "Second Scout Terr…"

"Why am I not surprised to see him connected with Tanard? We may need to keep an eye on this young man. Speaking of Tanard, what do we do with him?"

Ti Inai stared suspiciously at Ed-Kani, took a few deep breaths and relaxed. The man could be such a pain.

"Send him to Italan," he said after a time. Ed-Kani frowned and pulled at his chin.

"It might not be such a bad idea at that. Provided he refrains from attacking Fleet escorts," he added dryly. "As it is, he won't be able to parade around in that M-3 of his. It's likely the Fleet has him targeted already. Pits!" He ground his teeth and stirred in his seat. "Our life would be so much simpler if we didn't have to deal with those nonaligned independents."

"Unfortunately, we *have* to deal with them. Especially the Unified Independent Front. I know you don't consider the UIF dangerous, friend Ed-Kani, but in this you are mistaken. Be warned. Before the next General Assembly elections, they will petition for recognition as a nonaligned block and claim a seat on the Executive Council."

"Hah! In round numbers, Kaleen and Orgomy between them may hold enough systems to push them over the five percent needed for an Executive seat, if they were united, but they're not! What you're forgetting, Kaleen and Orgomy systems are still very much fragmented. They continue to behave as loose associations, cooperating only as long as it doesn't threaten their parochial interests. That's where they're vulnerable."

"That's true now, but it's changing. I tell you now before they make their petition, Kaleen and Orgomy will be a united front. Director Marrakan is a formidable force—"

"Him and his Wanderers, superstitious worm crap," Ed-Kani muttered sourly.

"That might be, and your prejudiced sentiments do not diminish him as a threat to our objectives," Ti Inai pointed out smoothly, comfortable in his element. He knew the Wanderers and the power they held in check, and prayed it would never be unleashed against them. He also knew Marrakan. As Prime Director of Kaleen's eight star systems and Controller of Anar'on, Marrakan's magnetic leadership and sheer personality finally convinced Orgomy's five systems to form the Unified Independent Front. As nonaligned independents, they were merely irritants to the major power blocks; the Servatory Party and the Revisionists, vociferous in the General Assembly, but impotent to affect Serrll politics. All that would change if the UIF is permitted to breathe life, and that must not be allowed to happen.

Ed-Kani looked thoughtfully at the Palean and nodded. "You may think I'm playing a dangerous game by giving lip service to the UIF threat. I'm not, and I didn't forget why we set up Italan. Even if Pizgor is absorbed, convincing three or four independents hovering around Kaleen not to join the Unified Independent Front would be useful, very useful. Our merger will bring us control of the Servatory Party, but if the UIF takes an Executive seat the Revisionist idolaters will continue to rule and our efforts will be for naught. I understand the threat, all right."

"All the more reason then to maintain our, ah, *encouragement* on wavering systems to join the Palean Union, friend Ed-Kani," Ti Inai pointed out with an oily smile that drew an appreciative grin from Ed-Kani.

"Subtly put. If for some reason, Pizgor is *not* brought into the fold, those systems could make all the difference. Yes, Italan may turn out to be more important than the Committee, or either of us, envisaged."

The merger would mean nothing if they failed to hold more than twenty-five percent of all inhabited Serrll systems, the magic number that would allow them to claim that third Executive Council seat; and with it, wrest control of the Servatory Party from the Karkans.

Ti Inai bobbed his head, reading Ed-Kani's thoughts. He worked hard as anyone to affect the merger, and he could not fathom Sargon's need for the urgency, to Ed-Kani's intense and ongoing irritation. Could they achieve the merger within eight years before the next general elections? It hardly seemed possible. The infrastructure disruption alone…

As far as Ti Inai was concerned, if the merger took another twenty years to crystallize, he would still be satisfied. Not for the first time, he wondered whether Ed-Kani's rush was driven by a personal desire to see it as a crowning achievement to his career in Captal. In eight years, his third term in the Assembly would be over. Under the Articles of Association, he would be out, a civilian again. Ti Inai, now only in his second term, would still have ten more years of power.

"Are the raids on Kaleen having an effect?" Ed-Kani demanded.

Ti Inai smiled broadly and his fingers coiled. "When the Committee convenes, I will announce that one independent system is ready to declare for the Union. Naurun, a system within Kaleen itself, is sufficiently compromised that they're having second thoughts about the wisdom of joining the Unified Independent Front."

"That is good news indeed," Ed-Kani murmured. "Kai Tanard's talents may be useful after all."

Ti Inai shifted in his formchair and crossed his spindly legs. He took an appreciative sniff at the wine's delicate bouquet and tipped the balloon to his lips. The golden liquid slid like oil down his throat, leaving behind a lingering memory of open fields, flowers, warm sunshine, and clear skies. Nursing his glass, he regarded the Sargon Executive Director across the table. He could almost feel the man's energy, molding events by the sheer force of his personality. An interesting contrast to his own measured and more calculated approach to doing business.

"Friend Ed-Kani," he piped, "you know, of course, Illeran and Terchran are watching Pizgor as closely as we are. They will not allow us to wrest control of the Servatory Party from them without a measure of resistance."

Ed-Kani snorted. "The Karkans have grown soft—"

"They have learned statesmanship," Ti Inai suggested in faint rebuke, reminding him of everything unsettling about the Sargon Directorate—aggressive and impatient. Strangely, that also made them so exciting to work with.

"Which they're wasting in a misguided quest to dominate the Captal government," Ed-Kani said. "They don't have the numbers and still refuse to see the obvious. As long as the Sofam Confederacy holds four of the ten Executive seats, Karkan's efforts are an exercise in futility."

"Far from being an exercise in futility, friend Ed-Kani, it means they're not prepared to risk social dislocation in the pursuit of their objectives."

"Implying we are?" Ed-Kani's voice frosty.

"What we're doing to Pizgor and Kaleen can hardly be called an exercise in statesmanship."

"If the Palean Union cannot stomach—"

"It is a question of tactics," Ti Inai said with a suave smile, fingers twining. "We would be wise to remember that beneath their cold fishy stares the Karkans are polished predators. There is not much they can do about Pizgor, but formation of the Unified Independent Front would be a thorn in their side as much as it will be in ours."

Ed-Kani hissed, staring thoughtfully at the Palean. Ti Inai's enormous black eyes looked back at him without blinking. Ed-Kani reminded himself that oily smiles and an ingratiating attitude notwithstanding, the Paleans were also polished predators. They merely used different tools. A race did not conquer, occupy, and hold twenty-eight systems with mere smiles. Ti Inai smiled faintly as though he read his thoughts.

"About our Pizgor activities," he said slowly. "I'm not sure the Karkans *are* completely helpless. I've been getting reports from my Bureau about high access demands to our computers by the Diplomatic Branch—"

"Prima Scout Anabb Karr isn't known to waste his time," Ti Inai mused.

"—and the Bureau of Technology and Development."

"Terchran!"

"As a Karkan Executive Director, he has almost unrestricted access to all the Bureaus systems. I doubt his is a case of idle curiosity," Ed-Kani mused.

"I agree. Anabb, though, represents by far the most serious threat."

"In the short term."

"In every dimension, friend Ed-Kani. Should his intelligence services uncover Lemos, it will be more than merely inconvenient."

"Then the Committee will have to see to it that Anabb's efforts are frustrated."

"Direct action against Diplomatic Branch operatives?"

"Who said anything about direct action?" Ed-Kani observed with a predatory smile. "It's dangerous out there and things happen…"

* * *

"He's all right?" Anabb demanded, his eyebrows drawn together in a dark scowl.

"Of course, he isn't all right!" Rayon said peevishly and the amber flecks in Anabb's eyes glittered dangerously.

"You don't need to be testy about it."

"Humph! Have you read his after-action report? Read?"

"I have, especially the part where his ship is totaled and he allowed Kai Tanard to get away."

Rayon shook his head in disgust, his broad flat nose twitching. "You're a hard man, Anabb. Hard."

"Hard you would be too if you had to replace ships as fast as that boy manages to wreck them."

"That's what ships are for, and in this case, it isn't your ship. It's mine!"

"It's my operation and the Fleet will bill *me*!"

"Oh, stop whining already. This is an Executive Council directive, as you very well know. They're footing the bill for this."

"Thunderation!"

"Exactly."

Anabb stared ruefully at Rayon, then grinned. "A talent he has for getting himself into scrapes, doesn't he?"

"You're an asshole, Anabb."

"So I've been told."

"Terr was lucky to survive, lucky."

"Lucky nothing. He's just good, but don't tell him I said it. I've started checking up on this Tanard character. Unless he has a double, he's supposed to be at COMPALOPS on Palea."

"I suppose it would be too much to expect there were two of them. Suppose."

"I've just started, Rayon. If Tanard is a real Fleet officer and driving an M-3, I'll find him. A Fleet vessel doesn't tool around. He's got to be getting support from somewhere."

"Agreed. If the Paleans are behind this, you'll never find him. Never. Whoever this Tanard may be, he has disappeared, trust me."

"As far as raiding Pizgor commerce, perhaps. Worth losing an M-3 for that, I guess. I sincerely hope the Paleans *are* behind this. It would mean that COMPALOPS is compromised. Enough at least to show they're brazenly using Fleet units for political ends—"

"We all do that. All," Rayon said pointedly.

"—but I suspect Tanard is too valuable to their organization not to keep employing him. Unless they've killed him," Anabb added wryly. "Save us a lot of trouble, that would. No, sooner or later, he'll surface."

"You have a dark and morbid psyche, Anabb. Dark."

"I can live with it. Now, about Terr…"

"He's in the system and I expect him down this afternoon. Expect. The M-4 that piggybacked him from Banard was released."

"Tanard, must have pulled the same trick," Anabb grumbled.

"Very likely."

A small vessel, itself unable to transit, can clamp onto a larger ship and ride within its distortion field. There is a downside. The two-ship configuration distends the field's delicate torus geometry, greatly reducing speed. At least the smaller ship is retrieved, the alternative is to abandon it if the main drive cannot be repaired, tagging it for later salvage. Terr initially cleared the Banard system by riding on top of the Devon transport. Almost certainly, Tanard used the same maneuver to clear the engagement area as the M-4 found no trace of him or his auxiliary raider.

"That's left us with a problem," Anabb mused, "and we're no closer to locating the raider base. I almost wish Terr never engaged Tanard."

Rayon stared thoughtfully at the Diplomatic Branch director. "Young Terr might not have located the base, may not, but it doesn't mean we walked away with nothing. In fact, I would say his efforts have gained us quite a lot. We have proof the Paleans are using at least one Fleet unit—"

"Circumstantial!" Anabb interjected with a raised finger.

"—with an armed auxiliary in support of raiders. Wherever their base may be, it cannot be too far from Pizgor, otherwise it wouldn't be effective. Wouldn't. If the Paleans are indeed running the base, which we *do* want to prove, and are using a Fleet vessel—"

"Probably more than one."

"Probably."

"You're suggesting they're operating from a military base?"

Rayon shrugged. "Why not?"

Anabb shook his head. "I don't buy it. If the raiders knew the Paleans were running a shadow operation, they'd blackmail them. There is no way the Paleans would openly advertise an M-3 or any other military asset before a raider. You have to remember that raiders are probably only a tool, not an active partner."

Rayon licked his fat purple lips and grinned, looking sly. "Obviously then, the raiders don't know they're getting military support. Obviously."

"Ah, your low native cunning is showing. Why would they expect that their raids are anything more than mercenary, right?"

"Exactly."

"Humph, that's good, but Tanard getting pounded means they'll simply clamp down on their operations. That'll make it much harder to find them."

"So, where is all that high-powered intelligence support you're always bragging about? Where? Sitting on their hands are they?"

"We don't have time to be sitting on our hands, as you so colorfully put it. As soon as you debrief Terr, I want him out there, stirring things up."

"He won't be stirring anything for a while. Not in his ship. He's in for a major yard overhaul. Major."

"Give him another ship, then," Anabb said with gleeful satisfaction and a nasty grin.

"You waited for that one, didn't you?"

"Sorry, I couldn't help myself."

"I'll speak to COMPIZOPS. Maybe they have a spare M-3 lying around. Maybe."

"I should make you suffer, but I won't. When I got your report, I dispatched an M-3 to you with a rotation crew. It'll arrive tomorrow."

"You should have sent two," Rayon said dryly, his eyes twinkling.

"Oh, very amusing! That's a brand-new ship. If Terr bends it, he'll be filling forms into his next life!"

Rayon laughed, a deep throaty sound that shook his ample belly. Anabb's down-to-earth, take-no-prisoners attitude, was a refreshing change from the smooth and somewhat restricted exchanges he was accustomed to in Captal's corridors. He imagined Anabb fulminating through a diplomatic session and chuckled. No wonder Captal's bureaucratic sensibilities were left in shell-shocked disarray after one of Anabb's mission rampages. More than one civil executive must have breathed a huge sigh of relief when Anabb relocated himself to Taltair. Rayon personally thought that to have been a superlative idea. Having so much merit, he was mildly surprised the Executive Council approved it. His eyes drifted toward the window.

Warm yellow sunshine bathed the morning sky over Suratan. The color-reactive environment panels that clad the city towers glittered as they soaked in the free energy. Dark shadows huddled in corners and alleys, softened by a gossamer haze of humidity. Banks of thick gray fog rolled through the mountain pass and pushed over the delta in its march to swallow the city. For a few hours the mist would turn the metropolis into a swirling ghost before the noon sun burned its way through. Rayon tore his gaze away and ran his palm over his cheek and chin.

"Anabb, Commissioner Hiraki doesn't know this, and there is no reason he should, no reason yet, but CAPFLTCOM will be scaling down the Fleet presence in sixty days."

"I know," Anabb growled, looking disgusted. "We've only started. Bovine fools! It gives us a chance to clean out raiders in that sector and we're wasting it."

"You cannot be that naïve, surely," Rayon reproached him.

The emotional struggle evident in Anabb's face, the burn on his cheek coloring. He slumped into his formchair in resignation.

"Jaded perhaps, but I am certainly not naïve. Wishful thinking at worst. We have made an inroad into the raiders, but we won't eliminate them because they're part of us, albeit it's a darker side. Don't worry, Rayon. I'm a pragmatist and I have our objective in mind. It'll mean more ships lost and we can only hope we find that raider base before the Fleet pulls out."

"You're not fooling me one bit, Anabb. Once we find the base, and we will, you'll be slavering after them in earnest, won't you?"

"Like you said, why waste all that good intelligence material."

"Even in a futile gesture?"

"Who said it was futile? Gives everybody something to do."

"I suppose," Rayon said bleakly. "I sometimes wonder which is worse, Paleans and Sargon or the raiders."

"In Palean space they wear the same head. For now, at least."

Rayon pursed his lips and nodded. "You know, of course, Pizgor is not the only threat to Sargon's grand vision of a Palean merger. Kaleen and Orgomy seem to be coming in for more than their fair share of attention from raiders. Seem to be."

"I know. I've studied the shipping figures. There is a measurable increase in hull losses, but it doesn't prove the Paleans are running a second base. It could also be a Karkan operation. The idea of the Unified Independent Front holding an Executive seat would be unwelcome to them as much as it would be for the Paleans. I'm looking into it."

"I am glad to hear that. Glad. What are our pals Illeran and Terchran doing to thwart the Sargon/Palean threat? What?"

Anabb raised a surprised eyebrow. "Why, Rayon! You must know that your question is political and outside the Diplomatic Branch charter."

Rayon looked pained. "Don't give me that worm crap, not this early in the morning. The Diplomatic Branch meddles into whatever it wants. Whatever. It always has."

"That's been part of its problem, and why I'm on Taltair," Anabb muttered darkly.

"Okay, you're the guardian of Serrll's security. So what are our Karkan friends up to?"

"Nothing."

For a second, Rayon stared, not sure he heard right. "Nothing? I find that difficult to believe. Difficult."

"Ah, that famed diplomatic façade has finally cracked," Anabb observed with evident satisfaction.

"I think you enjoy tormenting people. Enjoy. Did you move to Taltair voluntarily or did someone threaten to have you sanded?"

Anabb grinned. "Why? You're thinking of taking out a

contract on me?"

"The thought had crossed my mind once or twice. About Illeran…"

"Okay, this is how I see it. The Karkans are sitting back, doing nothing, allowing the situation to develop. At first glance they're committing a cardinal sin by not honoring the threat. However, this isn't a military confrontation and they may be handling it behind the scenes in ways I cannot see. Then again, from their perspective, things may not be that bad, although Pizgor might not agree with me on that one. With their martial philosophy, Sargon has always looked on inaction as a weakness. By aggressively pursuing the merger, in the process, they've revealed their tactics and players. That's always a questionable move in any high-stakes game. They've pushed too hard, as always, under the mistaken belief the Palean Alikan Union Party faction were just as anxious to consummate the merger, despite all evidence to the contrary. Oh, they're keen enough to make themselves a force in the Serrll political arena, but the Paleans are a cautious and wary lot. Illeran may be betting that Ed-Kani Takao's efforts will flounder from lack of critical mass."

"Hmm. A dangerous assumption, my friend, on which to gamble Serrll's security. Dangerous."

"Perhaps not. Attacking Pizgor commerce is a typical Sargon tactic, and although effective in the short term, I feel it may ultimately turn out to be a major strategic blunder. It's pissed off too many independent systems and now they're vigilant against any covert moves by the major blocks to swallow them. I am including Sofam and the Karkans, of course. Naturally cautious and afraid of ridicule and possible sanctions for their duplicity, the Paleans may be having second thoughts at the wisdom of pursuing the Pizgor policy so vigorously. Should their involvement be exposed, as the point operation, they'll be the ones with the most to lose. They were always leery of Sargon's proclivity to leap into dark waters."

"An interesting dissertation, interesting. However, it rests on some major suppositions which makes for a very shaky scenario."

"Your irreverence for my abilities—"

"Alleged abilities!"

"—is showing, Rayon, and someday, I'll take you to task on it."

"Pursuing this line of fanciful reflection further, how does all this begin to help the Karkans?"

"I'll explain this so that even you can understand," Anabb said. "Direct action against Pizgor has turned out to be precipitous and backfired on Sargon."

"How?"

"The Fleet is involved and the Diplomatic Branch is digging, no?"

"Right."

"Unfortunately for Sargon, being what they are, the tortuous diplomatic filing down is too devious for their taste and too time-consuming, something the Paleans excel at."

"As do the Karkans," Rayon mused softly.

"Exactly!"

"I'm beginning to see where you're getting at with this. Beginning."

"Ever patient, the Paleans are in no rush to affect the merger, no matter how desirous they may be of the outcome. Illeran and Terchran know this. They must be laughing watching Ed-Kani's efforts go into a meltdown."

"They won't be laughing if Sargon pulls it off."

Anabb shrugged. "Death is the only certainty."

"It places them in an unenviable position, though. Unenviable. The Paleans *could* be raiding Kaleen commerce in order to induce skittish independents to join the Union in case the Pizgor gambit fails. That *could* mean a second base. Still, Illeran and the Karkans are caught between two intractable problems. Intractable. He wants to see the Sargon/Palean merger fail, but he's going to get an attack of hives if an Executive seat is lost to the Unified Independent Front."

"Which would you pick as the more significant threat?"

"The merger, of course."

"Hah! That's why he is wooing Marrakan and the Kaleen systems, and Tarim Alai Kamara of Orgomy. If the UIF becomes a reality, Illeran would prefer to see its seat within the Servatory Party camp, rather than fight a hostile Alikan Union Party."

"He would much rather not have to do either, I'm sure," Rayon murmured.

"I don't doubt that."

"Well, with the Revisionists also wooing him, Marrakan must be feeling mightily pleased with himself. Pleased. He's got everybody running around in circles."

"It's a long way to the next general elections, my friend," Anabb warned him. "Plenty of time for things to go wrong."

"For everybody," Rayon agreed.

* * *

SC&C took over nav control and *Ramora* tilted and slanted down toward the curve of the world below. Near the equator a giant storm stood frozen in time, its black central funnel somehow magical and beautiful from above, belaying the terrible wrath of its eye. Tentacles of white wispy cloud trailed in the grip of its spiral, making the dazzle of the surrounding ocean more startling. Detail disappeared in the hazy curve as Pizgor grew large in the transparent nav bubble. Without wavering the ship moved across the azure of the glittering waters toward the lush greens of the northern hemisphere.

Katar Field came up quickly, with Suratan outlined against the backdrop of two mountains, brightly lit by the afternoon sun. *Ramora* shifted slightly and leveled as it glided in its descent toward a complex of maintenance yards. Civilian and military terminus buildings crowded each other, surrounded by landing aprons congested with ships coming and departing. Bulky, ungainly liners squatted on their landing rings, connected to the terminus by a myriad of multi-lane access tubes.

Bulk carriers towered over lesser vessels, serviced by automated loading and unloading systems, while enormous flat cargo pads played around the resting behemoths like swarming insects. At the military end of the complex, brooding M-4s, M-3s and one sinister looking M-6 kept sullen watch. Clusters of M-1s and smaller craft nudged each other unobtrusively among the giants.

Ramora slipped over the bunched military ships and glided toward an enormous hangar. A section of its roof retracted, revealing a gaping cavern that could have swallowed an M-4 and still had space left over. The ship barely paused as it sank. It cleared the roof and descended. After a momentary hesitation it squatted on the supporting landing ring below. The roof closed silently, cutting off the last of the afternoon sky and the hangar burst into brilliant light.

Along railed walkways that hugged the support levels, maintenance crews gazed down curiously at the burns running along the hull, the melted plating, and jagged scars of explosive decompression. The blurring shimmer of the nav grid faded as the battered M-3 shut down. Power umbilicals snaked up from the apron and connected automatically to points in the ship's belly. Hovering two katalans above the landing ring, the ship now fully under ground power. Access tubes extruded from the wall toward it and connected with a series of clangs.

Not wasting any time, Terr mused and glanced through the nav bubble at the closed roof section. He stretched his arms, sighed, and turned to Mati checking the patched engineering display plates.

"Docking sequence completed, sir. Ship is now on external support."

"Very well. Mr. Dharaklin, secure in-flight routine. Stand down the watch and prepare for crew disembarkation. I want everyone in the main maintenance hold in ten minutes."

"Maintenance hold, aye, sir," Dhar said gravely and started issuing commands to section heads.

"Sir, there is a Field Mater Scout on the main deck," the comms watchstander said and Terr nodded to her, noting her bandaged wrist.

He could relax now; let it go, but not yet. Looking around the silent deck, others were sitting back, also reflecting. Little evidence remained of the scars etched deep into the crew. The dead were beyond caring and the wounded at least had a future and something to complain about. It could have been worse had the ship gone into action with a full complement on board. Yeah, he'd been lucky, all right. Tired, mentally exhausted, he gripped the armrests and heaved himself up.

"Mr. Mati, you have the deck. You know what to do. Dhar, you're with me," he said and strode to the cable-tube hatch. He paused as the hatch hissed aside and they both stepped in.

"Main deck," Dhar said, keeping his eyes fixed on the tube wall, painfully conscious of the emotions warring within his brother. He wanted to say he understood, but he wasn't sure he did. There would be a time for healing later, he told himself.

Below, an elderly Karkan Master Scout shifted his wide, slightly flattened head and fishy black eyes focused from horizontal slits. Broad scales covered the green head, glistening, changing color as it moved on a long slender neck. The green looked faded and the luster not as bright as it used to be, but the Karkan carried himself with authority and poise.

Terr walked to him and stood to. He looked for some sign of expression in those black eyes and found none. Well, it took all kinds. He raised an eyebrow at the familiar tall figure of the Pizgor native waiting behind the Karkan.

"Master Scout, welcome aboard," Terr said lightly.

"Thank you, Second Scout," the Karkan said with a hiss. "I want to inform you that I am taking charge of the ship, sir."

"Your ship, sir," Terr said with equal formality, effectively relinquishing command to Maintenance. "Mr. Dharaklin will be coordinating crew disembarkation and quartering."

A flicker of emotion brightened the Karkan's eyes and he glanced at the Pizgor native beside him. The youth stepped forward, touched his chest with an open hand, and nodded to Terr.

"Sir, you and Mr. Dharaklin are requested to report to Ambassador Rayon at your earliest convenience."

Terr looked at him with a grin. "And you're here to make sure I get there, right?"

"Yes, sir," the youth deadpanned without expression and Terr shook his head.

"It will be convenient in a few minutes," he said and turned to the Karkan. "If you would care to accompany me, sir?"

The Karkan gazed curiously at the young commander, aware of the honor extended to him. Giving up a ship that had become part of a commander's very fabric never easy, no matter what the circumstances. He knew what Terr was going through, despite the young man's veneer of calm and relaxed informality. He had been there himself.

"Thank you," he hissed slowly. "If you are sure I will not be intruding?"

Terr smiled faintly, nodded, and glanced at Dhar, who stepped back and touched a pad next to the cable-tube hatch. It didn't take long. The hatch hissed open and they filed in.

Against the Gods of Shadow

The ride down made in silence. The sound of the hatch opening seemed unnaturally loud in the echoing spaces of the maintenance hold. They were all there, the officers standing rigid in front of their divisions.

Mati marched briskly toward Terr, stopped, and stood to.

"Sir, the assembly is accounted for."

Terr gave a terse nod and swept his eyes over them. "Stand easy," he said and waited for the crew to relax. They were curious, expectant, and there was something else there. They looked confident, he decided. They faced Death and their mortality and beaten it.

"We'll be here four days and I won't keep you from your well-deserved leave and your, ah, distractions." Smiles and appreciative chuckles rippled through the ranks. "I do want to say this. Your performance has been exemplary and you can be justifiably proud. We are here only because of those who were prepared to sacrifice all. They'll be missed, but we shall keep them alive in our memories."

In a moment of tense silence, everyone realized they had indeed experienced something special. Service in the Fleet could mean a career filled with patrols and years of uneventful routine. They fought an enemy and lived. Death might claim them all next time, but that was an imponderable.

"*Ramora* brought us back from the brink, but at a price. As we continue the hunt, remember that price, for it has been a good ship to us." Terr paused, allowing them a moment to reflect. "We're getting *Psandra*. It's a new ship and a new beginning for us. I hope to see our wounded back with us once they finish goofing off." That brought more smiles and chuckles. "We're also getting replacements. All I ask is that you go easy on the gags. I need them in reasonable condition to continue our mission." This time there was open laughter as they nudged each other in anticipation. The new swabbies weren't considered part of the crew until they were *initiated*—sometimes a tortuous process.

187

Terr nodded slowly and turned. "Mr. Mati, get them out of my sight."

"Sankri!" someone shouted and Terr's head jerked around in shock. "Sankri!…Sankri!" Others took up the chant and he stood there, letting it wash over him. He felt their pleasure, their pain, their relief, and an eagerness to please.

Only ingrained discipline prevented them from breaking ranks to surround him. He felt a surge of emotion. They were so innocent at times. They may be rogues and troublemakers all, but they were his to care for and protect, even the dead. A familiar twitch crawled up his spine and the hair on the back of his neck stiffened. He shivered as the power flowed through him. No, not here!

But he couldn't resist, couldn't hold it back. Blue sparks danced in his hands and without wanting to, he held them high. They would see him then for what he really was.

"I am Death and I shall protect you, and my touch will make you whole," he chanted in a deepening voice that rumbled like dying thunder, the words from the *Saftara* echoing in the hold. "They have no fear who stand in my shadow."

Some did fear, in their awed faces. He dropped his arms and they were around him; touching him, chanting, laughing, and the lightnings slithered over them, but didn't burn.

When the fires died, Terr finally turned to Mati and grinned wildly as his second officer spluttered in outrage at this flagrant familiarity. He caught sight of Dhar's broad approving smile and laughed and felt the weight on his soul lighten. Perhaps the dead have forgiven him, even Shan. As they pressed around him, he returned their touch.

The Karkan Master Scout stood back, watching the spectacle with startled wonder. This spontaneous display of affection for a commanding officer left him dazed and bemused. Naturally reserved, he could not conceive of a situation where the barrier that existed between crew and commissioned officers could ever be lowered. Yet here he was, seeing it done.

Against the Gods of Shadow

Cloaked in Death the young commander's terrible power did not cower his crew, but bound them, knitting them into a single will—his will.

* * *

"Come in, Second Scout, come in." Rayon beamed, standing behind his palatial desk.

Dusk shrouded the city towers behind him, framing the jeweled buildings that now shimmered with inner light. He nodded to the Pizgor native and the youth withdrew unobtrusively.

The office walls glowed soft green, offsetting the blue of the ceiling. A Wall display station, pooling through orange, red, and purple contortions, took up half the wall on Rayon's right. Large potted plants overflowed to the carpeted floor on either side of his desk. Shelving held vases, trinkets and data cubes, otherwise the office was unadorned. Soft formchairs took up one corner, capturing a low crystal-topped table between them.

Rayon extended his arm at the seats.

"Make yourselves comfortable," he said as he strode from behind the desk and eased himself into one of the chairs.

Terr followed, sensing Dhar close behind him. With some squirming and shuffling, they allowed the seats to cradle them. Rayon leaned forward and looked at each of them in turn.

"You are both well? Rested?"

"Well enough, thank you, sir," Dhar answered seriously.

"Good, good. Your flight from Banard?"

"Uneventful, but it did give us a few days to reintegrate the crew," Terr said.

"A third of them were in *Hronin*, weren't they?"

"Yes, sir. I want to express my appreciation and thanks to the M-4's commander for carrying us to Pizgor."

"His duty," Rayon said simply. "And while we're talking of ships, your new command will be here tomorrow. *Ramora* is far too badly damaged to be returned to service anytime soon and I cannot have you two hanging around waiting for it to be repaired. Cannot."

Just polymer and ceramic, Terr told himself, knowing it to be a lie as he pushed back the crowding memories. His eyes wandered to the sprawling blaze of the city. Rayon followed his gaze.

"Looks peaceful, doesn't it?" Rayon murmured. "I wonder how many of them actually care what's going on around them. Wonder."

Terr wondered the same thing, but that wasn't his concern. When boiled down, his job was to kill and he drove one of the best killing machines in the Serrll that enabled him to do it. Men like Rayon and Anabb and others worried about the why. He certainly couldn't do it, not if he wanted to remain sane. Did he really believe that?

"If we do our job, sir," he said softly, "they don't need to care."

Rayon's eyes were penetrating as he searched Terr's face. The young man had changed in the four years since they were both on Elexi, that was obvious, but what had that change wrought? He sensed Terr's pensiveness, a need to reflect, and he suspected, an opportunity to unburden himself.

He had another reason to draw the boy out. Terr was unique, a Wanderer, not a native of Anar'on, and that's what made him unique. Rayon never ceased to marvel at how the boy ended up walking in the shadow of Death. He knew Dhar was instrumental in saving Terr from insanity, the process merging their personalities, leaving behind the seeds of the Wanderer Discipline and the shadow of Death. To restore himself and regain his memory, Terr had to face the god of Death. He survived the trial and walked away with the power to wield the lightnings. The boy was exceptional and his insight could be very useful in Captal's dealings with the Wanderers and the Unified Independent Front. Was he using Terr? His conscience hardly gave a twinge. Everyone was used all the time.

"And do *you* care?"

Terr allowed himself a fleeting smile. "I can only afford to care about my little corner of it and hope what I'm doing is right."

"Ah, but then, what is right? Who judges? Who?"

"That's unanswerable as it deals with perspective, and I must work within my own. What I *can* deal with is the how. I don't judge the right or the wrong of the Sargon/Palean merger. That's merely a case of political evolution."

"Even when the how resorts to plunder and slaughter?"

"Plunder is a social restriction, not a moral position." Terr sensed Dhar's eyes on him.

"An interesting interpretation. Interesting." Rayon smiled and his eyes flickered quickly at Dhar. "And the other?"

"Imposition of a political order on another may be uncomfortable for those on the receiving end. As to whether the method used is right or wrong is again a matter of perspective."

"So, you are prepared to condone oppression, denial of personal freedoms, torture, murder, slavery? Condone?"

Terr sat back and allowed the formchair to mold itself to him. His eyes burned as Death stirred within them. Rayon saw the fires and felt a twinge of apprehension, which quickly passed. He had nothing to fear here.

"Mr. Ambassador, I walk in the shadow of Death, but I am not that which casts the shadow. With free will, everything is possible. To exist, we restrain the excesses of free will through mores, customs and laws—"

"Then there is no evil?"

Terr paused, confronted openly by a question he often

debated within himself.

"Causing willful suffering, bodily or mental, for no other purpose, I would call that evil."

"You don't hate Tanard, then?"

Terr clasped his hands and pursed his lips, admiring the skillful ease with which Rayon had manipulated him. Still, it was a fair question. He realized by opening himself like this, his views could be used to control him. In the end, he didn't care, a road yet to be crossed. If he learned anything of the Discipline, by denying the truth to himself, he could not hope to recognize it in others. He needed to be himself.

"When I ordered my chief engineer into the secondary drive reaction chamber, knowing he would lose his hands, I hated Tanard then. I wanted to hurt him as he hurt me." Terr felt Dhar stiffen beside him. He gave him a tight smile, then turned to Rayon. "No, I don't hate him for what happened between us. I had a job to do and he had a job to do. The action I took to save my ship was my choice. Is he deserving of hate because he happened to be a causal factor? A moot point. Perhaps no one is. As for actions he may have done elsewhere, he must confront himself and others for judgment. To hate is to risk the vengeance of the god of Death, and that's too terrible to unleash. Once loosened, it is a destroyer without recall."

"Standing in the shadow of Death as you do, could you have destroyed Tanard's ship?" Rayon whispered, his dull-brown eyes intense.

"Only at the cost of my own destruction. I know that in my hands, I hold the fate of worlds, but I cannot exercise that degree of control. Should I survive my two remaining trials with the god, one day perhaps, I may have the wisdom to judge and act. Until then, sir, my problem is learning restraint and not giving into temptation."

"And for those who fail?"

"Death becomes their ultimate judge."

Against the Gods of Shadow

Rayon sighed and shook his head. Incredible! This mere Second Scout had the capability to turn history if he wanted to. Glancing at Dhar's stern features, he garnered a measure of understanding of the awesome power held by the Wanderers. It chilled him. Intellectually, he had always known, but hadn't appreciated its emotional impact, even when Terr returned to Elexi after his crash. Always an amusing topic at diplomatic cocktail discussions, a novel curiosity good for a few chuckles, barbaric desert nomads with delusions of godhood. Not really the case at all, was it? The Wanderers truly possessed a power to destroy worlds.

Did Anabb know what Terr represented, what the Wanderers represented? Looking at the boy, he realized Anabb had known all along, must have known, and that's why he had Terr here. Anabb possessed a sneaky streak wholly unappreciated. Rayon spent fifteen years in Captal as an un-elected representative, all of it in diplomatic service, before getting into the Assembly. Now in his third and final ten-year term, to have this land on him? He simply could not accept that the Executive Council did not realize what Anar'on represented—or perhaps chose to ignore. Anar'on a much more complicated and multi-dimensional problem than he suspected, as were the drivers behind the Unified Independent Front. If the UIF were really threatened, would the Wanderers take affirmative action to thwart its opposition? He shuddered at the extreme possibilities of such action. Can Captal rely on the *Saftara* to restrain the Wanderer's hand?

He stared thoughtfully at the boy. Terr had given him much to think about.

"If I had any sense, Second Scout, I would see to it that you never commanded a ship again. Never. You would be on Cantor! After what you just said, it would be the height of hubris to condemn or judge you merely for being what you are, what both of you are. With the power they hold in their hands, I can only pray the Serrll never feels the wrath of the

Wanderers. Pray."

"Sir, if you want me to withdraw from this mission—"

"Withdraw?" Rayon demanded sharply. "Don't talk foolishness. Anabb will never say it, but I can. Your performance has been estimable. Yes, estimable. More noteworthy, it was honorable. Withdraw? Rubbish! You've achieved much, but we need you out there to finish it, to find that base. Find it."

"As I mentioned to Anabb, sir, a tall order."

Rayon waved his hand in irritation. "But not an impossible one. I understand the limitations facing you, and we were not altogether idle either. Weren't. A lot of useful information has been gathered and raider ships identified from their fuel cell signatures and other indicators," Rayon said with a shake of his head. "That's not to say we can get them all. A fool's dream, probably. What the data *has* allowed us to do is begin to build the bare outlines of the various support networks and cargo disposal routes. This, my boy, is far more valuable than bagging the raiders themselves. Far more."

It was to go on, then. More pain? More deaths? Terr did not really expect anything else. He'd had his time feeling sorry for himself. Did he feel ready to take that next step?

"One of the information requests I made to Anabb, sir, were details of any new commercial and support ventures established around Pizgor in the last five years. Any returns on that?"

"Several. So far they all seem legitimate. So far."

"Do you know if any of them are near a Fleet base?"

"Hah! Given your encounter with Tanard, I expected you to ask that one. As a matter of fact, there are two. Porpureen is on the ragged edge of your search criteria and I am tending to discount it."

"Why is that, sir?"

Rayon smiled and turned to Dhar. "Care to answer him?"

Dhar barely paused. "Because it is in Karkan space?"

Rayon laughed with delight and Terr chuckled. "You are

absolutely correct, Mr. Dharaklin. Correct. The Paleans would be most foolish to run an operation from there."

"But not altogether out of the realm of probability, sir," Dhar said with a mischievous glint in his eyes.

"Agreed, and we're checking it out."

"Do you know, sir, whether it's manned by Karkans or Paleans," Terr added and Rayon's smile turned grim.

"A very astute observation. Very. We will check that out too."

"And the other site?"

"Lemos. It's one of Praxa's moons. Lemos runs extensive gas mining extractions. It's been around for decades, as has the Fleet outpost there. Of interest is a relatively recent establishment of an import/export venture, the Tai-Mari Line. In itself the information doesn't make it noteworthy, except for the fact it offers maintenance support facilities to other shipping lines. All this could be perfectly innocent, of course. Perfectly, and logical. We don't want to tip off the civilian operator by barging in and being crude. A routine visit by a Fleet unit, quite natural under the circumstances, should not arouse more than fleeting suspicion."

Terr raised an eyebrow. "I thought—"

"Anabb and I will be checking out the commercial operation of both sites. Any support the raiders may be getting will certainly not be coming from a Fleet base, and definitely not anything the raiders would be able to recognize. The Paleans would not be *that* asinine. They may be foolish perhaps, but they don't lack in guile. By necessity my end of the investigation needs to be more, shall we say, circumspect? Yes, more."

Terr grinned. "I understand, sir. A hovering M-3 with a charged projector is hardly the subtlety required here," he said and Rayon laughed, looking at Terr with fond indulgence, his eyes full of amusement.

"It is gratifying to be working with someone who can

grasp all the nuances. Gratifying. However, it does seem to me you dropped the ball with Tanard. Tell me, why did you respond to his comms ping in violation of your own orders? Why?"

"He blew his cover with that ping, sir."

"Oh?"

"Yes, sir. Every Fleet unit in this sector knows about the level two comms protocol. Sector TACOPSCOM would have informed any ship entering the ops area. When Tanard pinged me, I had him. When he made contact, he saw an M-3 and a bulk hauler. Nothing about me that would force him to break protocol, unless he wanted to plant a suspicion in my mind that he thought I was a raider. He tried to draw me out. What made me almost certain, he never asked for *Hronin's* ident ping. He must have known who we were. The other thing was his approach. His course for Karkan space didn't feel right, coming out of Banard's detection shadow like that. No, he deliberately stalked me."

"But your ping!"

"I wanted him to get an impression he was dealing with a young and rash amateur."

"Which he was," Rayon said dryly and Terr grinned.

"Yes, sir. As soon as I returned his ping, he should have broken off. I was an unknown variable, but he had a powerful ship and an armed auxiliary. He felt confident he could take me."

"He almost did. Next time you get a ping from someone, even if it's a survival blister, you run. Is that clear? Run."

"I shall keep it in mind."

"What's more, you revealed yourself to him. Revealed. They now know you for what you are."

"Ah, not exactly, sir. New ship, new IFF."

"Hah!"

"And I would like to keep it that way, for a while at least. I would very much appreciate if you could arrange for

Psandra's landing data pack dump to be wiped from Pizgor SC&C. I won't be dumping on lift either."

Rayon looked speculatively at Terr. "Under the circumstances, it wouldn't do to advertise to Lemos that you're coming. It wouldn't."

"Thank you, sir. If I may? What's the search area for Tanard?"

Rayon gave a small shrug. "In theory, he could be anywhere. Without a main drive, his choices are likely to be limited. Yes, limited. The Et-Aran Nebula is one possibility."

Terr absently scratched the scar on his left temple. It made sense. Et-Aran only eleven light-years from Banard, well within the flight profile of Tanard's auxiliary *Zaradej*. Also a long way from anywhere. Tanard would be really exposed, no support or resupply, and no way to repair his drive—maybe. If he had casualties, they would need help. The auxiliary would not be of much use there, its facilities basic. It could have transported them somewhere else, and that raised another question. Terr lifted his eyes and Rayon smiled.

"In answer to your next question, we're also looking for his auxiliary. I am much more hopeful about locating it than I am of finding Tanard. Much."

"They could have destroyed it," Terr said. "No evidence, no case."

"Perhaps."

"Sir, whatever happened to that suspected raider on Mitlan mounting stolen fuel cells?"

"Glad you asked. Glad. They scooted off to Askaran, but Anabb's people are keeping an eye on it. It's still there, apparently undergoing drive maintenance. Of course, there is no way to tell how long they will remain there. No way. I'll arrange to have the raider's ident dump loaded into your ship's computer. As for the fuel cells, they were definitely taken from the vanished Four Suns bulk carrier *Rakish*. To answer the obvious, the reason we didn't jump them is because we're hoping they will lead us deeper into their network." Rayon noted Terr's wry smile and nodded. "I know, my boy. Where is *our* morality, eh?"

"Partly, sir, but I acknowledge it's more a question of expediency. Allowing immediate harm in order to later prevent an even greater harm."

"We are riding a slippery slope here, nonetheless." Rayon remained silent for a moment. "Is that why the Wanderers don't march between the stars spreading the Discipline?"

"You already know the answer to that question, sir," Terr said softly.

Rayon sighed heavily. "Well, should you happen to run across that ship, I know you will take measured and appropriate action."

"You can rely on me to do the right thing, sir."

"I always have, my boy. Always."

Chapter Seven

Re Nette sat back, crossed her legs, and cast a critical eye around the command deck. The watchstanders were chatting among themselves, probably retelling tales of conquests and hard play after arduous days of unremitting labor to get *Drakin* resupplied and squared away for another sortie. The forced layover hadn't come cheap. She pushed the ship as hard as she pushed the crew. Despite several postponements and extensive overhauls, she had to face the inevitable and have the main drive reactor rebuilt. She howled in outrage at the two-and-a-half million Serrlls bill, but the stone-faced ground superintendent remained unmoved. The figures were simple. She could spend another three hundred thousand on a patch job and be back in the body shop after only one of two runs, or get the thing done properly. But two-and-a-half million? Take her blood instead!

After raging and storming through the maintenance yard, threatening to have it blown up along with all the thieves inside it, she told the superintendent to go ahead. It wasn't like this came as any surprise. She should have done the overhaul two runs back when her balance sheet looked healthier. Things could have been worse. Unlike normal maintenance, which came off any raid proceeds and crew shares, infrastructure investments were borne by the owners. Thankfully, she was up for only a third of the cost, the other two-thirds met by her two silent partners. They didn't like it, wanting to push the ship further. In the end, they acquiesced, just as she had to.

Mitlan had been good to them. She offloaded her plunder from the Four Suns hauler and the proceeds from her previous raid came through. Awash with cash again, and that made

199

everyone happy. Intended to be a small celebration, issuing the share chits, but after only an hour it quickly degenerated into howls of delight from the crew as she called each name, accompanied by good-natured ribald commentary. Things went rapidly downhill after that. She didn't mind. They earned it. They may have been each one of them rejects from some past or better life, but they were hers. She hadn't even minded the casual groping of her butt and an odd peck on her cheek, but drew the line when an offending hand strayed to her breast. A hard fist into the malefactor's jaw settled that one, amid roars of appreciative laughter. Some lines couldn't be crossed if she wanted to continue commanding them.

After the party, she decided to have the drive overhauled on Askaran, rather than commit to a prolonged layover on Mitlan. Askaran only eight lights off and her partners had better facilities at their Otilando base. The trip would hardly raise a sweat. Besides, she needed to see her two partners. They didn't mind the profits, but they were also impatient for her to go out again, which she was not too keen on doing. With the Fleet on the prowl, the risks were suddenly serious and she needed an overhaul herself. She'd been out cruising for almost four straight months and the strain told on her. Her partners were sympathetic, but unmoved. She wondered how they would feel if one of *them* had to lay his butt on the line with the ship. To go hunting, she would need solid intelligence to keep herself out of trouble. That meant crawling to the high and mighty five percent Tanard! The image of his haughty smug smile made her blood simmer. In the end, she swallowed her pride and contacted Lemos, only to find Tanard wasn't available. One of his flunkeys gave her the dope. In a way, she was glad not having to face Tanard, having to argue again. Infuriating man!

One day, friend Tanard, there will be a reckoning.

Re Nette looked up. The nav bubble transparent, the sky still had the deep blue of dawn. Threads of white mist hugged the cracked apron. Golden light peeked over the maintenance sheds. The field small, but equipped with a terminal, landing rings, and modern repair facilities. Her partners obviously didn't spare any expense here.

The place offered other attractions. Askaran was a delightful tropical world with warm airs, azure seas and white, long sandy beaches. She enjoyed four days of absolute laziness and isolation in blissful contentment. She dived in crystal waters, speared fish, and took long sunset walks along the shore. Exactly what she needed to restore herself. Now it was time to get back to work.

She nodded, satisfied with herself and the world.

"Taplan?"

Her deputy and nav officer looked up. He ventured a few gropes himself the other night and wouldn't have minded a lot more. Impossible, at least while Re Nette sat in that chair. That wasn't going to be forever. Afterward, well...

"Ready to get underway," he said smoothly, his eye locked on her face. Her mouth barely twitched in acknowledgment.

"Tay-nee?"

"Power is up," he rasped and rubbed the scars on his inflamed cheek.

He'd caused minor mayhem around town, and last night, Taplan had to bail him out of the local hock. Which was just as well. *She* didn't know about it and he saw no reason why she should. He didn't mind leave, but he always looked forward to going out. He knew that one day, he probably wouldn't be coming back, none of them would, but that was the deal. It certainly beat the hell out of being a First Powerman in a lousy M-4.

Let's lift and be outta this dump.

"Right. Taplan? Pull her up," Re Nette ordered.

Drakin lifted three katalans, hovered for a moment while the support umbilicals disengaged, then streaked into a brightening sky. A low rumble of thunder followed in her wake.

* * *

"Approaching Lemos Surface Command and Control," the computer said flatly. "Initial interrogative verified. Insertion in eleven minutes. All systems nominal for orbital approach. Landing configuration procedure initiated. Ship within acceptable flight parameters."

Terr wasn't listening. He gazed at the ragged shape of the Et-Aran Nebula high on their port quarter. Barely eighteen light-years away, it made for a pretty sight. Lemos hung as a bright crescent beneath them, outlined against the deep black of Praxa's shadow. The configuration strikingly similar to Banard-Two and the memories lurked within reach, ready to be unleashed. He pushed them back and watched Lemos grow in the nav bubble.

"Standing by for orbital insertion."

He swept his eyes around the manned stations. It hadn't been much of a shakedown flight. *Psandra* crisp and responsive, and so were the crew. There were a few minor differences in the console layouts, but still a K/11 M-3, and he could have been in his *Ramora* for all the difference it mattered. It felt good to have a deck beneath his feet again.

"SC&C link enabled. Ready to copy."

"Approved," Dhar said gravely and stole a glance at his brother.

Sankri looked perky, impatient to get into action. The days leading up to departure from Pizgor were hectic. He hadn't begrudged the crew their leave, but once he got them back, he drove them and the support crew mercilessly. Every system check that could be done on the ground was done. He was particularly hard on their new chief engineer, a taciturn Karkan, wizened and unflappable, refusing to be goaded by his young commander. In the end, Sankri relented. Hadrian was simply doing his job, and doing it well as far as his brother could make out.

Once in space, Sankri became transformed, in his element, and things settled down, much to the crew's relief. A few speed runs, a weapons test, emergency procedures; *Psandra* took it all, everything he had thrown at it, and the crew started to enjoy themselves. They were hungry to hunt and looked forward to action, as did their commander.

"Entering IP," the computer said.

Terr slapped the armrest with an open hand. "Okay, Mr. Mati. Let's take this bucket of stale worm crap down before she falls down."

"SC&C enabled, sir," Mati said, wearing a broad grin. The comms operator leaned toward him and murmured something. He blinked at her, then looked at Terr. "Sir, it's SC&C. They're querying our denial to dump the data pack."

"Ignore them. It doesn't carry mandatory compliance. Mr. Dharaklin? I'll be wanting a full sensor sweep. Sow four S/14s into a one hundred talan orbit."

"That isn't going to make us very popular," Dhar murmured fatalistically.

"This isn't the time to be subtle. Ril Seen will know who we are soon enough and he won't like it anyway."

Unorthodox, but Dhar had come to expect the unorthodox from his brother. If Lemos did harbor a raider base, stirring things up might reveal a crack or two, unlikely as that seemed. Wherever the installation really was, it would have an impenetrable cover. That didn't mean it wasn't worth the effort looking for it. The most unlikely things were possible and they could always get lucky. He could try and wrap it up in strategy and tactics, but the plain fact remained that Sankri liked causing trouble.

"Full sweep it is," Dhar said with a resigned shake of his head.

Terr suppressed a smile. His influence had rubbed off on Nightwings and he could see his brother wasn't altogether sure he liked the change. They'd served together for four years...an eternity of experience. Terr never regretted asking Dhar to be his first officer, even though Dhar did not come close to holding such a position before. Dhar slipped into the role naturally, partly because he was extremely competent, and partly because of memories he acquired from Terr.

Over the four years, Terr felt an almost physical draining sensation as some of Dhar's memories slowly faded, or maybe they became more completely integrated with his own. He no longer felt the jarring divide between his experiences and those Nightwings left with him in that fateful moment of joining. He often wondered how his brother coped having another personality inside him. Probably far better than he coped with Dhar's, Terr decided. They talked about it in the quiet moments hanging between the stars. The merging they had undergone should have made them more alike. In a whimsical play of fates by the god of Death, it served to strengthen their individuality. Whatever the case, Dhar used Terr's memories and experiences to make himself an exemplary first officer. Terr helped, of course. A memory only a pale shadow of reality. As he knew from painful knowledge, doing it was something altogether different from merely knowing *how* to do it.

He would hate losing Dhar when he came up for his own command.

Terr watched the massive black hole of Praxa blot out the stars as Lemos shifted and grew large. How was *he* affected by Nightwings' heritage? Holding in his hand the power of Death had certainly tempered him and moderated his impetuousness. At least, he liked to think so. He could not deny it also thrust him into emotional turmoil. He hadn't sought the power and was damn sure Dhar certainly never intended to leave him with that burden, but merged they were and each was left to cope with the other's legacy. Terr could feel the power even now, lurking deep within him, waiting to be re-called and unleashed. It terrified him—and excited him. Wielding the lightnings of Death, he was immortal, a shaper of destinies. It had always been easier to destroy than to build or repair, and the temptation to loose the lightnings an ever-present seduction. He wondered to what extent it colored his thinking and behavior.

Even the presence of power is an influence. The words of his master echoed in his mind, and the desert sands were hot about him beneath the glare of an amber sky.

Rit!

SC&C didn't waste any time bringing *Psandra* down. They cleared the terminator into full daylight and the nav bubble polarized. The ship dropped quickly, making the surface a blur below them. Moments later the M-3 stopped in a brief hover, then plummeted down. Terr watched the Field instal-lations; arrays of holding tanks, service hangars and adminis-trative buildings, grow large in the main display plate. To port a cluster of low structures. According to the brief, it contained personnel housing quarters. Far to starboard, three ungainly Very Large Bulk Carriers, VLBCs, crowded the apron. Service vehicles maneuvered busily around the beached giants. Al-most directly beneath him, side by side, lay two M-3s. SC&C brought *Psandra* neatly down beside them. Grudgingly, Terr admitted the evolution had been very businesslike.

"Docking sequence completed, sir. Ship is on internal power and we're maintaining a two-katalan hover. No exter-nal umbilicals connected."

"Very well, Mr. Mati. Mr. Dharaklin, secure the in-flight watch and set ground routine."

"Sir, First Scout Ril Seen—"

"Put him through," Terr said and waited for the main plate to clear.

The Palean's features were long, gray and stern, and he

gave Terr a measured appraisal. Fingers twining before him, he jutted out his small pointed chin.

"All right, Mister, what's this nonsense about refusing to download your data pack?" he piped, his matte black eyes unblinking.

Terr sighed. This was going to be difficult. "I would prefer to discuss this with you in private, sir."

"Why don't we discuss it now, all right?"

"I would *really*—"

"For the last time, *Second* Scout!"

"Very well, sir." Terr glanced at Mati, nodded, and turned back to Seen. "You've just received a message burst giving you my orders, clearance and authentication codes."

"What the…" The Palean pursed his lips in annoyance as he craned to look at another display plate. His frown deepened, then his eyes brightened. For a moment there, Terr could have sworn that…no…

"Terrllss-rr…" Seen mused, his fingers trying to tie themselves into a knot. Then he smiled, all oil and friendliness—and phony. "Very impressive credentials, I must say, Mister; a Captal ambassador looking over you, no less, and director of the Diplomatic Branch. My, you travel in exalted company."

Terr decided that Seen must be giving him the benefit of his refined sense of humor, otherwise, it would be very easy to develop an intense dislike for the shifty, sly, condescending piece of worm turd.

"The impressive credentials bit is slightly overrated. Everything else is true," Terr said smoothly.

"I see. All right, Second Scout, it looks like we'll be having that private chat after all."

"I appreciate your cooperation, sir."

"I'll send a sled-pad," Seen said and cut contact.

Terr shook his head and sighed. He turned to Dhar and gathered Mati with his eyes.

"You two know what to do."

"I have never been a spy before, sir," Mati pointed out reasonably. "I'm curious to see what it feels like."

Terr grinned. "You'll be feeling more than just curious lying on a cold slab," he said and tapped a pad on his armrest. "Mr. Hadrian, you have the deck."

"Sir," the Karkan hissed from the engineering spaces.

Terr stood up and stretched his arms. "Right! It wouldn't do to keep the base commander waiting."

The cable-tube took him down to Hangar One. There, he got into one of the two cargo loading bays and descended to ground level forward of the projector dome. The protective rail lifted and a blustering, biting wind swirled through the compartment. The air smelled raw and grated in his throat.

"Glorious," Terr muttered and strode out.

Praxa hung above him, huge and brooding, waiting to squash him. It was an awesome sight. He looked around the bleak expanse of the apron. From ground level the Field didn't look all that big, but it felt lonely. He wondered what passed for attractions at this end of nowhere. The two M-3s beside him loomed dark, silent and lifeless. The sleek pebble shape of an M-1 farther off rested on its landing skids, probably Ril Seen's personal ship. A sweet craft any way he looked at it.

A whisper behind him made him turn. A sled-pad silently glided up to him and stopped to hover a few tetalans above the weathered apron. The wind gusted and Terr felt his skin crawl. He didn't need further encouragement and promptly stepped on the sled. It barely shifted beneath his weight. He touched a pad on the simple console. The sled lifted as the repeller field snapped on, blessedly shutting out the wind, turned and streaked toward a low two-story building.

Standing beside a doorway, a Third Scout stood to when the sled stopped. Terr climbed off and nodded to the Palean.

"Sir, First Scout Ril Seen is expecting you," he piped in a

thin, high voice. "If you will follow me, please."

Terr extended his hand. "Let's not keep him waiting, then."

Another biting gust stirred the dust around his legs. He shivered and hurried after the short figure. The place reminded him of Elexi, it had the same refrigerated welcome and climate.

The cable-tube took them up and the doorway hissed into the wall. Floor-to-ceiling window screens, giving an unrestricted view of the Field, surrounded most of the open area. Manned SC&C, nav and comms consoles lay arrayed behind each other. Curious, suspicious faces turned toward Terr. A full-dimensional Wall station stood gray and cold on Terr's right. A schematic of the Field took up a fair portion of one wall: run-up ramps, parking aprons, loading zones—bright lines everywhere. He didn't figure the place to be that busy.

"Ah, this way, sir," the young Palean said and walked left toward the corner of three closed-off offices. A hard beige carpet beneath their feet gave nothing away. The youngster paused before a double-paneled door and touched a waist-high glowing yellow pad. The pad turned brown and the panels hissed into the walls. The Palean nodded to Terr and stood to.

It looked like any other office, Terr noted as he stepped through. The two corner walls were transparent window screens giving a grand vista of the Field. His eyes swept over the bare walls and plain furnishings and came to rest on the Palean standing behind a desk. The door panels hissed shut.

"If you please, Second Scout," Ril Seen said smoothly and extended a thin hand at the formchairs.

"Thanks." Terr adjusted the seat to more comfortably study the Palean.

Seen looked a bit old for a First Scout, but that could mean many things. Terr reminded himself to check how long Seen held his present assignment. It wasn't much of a posting for an officer on a high-speed, low-drag career curve. He watched the Palean sit back, clasp his hands over the desk, and allow himself a wintry smile.

"You must excuse me if I appeared less than enthusiastic when you dropped in. TACOPSCOM has been on my case lately. Least of all about your, ah, encounter with that M-3. It is disgraceful to think a fellow officer…"

"It's a delicate situation for everyone," Terr ventured, weighing up Seen's words. If the Palean was outraged, he concealed it well.

"Delicate, yes. That's one way of putting it, friend Terr. Tanard a fellow Palean, well, I'm sure you understand. I am not unaware of the disruption raiders are causing to general commerce in this sector, and Pizgor in particular. Scum, all of them. That's a personal view, of course," Seen said easily and smiled broadly, his hands clasped tight to prevent the fingers from working. "I am also aware of the political dimension surrounding these raids, Second Scout. If there is a support base out there, and I'm not saying there isn't, what are you expecting from me? More patrols?"

"That's an operational decision for you to make, sir. What I would like is a copy of all your SC&C dumps taken over the last two years," Terr said and watched Seen's reaction.

The Palean merely blinked without a change of expression. That was…disappointing. Terr hoped for some reaction or something. Did he seek to nail Seen out of personal bias?

"Let me get this straight. You're checking up on *me*? You think *Lemos* is the support base?"

"It is merely one of a number of possibilities being investigated, sir."

Seen chuckled. "With me breathing down on them? Well, it's your time to waste. You know that all Fleet SC&C dumps are sent on a regular schedule to TACOPSCOM?"

"Yes, sir."

"Why then do you want the dumps?"

"Me? I don't want the damned things. It's the Diplomatic Branch. Pattern analysis, traffic movement; that kind of thing."

Seen stared at Terr, then smiled. "All right, Second Scout, what are you really after?"

Terr put on his trusting grin. "Well, Lemos is pretty far off the beaten track, sir. There *could* have been an instance where some stray carrier happened to drop in looking for supplies and some odd maintenance work."

"And you think one of those 'odd ships' might have been a raider?"

"It's possible."

Seen leaned forward slightly. "Let me tell you something, Mister. This might be the ass end of nowhere, but nothing happens around here I don't know about. Nothing!"

"Naturally. Do you also monitor all civilian installation activities?"

"Eh?"

"Well, I couldn't help noticing that the Tai-Mari Line shares the Field facilities."

"They provide service maintenance for some of the VLBCs, friend Terr. It's more than likely they carried out maintenance for an odd ship or two, as you put it. As to whether any of them were raiders—"

"That's why I want your SC&C dumps. The information will be correlated with data from other locations. Maybe we'll come up with something, however unlikely. I would also like to see for myself the Tai-Mari facilities."

"Mmm, damn awkward. As a civilian installation, I don't have any authority over them, you know. I cannot simply barge in and ask them to bare themselves for you."

"Sure you can, if you explained to them that the Fleet is trying to rid the shipping corridors off those raiding vermin, thereby protecting their operations…and profits. If that one doesn't work, it might be worth pointing out their Field facilities are rented from the Fleet. We are simply looking for some cooperation."

Seen laughed and shook his head. "Not that simple. They're providing service maintenance for *me*! At no cost! I don't want to jeopardize that. However, I can see you're not going to go away without getting what you want. It's a fool's errand, though."

"Probably, and I'll try not to upset anyone, but I have my orders, too."

"Yes, surely."

"Besides, if anything happens, you can always blame it on me."

"Oh, I will! You'll be out of here no matter what, but I've got to live with these people."

Terr got up. "I appreciate your help, sir. You don't have a problem if I take a look around?"

Seen stood and walked around from behind the desk. "This is a pretty barren place, friend Terr, as you've already seen. If you want to nose around, be my guest. I'll call you at your ship when Tai-Mari are ready for you," Seen piped and bobbed his head, fingers twining.

"Thank you, sir. I will notify my comms officer to expect your SC&C download."

Seen's smile vanished. "You still want those dumps?"

"I do."

"Mmm, I will need to get clearance—"

"Sir, you have my authentication codes. That's all the clearance you need."

"Pushy little shit, aren't you."

"I regret if I gave you that impression."

"All right, Second Scout. You'll get your damn dumps. Now, if you will excuse me…"

Terr nodded, waited for the door panels to slide open and walked out. *Well, that could have been handled better.* The Palean simply rubbed him the wrong way. Stalking toward the cable-tube, faces turned and hostile eyes scrutinized his every step. Each one of those large, black, expressionless eyes was Palean.

Rit!

He was starting to get paranoid, for pit's sake. Professionalism! He needed to keep things objective. If he were in Seen's position, he would have resented just as much having some young pup poke around his bailiwick. No, that was worm crap. Seen took this personally, and that was the difference. Still, Terr admitted he could also have been a bit more diplomatic.

The tube door hissed open and he walked in without a backward glance. Personal or not, he had a job to do and everyone the hell better get out of his way before he shoved a bolt up their exhaust end.

Outside, the wind still gusted and he pulled his zip-jacket close about him. Praxa had sunk farther, hanging low above the horizon, ponderous and moody. Staring at the giant, he told himself he would need to see the mining operations. It must be something of a setup. A flattened oval bulk carrier lifted off the far side of the Field, its nav shield barely flickering. It paused for a moment, then lumbered heavily into the sky. Terr followed it until it shrank into a black dot and disappeared.

He mounted the sled-pad and activated the repeller field. As the sled turned, he looked at Seen's two M-3s sitting silently side by side. There could be any number of reasons, some of them even valid, why those ships were sitting there, except they looked odd and out of place instead of being out in space, in their element. He reminded himself to ask Seen about that.

As the sled approached *Psandra's* curved underbelly, Terr saw the landing ramp was down. Four sleds lay in a neat row beside it. Obviously, Dhar had not wasted any time getting things organized. He parked his sled next to the others, killed the repeller field, and squirmed as the wind played around him. Muttering, he stepped off and hurried up the ramp. In the docking bay, he relaxed as a blanket of warm air enveloped him. He strode to the cable-tube and punched the request pad.

"Level two," he growled as he stepped in, "and get me the command deck."

The hatch snicked shut and the tube surged up.

"Dharaklin here, sir."

"You and Mati meet me in the briefing lounge."

"On our way."

Terr got out of the tube and strode quickly toward the briefing room. Inside, he brought up the Field schematic in the Wall, and Dhar and Mati appeared. With a last glance at the Wall, Terr stepped to the table, planted both hands down, and leaned forward.

"Gentlemen, this one is going to be a pain. First Scout Ril Seen has a little empire here, likes it that way, and doesn't relish intruders messing things up. That means us. If you're asking me whether we're chasing our tails, probably. Maybe I'm naturally suspicious and I'm seeing ghosts, but I'll want hard facts before I sleep easy. Forget finding the big things, there won't be any. Okay, Mr. Mati?"

"A true spy should never ignore evidence, sir, big or small," he said earnestly and Terr grinned.

"Right. Just don't trip over the small while your head is stuck in the clouds looking for the big."

"It would never occur to me, sir."

Terr straightened and clasped his hands behind his back.

"Something we should all keep in mind. While we're talking about the small, here is an item for you. On our way down when we contacted Seen, I had the strangest impression he knew me. There was a barest flicker of recognition. I'm probably imagining things, but if I'm right, there is only one way

Seen could know."

"Tanard told him," Mati murmured.

"That's right." Terr nodded and stepped away from the table. "Tanard told him. Whatever I saw or didn't see isn't evidence. I want evidence. Seen has given us permission to nose around and I intend taking him up on that. Dhar, set up parties of two and let them loose. Mr. Mati, we are getting his SC&C dumps. Once they're in, send them to Ambassador Rayon."

"Yes, sir, but—"

"I know. Director Anabb Karr should already have them. As I said, I'm the suspicious type. TACOPSCOM gets a pre-digested version of mush. The raw dumps could reveal differences between the two. One other thing. Seen is organizing clearance for us to pay a social call on the Tai-Mari Line. When he calls, I want to be ready to move. Dhar, you'll be with me. Mr. Mati, you and Hadrian shake down their support facilities, especially that big hangar of theirs."

"Is there anything specific we're looking for?"

"Anything and everything. If you happen to come across a spare Koyami or Terrasec projector, that would be good." Dhar and Mati both chuckled. "Otherwise, exercise those famed spy skills of yours."

Mati grinned broadly, his eyes already bright with anticipation of unmasking the raider base. It wouldn't do his career any harm either.

"Do we use sensor packs, sir?" he inquired.

Although possible, it's unlikely they would find any incriminating evidence left lying around.

"Good point. Take the place apart if you have to."

Dhar shifted in his seat and cleared his throat. "Sir, should this indeed turn out to be the raider base, we could be in some personal danger. Poking around a sensitive spot often leads to unpleasant consequences."

"Yeah, I've been there," Terr said dryly and Dhar

grinned. Terr's poking around Elexi and the mining world Anulus that landed him on Anar'on. "Our four-hour pings to Rayon on schedule, Mr. Mati?"

"The next one is due within the hour, sir."

"Lemos SC&C can pick them up?"

"Loud and clear with the cipher block removed."

"Good. Seen won't try anything. I hope. There is a lot at stake here and we're playing with large chips. Things could get awkward, but I consider the risk minimal. Seen knows we're covered."

"I will remember that when the phase rifles start to sizzle," Mati muttered.

"Mister—" Dhar wanted to squash this impertinence, but Terr raised his hand.

"Mr. Mati has a point. We cannot go around armed. That would kill our investigation there and then, not to mention the stink it would raise with TACOPSCOM, COMPALOPS, Ambassador Rayon, Director Anabb Karr, and Captal. Compared to that, dying would be easy. We'll use the soft approach first. If Seen tries any mind games, I'll get an M-6 to sit on him." Terr pushed back a formchair and sprawled across it. "Right, what have you two got for me?"

"The sensor sweep has come up empty," Dhar said.

"Well, it was a long shot anyway," Terr mused.

"Maybe not that long. We have a possible anomaly on the Tai-Mari support hangar. The computer says no, but Mr. Mati here insists we have decay residuals from a Terrasec projector."

"Mmm, not conclusive in itself. Some Palean tubs carry defensive weaponry. That's not unusual, given their problem with raiders." Terr said, appraising his young comms officer.

The boy was smart, aggressive, and not afraid to speak out. It looked like Terr's irreverent and relaxed attitude to discipline may be rubbing off on Mati, and he wasn't sure he liked that. He could not deny that action with Tanard had given the boy a level of confidence previously missing, and Terr definitely liked that.

"The sweep shows a pattern of layered decay, sir," Mati said. "And it's from the same signature source. Meaning, the same ship has spent a lot of time in the hangar, and recently."

"How do you read that when the computer is telling you have nothing?"

"I checked out the raw data from the sweep, sir," Mati said simply. Terr looked at Dhar.

"What do you think?"

"It's possible he is right. The computer did detect the residuals, but its discrimination logic might not have picked up on the significance."

"Those residuals could have come from a Koyami projector, you know," Terr pointed out. "Did you two consider that? Tai-Mari provides maintenance for Seen's M-3s."

"The signature patterns are different, sir, but it's possible," Mati conceded glumly.

"When we go visiting, have the hangar checked out. Anything else?"

Dhar shook his head. "There is nothing to indicate Lemos is anything other than a VLBC mining and transit facility."

Terr stood up. "You've done well, both of you. No one said this was going to be easy. Right, let's go to work."

* * *

"Quite an operation," Terr said quietly, impressed despite himself.

Hands on hips, he took in the cavernous interior of the brightly lit hangar. Overhead, three giant cranes, chains and grappling hooks dangled limp, hung suspended from two enormous H tracks that ran parallel the length of the hangar. A long oval landing ring stood empty beneath each crane. At various levels along both sides of the twenty-story high walls, blunt-nosed access tubes waited to slide out. At ground level, almost three hundred katalans away, a sharply lit control complex hugged the left wall. An M-6 could have sat here without dwarfing the place. Despite its size, it was eerily quiet. Big as the facility was, Terr could not see how a VLBC would fit here. He turned to the Tai-Mari maintenance manager. The Palean noted Terr's puzzled expression and smiled oily.

"That's the first question they all ask, Second Scout. How do you get one of those monsters into this small space, relatively speaking, of course." He pointed at the ceiling. "Special retractable roof."

Terr glanced at Dhar and grinned.

"Seems quiet at the moment, Mr. Kataki," Dhar observed.

The maintenance manager bobbed his head. "We are getting a Karkan bulk carrier in two days, main drive maintenance. We don't use this setup all the time. A lot of work can be done on a hull while it's docked down loading or unloading. We get a major job once every fifteen to thirty days. Pizgor makes for stiff competition. I worked there and their facilities are first-rate, as much as I hate to admit it."

"Considerable investment to be lying around not used," Terr reflected, looking at Hai Kataki from the corner of his eye.

"Not as much as you'd think, Second Scout."

"Oh?"

"COMPALOPS funded most of the infrastructure and the Fleet supplies about a dozen engineers. Besides, we're renting this from them, so it's not costing us in overheads. Tai-Mari provides support to First Scout Ril Seen's ships and any Fleet unit that needs some work done."

Terr nodded to the Palean. "Yes, he told me."

"It is still a relatively new business line, you understand, which we're hoping will one day show a substantial profit,"

Kataki explained smoothly, his fingers fluttering.

"I appreciate you letting us poke around, sir—"

"Don't mention it, Second Scout. Raiders are a menace to free trade everywhere and you have your orders. I hope you don't find anything *here* that will make you think we're a raider support base, heh heh."

"So do I, sir," Terr said with a small smile.

Kataki bobbed his head and waved his hand into the hangar. "Feel free to look around. Now, if you will excuse me…" He gave a small nod and walked briskly to a sled-pad. The repeller field sprang up and the sled sped silently over the expense of the apron.

Terr exhaled noisily. "Well!"

"Sankri, did you notice what he said? He referred to Fleet *units*. It is a military reference."

Terr continued to stare into the hangar. Rented or not, it was one hell of an investment.

"Yeah. Civilians tend to call them hulls, or worse." He turned to Dhar and prodded him in the chest. "Kataki's been hanging around Seen too long and this is in part a military facility."

"Years of ingrained habit don't die easily, my brother," Dhar rumbled, unconvinced.

A black speck rushed toward them from the far side of the hangar and grew. The sled-pad stopped and squatted slightly. Mati and Hadrian alighted.

"Anything?" Terr demanded.

"Inconclusive, sir. We've confirmed decay residuals from a Terrasec projector. Mr. Hadrian figures it's a sixty TeV job."

"And?"

"Sir, the place is clean, and I mean clean!" Hadrian hissed. "I've been an engineer all my life and I have never seen such a swept facility. Usually, workshops will have odd stuff lying around: spares, tools, metal shavings, solvents, cleaning rags, whatever. This place looks like it's just been unpacked."

"Maybe they're simply neat," Terr offered. "Or maybe we're trying to find something that isn't there." He looked at Dhar. "What do you think?"

"Let's wait to hear from the other parties."

Terr grinned broadly. "A very sensible suggestion. Gentlemen—"

Mati lifted his hand and pointed. "Sir, one of the M-3s is taking off."

Terr turned in time to see the M-3 slowly rise, its nav and main shield barely flickering. It paused, then surged up. He reached into his zip-jacket pocket and hauled out a little flat pebble communicator.

"Command deck?"

"Osinara, sir."

"Track the M-3," Terr ordered, his eyes fixed on the point where the ship vanished.

"Track the M-3, aye, sir."

Terr tapped the communicator against the palm of his hand. Praxa hung above them, blanketing the sky.

"We're missing something here," he said and gazed absently at the orange and yellow whorls that tumbled along the gas giant's equator. He looked at Dhar and raised an eyebrow. Dhar turned his head and stared hard at Praxa.

"It's possible."

Terr pointed at the gas giant. "That's where I'd hole up if I were him. It's perfect. All his needs are just over the horizon; medical, support, logistics, the lot."

"It would be a long haul from Banard for *Zaradej*, sir," Dhar pointed out reasonably. "Sixteen lights and exposed to detection."

"Still worth the risk and a far better tactical choice than slinking inside Et-Aran. Check SC&C if one of Tai-Mari's haulers was on Lemos in the last eight days. Mr. Hadrian, how old would you say those decay residuals were?"

"Six days, perhaps?"

Dhar shrugged. "The auxiliary could have dropped him off at Praxa, landed here, made repairs, picked up supplies and..." he trailed off.

"Exactly!" Terr said. "Where would he go?"

Mati pointed at Praxa. "There, with Tanard."

Terr grinned and patted him on the shoulder.

"All this conjecture would make sense only if Lemos *was* the support base," Dhar said guardedly.

"You know how to spoil things, don't you," Terr told him and everyone smiled. Then, his communicator gave a ping.

"Osinara, sir. The M-3 has dropped below my visual horizon, but one of our S/14s picked him up. His heading was taking him toward Et-Aran when he transited."

"Very good, Mr. Osinara."

"Et-Aran?" Dhar inquired mildly with a raised eyebrow.

"Seen could be out on a simple patrol," Terr said. "Mr. Osinara, relay a message to Ambassador Rayon requesting a frag order to detach two M-4s to check out Praxa. Emphasize that the units must not be under Palean or Sargon command."

"Will do, sir."

Terr slapped his hands together. "Right! Briefing room, nineteen hundred. Until then, we keep digging."

* * *

Lemos fell away into the black void of Praxa's shadow. Terr leaned back into his couch and watched the approaching terminator. With the command deck darkened, the gas giant's colors blazed across its roiling upper atmosphere. Stars filled the blackness as the giant slid beneath them. The deck quiet, everyone lost in thought. An occasional flicker from the consoles played with the shadows. There was no sense of movement as *Psandra* rushed toward its transition point. Terr felt the underlying hum of the ship around him and was comforted, sheltered from the unknown perils that lay waiting outside its secure confines.

He did not find what he came for. Despite that, he didn't feel disappointed. Even now two M-4s were scouring Praxa for any sign of Tanard and his auxiliary. He even took a crack at the place himself, but it was hopeless. The gas giant simply too enormous to search, offering too many ways to avoid detection for anyone not wishing to be found. Hundreds of low orbit probes raked the atmosphere envelope and upper boundary layers without getting so much as a stray energy spike, discounting the atmosphere extraction factories. It was depressing. If Tanard parked himself somewhere in that impenetrable soup, the brute approach wasn't going to find him, and Lemos turned out to be virgin clean. The Tai-Mari Line left him with an odd question or two, but no amount of probing on his part managed to pry open their cover—if there was one. Maybe Rayon's discrete behind the scenes digging would unearth something. Seen's SC&C dump provided a lot of routine traffic data, boring as it looked. Terr didn't expect Anabb's analysts would find anything, but they were just starting.

Seen and Kataki were full of oily smiles and fulsome praise for his diligent execution of orders when he told them he was leaving. Terr acknowledged that he could not win them all. Whoever set up the raider base would have made sure it was capable of resisting scrutiny at a far more intense level than his amateurish part-time efforts could bring to bear. Yet, as he told Mati, little things still worried him about the place. He kept seeing that flash of recognition in Seen's face. A case of overworked imagination? Then again…

Was he so fixated on pinning Lemos as the raider base because he lost his objectivity? Then everyone else had been swept along with him, and he could not accept that. Without evidence or a single item of proof, he only had his imagination, and it told him Lemos was as phony as a three-Serrll note. Whatever else Rayon may have thought of his report, at

221

least he hadn't laughed at his flights of unsupported conjecture. Others could now pick and sift through the details.

The stars suddenly blazed and seemed to rush at him as the M-3 transited. He listened absently to computer reports and an occasional verbal order before silence returned. Dhar swiveled his formchair.

"Ship has transited, sir. Flight time to Porpureen at half boost is thirty-one-point-seven hours."

One-and-a-half days. Terr nodded and folded his arms across his chest. On the edge of Karkan space, Porpureen was isolated and a long way from anywhere. A major transit shipping corridor went through it from Pizgor, which wouldn't normally justify an active Fleet base. Still, the Karkans were a strange breed and did things in their own particular style. Could the Paleans have staged their operation from a Karkan base? It would have been a brilliant stroke of audacious cheekiness. According to Rayon, Porpureen's complement over sixty percent Palean. Unless the Karkans were active collaborators, Terr couldn't see how the Paleans would run a covert operation under their very noses. When it came to sneakiness the Paleans had it down to an art form.

The idea tickled him, but such a base would be too complicated to implement and maintain, with a correspondingly high risk of exposure. Keep it simple and direct, and why he liked the Lemos setup.

The stars were hard and bright and cold. He settled back more comfortably.

* * *

"At half boost, we can reach IP in thirty-nine minutes," Taplan said with some reservation, pointing at a white A dwarf in the main display plate that made up the second star of the Zeller binary thirty light hours away. He disliked the idea of prowling this close to a major shipping corridor, and uneasy having the Porpureen Fleet base practically next door. So near to both asked for trouble.

Re Nette pursed her mouth and tossed back her hair.

"If we can trust the Lemos data, that Sargon container will be in the corridor in four hours. Plenty of time for us to get set up. Once we're in position, we'll wait—"

"To be picked off by a prowling M-3," Taplan added acidly. "I don't like it. They've got the shipping lanes bottled."

"That's where the targets are," Re Nette said reasonably, "and we already passed up one opportunity on your say-so."

Taplan grunted and nodded. "I know, but I have the strangest feeling. We need to hunt and everyone is getting restless, but this is a risk we don't have to take! Not now. Not with the Fleet on the prowl."

"We either hit the container or pull out," she said, allowing a trace of exasperation to creep into her voice. "I'm not going to simply sit here."

She understood Taplan's caution. Sitting snug and tight in a cloud of icy rubble that surrounded the two dwarfs, she could afford to sit around and bide her time. Everyone knew she liked to play it safe, and appreciated the reasons for it. So far, she managed to keep herself and the ship alive. She did it by not taking unnecessary chances. Trawling along a major shipping lane was a deadly lottery of diminishing returns. The smart thing to do would be to lay low for a while and wait for Fleet patrols to get tired of their game. Beyond the short-sighted attention on the bottom line, would her two partners understand the need for vigilance? They were not here, and the crew wanted to hunt.

Taplan looked around the deck. No one cared to face him, but he could see their silent accusations. Just because he was wary, didn't mean he had gone soft. It was his job to give Re Nette the bad news. Profits would mean squat if they were dead. Well, to the pits with them.

"If this blows up in our faces—"

"I shall be suitably apologetic," Re Nette said.

Taplan snorted amid nasty chuckles. "I'll remember that when we're on Cantor. Besides, are you sure you want to hit a Sargon merchie? Our agreement—"

"Covered shipping intelligence, for which Lemos is taking a hefty cut off the top, remember that. As far as I'm concerned, it's a target. Okay, we move."

Whoops of exultation and hearty back slaps forced a smile from her. Re Nette shook her head. They were so like children sometimes.

"Once we're in position, how long to intercept?"

Despite his misgivings, Taplan became a cold professional again. With the decision made to run, all debate ended.

"Nineteen minutes at full boost. Less if the container skirts Zeller II."

"Very well. Tay-nee? Get us rolling."

As the ship began to move, her pulse quickened and her senses tingled. She was running again, alive and free.

* * *

In the silence and quiet of the night watch, Dhar allowed his thoughts to drift. Ever since their meeting with Ambassador Rayon, he felt troubled again by the conflict his brother appeared to endure with his Discipline heritage, and the evident pain it caused him. The revelation somewhat startling, as Sankri did not openly speak to him about it. What he could have done to help, he did not know. After the trek to Katai Than all those weeks ago, he had seen Terr's spirits lift. Their mission against Tanard changed all that. He thought Sankri had come to terms with what he had become. Clearly not the case. Could he have helped his brother more? For a Wanderer the seemingly natural progression from training in the Discipline to the first trial with the god of Death came naturally and an expected thing. Every male child knew almost instinctively the path his life would take. Of course, for Sankri hardly instinctive, thrust into Death's embrace.

"Anomaly track identified as a type two transport hull," the computer announced, shattering the drowsy familiarity of the watch. "Range, one-point-eight light-years. Speed, half commercial boost. Closest approach, point-four light-years with present flight parameters. Time to intercept, three hours."

"Tactical," Dhar commanded briskly. "Project on nav bubble."

Immediately the dome became opaque on which a pulsing red dot painted the contact. An unusual location for a vessel on the edge of a debris ring in a cloud of rubble that surrounded the Zeller binary. Next to the second dwarf ran a broad bluish band indicating the Porpureen/Pizgor commercial corridor.

"Project track."

A faint orange line extended behind the contact into the ring as another traced its way past Zeller II.

"Could be a lone hauler wanting to get into the corridor," Mati offered.

Dhar's deep orange eyes probed him, the vertical red slits closed to fine lines. Uncomfortable under the first officer's stare, Mati knew the look only indicated Dhar was deep in thought.

"Perhaps," Dhar said at length. *What was it doing coming through the debris cloud?*

The command deck basked in pale amber light, he liked to see what was going on around him. He found Sankri's penchant for a darkened deck unsettling. He noted that Mati and the two watchstanders were relaxed, absorbing the situation, ready to spring into action if required.

"Warning, contact ident profile matches a known raider," the computer said.

Dhar raised an eyebrow. They carried only one raider ident.

"Display ident," he ordered. His eyebrows climbed still higher when the data sprang up.

Mati slapped his thigh in delight. "Got him! It's *Drakin*!"

"Mr. Mati, bring us to initial alert, but hold primary and secondary shield grids." Dhar tapped a pad on the armrest.

In his cabin, Terr settled himself more comfortably, the blanket tucked in just right behind his back, and sighed with contentment. In the darkness of his sleeping quarters, the ship softly hummed to itself. He closed his eyes and emptied his mind.

The comms alert beeped. His eyes snapped open and he muttered a curse. He stuck out an arm and groped for the comms pad.

"What is it?" he demanded, not bothering to sit up. Just a few moments longer of uninterrupted peace. He needed a nice, boring run to Porpureen to cleanse himself, heartily sick of Lemos and raiders. He wanted sleep!

"Sir, we have the Askaran raider," Dhar said apologetically. Terr grunted and threw back the covers. He really had no choice.

"I'll be right up."

On the command deck the cable-hatch opened and Kieran strode through. With a glance at the nav bubble plot, he took up his weapons station. Two more watchstanders came in after him. A minute later Terr appeared, paused in the hatchway, and swept his eyes around the deck, instantly taking in the tactical situation. Dhar climbed out off the command couch and waited.

"Any sign we're detected?"

"No, sir. Their sensor suite is either not as good as ours—"

"Or he's keeping a low profile, imitating a small hauler."

"That would give them a one light-year acquisition envelope."

"Computer, indicate intercept time at two-thirds boost," Terr ordered.

"One hour sixty-four minutes."

"Shipping activity?"

"None within detection range," Dhar said.

"Right. Mr. Mati, let's go after him. Two-thirds boost."

"Two-thirds boost, sir," Mati answered with a broad grin.

Terr settled himself into the couch and tapped a pad on the armrest.

"Mess," a bored voice came through.

"Bring up some hot drinks and nibbles. Enough for the whole watch," Terr said amid appreciative nods.

Even though in the middle of the night watch, he felt ravenous. Ignoring regulations, he didn't see any reason why everyone else could not have a bite as well. Besides, if they were going into action, it might be a while between meals. He placed the back of his hand against his mouth to stifle a yawn. Time to shake the cobwebs out of his mind.

"What do you intend, Sankri?" Dhar asked, looking up.

"He might be moving into Zeller II's shadow, positioning himself for a strike. That's what I would do."

"Once he is tucked in there, all that gravitational distortion and radiation flux will make him difficult to detect."

"It will also make it difficult for him to detect us. If he keeps going into the corridor, playing a legit hauler, we have him cold."

"But you don't expect him to do that?"

Terr grinned, a predator anticipating the thrill of the hunt. Dhar considered this side of his brother's personality. Did this thirst for the hunt give Sankri his edge? What disturbed him more was the certainty that cloaked within the shadow of Death, his brother had merely become a more efficient executioner. What of himself, then? He didn't have a ready answer for that.

"We'll know when he reaches Zeller II," Terr said with relish.

"Once he *does* detect us, he could turn back into the debris cloud. The rubble rings will make them a nightmare to search. He could crawl into some asteroid fissure, shut down and wait it out. It will not be easy to dig him out."

"Easy or not, we'll get him, in one piece if possible. Then we'll have a nice chat with its crew. They may have things to say, eh?"

* * *

"Oh crap!" Taplan swore and gave a low growl. "We have a contact at our one light-year perimeter. Profile matches the Sargon container."

"He's early," Re Nette muttered softly.

Early or not the deck crew were smiling, also anticipating a kill.

Drakin had sat parked in a slow orbit for fifteen minutes a bare three million talans above the white dwarf. Holding a fixed position above a star never advisable, as the star's close proximity made hash of sensors. It might be unadvisable, but she had no choice if she wanted to avoid detection by the container.

"Closest approach?" Re Nette husked.

"About half a light if he maintains present course. That's twenty-six minutes at full boost and combined closure rate. Recommend we commence our run in twenty-four minutes."

She sat back and allowed her slender fingers to drum on the armrest. They shaved it too close. Taplan looked at her, face pale.

"Another contact! His signature makes him an M-3, doing two-thirds boost. He'll be on us in eighty minutes. Sooner

228

if he goes max."

"Pits! Has he got us?"

"Probably. If we can detect him, he has certainly acquired us, and his sensor suite is better than ours."

"What a delicious little dilemma," Re Nette murmured and snorted in frustration, all thoughts of attacking the Sargon container now an irrelevancy. The M-3 must have tracked her all the way to Zeller II, almost certainly thinking she was a merchant trying to get into the corridor. She damned herself when she assumed a holding position above the star. No legitimate merchant would take such a posture.

The emergency comms band channel suddenly burst into life.

"Sargon registered container, this is a Scout Fleet M-3 sweeper *Psandra*. Alter port sixty degrees. Immediate execute. There is a known raider in orbit around Zeller II."

The message repeated and silence returned to the deck.

"Well, that's torn it," Tay-nee swore and rubbed his chin.

"The M-3 has gone max," Taplan said with finality. "We have fifty-eight minutes to lose ourselves."

"Tay-nee, break holding position and go around Zeller II. When we are occulted, we'll be undetectable, then make for the nearest rubble ring. Max boost."

Taplan shook his head. "No, Re Nette! That'll leave a signature trail in our wake. It'll dissipate some before he gets here, but not enough. It could lead him right to us. I would recommend not more than three-quarter boost."

"He'll know where we are anyway!"

"But we don't want to lead him directly to our hiding place, do we?"

She bit her lip, torn between a desire to flee and Taplan's sound advice. "Very well. Do it!"

* * *

"The Sargon container has altered course, sir," Dhar said quietly.

Terr nodded, only half watching the main display plot. The raider had disappeared. It wasn't hard to figure out what it had done.

Dhar looked at him. "He is in Zeller II's LOS zone. The closer we get the larger the avoidance cone will become."

"Yeah."

By the time they reached the dwarf, the raider would be safely tucked away somewhere. Dhar didn't need to tell him that. All right, then, he would turn over every rock out there if necessary. This one would not get away. Not now.

The food and drinks were cleared away and the ship brought to full alert, shields up. The white dwarf slowly grew visibly larger. At ten light-minutes, *Psandra* dropped normal, closed on its secondary drive, and went into a tight orbit. On the far side, six S/14 monitor probes peeled away from the ship, scooting into extreme low positions above the star. Although Terr didn't believe *Drakin* would be so foolish to pull such a trick, it could have gone low, hoping to lose itself against the star's interference. In a cold gas giant, yes, but it took a lot of energy to maintain shields and a fixed position against a star's gravity well and radiation flux. The S/14s were very good at tracking such energies.

After twenty-five minutes, Dhar shook his head. "All search modes negative, sir."

"Very well. We had to check. Retrieve the S/14s. Anything in the search cone?"

"Faint traces of residuals that match the raider emission signature, sir. They're hopelessly dispersed long before they hit the first rubble ring."

"He's in there somewhere. Distance to the ring?"

Dhar briefly spoke to the computer. "Eleven light-days. That's two minutes at maximum boost and there is nothing along the way large enough to disrupt the distortion field. I

230

have three masses within the projected search cone that are probables where he could hide. The next ring is thirty-nine light-days. That is seven point-two minutes from here. It gets pretty thin then until the next major ring, a fair way off—forty minutes at half boost."

"He could have reached it, though," Terr mused. "What do you think?"

"He could have, but I don't think so. That would give him only eighteen minutes to locate a suitable asteroid, check it out, and take cover, mindful that our sensors would penetrate everything non-metallic. He'd be cutting it too fine, Sankri. I would consider the possibility if the loss of signal cone was along his original insertion track to Zeller II. He could then have scooted to his initial hideaway, which is not the case here."

"Mmm. What's in the second ring?"

"Eight or nine possibles. Hard to tell from here." Dhar paused and Terr smiled at him. If he couldn't discern enough detail of the asteroid masses with his equipment, the raider with his poorer sensor suite would have had even more difficulty. Dhar climbed out of his couch and stood next to Terr.

Kieran looked up from his weapons console and turned his button blue eyes on Mati, pale gray folds of skin quivered as they hung down his face. His large flap ears pricked in anticipation. The first officer and the commander were discussing tactics again, totally absorbed. Terr had that faraway look, like he already considered all possibilities and the first officer only confirmed his thoughts. Almost like watching a rehearsal before a game.

Mati blinked at him and inclined his head slightly in a shrug.

"Running at three-quarter boost, if he stopped at the first ring and searched all three asteroids," Dhar said, "say nine minutes per search, including the hops between them, he would use up thirty-one minutes. It is a further nine minutes or so to the second ring. That's forty minutes. He couldn't check out more than two asteroids before he needed to hide, or we would have picked him up as we rounded Zeller II."

"And if he boosted directly for the second ring?"

"Thirteen minutes to reach it…he could have sorted through five or six possible contacts at most. More likely, three or four before he snuggled down without having to be rushed."

"I think that's where he is," Terr said comfortably and pointed at the second ring displayed in the tactical plot. "We still have to do this the hard way, though. Mr. Mati, as soon as the S/14s are secured, shift to our transition point and move us out to target one at max boost."

"Aye, sir."

Terr turned and grinned at Kieran. "Got that projector warmed up, Mister?"

"Synchronized and ready to toast him, sir."

"Good man."

Looking fondly at Mati and Kieran, Terr liked what he saw. They had grown more confident in themselves and their abilities, and were less formal with the crew. All good. An officer should not rely on his rank to command.

In the nav bubble the stars shifted and *Psandra* surged. It took a few minutes to clear the local effect of the dwarf's massive gravitational field, enabling the ship to transit. The stars rushed at them and they were in subspace. Plowing through an ice and rock garden had its dangers, but nav scans didn't show objects along their track for any concern. That, of course, would change once they entered heavier concentrations near the first debris ring.

Short of two minutes to the ring, Mati slowed the ship to one-third boost. A few seconds later, he dropped normal and immediately went to full secondary boost toward the first asteroid.

"Closing with target one in sixty-four seconds," Dhar

said quietly. "Sensor search initiated."

Mati enjoyed running maneuvering. Terr gave orders and didn't elaborate much, expecting him to sort out the details. Difficult at first, but the first officer helped and he had grown into the role. One of his first commanders was an antithesis in his penchant for the minutiae. He needed to control everything; no detail too small for his attention. It drove Mati and others to distraction. Of course, freedom to act also meant more room to stuff things up, but the first officer helped there, too.

Nothing out there to see in the nav bubble except the black of space and cold white stars. Little orange dots cluttered the tactical plot and vanished immediately as small grains of dust impacted the secondary shield grid. Larger pieces were swept aside by the nav grid's deflector near-field effect. The ship studiously shifted in respect to the more troublesome objects.

From one talan the cratered rocky asteroid appeared as a black and white crescent. Eleven talans of elongated, almost cylindrical conglomerate of rubbish. The surface pitted with countless impact craters, the larger peppered with smaller ones inside them. The topography looked much too smooth to contain fissures or valleys into which a ship could slip into.

"No anomalous energy or mass readings, sir," Dhar announced after two orbits and Terr scratched the scar on his temple.

"Very well," he said and nodded to Mati. *Psandra* shifted position and accelerated.

The second asteroid a simple flyby. Twenty-six talans of dirty water and ammonia ices. Although there were plenty of places where an M-4 could hide, the low mass density made the asteroid almost transparent to sensor sweeps. With the last candidate, they spent almost forty minutes scanning up and down the rugged, craggy metallic planetary remnant. Terr even took *Psandra* into two narrow deep fissures that seemed to run right through the body, much to Dhar's consternation. Eventually, they abandoned the search. Although Terr didn't believe the raider to be there, he left two S/14s hanging six hundred katalans above its surface, just in case.

During the brief flight to the second debris ring, Terr leaned back against the command couch and closed his eyes. Not tired or sleepy, the expectation of catching the raider made sure of that. He did not doubt he would catch it, the mission ideally suited for the M-3. Its speed, range, maneuverability and firepower made it deadly for anything less formidable than an M-4. Nevertheless, the quality of the person sitting in the command couch, not technology, often decided the outcome.

He tried to place himself in the raider's position. What would its commander be thinking right now? Concerned? Probably. Panicked? Terr didn't think so. It took coolness to decide to run for it into Zeller II's shadow. With only a limited number of asteroids to pick from and not much time to decide, would he necessarily hide in an asteroid? He must know Terr would search every likely rock. Even shut down cold, the raider emitted residual radiation, especially in the infrared. Any object in a temperature gradient would radiate. It would take a sealed cave to mask it, or...

"Mr. Dharaklin," he said softly, keeping his eyes closed. "Scan for rock clusters."

Dhar looked up from his tactical console and raised an eyebrow. The raider *could* be making out simply another piece of rubble among other rubble.

"Two large clusters beyond our search line," Dhar said heavily a moment later, "but I'm not detecting any residuals or mass density variations that would indicate a hull."

"Composition?"

"Nickel and iron mostly, with some rock aggregate. Mean diameter of the main masses is nine hundred katalans."

Terr opened his eyes and looked at him. "What if he attached himself to one of the pieces?"

Dhar pursed his lips in a deep frown. "I suppose it's possible. The nickel composition would prevent us from detecting him," he said slowly, the effort obviously paining him.

"Ah, sir, that means he could be anywhere, then," Mati ventured, risking a rebuke.

Terr glanced at him and shook his head. "Perhaps, but I don't think so. I still think our best bet is one of the asteroids. Still..."

"Nineteen seconds to IP on the first asteroid, sir," Mati said briskly. Kieran swept his eyes over the weapons console.

A snowball and they moved on.

Two hours later they came up empty. No radiation, no residuals, no emissions, nothing. The raider had vanished, swallowed by the rubble ring. Two of the asteroids were ideal hiding places with plenty of fissures and crags to hide in, but they lacked caverns or other spaces where a ship could effectively take cover. Frustrating.

Time to look at other options.

"Dhar, what's the range to the nearest rock cluster?" Terr asked.

"Three hundred and sixty thousand talans. One minute thirty-four seconds at half secondary boost."

"Very well. Mr. Mati..."

Chapter Eight

"*Psandra* has changed course," Taplan said with a catch in his breath. "He'll be here in one-and-a-half minutes." It had only been a matter of time after all.

Re Nette frowned. It took the warship almost three hours to determine she did not hide in one of the obvious places. The fact gave her scant comfort. For the first time in her life, she faced the prospect of death, the realization a little unsettling. She swept her eyes around the deck and saw resignation in their faces. How quickly the fates cast their dice.

"What are you going to do?" Taplan demanded.

She looked at him and frowned, tired of his defeatist attitude.

"Order you to resume your station!" she snapped. Taplan opened his mouth, shrugged, and sat down. The watch around her silent and expectant, the tension palpable.

"We're in a box," she told them quietly, lingering briefly on each face, "but we've been through worse. I will not tell you not to be worried. We could lose our ship and our lives here. I'll try to see that we walk away from this one, one way or another." Her fingers drummed on the armrest. "Tay-nee? The M-3 will either close and extend an access tube to board us or they will send an ABP. If they close, they'll be vulnerable. I'll want maximum yield fire when I give the order."

"No problem there," Tay-nee whispered hoarsely. "But our Terrasec 14/E won't make much of an impression against his shield grid—"

"Or the seventy-two TeV of his Koyami 9A," Taplan snarled.

Re Nette whirled at him. "Unless you have something constructive to contribute here, why don't you just shut your mouth! I'm tired of your crap!"

Taplan flushed and his hands closed into fists. No one talked to him like that. "I *have* something constructive. Pull us back and transit!"

"Can we transit?" Re Nette demanded in surprise and Tay-nee gaped.

"With the mass of the asteroid below us? We would need to clear it by at least six talans or the precursor would never form. We'd also be out of the asteroid's shadow and exposed. Besides, where would we go? With its speed advantage, the M-3 has got us."

"If you listened to me, we wouldn't be in this fix now!" Taplan snarled.

"You're free to take a survival blister any time you want a change of scenery!" she snapped.

The idea so ridiculous, he was startled. Then he roared with laughter. He turned to Tay-nee and slapped him on the back. Tay-nee chuckled, glanced at Re Nette's stern expression, and also laughed. In minutes the whole command deck crew were convulsing, tears streaming down their faces. Re Nette couldn't help herself as a giggle forced its way from her. They were all mad.

A few moments later, still chuckling and wiping eyes, they settled down after release of tension and anxiety. Everyone felt better despite the fact they probably faced death in minutes.

Taplan looked at Re Nette and cleared his throat. "I think I'll hang around, if you don't mind."

"Fine. Tay-nee? When he closes, fire. Keep firing until we see what he'll do. We might get lucky. Be prepared for some lithe maneuvering."

"Passing eighty thousand talans," Taplan said from his tactical plot. "The M-3 is slowing to quarter boost. We have forty-six seconds…twenty-two—"

"Stand by," Re Nette warned. "Raise the ship one hundred katalans and fire."

Nestled in a valley between two razor peaks of twisted nickel-iron, *Drakin* gingerly lifted to bring its projector dome to bear on the slowing M-3. With shields down, it gave no warning of its presence. Force lines arced along the dome housing and a searing yellow beam ripped toward *Psandra*. The M-3's secondary shield rippled, channeling the energy along the force lines in white and blue slithering discharges around the impact zone, but it kept coming. The raider fired again without effect, then settled into its protective hole again.

Psandra stopped.

Tay-nee glanced at Re Nette. He didn't have to say anything. They had to try it.

The comms alert beeped. "The M-3 requests a visual," Taplan said in disgust.

Re Nette's shoulders drooped. End of the line. She could keep dodging *Psandra's* fire for a while, keeping the asteroid between herself and the warship, but the Scout commander would quickly tire of the game and send in his ABPs. With the M-3 denying her the ability to maneuver, the ABPs would attach themselves to her hull, burn their way through and that would be it.

"If we surrender, at least we'll be alive," Tay-nee ventured, voicing their unspoken thoughts.

Taplan leaped out of his seat and whirled at them. "No! As long as we keep this rock between us and *Psandra*, the M-3 cannot touch us."

"Nuts!" Tay-nee snapped. "He can keep us pinned down and send for support."

"If we surrender, then what?" Taplan demanded. "A quick execution if you're lucky, and a slow death in some prison if you're not. I would rather end it right here."

"Well, I'm not," Re Nette said quietly. "That blister is still available if you want it."

Taplan glared at her.

"It's over!" she told him and swept her eyes around the deck. "We can evade for a while, but we'll only be postponing the inevitable. We're in this together and I won't make this decision for you. You tell me what you want to do."

A pulse of bright yellow light lanced from *Psandra* at one of the peaks that sent a stream of molten metal gushing out in a jet where it struck. The near-field effect of the beam made *Drakin* stagger. Re Nette grabbed the armrest and waited for the ship to settle.

"A ranging shot," Taplan observed dryly.

"I guess they want an answer," Re Nette murmured with a forced grin. "Well?" She looked at each one of them in turn.

"I'm not ready to die yet, and tomorrow is always a new day and a new possibility," Tay-nee said reasonably. Others nodded. Taplan snorted in disgust.

"Cowards!"

Tay-nee half rose, but Re Nette restrained him with an outstretched arm. She climbed out of her seat and stood beside Taplan.

"Destroy all logs, nav data, and trash the computer, then open a channel for me."

Taplan glared at her, then complied. She waited for the comms plate to clear. The young Second Scout's gray eyes were hard and bored into her without emotion. More than anything, his cold look unsettled her.

"*Drakin* Pilot, you are ordered to surrender your ship. If you resist, I will destroy you in place."

"My terms—"

Another beam struck the metal outcrop and sheared through the peak. Several hundred mikans of metal and rock tumbled away in a lazy dance of the asteroid's weak gravity. She knew her hull was now exposed to direct fire. She could pull back...

The *Psandra's* commander didn't say anything as he

waited, his eyes stone.

"Scout warship, I surrender my ship," she said softly with a ring of finality. Taplan pounded the console in outrage and frustrated helplessness.

"Power down immediately and prepare to be boarded. If I detect any change in your energy levels, I will open fire and I'll not stop until there is nothing left of your ship."

Re Nette bridled. "I surrendered! We have rights under law—"

"I am the law here," the *Psandra's* commander said with such chill and indifference that her skin crawled. "Take to your survival blisters, but do not jettison. Anyone found outside a pod will be shot!"

She bit her lip. "Very well, Second Scout. Powering down now."

* * *

Terr heard the hatch hiss open behind him. He did not turn, watching *Drakin's* dead hull and the ABP glued to one of its access hatches. An ugly, boxy vessel, with large doors along its sides designed for rapid cargo loading, the raider hid the menace that lay within. It might be functional, but he wouldn't be caught dead commanding such a tub. Ugly or not, he could not afford to forget that death lurked within that hull.

Drakin's crew were secure in Hangar Two. With Razzo's men looking for any excuse to pound them, he figured he wouldn't be hearing any complaints from the raiders. He should have shot them! As it is, thirty-eight additional bodies would be an infernal nuisance until he got them to Pizgor. Hands clasped behind his back, he turned to face his prisoner. He lifted his eyes and Dhar quietly withdrew. The closing hatch sounded unnaturally loud in the silence of the briefing lounge.

Against the Gods of Shadow

Re Nette stood proud, regal, and defiant. A tall woman for a Palean, she reached to his shoulder. She tossed back her head and black hair swirled and swayed behind her. She possessed a command presence and raw magnetism that could sway men. Any man. There was nothing outwardly barbaric about her. Sophisticated and smart, she knew how to wield power. Her black eyes regarded him without emotion. He reminded himself that beneath the façade of beauty lay a streak of ruthlessness and cruelty of a cold-blooded killer.

She did not have to destroy *Rakish* or murder its helpless crew. The knowledge helped steel him for what he had to do.

"Sit down, please," he said pleasantly and waved at the formchairs.

Re Nette looked at him warily before pulling back one of the seats and gingerly lowered herself into it. Terr swung around a seat and sat down.

"How did you know?" she demanded, her voice musical and pleasant. Some of the certainty and bravado drained from her, as the aura of authority.

"Your fuel cells."

"Fuel cells? I don't understand."

"SC&C takes data dumps every time a ship enters or departs its controlled space. The dump contains fuel cell signatures."

"Damn, but that's clever," she hissed with admiration. "All this time…"

"When you landed on Mitlan, we matched your cells to the Four Suns bulk carrier *Rakish*."

"Why didn't you…ah, I exposed my Askaran operation, haven't I?"

"You're run by an interesting network," Terr said, watching her face.

"No one runs me! I—"

"Your two partners…Never mind. I'm not interested in that, for now."

241

She pouted and lifted her head. "I'm not telling you anything, Second Scout."

"I will ask you just one question."

"You're wasting your time, sonny. As your prisoner—"

"Remember what I said about law?" He gave her a moment to think about it. "As raiders, I could eject you all out the nearest lock and get a commendation for it. Give me one excuse and I'll do it."

Re Nette chewed that one over and didn't like it. This Second Scout may only be a boy, but she kept coming back to his eyes. Something icy lurked in them, waiting to be unleashed. That Wanderer first officer of his…Death lurked in those eyes, both their eyes. The boy looked determined, but as a Serrll Scout Fleet officer, he played by fixed rules. Rules she could exploit.

"A name," Terr repeated slowly. "I want to know who is supporting you."

"Askaran," she said sweetly and smiled.

A cloud passed across Terr's face. "Enough!" He slammed an open hand against the table, the sound like a crack of lightning that made her jump. "Who is supporting you?" he repeated in a fierce whisper. "I can get it from one of your crew and I won't be as polite."

Re Nette felt her face drain and her mouth suddenly became dry.

"A deal," she croaked and cleared her throat. "If I talk, I'm dead. They will find me no matter where you stash me."

"You're already dead, Re Nette, and I gave you a better deal than you deserve—your life."

"Hah! It's not just me, you fool! They will be after you, your friends, loved ones, everyone you know will be killed. Everyone I know! You may think I'm a monster. I don't mind. I don't even mind dying. Well, not much, but I will not destroy lives who had nothing to do with what I am."

So, a shred of honor remained behind the brutal façade

after all, Terr mused. Or perhaps some well-orchestrated psychological intimidation.

"Last chance," he said coldly.

Re Nette clamped her mouth and sat back. Terr nodded. Forgive me, master…

The words came and he found himself in another reality. He felt the hot desert wind stir the cape of his surtaf robe. The white sun sucked the moisture from his skin and the burning sands stirred beneath his sandaled feet. The amber sky had a hard coppery sheen to it. Death settled on his shoulders and he welcomed its embrace.

Small blue lightnings danced between his fingers. Re Nette's eyes grew large and she shrank into her seat. The *Psandra* commander was a Discipline adept! She heard stories, hardly believable, but this display of raw power chilled her. He reached for her and Re Nette gasped. A coil of light reared up from his hand and struck her shoulder. The pain burned as it bored through flesh and bone. She fell back in shocked agony and screamed. Fat tears flooded her eyes. On the deck, gasping, she gingerly prodded her injured shoulder. The material of her gray tunic charred, and tiny wisps of smoke curled above the ragged edges of the burn, colored by welling blood. She sniffed, wiped her eyes and glared at him.

"You bastard! If you think—"

Terr lowered his hand and a blue flash struck the deck beside her head. She screamed again at the crack of thunder and involuntarily raised her arm before her face for protection.

"That could just as easily have been your face. You're a smart woman and a beautiful one…"

Re Nette whimpered. She knew much of her power over others, especially men, came from her looks. Without that, she was nothing. To pits with everyone! What did she owe them anyway? Would any of those slime help her now? The high and mighty Tanard expected her to die and keep her mouth shut to the end. For what? Screw him!

"Kai Tanard," she hissed, hating Terr for making her do this. "He runs the Tai-Mari—"

"On Lemos?" Terr felt a hot flush of excitement.

She stared at him in surprise. "You know him?"

Terr nodded, expression grim. "Let's say we had an encounter. Mr. Dharaklin!"

The hatch immediately slid aside and Dhar stepped in. He paused when he saw Re Nette on the deck.

"Take her away. Have her treated."

Dhar's eyes burned into him. He bent down and almost lifted Re Nette's small frame to steady her. At the hatch, she shook him off and turned.

"Would you have…"

Terr ignored her. After a second, Dhar pulled her out and the hatch hissed shut. Would he have carried out his threat? With the power still coursing through him, aroused, the god of Death demanded blood. It would have taken almost no effort of will to loose the lightnings at the raider scum.

The conversation with Rayon echoed in his mind. What price *his* morality?

He sat down and allowed the power to slowly drain away. Death lingered for a moment, then it was gone, leaving him empty and drained. His eyes slid to the raider hull. After a time, he didn't know how long, he reached with a weary hand and tapped a comms code into the inlaid console in the desk. The Wall grayed, then cleared. His young Pizgor friend peered gravely at him.

"Second Scout Terrllss-rr. I presume you wish to speak to Ambassador Rayon?"

"Correct."

"He is detained—"

"Interrupt whatever he is doing. He will want to talk to me."

The youth stared at him, then nodded. "A moment, sir."

His image faded and the Wall cycled through whorls of yellows, reds, and purple storms. The image could have been of Praxa.

Barging in on Rayon like this was tricky. If the Ambassador got pissed at him, Terr could be in for some serious career adjustment. Did he presume too much on their relationship?

A few minutes later the Wall cleared and Rayon's red face filled the image.

"My apologies, Second Scout. You tore me away from a session with Commissioner Hiraki."

Terr blinked. A Captal ambassador apologizing to a second scout? Who would believe him!

"Sir, I should be the one apologizing."

"Nonsense, my boy! I know you wouldn't have called unless it important. Yes, important."

"I appreciate that, sir."

"So, what have you got for me? What?"

"It's Lemos."

Rayon sat back and nodded, his smile grim. "Go on."

"I happened to run into the Askaran raider and its commander talked."

"Talked?" Rayon remarked with an amused grin.

"I would like to think I did the right thing, sir."

Rayon studied the boy, trying to read beyond the words. Something had clearly happened out there, but he didn't have time for that now.

"I am pleased to hear that. Pleased. Who is implicated?"

"The Tai-Mari Line. Tanard—"

"He was named?"

"Yes, sir. He operated a raider support arm behind a front of being an import/export hauler. First Scout Ril Seen must know, sir. There is no way Tanard could have run an M-3 without Seen's collusion."

"Quite right." Rayon nodded approvingly. "This is a grand haul, my boy. Grand. Hiraki will no doubt be beside himself. I dare say Sargon and the Paleans will soon be in for some very uncomfortable times. Very. Where are you now?"

"Zeller binary, sir, nineteen hours from Porpureen. I'm getting ready to transport the raider hull and the prisoners to Pizgor."

"Negative! Sit tight. I will dispatch the nearest Fleet unit to you and relieve you of both problems. Both. When you make the transfer, I want you on Lemos at your maximum speed."

"Sir?"

Rayon grinned broadly. "I want you to place Ril Seen and his command under close arrest and interdict all civilian operations until we get to the bottom of what's going on there. Yes, bottom. I feel I owe you that much."

Terr gaped in astonishment, then gulped and cleared his throat.

"Thank you, sir."

"You won't be going in alone, my boy. Won't. Those two M-4s are still combing through Praxa. One will accompany you down in case you need a force multiplier. The other will cordon off all approaches and departures from Lemos. All. They will not get into position until you get there."

"I must thank you again, sir—"

"Rubbish! You have done well, Second Scout. Very well."

* * *

"Pizgor Order of Merit with cluster," Anabb muttered darkly. "*And* the Fleet Meritorious Achievement ribbon. It's a damnable nuisance. It'll just swell your head."

Terr stood at rigid parade rest wishing Anabb would stop fulminating and get on with the debrief. He would have thought the old fart would be pleased instead of being vinegarish about it.

Rit!

Against the Gods of Shadow

Sour or not, Terr wasn't about to let Anabb spoil the moment for him. He didn't mind basking in the limelight for a change either. Worth the rush back to Lemos to confront Seen and see the Palean's expression of smug insolence turn to consternation as Terr read out the charges. The assault troops took him away, still stunned by the sudden reversal of events. Mopping up the base and Tai-Mari personnel most satisfying. Nabbing the smooth maintenance manager, Mr. Kataki, an anticlimax. The civilian and ship crews looked amused at the sight of swarming military rushing about, but that turned to outrage when Terr suspended all commercial activity.

The look on Seen's face…that had been a sweet moment, but nothing to what Rayon pulled on him back on Pizgor. When the Lemos story broke, the media went into a frenzy. Some editorials wanted the Palean Union attacked. A special session of the General Assembly on Captal issued a formal censure against Sargon and the Paleans. Politically, it may have been just a slap on the wrist. However, Sargon and Palean commercial interests took a savage hit. Common stocks were ravaged. Captal could not very well allow the major market exchanges to go into free-fall without destabilizing the whole Serrll economy, but speculators raked it in huge while the dust settled.

Mercifully, they kept Terr's part in the fall of Lemos confidential, for which he was especially grateful to Rayon. Such notoriety could be the kiss of death to a career. The Fleet appreciated heroes, but on its terms. The news release merely stated the Fleet had broken a major conspiracy—which was true—and even now, raiders were being swept up. The media grumbled, sensing more behind the simple statement of facts, but that's all they got. Over time the details would leak. By then it wouldn't really matter anymore. Lemos lay uncovered and Pizgor's immediate political concerns were resolved. Anabb still had running covert ops and didn't want too many details in the public domain. The last thing he needed was a mob of investigative reporters sending all his undercover contacts into flight.

Although Terr's part not made public, Rayon saw to it that Captal knew the full story. Commissioner Hiraki and Prime Director Kernami gushed their grateful thanks on behalf of the Pizgor Triumvirate. Treated like a celebrity were heady vapors and he figured it would be very easy to get used to such handling. Dhar cautioned him against misguided pride and Terr told him not to be a sour puss.

Reality hit with a thud when Terr received orders to report to Taltair. The message wasn't delivered by some eager prima scout, hands trembling with excitement at being in Terr's exalted presence. It wasn't even delivered! Simply a file in the ship's computer. Still very much a lowly second scout, the reminder dampened his exuberance.

Anabb looked fondly at Terr. Even though his Wanderer shadow Dharaklin towered over him, Terr's presence dominated. The boy seemed ready to tackle anything. Such arrogance! Anabb had gambled, playing a hunch that sent Terr on a seemingly hopeless mission. That it succeeded so dramatically due to a very large helping of luck, but he could not dismiss the fact Terr was the causal factor. Large gaps still needed to be filled, and a lot of work remained to be done. To him, Lemos was the visible tip of what must be a massive logistical, intelligence, and political operation, happy to leave the political dimension to Sill-Anais while he rooted out raider nests.

As far as he was concerned, the job remained only half done. He cleared his throat and touched the burn on his cheek.

"To shrink your swollen heads, I want you two to know BuePer on Captal has approved selections to the lower half of the officers' list. Mr. Dharaklin, your appointment to Second Scout second grade is confirmed, effective immediately."

"The honor is undeserved, sir," Dhar said quietly. "I only carried out my duty."

"An exemplary execution of that duty, too."

Anabb measured the Wanderer, trying to see beyond the impenetrable orange eyes. Did he see a slight flush of pleasure in that stern face? Impossible to tell, but he would not have been surprised. Eminently satisfied to see Dhar and Terr still together, he did not doubt whatsoever Dhar's calming and steadying influence had more than once restrained Terr's exuberant efforts. They made a formidable pair.

He looked at Terr and glared. "As for you, I am authorized to inform you that you've somehow managed to get yourself on the First Scout, second grade list."

Terr felt a flash of fire race down his spine. It was a long and tortuous step to field rank and he wanted to savor the moment.

"Well? Nothing to say?" Anabb demanded, his eyes kindly.

"I am grateful…"

"So you should be. Now that we've completed the official nonsense, I want to add my personal congratulations to both of you. Sit!" he commanded and waved at the formchairs.

First Scout Terr…he liked the sound of that. He realized he had done Anabb an injustice and felt a momentary twinge of guilt. He thought the crusty old fart would give him and Dhar a reaming, but it seemed Anabb came down hard on everybody.

He settled himself and the seat molded itself around him. The office a touch warm, just right for relaxing. He remembered Anabb's aide. Like a protective angel, Ariane stood guard outside the office. She had delicate high cheekbones, full lips, and a long neck. Her head narrow and oval. She had no hair and was gorgeous. Terr had to restrain himself from gawking at the creature, his hormones sizzling in an emotional frying pan.

"If you're quite comfortable…" Anabb remarked, bringing Terr up with a jerk.

"Sorry, sir."

"Humph! I have an offer for you, both of you, but if you want to sleep…" Anabb waited, but Terr was all attention. Impertinent young scamp. "I want you to join the Diplomatic Branch on detached duty from the Fleet as special operatives. You'll keep your commissions and your time will count toward your seniority. You already have an exaggerated sense of your own importance, and I shouldn't say this, but I am pleased with your performance, son; even though it cost me an M-3." He looked for an indication of an apology, but Terr appeared unmoved. Did he think M-3s grew in a pot?

Anabb cleared his throat to hide his amusement. The boy didn't have a shred of respect for his superiors. In this case, quite rightly so. Ships were meant to be used, and that included getting shot at sometimes.

"Well?"

More of Anabb's skullduggery? Terr had a good idea of the kind of assignments he and Dhar were likely to end up with; all the shitty jobs no one else wanted or was too smart to touch.

"I know what you're thinking. You're not intelligence officers and I've got plenty of skilled agents to be looking for a couple of amateurs. I need you for work that requires a more, ah, unorthodox and creative approach."

Terr winced. He knew all about creative approaches. "With respect, sir, such an approach usually lands one in a crack."

Dhar shifted uneasily. Newly minted First Scout or not, you did not talk to a prima scout like that—*and* director of the Serrll's intelligence service!

"If it were easy, I wouldn't need you!" Anabb snapped. "As Diplomatic Branch operatives, you'll have authority far beyond the strict interpretation of your Fleet ranks. As for landing in a crack, it's a risk, but you'll be supported by the weight of my whole Branch. You'll probably end up hating me if you accept, and you'll have plenty of strife and pain along the way. However, I promise you won't be bored."

Terr agreed with him there if his last experience was any guide.

Still, he faced a major life-turning decision and he needed a moment to clear his head. Things were moving too damn fast. He suspected Anabb knew this and wanted to waylay him while he was still on a high and feeling full of himself. A dirty lowdown trick and he admired Anabb's barefaced gall and cunning. Despite Anabb's glowing words of support, the offer nothing more than a chance to have his ass creamed in some dark alley and dumped in a gutter to be swept away with the rest of the garbage. He tangled with Anabb's warped sense of fun on Elexi, and still chuckled over that one, not sure he wanted another such thigh-slapper. The alternative being what? Patrols, raiders, fighting maintenance and logistics jerks? Even as a First Scout, he could look forward to at least another five to eight years driving an M-3. No one was about to gush over with sudden generosity and hand him a brand-new M-4, Lemos notwithstanding. Did he really want to push an M-3 for eight more years? The thought appalled him. He had driven one for five years already, but wasn't that what he signed up for? Perhaps. The rub, he *liked* independent action, and there were only so many tolerant commanders who would be willing to indulge him. Did he want to give up his crew and command?

What *did* he want? When boiled down, he had his answer. He wanted to make a difference. Would joining Anabb's screwball outfit enable him to do that? Didn't he make a difference with Lemos, though? He realized then, it was a qualitative difference that would never have come his way had he not been under Anabb's orders. Would Anabb be any more tolerant of his penchant for independent action than some

Fleet fossil? On reflection, he admitted Anabb had already demonstrated he would. Wasn't Lemos all about independence and freedom to take initiative in a situation?

At that moment, he felt an almost affectionate fondness for the crusty old prima scout. The chiseled narrow face may be stamped into a permanent scowl of disapproval, but he did not mistake the kindly twinkle in the close-set brown eyes. Anabb undoubtedly had his motives, but as an opportunity, the duty was certainly a career mover—if he survived. Terr suspected if he took on this job, Anabb's prediction about hating him would probably turn out to be true.

"I can see the questions on your face, son," Anabb said with surprising gentleness. "This is a big step and you may be feeling bruised after Lemos. You need a rest. Well, my boy," he roared, "you've *had* your rest! Twenty days it took to get from Pizgor to Taltair. Now, I have a job and it's yours if you want it."

Terr glared. Crafty old devil!

He was being bulldozed, but he wasn't about to simply cave in. He glanced at Dhar. Something passed silently between them and he felt warmed. Dhar understood. He didn't want to impose a decision on his brother that may compromise his ambitions in the Fleet. As a Second Scout, he could look forward to a command of his own soon, and an M-2 a nice way to start. When Dhar didn't say anything, Terr gave a barely perceptible nod. It would be all right. Nightwings would be there to cover his back.

"If we are together—"

"I can't promise that," Anabb warned and raised his hand. "Whenever possible…"

"I accept, sir," Terr said with relief and no small amount of trepidation. This could still turn out to be very messy.

Dhar grinned. "Sankri needs looking after, sir."

"So I know," Anabb said heavily, then rubbed his hands. "With that out of the way, I've got a deal that you'll love. You will keep *Psandra*, for the moment at least. Knowing that Paleans actively raided Pizgor's commerce, it's a small step to make the next logical assumption. Care to hazard a guess?"

Terr didn't like where this headed, any of it. He'd been rolled and knew it. The slimy, evil, scheming…

Yet, his skin prickled and his mind raced. He couldn't help working the problem. Whoever ran the Lemos operation obviously expected to succeed. Anabb probably had a contingency position in case things became disagreeable. Terr understood why Sargon and the Paleans lusted after Pizgor's five lousy systems: numbers. They needed to secure enough systems to enable them to hold a third Executive Council seat. Without that seat, the whole exercise became a very expensive futile gesture. If the objective was just numbers, did it necessarily matter where they came from?

"They're after enough independent nonaligned systems to push them over the twenty-five percent margin needed to secure an additional Executive seat. Sargon may be wooing some systems in its sphere of influence, but the largest block of independents—"

"Go on," Anabb prompted with huge satisfaction.

"—is locked within Kaleen and Orgomy. Fourteen systems, to be exact, sir. Maybe the Paleans figure it would be easy to peel off four or five…" Terr trailed off, an ugly suspicion forming in his mind. He groaned and spread his hands. "You can't be serious, sir!"

Anabb beamed at him happily, turned to Dhar and raised a questioning eyebrow.

"You suspect, sir, the Paleans are running another base?" Dhar said cautiously.

"Very good, Mr. Dharaklin. That is exactly what I think. They're raiding Kaleen commerce not only to intimidate the independents, but I suggest they want to disrupt the formation of the Unified Independent Front."

"A bold initiative, sir," Dhar murmured.

He had not followed developments surrounding the fledgling attempts to consolidate Kaleen and Orgomy into the UIF as closely as he should. As a Wanderer, he understood Prime Director Marrakan's burning desire to secure not only economic freedom for the two independent blocks. More importantly, political freedom. Once ratified, the Unified Independent Front would hold an Executive seat in its own right, giving it a powerful voice in the Serrll's ruling council. Combined with the traditional one seat reserved for other independents scattered throughout the Serrll, the voice of those two seats would dilute the power of the major blocks. No wonder that the Paleans, Sargon, and the Karkans, for that matter, appeared prepared to go to any lengths to see the UIF died stillborn.

"Why waste a good idea that worked successfully elsewhere, right?" Anabb said comfortably. "Well, partly successful, and the Paleans can never be accused of wasting a good idea." These two would make a terrible pair once he let them loose.

Terr looked disgusted. "Sir, after Lemos, the base, if there is one, and I'm not necessarily saying there isn't, will be tighter than a canal worm's…ah…" Terr cleared his throat. "If the Paleans are really running one, they'd be nuts to execute sorties. I doubt raiders around Kaleen would be so gullible to go prowling after seeing their buddies mowed down around Pizgor."

"Your summary is crude and succinct, First Scout, and wrong!"

Terr ignored the thrill of hearing his new rank. Keep focused here.

"Sir?"

"The raiders are not being mowed down, as you put it."

"Ambassador Rayon said—"

"A slight misdirection on his part. The raiders know that Lemos is exposed and they're naturally wary now that the Tai-

Mari Line has compromised them. They're lying low, but they're not hunted. For now at least."

"Until that second base is found and the network exposed, is that it?"

Anabb beamed at him. "Exactly! I have Re Nette and her crew. As far as anyone knows, she disappeared and her ship is lost."

"Sir, the Paleans may not be using raiders around Kaleen at all," Dhar said quietly, and Anabb pointed a finger at him.

"Good point. They could have Fleet vessels."

"Like Tanard's," Terr said slowly.

"Like Tanard's. With COMPALOPS turned inside out, they'll find it difficult doing that."

"They could still have plenty of armed auxiliaries. If a carrier disappears in an attack, all we have is a missing hull, unless you can catch them in the act," Terr mused, then his eyes widened and he groaned. "That's what you're planning, isn't it?"

Anabb laughed. He couldn't help it. The boy was smart.

"Son, that's exactly what I want you to do. Catch them in the act. As Mr. Dharaklin already surmised, for the Sargon/Palean merger to succeed, they need systems, at least enough to neutralize the Pizgor debacle. Right now, on Naklanor, Orgomy's capital world, delegates have gathered from all over the Serrll. Each is a representative of an independent nonaligned system. In thirty-one days, a converted liner, escorted by an M-2, will carry them to Anar'on for a plenary conference. They'll be hashing out ratification clauses for the Representatives Conference to be held in five years' time. A lot of powerful decision-makers will end up on Anar'on. You can imagine what it would do to the UIF cause if something were to happen to them while in transit. Getting rid of some could sway undecided independents right into Palean arms. It would certainly disrupt the UIF machinery. There will be talk of plots and sabotage afterward, but if no evidence emerged to implicate the Paleans, the damage would be done and the rumors will blow over in time."

"An M-2 is a pretty weak escort, sir. You're not really contemplating risking the lives of the delegates?"

"Of course not. Thunderation! If only one of them gets a nosebleed, I'm in trouble. The delegates will be in an M-4."

"The M-2 is bait, then. What can I use to counter the attack?"

"That, of course, is up to you."

Terr chewed that one over and didn't particularly like the taste. He imagined all the things that could go wrong. The list alarming in its length.

"With respect, sir, how will this deception serve to unmask the second base?"

"It won't, and your lack of faith in my abilities is disturbing," Anabb said darkly. "The mission objective is to link the Paleans with the covert operation. The resulting political fallout will shut down any base they might be running, effectively neutralizing the threat to Kaleen and Orgomy commerce—and the Unified Independent Front. They won't dare pull another stunt like that for a while. It will also relieve the pressure on Kaleen commerce."

"I hate to sound defeatist, sir, but after Lemos, they will be wary and suspect a trap."

"Wary or not, my boy, their hands are tied. Whether they act or not, the UIF initiative will keep moving. Whether they like it or not, Sargon will want the merger to keep moving as well. Ti Inai and his faction will be forced to act. Trap or not, this will seem to them a real opportunity to deliver a killer blow."

"You know, sir, the Karkans could also gain a lot if the Unified Independent Front failed. They might decide to attack that liner themselves. I would hate to wind up on the receiving end of a two-pronged end run."

"Your problem, First Scout, and that's subject to a different ops."

Terr and Dhar exchanged glances. Perhaps joining this fruitcake hadn't been such a bright idea after all. Too late now.

"You'll have plenty of time to work out the details," Anabb offered comfortably. "Before you route for Orgomy, this is not a junket for you. For the next three days, I want both of you with my debriefing team going over your Lemos report and its findings. Don't worry. This is a milk run."

Terr recalled what happened the last time on one of Anabb's milk runs and sighed.

Rit!

* * *

Enllss liked spring. After the harsh, jagged edge of winter winds and driving rain, he felt invigorated to be outside, enjoying the morning's crisp sharpness. Today the morning was special, the air warm and soft, filled with fragrances of new growth. The sprawl of Celean Park that surrounded Captal's Center a profusion of budding greenery. Ignoring the security detail around him, he could almost hear its satisfied whisper as he walked a meandering gravel path. The loose stones crunched beneath his strong purposeful strides. The sun caught the Center spires in buttery light that outlined the tall columns and the hanging tubeways in a glowing halo.

He needed to think.

Everyone indulged in serious and sometimes not so serious political and economic squeezing in order to make the other guy mend, or bend, his ways. The Sofam Confederacy knew all about the subtle art of covert influence. The Paravan Trading Association had written the manual on conducting influential subversion against an intransigent opponent. Over the millennia, those tactics served Sofam well, avoiding open war with Sargon and winning over the Deklan Republic with unrelenting filing down, until one day the Deklans found themselves bound to Sofam. Even today the Deklans were bemused partners, wondering how it all happened.

Sofam understood the application of power, all right. Perhaps it was time for a little refresher lesson for some who sought to emulate the technique in a manner a little too obvious. Finesse, after all, was everything.

The Paleans were caught with their faces covered in cream and their embarrassed squirming justified. Pizgor was a bold initiative and could very well have succeeded, but for one ill-advised detail. All political blocks exerted pressure to influence an outcome, but using the Serrll Scout Fleet as an instrument of domestic policy stepped over the tacitly understood line. Pizgor bore all the hallmarks of a typical Sargon operation: make your partner or intended victim take all the risk, then step in and mop up the proceeds. In failure, they can stand back with feigned indignation and deny any complicity. It worked well before and Lemos was another classic example of its type—with the Paleans taking the fall this time. This time, though, Sargon wasn't going to get away with it.

Whoever ordered Kai Tanard to raid Pizgor commerce with a Fleet unit had committed a cardinal error. The person did not understand the application of power. What Enllss needed to know, to what extent was the Palean Congress involved? He knew of Ti Inai and his merger faction, but did he operate with the implicit approval of the Palean government? He had to have had *some* support.

The Bureau of Colonial and Protectorate Affairs tower rose tall before him. Connected to other towers of the Center by tubeways, it was a slender needle of ceramic and reactive panels. Lost in thought, he ambled up wide, creamy stone steps and walked through the main entrance. His footsteps echoed in the dark vastness of the pale yellow marble hall. He picked one of the high-speed cable-tubes that went all the way to the executive offices.

Against the Gods of Shadow

When the tube stopped, he stepped out and his feet sank pleasantly into a thick green-tinged rug. A dull yellow-orange crest of the Bureau lay woven into the pile. Finely textured Catlan moss panels lined the walls. Background music filled the hollow spaces with muted unrecognizable sounds. He quickly strode to his office, ignoring the activity of his staff.

Enllss settled back his muscular and powerful frame into the luxurious formchair and inhaled the delicate aroma of the herbal tea before taking a sip: tangy, sweet, and redolent, just the way he liked it. Yellow sunshine streamed through the window screens. Electronic only, but indistinguishable from the real thing. Tapping the desk with long fingers, he reviewed the meeting held earlier in Tao Karam's office. Not a pleasant time for the Bureau of Justice Executive Director.

Sweetmeats lay in a shallow stone tray on a small table between the formchairs. Enllss glanced at Sill-Anais and suppressed a smile. Sill hated tea, especially the concoction Enllss favored. Enllss put his cup on the crystal saucer and laid it down with a gentle scrape. Opposite him, Tao Karam looked up, his large black eyes expressionless. Enllss admired the wily old Palean. He always considered him and his faction as Sofam's friends and a stabilizing influence within the Palean Congress. Was Tao Karam implicated? It didn't seem possible. His faction had always been openly pro-Sofam. So, it must be that little shit, Ti Inai.

"Mr. Director, the emergence of the Unified Independent Front might be seen by some elements within the Serrll as an unsettling development, better to have never started," Enllss said easily, probing for a reaction. Tao Karam's black eyes regarded him without expression. "Nonetheless, they're a natural culmination of factors that has set the process into motion and the Serrll government must deal with the emerging consequences. We all have reasons to influence the process in order to control the eventual outcome that will protect our various singular interests. No one objects to that. However, given the deplorable tactics used against Pizgor, there is a need to remind everyone there are limits to how far such action can be tolerated. In Pizgor's case, those limits were clearly exceeded. As the senior Revisionist Party coalition partner, the Sofam Confederacy wishes to inform the Palean Union of the possible gravest consequences should the coming UIF delegates conference on Anar'on be disrupted or any of its representatives interfered with."

Tao Karam blinked. The tactics may have been deplorable—only because they failed. He abhorred Ti Inai's desire to plunge the Palean Union into turmoil, but even more unpardonable that the exercise had been so clumsily executed. Enllss' words were soft and measured, but there was nothing soft about his square jaw, thrust out when emphasizing a point. Dark gray eyes probed and measured. His hair getting white with a fleck of brown here and there. The aquiline nose sharp above a firm mouth.

The fact Enllss that delivered the message, a commissioner, rather than receiving it through official Sofam channels, not lost on him. It signaled he had freedom to engage in a frank exchange, unencumbered by diplomatic protocol. However, he learned long ago that everything was subject to protocol in one form or another. Only the method of delivery sometimes allowed some room for interpretation of real intent. Even though the Palean Union and Sofam were political partners in the Revisionist Party against the Karkan-dominated Servatory Party, Sofam had informed the Paleans it would brook no direct interference with the Unified Independent Front. It wasn't the first time. Sofam prevented the Paleans from absorbing the Kaleen systems before and Tao Karam held no illusions that it would be prepared to do so again. He knew of no covert plan to annex Kaleen, although Congress had spoken of it from time to time. Enllss obviously referring to Ti Inai's Alikan Union Party faction and the merger with Sargon; such a stupid and unnecessary thing.

Against the Gods of Shadow

He clasped his hands in his lap, his delicate button nose glistened on his small, triangular face.

"Mr. Commissioner, the Palean Union has no desire to disrupt the proceedings of the Unified Independent Front conference. However, Sofam cannot hold us responsible for every act committed by one of our various factions."

"Sir, I understand the Alikan Union Party has strong traditional ties with much of what is now the Sargon Directorate, and those ties span a history of millennia. Sofam doesn't care if the Palean Union wishes to pursue a merger with them. That's an internal matter for you to deal with. Indirectly, however, we would not approve of any social dislocation such a merger may cause in your pursuit of expansionist policies."

Karam shifted in his seat, his fingers twining. He sympathized with Sofam's concerns and cursed Ti Inai for putting him into this awkward position.

"Believe me, friend Enllss, the Palean Congress understands and shares your grim view of the possible consequences in any such merger with Sargon. When Prime Director Kernami presented Pizgor's case to the General Assembly, I was shocked and outraged as anyone. The idea that we were raiding their commerce in order to bring political pressure to bear on their status as an independent nonaligned group monstrous. I could not believe that Ti Inai's faction would be so foolish. With Lemos uncovered, I met the news with consternation."

Sill-Anais cleared his throat. Thin white eyebrows outlined large, liquid wide-set green eyes. His face, pinched and dry, traced with age and responsibility. He ran a hand through the twin gray bands in his hair.

"Mr. Director, by actively using Fleet ships against Pizgor's commerce the Palean Union showed a disturbing level of disregard for the Constitution and the Articles of Association. Ach! The Serrll Combine exists as an entity solely on the basis and understanding the government's organs are

261

there to serve all. When one block usurps that faith it opens the doors to chaos."

Karam bobbed his head in an agony of embarrassment. "I appreciate that all too well, Sill."

"Sir, the Palean government might not be directly culpable, but as far as the Serrll is concerned these acts were performed by the Palean Union," Enllss said evenly. "Deklan and the Karkans don't necessarily care that an internal faction is the real perpetrator. With Lemos uncovered, the Pizgor gambit has failed. The issue will be dealt with by the Executive Council and is outside my concern. Sofam wishes to bring to your notice our concern that Ti Inai's operation may, if it has not already, turn its attention to Kaleen and the Unified Independent Front. Sofam urges you to dissuade any interested party from pursuing such an unwise course of action."

"I appreciate your candor, Enllss," Karam said smoothly, his thoughts raging. "I will not deny that one of our policy platforms is the absorption of Kaleen and the surrounding independent systems, but not through military or destabilizing means. We have used inducements and economic pressure and will continue to do so. This is universally accepted practice. However, the Palean Congress does not use raider mercenaries as an instrument in the execution of its policy."

"Evidently someone was prepared to do just that," Sill said dryly and Karam nodded.

"Evidently. Please convey my guarantee that Sofam's concern regarding the UIF will be discussed by the Congress, Mr. Commissioner."

"Sofam is looking at far more than simply discussion, sir," Enllss said and stood up.

When the two left, Tao Karam leaned back behind the polished expanse of his desk and cursed roundly. The day had lost its charm long ago and he was uncharacteristically concerned. Despite his mortification over Lemos, what irked him more, while a significant segment of the Congress supported

Ti Inai, the executive government purported to know nothing about it. That went beyond the credible. It meant they must have silently approved. The thought made him shudder.

A side door opened and Ti Inai strode through. He glanced briefly at the double translucent door panels through which Enllss and Sill exited, and sprawled himself comfortably into one of the seats in front of Karam's desk. He bobbed his head in greeting.

"You heard?" Karam demanded, his black eyes half closed in disapproval.

"Everything, friend Karam," Ti Inai piped oily, his hands twining. Karam glared at him.

"You fool! Do you realize what your scheme has done?"

"That's a little harsh," Ti Inai said with a hurt pout.

"Perdition! What were you people thinking? It's bad enough that you're pursuing questionable policies without government sanction—"

"You never understood—"

"I understand all too well," Karam hissed, trembling with repressed anger. "And I understand you and your ambition, friend Inai. Your objectives are not entirely without merit. What I cannot condone are the methods you're willing to adopt to achieve them. This is not how the Palean Union conducts its business! And it's certainly not how a prospective executive director should behave. Your faction's misguided zeal could bring general sanctions against us. What may happen to Sargon will be richly deserved, but the effect on us would be devastating."

Ti Inai sat straighter and sneered, contemptuous of Karam's timidity and lack of vision.

"You've been blinded by Sofam's rhetoric, friend Karam. In its days of pride and glory the Alikan Union Party boasted a conglomerate of Palean and Sargon worlds. I want us to live those days again, wielding real power in the Serrll as equal partners without having to kowtow to Sofam or anyone else.

Pizgor and Kaleen are mere irritants to be brushed aside if they resist."

Karam looked at the young commissioner and shook his head.

"I cannot believe what I'm hearing. Your faith is indeed misplaced, as is your knowledge of our history. The old Alikan Union Party had to make alliances to counter Sargon's military overtures to engulf it. The AUP *became* the Palean Union to preserve its identity, then driven to defend its borders with force after Sargon occupied some of its systems. After that struggle, you now intend to hand over the Union to them and expect me to sit idly by and watch an occupation take place? Who do you think will control the new Alikan Union? Remember one thing, friend Inai, in its whole history Sargon has *never* relinquished an occupied system.

"I have no doubt that over time, you could induce enough independents around Kaleen to give your merger the needed numbers, and with it, that third Executive seat, but have you counted the cost? Sargon has been your partner with Lemos, but who took the risk? In your next play, ask yourself who is again carrying the risk? You may gain your merger, but Captal will ostracize you. Is it worth forcing the issue now, when all the evidence suggests that in a generation the Karkan Federation will be a spent force. The Palean Union independently will be able to carve out enough systems from the collapse to claim a second Executive seat in its own right. Has your thirst for personal power and a place in history swept away your sense of duty and responsibility to the Union? Forcing this issue now will certainly win you a place in history, friend Inai, but is it really the one you crave?"

"An elegant speech, friend Karam, but unconvincing."

"Then I shall make my point in a more telling fashion!" Karam barked, out of patience. "You're coming up for preselection before the Congress as an Executive Director and senior Captal representative of the Palean Union. I can make that process very difficult for you, friend Inai. Very difficult. Another thing. Should I learn that you played an active role in subverting the due process by using Fleet ships to advance your faction's cause, your position as a prospective director will become more than merely awkward. You'll be sifting rocks on Cantor! As for the Unified Independent Front, after Sofam's warning, don't even *think* about it."

Ti Inai wrung his hands and bobbed his head to Karam, his smile oily and ingratiating. The old fool may not have the vision to make the Union great again, but he certainly had the power to wreck his career. After twelve years in the General Assembly, he would be out, a nobody. He didn't consider himself addicted to power, but used it as a necessary tool if he wanted to achieve his objectives. The old dodder might be right about the Karkan Federation becoming a spent force, but to wait a generation? Karam was a dope! Nonetheless, a pause might be in order, time for the Provisional Committee to reflect. He could well imagine Ed-Kani's reaction to such a suggestion and suppressed it. Damn him anyway! Ed-Kani wasn't the one risking all if Italan failed. Besides, why the damned rush to consummate the merger? Killing off the Unified Independent Front delegates would not neutralize the movement. A setback certainly, but would it deliver that decisive blow? Perversely, the action may serve to stiffen the resolve of the independents. If he pushed too far, his action may cause Anar'on to retaliate, and the Wanderers were not to be underestimated. There was a clear groundswell of support for the UIF whose birth may not be so easily stifled. He didn't need to kill the UIF. He only needed to frighten half a dozen wavering systems to join the Union and make the merger politically viable. A firm example would do that very well indeed. No, a strike against the UIF delegates would proceed.

"Friend Karam—"

"Get out. You make me tired," Tao Karam snarled, abandoning even the basic forms of politeness.

Chapter Nine

"Until the liner reaches the Haram'an waypoint, you will shadow it at four lights separation," Tanard rasped. "I will be sanitizing Haram'an. Once we engage, I don't want to worry about an M-4 jumping us. We distract or brush aside the M-2 escort, destroy the liner in place and clear out."

Val Keen bobbed his head, his long fingers fluttering. The tactical plan outlined in the Wall simple and lucid. In theory, a set piece engagement. A good plan, although he felt somewhat nervous confronting an M-2. *Zaradej* housed a comparable projector, but an M-2 was a real warship with hull shielding to match. He glanced at Tanard and grimaced. He could never get used to the two long disfiguring scars running down Tanard's right cheek and neck. Why the pits didn't he have the things removed!

Tanard glowered at the Wall.

Asinine orders! Even disguised as raiders, attacking a liner was questionable politics at best. After his encounter with young Terr, to attack another Fleet unit again sheer idiocy, even if it was a lousy M-2. He never doubted the disrupting influence on the Unified Independent Front that eliminating the delegates would cause. He didn't feel comfortable with the Committee resorting to such crass tactics. This would not be a commercial raid, but direct intervention into Kaleen's political process. Captal is bound to take a grim view of any such action, especially after Lemos. More disturbingly, if the Committee were willing to resort to such methods to achieve its ends, where were the limits? What else were they prepared to do? There were enough historical precedents of similar actions to be found in the Serrll's checkered past. He noted that most such efforts either failed or were only partially successful

266

at best. Lunacy!

Whatever the motivation, the mission didn't make him at all happy. The tactical disposition smelled like a setup and his inner alarms were clanging. They were committed and he didn't have a choice, none of them did.

Tanard pushed back his formchair and stood up.

"We'll keep adjusting the action plan until the moment the liner lifts. We have fifteen days to see to it that the crews and ships are ready. I'll want to go in clean, make a quick kill and disengage. Keep me advised on the logistics."

Val Keen stood and smiled. "You worry too much, friend Tanard," he piped softly and bobbed his head.

"I have cause to worry, friend Keen," Tanard said quietly. "That's what keeps me alive. When we engage the escort, don't go for any fancy maneuvers, not if you want to live. You won't be facing a dumb bulk carrier. Come in straight and go for the kill."

"I do have some expertise," Keen said, stung by Tanard's implication. He stood up and walked out. Tanard watched him go and sighed.

Expertise? Comparing his amateurish skills against a trained Fleet officer? A good man, Keen had never been on the receiving end of a projector. His brush with Terr wasn't an engagement at all. One of Le Maran's political cronies, Keen was a manipulator, not a ship driver. At any rate, Keen would have to handle it, the M-2 an even match. Tanard knew he should have pushed harder for an ex-Fleet driver for the second auxiliary. Even after Lemos, Le Maran still dismissed Tanard's warnings about the coming ops.

Lemos, what a debacle!

He could not believe how quickly the whole thing had unraveled. His friend Ril Seen exposed, the Tai-Mari Line broken up and raiders scurrying to escape the Fleet net. Lemos should not have fallen, not this easily. Part of the driving team that planned and put into place the layered defenses,

Lemos should have been secure.

He strode to the window screen and stared at the harsh black and gray contrasts of Italan's airless landscape. If Lemos was the ass end of nowhere, Italan was a purgatory. The caverns and tortuous tunnels that riddled the metal-rich asteroid held the barest of living amenities. Mining abandoned decades before when the returns fell below the break-even point. As a staging post for mounting clandestine jumps against Kaleen commerce, the free-drifting asteroid ideal. In fact, raiders used Italan as a base before the Committee mopped them up and moved in. This time, no partnerships, the raids mounted by converted armed auxiliaries owned by the Committee.

Setting up Lemos as a joint venture with raiders probably contributed to its undoing. He relied on intimidation and the threat of deadly reprisals to maintain security, and for two years, it worked. Did one of the raiders betray him? That had always been a possibility and Lemos' one great weakness. Staring down a hot Fleet projector a raider probably traded Lemos for his life.

Scum!

They might never know what really happened.

And how close he came to losing it all himself. He thanked the gods for rejecting Val Keen's urging to hide in the Et-Aran to repair his main drive. Instead, he ordered Keen deeper into Palean space and rendezvoused with a support ship. Had he listened to Keen, both of them might now be enjoying Cantor's famed hospitality, or worse.

What really galled him, the whole ironic mess could have been so easily avoided. The Committee were criminally stupid in their misguided direction to attack a Fleet ship. He clearly remembered a similar incident last year when Le Maran ordered him to attack an escort. That time, Tanard had been lucky and only an expanding plasma cloud was left of the luckless M-3 sweeper. Even so, the Fleet went orbital. For over thirty days, no one dared venture on a raid.

Against the Gods of Shadow

Ignoring the lesson, the Committee did it again. Should he have protested more strongly Le Maran's order? Did the Committee even care that Lemos was gone? He could not believe it.

His mouth widened into a rueful smile at the thought of his young adversary. Terr's role had not hit the media on Pizgor, but Tanard felt certain the Triumvirate had expressed its thanks discreetly. More than likely the incident would elevate Terr to First Scout rank, he noted with professional detachment. Any hopes he cherished of slipping back into active Fleet duty and advancing to Master Scout were now irrevocably dashed. He fervently believed in the Palean cause and some things were worth sacrificing a career for. What gave him a bitter taste was the casual ease with which the Committee seemed to have thrown that career away.

"We may yet meet again, friend Terr," he murmured.

Why send an M-2 to protect the liner?

Italan's black landscape remained silent.

* * *

Naklanor stood out as a brilliant blue jewel in blackness pierced by fragile starlight. The northern polar cap stretched long tentacles of glaring white ice toward the temperate latitudes. Bunched clouds crowded the equator. Two quarter moons peeked shyly in the background. Orgomy could not have chosen a more beautiful planet for its principal world.

SC&C picked them up and brought *Psandra* slanting in. The rapid descent took them over the capital Tanaree. Heat haze smeared the city as the M-3 settled and moved slowly toward the landing field. A typical facility with a mixture of civilian and commercial terminals that usually shared maintenance and support. Liners were tethered by several access tubes, while large cargo haulers lay grouped around automated loading and unloading ramps. The military terminus

269

tucked into one end of the field with its cluster of hangars and refurbishment yards. Two M-4s stood side by side on the landing rings, access tubes connected. A lone M-2 rested on its ring, hooked to the opposite side of the terminus. Two M-3s lay parked farther out on the apron, while the blunt triangular snout of an M-6 peered from a maintenance hangar.

Psandra hovered briefly, drifted slightly as SC&C positioned it above the landing ring, then settled beside the M-2. An access tube immediately extended from the terminal and attached itself to the hull with a dull thump.

After a quick glance at Terr's unresponsive expression, Dhar shut down the in-flight routine and set the ground watch.

Terr was moody.

He felt moody ever since they left Taltair, ever since Anabb dumped this nutty mission on him. No, that wasn't it. The consequences of his decision to join the Diplomatic Branch were beginning to sink in and he did not entirely like the feeling. Only on detached duty, he had a sensation of dislocation. The Fleet had been home for most of his life. Wherever he went, his uniform opened most doors. It had always been there, behind him, protecting, nurturing him. No matter what happened, he knew he belonged and they would not let him down. That sense of security and comfort always with him. In the background perhaps, but it colored his behavior and approach to duty.

He still belonged, but being out of the chain of command was disconcerting. Even wearing his uniform now felt uncomfortable, pretending to be something he really wasn't. He had never worn anything else! How would he feel then when on an assignment in civilian mufti? Yet, as one of Anabb's agents, he still carried out his duty. Part of the commissioning oath rang in his head:

'*...bear allegiance to the Constitution of the Serrll Combine and the Articles of Association...*'

Working for Anabb would not violate his oath of duty. The problem might be a shifting of loyalties. He gave unquestioning loyalty to the Fleet, and they never betrayed that loyalty. Would Anabb betray it? He didn't know and suspected that finding out was likely to be very uncomfortable—for him.

Time enough to be moody after the mission.

With ground routine set, the deck watchstanders stood about and chatted, waiting to be relieved by the skeleton watch. Boring duty for the two crewmen, however necessary. It served mainly to coordinate communication between shore parties, ground support and crew who had taken leave. As far as the crew were concerned, *Psandra* made a routine stopover to undergo a standard maintenance check. One unguarded word that Terr's mission was anything but normal could be disastrous. If the Paleans intended to strike at the Unified Independent Front delegates, Their intelligence operatives would be on the prowl and wary.

This undercover aspect of the operation made him uneasy. Mixing it with spook types could terminally end his career. He complained to Anabb, but the crusty old prima scout merely shrugged, telling him to handle it. That gave Terr a negative surge of comfort and did nothing to boost his confidence. Anabb relented, saying the local Diplomatic Branch Resident handled security. All Terr had to do was sweep up the raiders.

That's when he started getting moody.

He stood up, stretched, and made his way to the cable-tube hatch. The comms watchstander looked up from her station.

"Sir, there is a ground maintenance chief petty officer on the main deck. He says he needs to speak to you."

"To me?"

"Yes, sir."

As far as he knew the bottom had not fallen off the ship,

so this must be something more drastic. He scratched the scar on his temple.

"Okay. I'll see what's giving him the itch. Mr. Dharaklin, you have the deck."

The main deck crowded with ship and ground personnel, some anxious to leave, others clustered in small groups chatting. Terr spotted a marine rating standing guard over a Naklanor native. The petty officer stood to as Terr approached.

"What's going on?" Terr said to the rating and looked curiously at the native.

"Sir, the Chief doesn't have proper access authorization. When I denied him entry, he demanded to speak to you. I would have thrown him off the ship—"

"Quite right."

The native looked sharply at him. "First Scout, unless ground procedures—"

"Take it up with SC&C, Mister!" Terr snapped. "I'm going that way myself. You can come with me and we'll sort it out there."

The native didn't look happy as he gave a stiff nod.

"Good work," Terr told the rating, gathered the native with a glance, and walked briskly into the access tube.

The walk to the terminal a silent one. Although well lit, the utilitarian concourse stood mostly empty. Not a passenger terminal, the Fleet did not see the need to make it look like one.

"First Scout, this way, please," the native said beside him, and indicated with his arm at a row of cable-tubes.

"Mr. Sakariwan?" Terr ventured and the native nodded. "I wondered how you were going to get in touch with me."

The Diplomatic Branch Resident grunted. "I have a place where we won't be disturbed," the Resident said briskly, all trace of a frustrated ground chief gone. "I need to bring you up to speed and clear up a couple of points."

Terr blinked. He wanted to clear up more than just a couple of points.

The tube took them up two levels. Sakariwan strode down a gloomy corridor and stopped before a nondescript white door in a row of other white doors. He palmed a pad and the door hissed into the wall. The room small, and the large desk made it feel even smaller. Indirect ceiling and wall lighting did nothing to dispel the dreariness the room radiated. It looked more like an interrogation cell than a meeting room.

"Make yourself comfortable, First Scout," Sakariwan said and promptly sat on one of the formchairs.

Terr pulled back a chair and sat down more cautiously.

"Is this where you drag out the sandbags and truncheons?" he asked brightly. Sakariwan frowned, obviously not amused.

"Actually, First Scout, my methods are less subtle," he said and Terr grinned.

"Don't feel you have to demonstrate."

Sakariwan leaned forward and placed his hands on the desk.

"Terr…may I call you Terr? Good. Now listen to me. You're pissing on my turf now, Mister. I have a lot to do and not enough time to do it in. Listening to your wisecracks isn't one of them. Director Anabb Karr told me to cooperate with your side of the operation and I'll do that. You don't want to pick a fight with me, clear?"

"Mr. Resident, I'm not interested in messing with your side of the turf," Terr said soberly. "I apologize if we seem to have gotten off on the wrong foot and I appreciate I won't be getting off the ground if your ops is penetrated."

Sakariwan glared. "Anabb told me you were a hardcase. Okay, we'll start over." He stood up and paced. "Everything is proceeding as planned. All the preparations on Anar'on are completed and security is in place. No amount of investigation will show otherwise, simply because there is nothing to hide. However, from what I know of Director Marrakan's preparations, it would be a brave Palean to start something on Anar'on. For all intents and purposes the plenary will be held as scheduled."

"Any chance that someone might try getting at the delegates here in Tanaree?"

"It's one of the possibilities that's been keeping me awake, First Scout. I won't be sorry when *Zavian* lifts. The liner will become your problem then."

Sakariwan paced and Terr felt a stab of sympathy. The thankless job probably a nightmare. If everything went smoothly, no one would bother to thank him. If there was trouble, his career would probably be in the dumpster.

Sakariwan stopped, buried his head between his hands, and sank back into his seat. After a moment, he looked up.

"The M-4 with the last of the delegates will be here tomorrow afternoon. All the delegates will board *Zavian* day after tomorrow and lift with *Terraton*, the M-2 escort, in tow. A perfectly routine hop in case anyone is looking."

Terr liked it. The operation simple and uncluttered, with a minimum of twists. More importantly, there was nothing happening that anyone could construe as being suspicious or a trap. Could that be construed as suspicious?

"Have you spotted any counter-surveillance?"

"No, and I would be surprised if I did. The people we're dealing with here will be too professional."

"Anyone can make a mistake," Terr pointed out.

"If they do, we'll pretend not to have seen it. Of course, the Paleans may not be planning anything at all and we're simply being paranoid."

"Of course," Terr said, not believing it.

"Now, about your end. The two M-1s are in orbit as you wanted, including the extra assault forces marines. They are due to depart this afternoon, and will wait for you at the designated rendezvous point. You'll lift at midnight. The M-4 will follow you in the morning. You were right to insist on separate departures. It wouldn't look good to have several warships lift at once."

"The M-4's commander knows I'll be in tactical command?" Terr demanded sharply.

Sakariwan nodded. "She knows. I appreciate you people are a bit sensitive about such things. I do have one concern, though."

"Oh?"

"Yes. An M-1 isn't exactly what I would use against a raider. In this case, there could be more than one. If one of them is carrying anything heavier than a Terrasec 14, you'll be fried."

Terr nodded, impressed by Sakariwan's knowledge. "Unfortunately, the liner's holds cannot take anything larger and still carry six ABPs. If we go into action, I will overstress the projectors."

"That will drastically reduce their operating life."

"Better than reducing mine. The odds are not all one-sided, though. The raiders may pack heavier weaponry, but they're not military vessels. They don't have the hull armor and shields of an M-1. The pilots probably won't have tactical battle skills."

"You hope."

Terr shrugged. "There is always that. If I cannot take out a raider with an M-2 and two M-1s, I will humbly apologize to Anabb."

"I am sure that will more than make up for the loss of the liner," Sakariwan said with a straight face and stood up. "I won't see you again, it's much too dangerous. All the comms and authentication codes, if I have the jargon correct, were transmitted to your ship. Access is able, able, triple zero. Good luck, Mr. Terr," he said briskly and walked out without a backward glance.

Terr looked at the open doorway and slowly shook his head. Spooks!

Well, he had one of his concerns allayed. His image of an intelligence field operative was one of midnight meetings, secret drops, covert gadgets and silent murders. At least that is how the Wall thrillers made them out. Apart from the corner meeting, Sakariwan turned out to be sharp, focused and direct. He did not argue about Terr's side of the operation and even made helpful suggestions. If that was typical of Anabb's agents, Terr could work with them.

He made his way out and walked to the cable-tube, a short ride down. The tube pulled up with a sigh and he stepped out. The terminal concourse still almost deserted. Footsteps echoing, he walked briskly across the hard polished floor toward the guarded access tube entrance. The marine stood to as Terr strode past him. On the empty main deck, he stopped before the tube hatch and thumbed the access pad. The hatch immediately opened.

"Level two, and get me the command deck."

"Command deck, ground watch, sir."

"Issue an all-officers alert. Briefing room in two hours."

In his quarters, he pulled off his zip-jacket and sprawled across his day cabin couch. The Wall pooled through swirls of color.

"Computer, display commercial corridor between Orgomy and Kaleen."

The color pools vanished. Against an indigo background a pale yellow stripe connected the two interstellar blocks. Navigational hazards pulsed orange, highlighted by white rings. There were only two: a neutron star and Haram'an's protostar. The corridor split around the young star, one branch lanced into Kaleen, the other continued toward Palean space. He knew the routes by heart, but it helped him to think seeing the full-dimensional image. He traced and retraced every maneuver of his little fleet and the course changes the liner would need to make.

An hour later, he glanced at the same display in the crowded briefing lounge. He swept his eyes over his officers.

"I want all crew to be on board in six hours. Once we're finished here, no one is to leave the ship under any circumstances. No personal comms to be made by anyone, and I mean anyone. All preparations will be made to lift at midnight. Mr. Hadrian, are our maintenance check evolutions complete?"

"In four hours, sir," Hadrian hissed.

"I want all ground personnel off the ship by the time the last of the crew are aboard. I could not tell you this before, and this doesn't leave the room. You can inform the crew once we're under boost. Gentlemen, we're hunting raiders!"

There was a stir and an exchange of glances and subdued murmuring.

"Two M-1s will be waiting for us four lights off Naklanor outside the Orgomy/Kaleen shipping corridor. We will rendezvous with them and wait for an M-4 that'll give us extra assault marines and three ABPs. We'll then hang around for a converted cargo liner *Zavian*, to make its way into the corridor in three days' time. *Zavian* will be escorted by *Terraton*, an M-2. We will intercept the liner, take off its passengers and crew, load the M-1s and six ABPs into its holds and proceed to Anar'on like nothing has happened.

"What you need to know, *Zavian* is carrying delegates from independent nonaligned systems for the upcoming Unified Independent Front plenary conference on Anar'on. The plan is to draw the Paleans into attacking the liner. We made it attractive for them by having only an M-2 as escort. Normally, such an operation would rate an M-4, but that would scare off anyone contemplating an attack. If they fall for it, we will capture the raider ships if possible; destroy them if not. It's important we capture at least one of them to establish a link back to the Palean government."

"Sir, does the *Zavian* pilot know what you have in mind?" Mati asked diffidently.

"No."

"He'll be pissed," someone said to a ripple of appreciative chuckles.

"It is unorthodox," Terr agreed with a grin, "and just short of piracy. For obvious security reasons, he and his owners could not be told anything. The M-4 will take the delegates and the liner crew to Anar'on. The reason for that is also obvious."

"What about us, sir?"

"Glad you asked, Mr. Hadrian. You will command *Psandra* and accompany the M-4 to Anar'on. I will command one of the M-1s during the engagement. Kieran, you'll be with me." The boy flushed with pleasure and his drooping ears turned bright red. "Mr. Dharaklin will command the other M-1. Mr. Mati, you'll be with him. Mr. Osinara, you will command three of the ABPs. Senior Chief Razzo, you'll command the other three. Questions?"

"Sir, what about the M-1 crew?" Mati asked.

"Right now, each is commanded by a Base Scout and a skeleton watch. They will be relieved and taken off by the M-4."

"Am I to take it they don't know what's going on either?"

"You can, Mr. Mati."

"Man, will they be pissed," the same voice said to another ripple of laughter. Terr allowed the humor to die down.

"They understood we would pilot the M-1s. The M-4 commander will be filled in once we rendezvous." Terr looked at the crusty assault marine. "Chief, get your marauders told off. Mr. Dharaklin will coordinate with your pilots."

"I presume, sir, the M-4 will give me three fully *manned* ABPs?" Razzo growled with a heavy scowl.

"It will."

Against the Gods of Shadow

"Although he doesn't know it yet," Mati said, wearing an innocent smile.

* * *

"Message burst from Italan, sir," the comms watchstander announced.

Tanard touched the scar on his right cheek and swiveled his seat.

He cleared his throat, sore again and getting worse. He realized he had been lucky to survive what were intended to be killing slashes, but he'd had enough of surgery. Regeneration failed and he did not want to undergo the delicate reconstruction regimen that might very well leave him without a voice, unlikely as that seemed. He would rather suffer than place himself in a physician's hands again. The inept fools have almost succeeded where his attacker failed.

He cleared his throat and swallowed. Perhaps with this mission done, he would think about it again.

"Well?" he rasped.

"Surveillance in Tanaree has identified a First Scout Terrllss-rr. Down less than a day, he left at midnight local time. That would make it eleven hours ago, sir."

Terr! And a First Scout!

"Anything else?"

The comms operator shook his head. "His stopover appears to have been a routine transit."

Tanard felt it in his bones there was nothing routine about it, not with Terr. *What were you doing on Naklanor, friend Terr? Are you involved in any way with the Unified Independent Front plenary?* Possible, but unlikely. The Diplomatic Branch would have plenty of specialists on hand for that. What then? There were lots of possibilities and Tanard didn't like any of them.

"Send a query to Italan. Ask them to confirm *Zavian's* departure schedule and the delegates are indeed boarding. Get them to check any contacts that First Scout Terr might have made while down there. Ask for anything unusual. Fleet movements, anything."

"Aye, sir."

Winn stepped to the command couch. "We should also ask about the preparations on Anar'on."

Tanard's left cheek twitched. "I would if we had someone there to ask. We lost our last agent two days ago. Disappeared, and all embassies are quarantined."

"They can't do that! It's against—"

"They have done it. Oh, we filed a protest with Captal, as has Sargon, but the Anar'on government is unmoved. They seem determined that the plenary will not be interfered with."

"Sir, response from Italan," the comms operator said.

"And?"

"Our operative saw First Scout Terrllss-rr in company of a ground maintenance chief. He returned to *Psandra* and didn't go dirtside again."

"Was his M-3 undergoing maintenance?"

"Routine stopover checks only, sir."

"Continue."

"The delegates are boarding *Zavian*, and it's making all preparations for lift. No irregular Fleet movements detected."

Tanard rubbed his scar.

Something was going on, he could smell it, but what? Would Naklanor really entrust the lives of the delegates to a lone M-2? If he were Director Marrakan, he would have demanded an M-6. He grunted in frustration at the circular argument. He asked himself the same questions ever since Le Maran gave him his orders and he still didn't have any new answers.

He glanced at the nav bubble. Long even lines of gravity waves snaked past the ship. The stars looked back at him, cold and aloof.

Against the Gods of Shadow

* * *

"We have their ping, sir," the comms operator announced. Terr nodded to her.

"It took them long enough," Mati muttered with a sad shake of his head.

Terr had to agree. They were within half a light-year from the liner before the M-2 showed any interest in them. The approaching ships might be Fleet units, but given the sensitive nature of his charge, the *Terraton* commander should have issued a challenge at least a light-year out.

"Wake him up, Mr. Mati."

"SSF M-2 picket *Terraton*, please respond."

The main display plate cleared almost immediately.

"What can I do for you, First Scout?" The Karkan commander looked young and appeared unconcerned to have an M-4, an M-3, and two M-1s closing on him.

"Clean up your contact procedures, Mister!" Terr snapped and the Karkan bridled.

"Your IFF—"

"Could be faked for all you know." Terr paused. It wasn't worth getting upset over. "You have a message burst with my clearance and authentication codes, Second Scout, placing you under my command."

The Karkan's head squatted lower. "Your command?" he hissed, looked away quickly, then back at Terr. "Just a moment, sir," he said and cut contact.

After three minutes, Terr started to get impatient, the plate finally cleared.

"My apologies for the delay. Given my mission—"

"Understandable, Second Scout."

"Your authentication codes check out, sir. I don't know what's going on, but I acknowledge your command."

"I am pleased to hear that. I'll brief you once I transfer to *Zavian*. Be prepared to drop normal on station with it."

"Aye, sir," he said automatically, then frowned. "Transfer to *Zavian*?"

Terr glanced at Mati and the display plate went gray.

"Right, now for the liner. Mr. Mati, give them the bad news," he said, and Mati grinned, relishing to coming exchange.

"Commercial liner *Zavian*, this is SSF M-3 sweeper *Psandra*. You are requested to drop normal and prepare your passengers for immediate disembarkation."

It didn't take long. The main plate cleared and Terr looked at a senior Master Pilot. The Naklanor native's large eyes were icy, and the thin lips white with suppressed rage.

"What's the meaning of this ridiculous demand, First Scout? I want your explanation, Mister!"

Terr figured the pilot was probably the chief officer of the Naklanor Lines and clearly not amused by the proceedings.

"Sir, it's possible that your ship will be attacked by raiders before you reach Anar'on."

"Attacked by raiders? Ridiculous!"

"Given the special status of your passengers, the Orgomy government disagrees."

"Why wasn't I told this before?" the pilot spluttered. "Are you here to provide escort?"

"Not quite. Your passengers will transfer to an M-4 for the completion of their journey."

"Transfer? Are you crazy? In case you haven't checked lately, Mister, an M-4's accommodation facilities are not exactly what my passengers are accustomed to. You cannot shuffle them around like cattle. Each one of them has diplomatic credentials. Do you have any idea of the stink this will cause? It's the most asinine thing I have ever heard."

"Under the circumstances, sir, a few days of discomfort may be eminently preferable to the alternative."

The pilot frowned, eyes fixed on Terr's face.

"You're up to something, I can tell. I suppose it wouldn't do me any good asking what you have in mind, would it?"

"I am sorry, sir, I cannot discuss this now."

"Humph! There will be some hard questions over this, First Scout."

"Of that, sir, I have no doubt," Terr said bleakly.

"Hah! I suppose you cleared this with *Terraton*? Very well, Mister. It looks like I don't have much choice, do I?"

"I will explain more fully when I come aboard." The plate went gray. Terr wasn't looking forward to telling the old geezer he was not only going to lose his passengers, but his ship as well.

"Sir, *Zavian* has dropped normal," Dhar said. "We'll be on them in thirty minutes."

"Very well. Inform the M-4 and the M-1s. Have the ABPs power up and stand by."

"Aye, sir."

The little fleet dropped out of subspace half a light-hour from the liner, which cut it fine. Terr did not want to be under auxiliary boost longer than absolutely necessary. If anyone waited for them down the transit route, delaying too long from the expected schedule could make them suspicious. Even so, it took another forty minutes before they closed with *Zavian*.

Terr watched as the M-4 maneuvered beside the huge passenger ship, gingerly narrowing the gap with the massive hull. It stopped and extended an access tube. Even with the reduced ship's complement the delegates and their entourage would find the M-4 exceedingly cramped. It promised to be an interesting three days for the M-4's commander. He didn't waste too much sympathy on her. He would gladly swap places rather than risk his people on a mad scheme. *Psandra* drifted past the M-4 toward a lock in the liner's side. An access tube slid out quickly and mated into place with her.

The cable-tube opened and Hadrian walked in.

"Mr. Dharaklin, as soon as *Zavian* opens its holds, get the M-1s and the ABPs moving. I'm going across," Terr said.

"Aye, sir."

"Mr. Hadrian, you have the ship."

Down in the maintenance hold, he opened the tube hatch and walked quickly through the fifteen katalans of tunnel that separated the two ships. The liner's hatch opened before he reached it. A curious merchant rating stared at him with undisguised interest.

"First Scout, I will take you to the command deck, sir," he said diffidently and bobbed his head.

Terr followed the Palean to the cable-tube. The youngster's hands twitched and twined as they rode up in silence. The hatch opened to one of the largest command decks Terr had seen. The opaque nav bubble slightly flattened glowed creamy gray. An array of display plates and command consoles occupied half the curved bulkhead. In the middle of the deck stood a nav holosphere showing a full-dimensional plot. It all looked damn impressive. Two watchstander stations were spaced on either side of the command couch.

The tall, portly Master Pilot finished talking to one of his officers and turned as Terr walked in.

"First Scout, I'm going to have a rebellion on my hands unless you tell my passengers what's going on," he growled, his manner expecting instant obedience. Terr had met his type before and wasn't overawed.

"Have you started offloading luggage?"

"I have not!"

"Then please do so. Time is limited. As for the passengers, they are your responsibility, sir."

The pilot scowled and placed his hands on his hips. "Now look here, son—"

"Sir, I need to inform you I am taking command of your ship. You and your crew will transfer to the M-4."

The pilot gaped and his face slowly turned a bright red.

"This...this is piracy, Mister!" he roared. "I'm damned if I'll hand over my ship to you."

"Sir, unless you want to be in an engagement—"

"To perdition with your engagement! This is my ship!"

"I cannot force you and I could use a skeleton watch. I suggest it would be prudent to transfer all non-essential personnel. We won't be needing stewards where we're going."

The pilot clenched his fists in outrage. "Damnation! This is an insult, sir! When you told me you were taking the passengers, I thought I'd be returning to Naklanor."

"I apologize for the deception, sir. I didn't want to burden you with too many complications."

"Hah! Thoughtful of you."

"I also want to request that you retain your medical staff on board."

"Expect them to be busy, eh?" the pilot snarled, then glanced to the officer beside him. "First?"

"Unorthodox, but he is within civilian shipping regulations, sir."

The pilot glared at him, puffed his cheeks, and exhaled loudly.

"This is not the end of it, First. Not by a long shot! Very well. I'm staying, of course. I don't intend handing over my ship to this youngster to play with. If anyone else wants to stay, it will be strictly on a volunteer basis only. Double bonuses and hazard pay, naturally. Now, let's get our passengers off." He turned and his eyes bored into Terr. "Happy now?"

* * *

Tanard hated the waiting part.

Sitting deep within the cloud of dust and debris left over from the formation of the Haram'an sun, the armed auxiliary could have been just another piece of flotsam—dark, cold and silent. Burning blue-white, the star glared a quarter of a light away that cast frozen shadows around the dusky command deck. Winn and Railee held the graveyard watch, enjoying a heated discussion on the pending action before Tanard appeared wearing a deep scowl that instantly plunged them into silence.

Tanard knew he should not be up here. Absolutely nothing for him to do, and his gloom ticked people off, but he found it impossible to rest in his quarters. *Zavian* now over three hours overdue, even allowing for different approach vectors through the shipping corridor. At a standard half boost—nominal for a passenger hauler—it should have already reached the junction waypoint and turned into the Kaleen lane. Unless the damned thing had decided to go around Haram'an? No, *Zaradej* would have warned him. That is why Tanard put Val Keen close to the waypoint. They hadn't gotten lost, have they? The thought brought a wry tug of sardonic amusement to the left side of his face.

The comms alert beeped and everyone jerked. Winn leaned across the repeater plate, then grinned and looked at Tanard.

"We've got him! *Zavian* is one-point-three lights from Val Keen's position, doing slightly less than half boost."

"Hah! On a pleasure cruise, are they?"

"They are in the Kaleen corridor already, and if they maintain their flight profile, they will be within point-six of a light from us in two hours and fifty minutes."

"And *Terraton*?"

"The M-2 is barely a light-minute ahead of the liner. To intercept, we should make our run in two hours."

"Good. Tell Keen to time his run accordingly. Mr. Winn, check him. I don't want any fumbles here."

"Ah, he won't like that much."

"Don't be obvious about it," Tanard rasped and ran a finger down his right cheek.

"Aye, sir."

Against the Gods of Shadow

Tanard's fingers drummed the armrest of his command couch. Annoyed, he stilled them. A few seconds later, his fingers twitched.

If anything, the waiting was even worse now.

* * *

"How long have you been with the Fleet, Mr. Terr?" the grizzled pilot demanded kindly.

"Fourteen years, sir. Four of those were at the Academy on Captal, followed by a year in a training ship."

"And a First Scout already? You've done well."

"I've had my moments."

The pilot chuckled. "I dare say. For me, it's been sixty-eight years with the Naklanor Lines. I am Chief Pilot and they have me commanding this scow. Bah!"

"I am sure the delegates appreciated having the best."

"Flattering to think so, young man. I fear, though, their interests were more earthy."

The comms operator looked up. "Excuse me, First Scout, it's *Terraton*."

Terr nodded, reached toward the repeater plate, and tapped a pad. The Karkan's fishy features were expectant. Terr toyed with the idea of taking command of the M-2, but forced to reject it. Although he didn't entirely trust the young commander, he simply wasn't familiar enough with the M-2's systems and crew, and did not relish the idea of learning on the job. Equally importantly, the move would have critically undermined the young commander's authority.

"What is it?"

"Sir, I have two uncorrelated tracks on an intercept coming off Haram'an. They should be here in fifty minutes. They show no IFF and have not responded to my comms pings. Power emission profiles identifies one of them as *Zaradej*."

Terr frowned. Could this be Tanard's operation? Possible…

"You know what to do," he said and cut contact.

The pilot peered at him. "Raiders?"

"Two unidentified vessels, sir. They could be anything," Terr temporized.

"Don't bother sparing my feelings, Mister! I like it plain and hot."

Terr grinned. He should get the pilot and Anabb together, then step out of the way.

"I don't know if they're raiders, but it's unlikely. They never bothered passenger haulers before. No profit in it."

"Something else, then."

"Coming out of Haram'an, they're certainly not sightseers. That's the reason I'm here."

"You're decidedly cool about it, I'll give you that."

Terr grunted and stood up. "I need to get below, sir. When I call, open your hatches fast."

"What can I do, Mister?"

"Nothing. If they roll us up, they will probably come back and destroy your ship to remove any evidence. You may yet regret your decision to stay on board."

"Then see to it I don't have cause for regrets, Mister!"

"Aye, sir. Your ship, sir," Terr said crisply, turned, and strode to the cable-tube hatch.

The Master Pilot watched Terr leave and shook his head. The delegates were bound to raise a howl of protest at their treatment once they reached Anar'on.

Down in the hold, *Reena* loomed huge on its landing skids despite the cavernous space. A tight squeeze to get the ship through the hatch, judging by a single long, bright scrape along its port side. Three ABPs were tucked against the far bulkhead, barely clearing the overhanging M-1.

In full battle suit and armor, Razzo held court over his three assault teams sorting through personal equipment. He glanced at Terr and nodded. Dhar saw him and hurried over.

"Everyone is prepped up and both M-1s are preflighted. I just finished checking the command net with the ABPs and *Sheeva.*"

"Good. I'm going to Hold Two. Get everyone on board and ready in thirty minutes." Terr searched his brother's face for a moment, then reached out with his arm and touched Dhar's chest with an open palm. "Nightwings, take care. This one could go either way. One of the hulls has been identified as *Zaradej.*"

Dhar returned the gesture, his orange eyes burning. "The gods shall be with us, Sankri," he rumbled and Terr grinned.

"Of course, they will have to give us their undivided attention," he said, then turned abruptly and hurried to the cable-tube.

Dhar stood staring at the closed tube hatch, his feelings mixed. A wave of unreasoning fear and pending loss swept through him and he shuddered.

"Tah, the gods will tell," he whispered, but it didn't help. No emotion showed in his face as he walked to Razzo. The scarred marine turned to face him.

"Are we moving, sir?"

"Seal them up in thirty minutes, Chief."

"About time! I was starting to get bored."

"It should get plenty exciting soon enough. Remember, move out as soon as I clear the hatch. Stay close."

"Right on your...ah, right behind you, sir," Razzo growled and beamed hugely. The commander allowed him a lot of leeway, but the first officer somewhat of a tight ass frowned on such levity. Razzo didn't hold it against him. The first had it all together and didn't flinch when the shit started flying. That mattered. Anybody can sit in a formchair and drive a ship. Hell, the thing ran itself most of the time. How an officer handled a crisis that separated kids from their toys that mattered. He wished he could have been there when Terr had it out with that Tanard guy.

"Kick ass, Chief," Dhar said unexpectedly and strode to *Reena's* landing ramp. Before climbing up, he paused and turned.

Hands on hips, Razzo glared at his squads. "Ready to get it on?"

"Ready and able, Chief!" they chorused.

"How ready?"

"Always ready!"

He scowled at them. "Disgusting, all of you. Maybe you'll all buy it this time and I can start over and do it right. Let's load up!"

Dhar smiled, shook his head and walked up the ramp. A terror aboard ship, busted twice from Master Chief, Razzo headed for the ranks when Sankri picked him up from COMDEKOPS BuePer. The slide from being a top marine in an M-6 to nursing a squad of M-3 grunts brutally swift. For anyone else it would have been a terminal career move, but not for Razzo. In one of his mellower moods, he confided he had gotten tired of doing close-order drill. He trained and longed for combat, but M-6s never went into combat. From what Dhar saw, Razzo was the best he knew in small unit tactics—on the ground or with an ABP. To him, the only thing that really counted. What the hard-bitten chief did when he hit dirtside was his business.

The tube hatch hissed open. Mati looked up and gave a small nod.

"Status?" Dhar demanded gruffly, automatically scanning the displays.

"Flight mode enabled. Power management on standby. Comms net is active."

The first officer is moody again, Mati thought, phlegmatic enough about it not to let it worry him.

Satisfied, Dhar sat down. The command couch creaked slightly beneath his weight. He leaned back and looked up.

Against the Gods of Shadow

"Computer, tactical on nav bubble."

The neutral gray faded. A quarter of the bubble showed a washed-out blue of Haram'an. Two orange blips, one directly to starboard, the other coming up behind them, were visibly converging on the liner's position. The bright blue blip of *Terraton* slowed and fell back to close with its charge. The two contacts *could* be legitimate, Dhar allowed, not believing it. In a set-piece engagement the M-2 would be under a distinct disadvantage. When the raiders split into their attack, the most likely tactic, *Terraton* would be forced to engage one of them, leaving the other to pounce on the liner. At least that is how he would do it.

Several direct hits into *Zavian's* drive spaces and it would be all over. With their objective destroyed, they could concentrate on *Terraton* or withdraw. In his view, going after the M-2 first would be a major tactical mistake. Although the raiders held a numerical advantage, *Terraton* was a real warship and built accordingly. A raider might mount a more powerful projector, but its hull not designed to be a fighting platform. A frontal attack could leave both raiders damaged or even crippled without achieving their objective. A civilian raider pilot might be tempted by such a maneuver, although contrary to all accepted military doctrine. If this attack was indeed politically motivated, Dhar doubted the raider drivers were going to fall for such amateurish adventurism.

That meant a confrontation where no quarter would be given or expected. The stakes they were playing for were enormous, but its cold-blooded execution violated all the teachings of the Discipline. The life of a Saddish-aa Wanderer was a trial of personal discovery and a union with the gods of the Saffal. Anar'on had never known the devastation of total warfare. Its small and scattered population prohibited such confrontations. That's not to say the Wanderers did not understand conflict. It had happened. Challenged by an affront, two individuals would face each other in the open desert where usually only one returned. Often, though, the Saffal would claim them both. Unleashed, Death walked without restraint. Given the distances, feuds between villages were rare, but did happen. Blood, thunder, and lightning was the price paid for invoking the god of Death, leaving the survivors shattered and bewildered by what their power had wrought.

Dhar knew Death lurked now, waiting to be unfettered, waiting to feed. Closed within the protective shell of the ship, not having to see the raider faces he prepared to kill, he almost convinced himself only a ship stood at the end of the projector beam—polymer and ceramic, not living flesh. Would he have the moral conviction to fire? This time, he would not be able to hide behind a cloud of duty. Chagrined, he felt a wave of shame. He participated willingly enough in seeking Tanard's destruction, feeling superior in the conviction that Sankri committed the transgressions. Afterward, he had seen the pain in his brother's eyes and did not understand.

Perhaps the fates have given him an opportunity to atone for his moment of arrogance.

He turned his head to the second officer. "Mr. Mati, I will con the ship. You concentrate on weapons and power management. Don't wait for my orders. Try to disable their projector or drive. We must cripple one of them at least. The liner is expendable."

"That Master Pilot will go orbital when he finds himself stranded," Mati said, probing the limits of familiarity with the first officer.

Dhar nodded. "It might not come to that. As soon as the M-1s launch, the raiders will either force action or attempt to disengage. We cannot allow them to do that."

"I figure *Terraton* and two M-1s should be enough to bag one of them," Mati said comfortably, then his eyes widened. "They may want to transit as soon as the M-1s appear."

"You need to keep up your rate of fire to prevent them from forming the field precursor," Dhar said flatly and looked up at the nav bubble. The two raiders were close. "Not long now."

"I won't let you down, sir."

Dhar grinned at him. "I never doubted it, Mr. Mati."

The comms alert beeped.

"*Sheeva* to all units." Terr's voice strong and even. "The raiders are coming in high and low, forcing *Terraton* to commit to one of them. As soon as their shields start to synchronize, we'll drop normal to scramble their firing solution. When *Terraton* commits, and I don't care which one he picks, we will launch in support. That includes the ABPs. Questions?"

There weren't any. They had gone through the scenarios and simulations, and knew what to do. Once the battle was joined, it would degenerate into a scramble anyway.

"Keep it tight and close, and good luck to us all."

* * *

"Sir, we have a ranging ping from *Terraton*," Railee said, watching the warship close with the liner.

Tanard acknowledged with a nod, keeping his eyes fixed on the tactical plot. The M-2 did not declare an all-ships signify and hadn't bothered to jettison a beacon. Was it fatalism or could the escort possibly think the two ships moving in on him were friendlies? Unlikely, as *Terraton* already positioned itself to cover its ponderous charge—a futile gesture.

He felt detached and cold, part of the weapons system of his ship. No honor lay in destroying a helpless liner, only duty. He didn't care to dwell on that too much either. He long ago realized that duty often served as a convenient cloak wielded by those who had no honor or understanding of duty.

He bit his lip and touched the scars on his throat. Best not to think about that too much either. Not now. The small ship's noises filled the silence around him.

Winn stood up and leaned toward Tanard. "Sir, tactically,

I must point out that we should take out *Terraton* before engaging *Zavian*."

Tanard looked at his anxious first officer and smiled. The boy had matured. Winn had never before dared question his orders. That took courage of a different order to facing live fire.

"I would agree," Tanard said, "if this were a tactical engagement. Our mission objective is to kill the liner and its passengers, not the M-2."

"If *Terraton* knocks one of us off, we can kiss our objective."

"You want to face him first?"

Winn grinned. "I wouldn't mind."

"You may get your chance yet. Give me *Zavian's* energy profile."

Winn sat down and scanned his displays. Not the exquisite sensor array of an M-3, but adequate enough.

"Nothing unusual."

"Keep the reports coming."

"It's only a lumbering liner," Winn said, not understanding why Tanard was worried.

"Perhaps, and keep those reports coming."

Terraton did the expected and correct thing to close with and cover the liner. Soon, Tanard would give it a cruel no-win option. Whatever choice it made, it would leave *Zavian* exposed. He wanted to come in quick, make his kill, and withdraw. Why send a lone M-2 to protect the delegates? It grated on his nerves and made him suspicious. Was he getting paranoid? Sometimes things *were* as simple as they appeared, suspicious of that also.

Winn looked up. "*Terraton* has extended its secondary shield grid and is synchronizing. Energy profile shows him overstressing his power management system by some fifteen percent."

Tanard scowled. That wasn't going to do much for the

M-2's projector. A realistic option and the move negated some of the power advantage of his ship. Faced with two opponents with potentially superior weaponry, Tanard would have done the same thing.

"Very well. Range?"

"Three minutes to IP."

"Mr. Railee?"

"Ready on all systems, sir."

"Very well. Sync shields, unmask the projector and make ready for full yield bursts."

Railee touched a large brown pad on his console. Beneath the hull a hatch split and the two halves retracted. The dark projector dome descended and locked into place. In the engineering spaces stripped helium nuclei fuel flow increased, feeding the artificial antimatter convergence point reaction chamber, massively increasing the rate of particle annihilation. Energy surged through separation wave-guides into the massive secondary bus nodes in the hull, forming tight lines of force that expanded from the ship, allowing the shield grid matrix to form an eight-talan cylindrical cocoon around the hull. Some of the energy directed through a separate reaction chamber that flooded the single Terrasec 8/B generator. Coils fully powered up, the computer synchronized the firing pulse frequency with the shield management system.

Satisfied, Railee nodded. "Ready in all respects, sir."

"*Zavian's* energy profile still showing normal," Winn said.

Tanard sat back and followed the developing confrontation in the main tactical display plate. It looked like Val Keen's course would take him low beneath the liner. He glanced at Winn.

"Bring her up a tad," he said, cleared his throat and stared gloomily at the plot.

To the pits with it! Shake it or bake it. His crew did not need a moody commander in a combat situation when indecision could get them all killed. Emotion was a luxury he could not afford, especially now.

The nav ring around the liner brightened.

"Sir, *Zavian* has gone max on his nav grid," Winn said matter-of-factly.

"Fat lot of good that'll do him," Railee muttered.

"IP in thirty-two seconds," Winn said.

Which way would *Terraton* go?

The distortion field around the M-2 and the liner faded and collapsed, instantly dropping both ships into normal space. To Tanard, a questionable tactic that would merely delay the inevitable encounter. It also suggested the M-2 driver might be short on experience. That was all right with him.

He didn't have to say anything, Winn already plotting a new intercept point. They dropped normal and the auxiliary turned, doubling back to make up for the overshoot.

"Targets are maintaining course at half standard boost. Dropping normal now. IP in nineteen seconds. *Terraton* has withdrawn his secondary shield to five talans. No change in *Zavian's* energy profile."

The changeover brought Tanard below the liner. With the M-2 holding high, it looked like Val Keen would have the questionable opportunity to engage first. He wasn't sure he liked that. Handled smartly an M-2 could be a nuisance, and Keen was a trash hauler, not an experienced combat officer. On the other hand, the M-2 driver had shown he also lacked experience. Only a Third or Second Scout billet, an M-2 wasn't exactly a front-line Fleet unit. Still, Tanard felt uneasy. *Zaradej's* power advantage would be wasted if Val Keen blundered playing like an M-4. About to order Keen to sheer off, Tanard ran out of time.

"IP!" Winn said firmly without looking away from his displays. "Forty thousand talans."

"Ready with the projector," Railee piped, excitement tingeing his voice. The target may only be a lumbering liner, but still a worthy kill.

Against the Gods of Shadow

Terraton committed then and maneuvered to come over *Zaradej*. This forced Keen to roll his ship in order to bring the projector to bear. A gutsy move by *Terraton*, and Keen hesitated, which allowed the M-2 to send a long traversing burst along the length of the auxiliary. Its shields flared in a cascade of blue and orange discharges, but appeared to hold. The move may have been gutsy, but it also left *Zavian* exposed to Tanard's fire. He pursed his lips, concentrating on his objective. Keen would have to take care of himself.

"Mr. Railee—"

Winn's head jerked up, his face creased with concern. "Sir! *Zavian's* energy profile just jumped. I am reading two additional power plant signatures—M-1s!"

Tanard now knew what young Terr did on Naklanor.

* * *

With the hold depressurized, the enormous cargo hatch slid silently into the hull and spilled white light out to space. The nav grid around *Reena* showed as a barely perceptible shimmer that twisted along the force lines. The landing skids retracted and the sleek ship hovered momentarily, then surged through the open maw. Fully powered the three ABPs lifted off the deck and plunged into blackness after the M-1, already over nineteen hundred talans ahead of them.

Sheeva emerged above the sheer curve of the liner and became a blur as it flashed after its sister ship. The ABPs, ungainly and less nimble, followed quickly enough, forming a string of six assault craft in desperate pursuit. At 1,700 talans per second, they could not match the M-1's 7,400 tps maximum boost and quickly fell back. They were not meant to mix it up with the raiders just yet.

Zavian immediately increased boost and surged past the tangle of engaged ships, effectively placing them between itself and the remaining raider.

In the leading ABP, Osinara sat in the pilot's seat scanning the tactical plot, shield status, environmentals, power management, and the penetrator deployment readiness. He took it all in subconsciously, concentrating on his situational awareness. In the ready cabin behind him, the six suited marines quietly discussed the coming action.

Thirty-four thousand talans ahead of him, *Terraton* exchanged fire with *Zaradej*. One long burst from the raider staggered the warship and its shields flickered briefly before they stabilized. Osinara growled, unconscious he had done so. Large and powerful, and what he could glean from the basic sensor suite of the ABP, *Zaradej* showed no damage.

One of the M-1s, its IFF identifying it as Mr. Dharaklin's *Reena*, positioned itself above *Zaradej* and poured continuous bursts into its drive spaces. The raider's shields sparkled along the force lines in unremitting discharges. Commander Terr's *Sheeva* stood off below *Zaradej's* stern and fired deliberately at its projector housing. Unable to shake off the irritating M-1 hanging above it, the raider attempted to maneuver to place itself ahead of the three warships, allowing it to bring all three under fire. More importantly, it needed to increase its boost to escape the approaching ABPs. Almost lazily, *Terraton* moved to cut off the attempt.

His ABP closing rapidly, Osinara checked the boost rate. Absorbed in following the action it would be easy to overshoot the target, to his lasting chagrin. He touched one of the designated comms pads.

"Force One, form up."

The two trailing ABPs acknowledged and fanned out, forming a classic triad attack formation, their forward shields at maximum. With *Zaradej* almost in sight, he readied the penetrator coils.

"Prepare to attach over the target's engineering spaces."

Osinara steered to place his formation above the raider, rendering the ABPs immune to its fire. *Zaradej* rolled to bring its projector to bear and a series of long traversing bursts raked the port ABP. The ABP's shields flared in point collapses as several direct hits struck the armored hull. Able to withstand six seconds of direct M-4 fire the raider's forty-eight TeV yield could not hope to penetrate the sixteen tetalans of armored hull. Nevertheless, the assault craft jinked to scramble the raider's firing solution. An unexpected back-surge could always burn away sensor pods, allowing an inrush of devouring energy to leak into the hull along exposed circuit lines, destroying everything connected to them.

To deal with the closing ABPs, *Zaradej* slowed down its rate of fire against the warships. It also needed to get rid of the pest stinging its back. It rolled with unexpected agility and exposed its projector to *Reena*. The small warship shifted, not quickly enough and received a raking burst along the length of its belly. *Reena* staggered from the blow, its shields a mess of discharge lines. Backsurges teased through the primary shield and arced against the exposed hull, ablating away the plating.

Osinara winced as the M-1 recovered, but he didn't have time to worry about it. He maneuvered to close with *Zaradej*. At four talans the ABP's specially modulated shields sheared through the raider's secondary grid in a ripple of blue-white discharges. *Zaradej* executed a quarter roll and fired a burst directly at the nose of the starboard ABP. The energy stream slammed through the assault craft's shield and flipped the ABP over. Massive backsurges rippled along the craft's hull as it fell out of formation, tumbling end over end.

Gritting his teeth, lips pulled back in a snarl, Osinara forced himself to remain calm. It wouldn't do to get emotional now and play the hero. They would recover the ABP later—if he lived through this, he reminded himself. His ABP rammed through the raider's primary shield and the black hull loomed massive before him. Watching the sensor outputs, he shifted the ABP slightly to bring it farther aft. The results would not be desirable if he burned his way into one of the drive reactor compartments. His finger stabbed at several touch-sensitive pads and the ABP slowed.

In the nose of the craft, four powerful coils glowed into life and cut swiftly through *Zaradej's* thin hull. Great clamps fixed themselves through the openings, splayed and secured the craft firmly against the plating. The penetrator discharge coils hummed and burned an oval line through the ship that matched the diameter of the ABP's forward hatch. Drumming his fingers impatiently against the console, Osinara waited for the coils to finish their work. When the display flickered brown, he touched a large triangular pad, and the thick forward hatch retracted. He pulled out his needler and leaped out of his seat. Grinning insanely at the six men seated in the main part of the assault craft, he strode between them and paused at the hatch.

"What are we waiting for? Let's get it on!" he bellowed and rushed through the opening into *Zaradej.*

The leading petty officer shook his head and charged after Osinara. The kid wasn't even wearing a pressure suit, let alone armor!

* * *

"Landing skids retracted," Dhar said.

"Lift sequence enabled," the computer said.

"Proceed with lift."

Reena hovered, ready for flight, waiting impatiently for the huge hatch to retract. It barely locked into place and Dhar gently nudged the ship out, then surged through the opening. In the tactical plot, one of the raider ships low and astern of the liner a bare forty thousand talans off, well within its acquisition envelope. *Terraton* engaged *Zaradej* high above them. Coming out of the port side hold, *Sheeva* increased boost to close. Ignoring the second raider below him, Dhar maneuvered the M-1 to clear the massive bulk of the liner and accelerated at max toward *Terraton*. He nodded approvingly as the plot revealed Razzo's three ABPs clearing the liner. Osinara's group strung out as they streaked toward their target.

He saw *Zavian* accelerate.

"All shields extended and synchronized. Yield stressed to one hundred and fifteen percent. Ready to engage," Mati said quietly, his voice slightly tense.

In the plot, the engagement had already degenerated into a bar melee. *Terraton* maintained steady fire, and *Zaradej* returned it just as effectively. Sankri positioned *Sheeva* below the raider and sent continuous bursts into *Zaradej's* projector housing. Dhar moved his ship above the hull, and Mati began pounding the exposed drive spaces.

Zaradej sprayed the approaching ABPs, then rolled. Dhar pulled *Reena* into a slide to maintain his position, but the raider had already unmasked its projector. A continuous burst raked along the M-1's belly and the ship shuddered under the impact. The restraining field gripped the fragile cargo as the internal gravity shifted. Panels flickered pale green in overload. Dhar's fingers moved over the pads trying to strengthen his belly shield grid. With the weapons pod drawing extra energy, precious little remained for anything else. From the displays, the grid had suffered several backsurges, but the hull appeared intact. He glanced at Mati.

"The projector—"

"We took some damage, but we can still fire," Mati husked, collecting himself from the shock. He stabbed at the commit pad and a line of searing yellow ionization lanced at the rolling *Zaradej*.

In the tactical plot, *Terraton* and *Sheeva* were maintaining steady fire. He was amazed that *Zaradej* appeared not to have suffered damage. The M-2 barely matching it, and the M-1s appeared to be mere distractions, albeit dangerous ones. Dhar moved *Reena* closer to the raider to cover the approaching ABPs. As the assault craft punched through the raider's secondary shield, it fired directly at the starboard ABP and flipped it over.

One of Mati's bursts penetrated *Zaradej's* hull. Air gushed through from a tearing rend as the thin plating deformed and melted. Dhar prepared to move in closer when a beam from the second raider slammed into *Reena's* stern. The ship reared under the impact and the restraining field snapped on as the command deck suddenly went dark. Small blue sparks slithered over exposed equipment and the air smelled strongly of ozone. Display panels were protests of green and white as subsystems reported severe damage or went offline.

The ship bucked again and Dhar was thrown out of his seat. A flash of intense pain along his left shoulder, and light burst in his head.

* * *

"Nightwings!" Terr screamed as his left shoulder burned and the anguish made his stomach knot. "No!"

Even as the terror of losing his brother coursed through him, he pulled *Sheeva* into a tight arc to bring his projector to bear on the swooping raider. He could not allow it to close on *Zavian*.

"Cover him!" he snarled at Kieran.

Ears pricked high, Kieran grimaced in concentration and waited for the firing lock. As the enable pad lit bright brown, he stroked it lightly. At sixteen thousand talans, point blank range, and he grinned as the raider's shields flared around its projector housing. The raider didn't even slow down, returning a sweeping beam that made *Sheeva* shudder and the air crackle from the near-field effect. Small blue sparks jumped over the consoles.

Terr brought *Sheeva* above and behind the drifting *Reena*, shielding it from direct fire. Kieran's bursts deflected the incoming raider from its course, forcing it to go high over them, rotating to keep its projector exposed. Terr was tempted to close, but that would engage him in a duel he could not hope to win. He would also be abandoning his responsibility to the attack force. Grinding his teeth in frustration, he worked to reacquire situational awareness.

Osinara and one of his ABPs were latched against *Zaradej's* hull. The third assault craft checked its tumble and moved slowly toward the raider. Razzo's ABPs were standing off as ordered. The crusty old chief probably not too happy about that, but Terr was adamant. He could not commit all six ABPs against a single target. A matter of luck. Had *Terraton* decided to engage the other raider, Razzo's team would have gone into action first.

Suddenly the shields around *Zaradej* faded and vanished, the ship visibly slowing. In the tactical display, he saw an energy bloom flare beneath the raider's hull and *Terraton* stopped firing.

"*Terraton* to *Sheeva*," the Karkan commander hissed. "Target's shields are down and the projector is disabled. Engaging secondary target."

"Acknowledged," Terr said and followed the M-2 in the plot as it cleared the hull and boosted toward the other raider, firing. *Terraton's* commander had performed very well in the engagement.

"*Sheeva* to Force One, give me a sitrep."

Osinara's excited voice came through: "From Force One, have secured the engineering spaces and proceeding to *Zaradej's* command deck."

"Acknowledged. Force Two, proceed to engage the secondary target." That will make Razzo happy, Terr mused as he rolled the M-1 to cover the raider above him. Kieran fired immediately. "*Reena*, respond!" His fingers tightened above the comms panel. *Come on, Nightwings, answer!*

Rit!

The plot showed *Terraton* exchanging long bursts with the surviving raider, the shields of both ships flaring. Terr's weaker fire seemed to have little effect. The raider momentarily disengaged, then plunged directly at *Terraton*, firing a long burst into the warship's side. The M-2 staggered as its shields discharged in a cascade of flame. Point collapses allowed the ravaging beam to rake the exposed hull. The tough polymer ablated and glowed from bright yellow to searing white. The weakened material deformed and bulged from internal pressure, then blew out in a jet of escaping air.

The raider sheered off and streaked toward *Sheeva* as *Terraton* tried to stabilize its shields. Armored hull or not, at close range, Terr did not relish receiving direct fire from a more powerful projector, but the raider ignored him, flashing by to swoop on *Zaradej*. At three thousand talans the raider loosed a raking burst along its consort's already weakened hull above the drive spaces. With its shields down the hull vaporized almost instantly, venting jets of white atmosphere through the gaping rends. Kieran fired a sustained burst. The raider's shields shrugged off the bombardment as it maintained its assault on *Zaradej*.

The ravaging energy streams penetrated *Zaradej's* main drive reactor chamber and the containment field tore apart. Even with a disengaged drive, the residual fuel turned into plasma that added to the fury of the incoming beam. The antimatter chamber lining flashed into vapor and a runaway reaction instantly consumed the reactor housing. The sphere of energy expanded into a four-million-degree flash of consuming white light.

On *Zaradej's* command deck, Osinara staggered as the ship heaved under him. He heard a dull thump from below and the engineering panel went white. Immediately, an almost subsonic hiss became louder. He glanced at his leading petty officer and read death in his eyes. An instant of unbearable pressure, and he was enveloped in a blue-white corona. He didn't even have time to scream as his body flashed into plasma.

As the wavefront absorbed the less dense interior and hull, dazzling beams streamed out from the stricken ship, the skeletal frames were monetarily outlined a stark black, then *Zaradej* vanished. The expanding sphere swept over the two attached ABPs, vaporizing the enormously tough hulls like tissue paper. They were consumed before the assault craft's power cell containment field could fail and add its energy to the conflagration. The shockwave front reached the lone ABP of Osinara's force and its shields flared and the craft shuddered, then steadied. By the time the front's shell reached *Sheeva* the ship barely trembled.

Appalled at the cold-blooded decision by the raider to destroy *Zaradej* rather than have it fall into his hands, Terr grimaced as the realization hit him that Osinara and twelve assault marines were dead, including two pilots. The third ABP appeared to have survived, but its crew might be less fortunate. That would make it twenty-two so far. How many dead or injured in *Terraton*? How many more would it take before it ended?

Nightwings…

Thoughts of death and destruction flashed through his mind, tearing at him. He wanted to reach out for that raider and snuff him. Instead, he clamped his mouth and swung *Sheeva* to keep the raider from closing with *Zavian*.

The raider rolled to present its projector at the two Fleet ships and fired in quick succession…a mistake. A direct hit from *Terraton* penetrated its shields above the dome housing and burned through. Massive backsurges arced around the housing, discharging into the dome that tore through the containment seals and the delicate circuitry inside, effectively cooking the projector.

The raider broke off and immediately accelerated to half

boost to clear the datum point. Terr grinned savagely, sensing the raider pilot's intention to transit and escape, leaving no evidence behind of his assault.

"No, my friend, it will not be that easy," he muttered grimly and boosted after the fleeing ship. This is where the M-1 held the tactical advantage. Almost as fast as an M-4, at full military boost, *Sheeva* swiftly closed the range. Terr needed to close quickly with the raider and had three seconds at most before the raider brought up its precursor. *Terraton* maintained relative position, the hole in its side apparently not interfering with its fighting effectiveness.

In the tactical plot, a fuzzy ring sprang around the fleeing ship.

"Target's power profile showing activation of primary drive systems. Detecting distortion field precursor modulation," the computer announced calmly. "Range, forty-six thousand talans. Optimum firing point in two seconds."

"Firing!" Kieran shouted immediately.

The first burst dissipated before reaching the raider, but subsequent bursts rippled along the raider's secondary shield grid. The energy surge disrupted the fluctuating force lines of the field precursor. It destabilized and failed. The raider pilot attempted to bring the field up again, but Terr's fire collapsed it.

Terr brought the M-1 to nine talans separation off the raider's port side and tapped a comms pad.

"*Terraton*, close to fifteen talans and fire a single max yield burst into its aft side."

"Acknowledged."

The M-2 swooped in and fired without ceremony. The raider's shields flared in point collapses and the exposed hull glowed and ruptured. Plating tore open along an eleven kata-lan seam and air vented through the gash. The raider had given up trying to transit, still plowing along at half boost. Tired of the game, Terr touched the general frequency comms pad.

"Raider Pilot, you are ordered to drop your shields, assume neutral status and surrender your ship. If you resist, I will destroy you in place." Without waiting for a response, he tapped another commas pad.

"Force Two, your ETA to close with me?"

"Be with you in six minutes, sir," Razzo's cheerful growl throaty with anticipation. The cold-blooded destruction of *Zaradej* had shaken everyone.

"Very well. Close and penetrate. Your objective is to neutralize the drive spaces and command deck."

"Acknowledged."

Terr could stand off and pound the raider into a drifting hulk, but he needed the ship intact. He also needed prisoners. A riddled dead hull just wouldn't do. Even if the raider stopped, Terr would never consider boarding it. Dashing around with a needler in his hand only looked good in a matinee thriller. Also an excellent way to get one's self killed. For this, he wanted Razzo and his armor-suited assault grunts. His threat to destroy the raider genuine, but it would be an action of last resort. He needed it in one piece.

The raider slowed to a stop and its shields dropped.

Terr tapped the comms pad. "Deactivate your primary and secondary reactors," he ordered and glanced at Kieran. "Tell me when they're down."

"Coming down now, sir," Kieran said, still ready to fire into the raider. The tension of the last few minutes began to ebb and he sagged slightly in his seat. For a while there…

"Mr. Kieran!" Terr bellowed and Kieran jumped in startled astonishment.

"I need you sharp and frosty, Mister! You'll have time to daydream when this is over, understood?"

Kieran flushed, ashamed at his lapse in duty. They didn't have the raider yet.

"I apologize, sir," he mumbled, not daring to look at his

commander. "It won't happen again."

Terr nodded and slapped him on the back. "I know. Just keep your finger on that commit pad, okay?"

"Yes, sir," Kieran said and managed a weak grin.

Terr turned away and smiled. Kieran wasn't about to forget this in a hurry and the warning serious. It took one momentary distraction, a forgotten detail, and you were dead. He cleared the nav bubble.

At nine talans the raider barely visible, the light from Ha-ram'an too weak to see by this far out. His eyes automatically scanned the plot. Razzo's ABPs were boring straight in. At four hundred talans the assault craft slowed and moved purposefully toward the raider. Terr wondered what the raider pilot thought about right now. Ready enough to take out *Za-radej*, but not so keen to go out in a blaze of glory himself. What did that tell him about its commander? He didn't bother wasting time moralizing. The situation too complex for that. The ABPs looked tiny beside the dark drifting hulk. Two of them clamped on low near the engineering spaces, the third went high, all of them on the same side of the ship.

It was a long eleven-minute wait before Razzo reported.

"Force Two to *Sheeva*, the ship is secure."

"Very well, stand by for my dock. *Terraton*, maintain position."

"Acknowledged."

Terr allowed himself a small sigh. Even with armored suits, boarding a hostile ship was always chancy. The fact Razzo hadn't reported casualties, at least not among his men, probably meant the raider pilot had simply surrendered. Short of self-destruction the loss of his offensive capability did not leave the raider with too many palatable alternatives. High politics notwithstanding, few men were willing to end it all in a senseless death. Well, it would not be all that senseless if they managed to take *Sheeva* out as well.

The M-1 drifted slowly toward the looming raider and

rotated to bring its access tube to match with the flashing docking ring. The tube slid out quickly and mated with a silent clang. Terr turned to Kieran.

"As soon as I board, I want you to withdraw to five talans."

"But, sir—"

"Don't argue. Just do it."

"Aye, sir." Kieran not happy letting his commander walk into danger, but he could not very well disobey a direct order.

Terr stood up and strode to the cable-tube hatch. On the main deck, he cycled the access hatch and walked through. A single pad glowed brown on the right side of the raider's lock. Terr touched it. The lock cycled and a petty officer on the other side stood to.

"I will take you to the command deck, sir," he growled good-naturedly.

Terr looked around the large hold. Apart from Re Nette's ship, he never had an opportunity to see the inside of an armed auxiliary. A small difference in lighting, but the hold could have been in any ship. He followed the marine to the cable-tube.

"Any trouble?" he asked and the marine smiled.

"I looked for it, sir, but it was sad. They didn't even raise a finger. Too bad," he murmured and stroked his worn rifle.

Terr's mouth twitched. Regrettable that the Serrll Combine was not in a position to employ all their marines in combat situations. Then again, maybe not all that regrettable.

The tube hatch opened and he stepped through. Razzo and two of his marines held four raider crew covered with rifles. They were all Palean. One of them stepped forward and Terr felt a shock of recognition.

"Kai Tanard!"

"Well met, young Terr," the scarred Palean rasped and a faint smile tugged at the left side of his face. He reached into his tunic, pulled out a needler, leveled it, and fired.

* * *

A moment that transcended reality and time ceased. The First Scout stood frozen, his deep gray eyes beginning to register astonishment. Tanard felt a glow of satisfaction as his gaze swept over Terr. He was right in his assessment. The youngster exuded a presence, that indefinable something that would immediately identify him as a commander in any crowd. They were a kindred spirit, and Tanard regretted keenly that fates had chosen them to walk different paths.

Ignoring the two assault marines and their extended rifles, he slid his hand into his tunic. The feel of the needler's grip a comforting weight. He drew the weapon slowly, expecting to die, but the figures before him were statues and he seemed to have an eternity of time. He didn't mind giving up his life all that much. He sacrificed everything else for the Provisional Committee and the cause. Too late, he recognized the flawed nature of his loyalty to an ideal that meant nothing to the faceless men on Captal, intent on gaining personal power only. The Alikan Union Party merely a cloak that legitimized their operation. His own efforts have failed, but he liked to think the idea of a union was now planted and that Paleans in general may nurture it yet, even if he wasn't going to be around to see it flower.

Of all the unpleasant things his struggle forced him to do, the innocent lives he destroyed—was anyone ever innocent in a war—he genuinely regretted having to do this one last thing.

You were a worthy opponent, friend Terr, but you're just too good to live.

He leveled the weapon at Terr's chest and began to squeeze the contact. He could see Terr only now realized his predicament, but too late. As the contact closed, Tanard saw the burly assault chief fling himself across Terr as the needler fired, astonished to see such a powerful man move so fast.

Against the Gods of Shadow

The fine collimated white beam struck the chief's armor beneath his left armpit, melted through, and burned its way into the body. The chief's movement caused the beam to slice across his side, cutting away flesh and bone and his outstretched left arm. The chief grunted from shock and searing pain and slammed heavily onto the deck.

One of the marines standing guard hesitated, unable to believe the Palean had actually pulled a weapon. Instinct and training took over. His rifle twitched and he fired a split second after the needler went off. Its beam lanced through Tanard's gun arm and sheared it off below the elbow. The hand, still grasping the needler, fell to the deck with a meaty thump. One of the Paleans gasped, doubled over and retched.

Tanard saw the rifle glare and felt a numbing shock in his arm. The severed nerve ends protested with fire and waves of hot agonizing pain shot through his shoulder. A blinding light burst in his head and he cried out. He staggered and fell to his knees, clawing at the burned stump of his arm. Warm blood pulsed between his fingers. The marine slowly walked to him and without emotion, kicked away the needler and the attached hand. *The scum dared threaten his commander?*

Terr twisted his mouth and grimaced at the sudden powerful stench of burnt cloth, flesh, and blood. He spared a single glance at Tanard, then quickly knelt beside Razzo and gently turned him on his back. There was an awful lot of blood everywhere, mostly from Razzo's arm. A large gash went right through the major muscles and Terr wondered if the beam had completely cut the bones.

"A damn silly thing to do," Terr told him gently and Razzo grinned.

"Yeah, I should have let him shoot you. My fault...didn't check if the bastard was armed."

"Don't talk," Terr said and looked up at the cowering Paleans. "You have a medic?"

Winn didn't feel steady and wondered if he would lose it

like Railee. He stepped forward, glancing nervously at the marines and their leveled rifles.

"Sir, I am Winn, first officer—"

"Get some emergency first aid here!" Terr snapped at him.

Winn recoiled at the fierce intensity of the first scout's voice, then turned to the comms panel. He gave brief terse orders.

Terr tore off his zip-jacket and wound the material around Razzo's arm. The chief groaned, but didn't cry out. At least it helped to stem the flow of blood. Terr looked down at Tanard and his eyes flickered at the stump of his arm. Sweat beaded down Tanard's forehead as the Palean met his eyes.

"You should have killed me, friend Terr," he gasped through gritted teeth. "As one brother officer to another."

Terr's mouth tightened. "You betrayed your uniform and the Fleet you served. You have no right to call me a brother."

Tanard smiled. "The uniform merely hides our darker side."

"No matter what the cause, you didn't have to do it like this!"

"Ah, my young friend, if you only knew."

"You should have vaporized your ship, like you did with *Zaradej*. It would have been better for you."

"Dying is the easy way out, friend Terr," Tanard muttered and slid to the deck, still clutching the bleeding stump of his arm.

The cable-hatch tube opened and two Paleans hurried in carrying bags. Terr motioned them to Razzo. One of them hesitated, his eyes flickering to Tanard. Terr stood up. Blood soaked his trousers, tunic, and hands. He shoved his face at the first medic and stared hard at the Palean.

"You treat the Chief now or I'll have you burned down where you stand!"

The Palean didn't say anything, but both immediately

knelt beside Razzo.

Terr turned to the petty officer standing behind him.

"Clear the prisoners off the deck. Put them all in one of the holds and mount a guard. Shoot anyone who even blinks."

"Aye, sir!" The petty officer smiled and pointed his rifle at the three raiders. "All right, you! Into the tube! You two," he motioned to the other marines, "fall in behind them."

The deck cleared quickly and Terr again knelt beside Razzo.

"How're you doing, Chief?"

Razzo grinned, coming out more as a grimace. "I'll trade places with you."

Terr nodded and looked at the medics.

"It's messy," one of them said, "but it looks worse than it is. A lot of muscle is cut, including two ribs. His arm is a problem. Even with regeneration and genotherapy, it's unlikely he'll regain full use of it." The medic glanced at Tanard. "Ah, may I…"

"Of course," Terr said absently, not taking his eyes off Razzo.

The chief out of it now, end of a career. What would he do? Being a marine was probably all that Razzo knew. Terr stood up. Razzo had become his responsibility now and he had to do something to secure his future. The chief wasn't going to have a future if he didn't get expert treatment and quickly. Terr strode to the display panels, located the tactical plot and touched several pads. Satisfied, he leaned over the comms console.

"*Zavian*, this is First Scout Terrllss-rr."

"It took you long enough, Mister!" the Master Pilot's unmistakable gruff voice came through. "I was beginning to think you'd forgotten us."

"Not likely, sir. I'm about to have my units dock on you. Please have your medical team standing by."

There came a moment of silence. "I saw what that raider

313

did to one of its own. I hope you got the bastard."

"We got him."

"Okay, son. We'll be ready."

"Thank you." Terr cut contact and reset the pads. "*Terraton*, report status."

"*Sheeva*, I am tactical capable. There is a major breach on my hangar deck and I lost a man there. Three wounded, nothing serious."

"Very well. The raider is secure and we have casualties. Have an engineer, two deck watchstanders, and four skeleton crew stand by to man the raider. You will proceed to recover Force One ABP, then dock with *Zavian* and transfer your wounded."

"Acknowledged and understood."

Terr touched another pad. "Mr. Kieran?"

"Is everything all right, sir?"

"Dock immediately and have one of the marines bring you to the command deck."

"Aye, sir."

The medics placed the unconscious Tanard onto the command couch. A crude gauze pad covered the stump of his arm and the severed hand sealed in a sterile bag. One of the medics looked up.

"He's out, shock. I imagine *Zavian's* facilities will be first-class. We may be able to reattach his arm, but the sooner we get him there the better."

"How is Razzo?"

"The Chief? He's comfortable. I've given him a shot of tailored nanobods to ease his pain and start the regeneration process."

Terr clenched his teeth and his cheek muscles jumped from tension. He nodded reluctantly to the medic. He may be raider scum, but he had done him a service.

"Thank you," he said coldly.

The tube hatch opened behind him and Kieran walked

in. He looked around curiously, then paled when he saw Tanard and Razzo.

"Holy gods!" he murmured, then gaped at the blood on his commander's uniform. His ears pricked high. "Are you all right, sir?"

"You will command the raider, Mr. Kieran, and take her to Anar'on. First, dock with *Zavian* and transfer the wounded. *Terraton* will have a watch crew ready for you."

Kieran's ears turned red and his eyes sparkled. Only then, he noticed the stench of blood and burned flesh and his nose wrinkled.

"And you, sir?"

"I need to check on Mr. Dharaklin," Terr said absently and walked to Razzo. He looked down and smiled.

"I hate to run out on you like this, Chief—"

"Go! I'll look after Mr. Kieran."

Terr bent down and lightly touched Razzo's good shoulder, then abruptly stood up and walked into the tube.

"Ah, sir." Kieran coughed behind him and Terr turned. "Pardon me, your uniform…"

Terr glanced at the drying blood on his working grays and grinned. "I'll clean up," he said and the hatch hissed shut.

Inside, he leaned against the bulkhead and closed his eyes. The image of Tanard raising his needler and Razzo throwing himself into the line of fire would stay with him forever. The cold data part of him blamed Razzo for not searching the prisoners, but he thrust the thought aside. Merely one of the cusps in life, and it was over. There would be no more deaths, not for a while.

The four marines guarding the access hatches on either side of the hold looked startled when the bloody figure stepped out of the tube, then stood to.

"*Sheeva?*" Terr demanded and one of the marines pointed at a hatch. He hurried through.

In the M-1, he sealed the hatch and retracted the access

tube. On the command deck, he gave the displays an automatic scan and lowered himself onto the couch.

"Computer, report *Reena's* status."

"Drive reactor is in standby mode. The shield grid is down. Structural integrity unknown. Have not detected debris or atmospheric venting."

"Execute a max secondary boost to *Reena* and attach."

"Acknowledged."

Sheeva immediately backed away from the raider, rotated and boosted. The range closed rapidly. Not daring to think what he would find, Terr felt his stomach knot and his mouth go dry. He felt his face drain and his body turned cold. He took two deep breaths, which only made him nauseous.

"Nightwings…"

He cleared the nav bubble and squinted anxiously, trying to spot the other M-1. It appeared suddenly and rushed at him, making him pull back involuntarily. Not a normal way he would have made an approach, but the computer's reactions were much faster than his. *Reena* almost on top of him, *Sheeva* slowed and rotated as the computer maneuvered the ship into a docking position. The stars stopped wheeling and the deck silent.

He hesitated, his mind filled with all the possible horrors that could suddenly turn into numbing reality. Steeling himself, he let out a loud breath and got up.

At the end of the access tube, he touched a glowing brown pad and the hatch slid away. The lower deck identical to his own. He fought off a second of disorientation. At least life support seemed to be working.

The hatch opened to the command deck and he paused before stepping through, drinking in the tall figure standing before him. Dhar smiled faintly and Terr felt a surge of heat flash through him. More than anything, he had a sense of overwhelming relief, and the crushing weight in his chest dissolved into euphoria.

"Nightwings," he whispered. His eyes shone with joy and his heart soared. The next moment, he hugged his brother, head buried in Dhar's broad chest. "Thank gods! I was beside myself with worry," he mumbled, drinking in Dhar's smell, feeling his brother's powerful arms around him.

After a time, he pulled back and gazed into Dhar's orange eyes. A rush of love and affection coursed through him and he blinked away the sting in his eyes.

"The fates seemed to have smiled on both of us," he said gruffly, even as Death settled on him and small blue sparks crackled over his body.

Dhar laid his open palm against Terr's chest and blue fire slithered along his arm.

"All is well, Sankri," he said softly and the blue glow grew and brightened, enveloping them both.

Content that his brother lived, nothing else mattered. All that ever mattered. The sick dread of loss gone, Terr basked in the glow that made them one again. Then the fires died, but the bond between them burned strong.

"I'm sorry, Nightwings. I couldn't come earlier," Terr started, then saw the angry bruise that ran down Dhar's forehead and cheek. "You are hurt!"

"It is nothing, Sankri. I was thrown out of my seat and the deck got in the way," Dhar said easily and Terr grinned.

"You always did have a hard head."

"I hope that's not your blood on the uniform."

Terr grimaced. "It's Razzo. He took a hit when Tanard tried to kill me—"

"Our Tanard?"

"The same."

"By the look of all that blood—"

"It's bad, but Razzo will live. They've taken him to *Zavian*, and that will include you!"

"I am all right, truly."

"Get checked out anyway. Is *Reena* flight capable? Can

317

you dock the ship? I can have *Zavian* come here."

"The mains came up a few minutes ago and we can transit. The secondary is online."

"Where is Mati?" Terr demanded and looked around the deck.

Dhar's eyes clouded.

"What happened?" Terr insisted, fearing the worst.

"When the raider made his second pass the shields went and the restraining field failed. Mati landed against the bulkhead and broke his neck."

Mati, a most promising young officer. Another death to atone for.

"The computer initiated the autonomous diagnostic and repair cycle, but we lost voice comms. I watched you take the second raider in the tactical plot."

Terr looked deep into Dhar's eyes. "The thought of you gone…"

"We will have time to talk later, Sankri," Dhar said, his voice rough with emotion.

Chapter Ten

Anar'on shifted ponderously above them as *Zavian* made its approach. In full sunlight, the planet swirled in yellows, reds, and browns. Even from space, it looked like a desolate and harsh world. Leaning back in his seat, Terr watched as Anar'on filled the nav bubble. After three days of writing reports, checking the wounded, and reliving through the action over and over, he finally felt peace. Warmth stole through him that started from his middle and slowly spread through his body. A feeling akin to religious satisfaction. It happened every time he approached Anar'on, a welcome that came from the world itself. Time did not exist. There were no tomorrows, only the now. He allowed himself a few moments to savor the sensation.

There were few onlookers hanging about when the three ships came down. The liner dwarfed the raider and the M-2. The fierce afternoon sun glared from an amber sky and made the air twist and sway above the landing apron. A misty fog hung above a topaz sea—wispy clouds that evaporated and reformed constantly. Kanarath rarely saw rain, perhaps once or twice a year. In the desert a wall of dark dust rolled across the sands. Between the city and the curving coastline, rectangular patterns of green and olive vegetation held the sands at bay. By outworld standards, Kanarath wasn't even a city. Nonetheless, at almost one million inhabitants, Anar'on's administrative center, and capital of the Kaleen group, Kanarath was a sprawl. The fabled hanging gardens were ribbons hung between buildings. Communals, combies, and cargo haulers crowded the sky.

Zavian squatted daintily on its landing ring next to the passenger end of the inter-star terminus. Two access tubes slid out from the terminal and connected. *Terraton* landed next to *Psandra* at the military end, the raider parked on the apron beside a large maintenance building. Three black Personnel Carriers raced toward the grounded raider. One of the hold hatches in its side split and retracted into the hull. A broad landing ramp protruded several katalans from the hull. The PCs slowed, then stopped and squatted on the apron. Armed assault troops piled out and stood guard around the ramp. The raider crew were herded onto the ramp and it slowly descended. They were hustled unceremoniously into two of the PCs, while the marines boarded the third. The PCs lifted and sped toward the terminus building, leaving behind a grim-looking squad facing away from the ship, their rifles held at port arms. Uncomfortable duty in the open sun.

When the nav bubble polarized, Terr stood up, placed both hands behind his back and stretched with a satisfied grunt. Dhar looked at him and smiled indulgently, the bruise on his face hardly noticeable. His shoulder still throbbed, but on the mend.

The Master Pilot snorted and pushed himself out of the command couch.

"The sooner I get you and your pirates off my ship, Mister, the happier I will feel. I would also appreciate if you could clear my holds of all that military clutter."

Terr grinned, faced the grizzled pilot, and stood to. "Sir, the Serrll Scout Fleet owes you a great debt—"

"Which I shall collect!"

"—and my heartfelt thanks. My special appreciation goes to your medical team."

"Just doing their job," the pilot growled.

The comms operator turned from his console. "Sir, the Naklanor Lines regional manager is in the access lounge demanding to see you."

"I bet he is," the pilot said and snorted.

The operator smirked and looked at Terr. "There is an

official delegation waiting for you too, sir. They are at the terminal entrance and would like to see you at your earliest convenience."

"Tell them I'm on my way."

The pilot shook his head. "Well, it's started. Bureaucrats! Bah! And you!" He fixed Terr with a hard stare. "Next time you feel like using my ship for target practice, I'll ram you. Now get out of my sight!"

"Thank you, sir!" Terr gathered Dhar with his eyes and made his way to the cable-tube.

"First Scout!"

Terr stopped in the hatchway and turned.

"Good luck, son."

"Yes, sir. Don't take any crap from that desk pusher."

"Hah!"

The terminal spacious and modern, floor-to-ceiling window panels opened to the city. Subdued lighting added to the feeling of coolness. Sculpted murals depicted reliefs of open deserts, towering red escarpments, and village life.

Flanked by two unobtrusive security types in mufti, the three Wanderers stopped talking when Terr and Dhar cleared the access tube. One of them a senior master scout and Terr winced. The action with Tanard left *Terraton* and the M-1s badly scarred. He did not imagine the master scout would be happy about that. The other two had that indefinable about them marking them as bureaucrats. Terr stood to, his boots making a hollow thump on the polished yellow stone floor.

"First Scout Terrllss-rr, reporting as ordered!"

The master scout gazed curiously at him, his deep orange eyes missing nothing.

"So you are Sankri," he rumbled softly, turned to Dhar, and nodded. One of the tallest Wanderers Terr had ever seen, the master scout pushed back his flowing hair and grinned, revealing even brown teeth. "At ease. I am Monsaratt. Allow me to introduce the Diplomatic Branch Resident, and

321

Ronowan, from Director Marrakan's office."

"I am to tell you, Sankri," Ronowan began smoothly, "that you and Resident Sakariwan have done an inestimable service to the Anar'on government and the Unified Independent Front. Not only for protecting the delegates, but also for foiling the Palean's plans."

Tired and short of sleep, Terr hoped this wasn't going to turn into a mutual congratulations party.

"My duty, sir. As for foiling any Palean plans, that remains to be seen."

The Resident shot Ronowan a scowl. "Ignore him, Terr. He's just a backward provincial. Let's get you to the Center. Prima Scout Anabb Karr is anxious to talk to both of you."

"The raiders—"

"Not your concern anymore," Ronowan said. "My government has taken jurisdiction."

Terr could imagine what that meant, probably nothing pleasant for Tanard or his crew. Well, he wasn't about to shed any tears over that. He looked at Monsaratt.

"I saw *Psandra*—"

"No longer yours, Mister. It belongs to the Fleet and you no longer work for the Fleet." He saw Terr's dismay and relented. "Sorry, I didn't mean it to sound that harsh."

The Resident sighed and shook his head. "Another provincial. Forgive his lack of tact, Terr. Shall we go?"

The two security types moved ahead of them, their eyes wary and vigilant. Terr did not expect to be jumped or anything, not here, but the type attracted the paranoid and the neurotic. Who would want to attack him anyway? He hadn't worked for Anabb long enough to have made such enemies. The likelihood that in the course of time he probably would, did not overburden him right now.

A solid wave of heat hit him as they cleared the terminal. It seeped through his tunic and into his bones. He fancied he could smell burnt sand and rock in the air. More likely, he smelled pollution. In the open, the sun struck him and he felt a tingle of forgotten sensations race through him at its burning touch. He squinted at the amber sky, peeked at Dhar and smiled. Life was good.

Monsaratt saw Terr's reaction and marveled. The tales were true. The boy was indeed one of them, an alien Saddishaa Wanderer. Incredible.

They piled into a parked combie and Monsaratt took the controls. Their security shadows were already aloft in another combie. The bubble closed and polarized and the lithe craft surged into the sky. A cold blast from the air-conditioner chilled the mood and Terr snapped back to reality. He glanced at the Resident at his left.

"Do you have any idea what Anabb is after?"

His head almost scraping the bubble, the Wanderer shrugged. "Probably ream you out for scratching his ships," he said with a straight face, but his eyes were full of humor.

Terr smiled. "That'll be right. Technically, though, they are *his* ships," he said, indicating at Monsaratt.

The Resident smiled. "So they are. Don't worry, I don't think *he* will ream you out for denting them."

"You don't know what a weight that takes off my mind."

The Wanderer chuckled. The boy had confidence and handled his power well. A depth of maturity hung about him that only facing Death and surviving its embrace can bring. He glanced thoughtfully at Dharaklin. What a unique combination these two made, brothers in the shadow of the same god.

The combie sagged in its turn as it swung on final approach toward one of the executive towers of the Center. The shadowing combie swooped over them and peeled away. Protruding from the sheer wall the landing ramp looked awfully small. The combie slowed and descended quickly.

They piled out and moved into the entrance foyer where a burly marine straightened his polished rifle and stood smartly to. Monsaratt led them to the tube.

"We'll do this in my office, Terr, then get you to your quarters," he said briskly. "You'll have time later to carry out a change of command."

"I am losing *Psandra* then?"

"Orders."

Terr felt a chill breeze of change as the enormity of the impact hit him. He was effectively out of the Fleet. Intellectually, he accepted the blunt fact when he agreed to join the Diplomatic Branch, but the emotional consequence of that decision only struck him now. He felt a door had slammed in his face—a door that previously always opened for him.

Monsaratt placed his hand on Terr's shoulder. "Do not be concerned, my brother. Your home will always be here when you choose to return."

Surprised at the Wanderer's gentleness and understanding, Terr nodded in gratitude. He looked at the Fleet as a family, a place where he belonged. Monsaratt's insight made him realize the Fleet merely constituted one life's path. He *was* home and his family here.

His ship…just polymer and ceramic.

He looked deeply into Monsaratt's eyes and smiled faintly. "You are right, my brother, and I thank you for reminding me."

The tube door hissed open and Monsaratt extended an open hand inside.

"Make yourselves comfortable." He took his own advice and sprawled into a loose beige formchair. Tall narrow windows provided a panoramic view of the city and the shimmering jade sea on the horizon. Behind the seats the Wall pooled through whorls of merging color. A simple, yet elegant office.

The Resident helped himself to a glass of purple cordial from a bulbous pitcher, sipped, and laid the glass on a small table with a loud click.

"This is not a debriefing, Terr," he said. "You will have

your fill of that over the next few days. You must know yours was not an ordinary Fleet operation, even though Fleet assets were used."

"Abused, I should say," Monsaratt murmured and the Resident shot him a look of annoyance.

"Capturing Tanard has turned out to be far more valuable than anyone realizes. His ship is evidence of Palean duplicity Captal and the Anar'on government can parade before the media. More importantly, Tanard and his crew represent a mine of invaluable information that will unmask what we learned is called the AUP Provisional Committee. That knowledge will expose the men behind this Committee and their network. It takes years to set up such an operation, as I know from personal experience," he said with a toothy grin. "It will take them a while to reestablish it. There, gentlemen, lies the damage. By the time they get a new organization in and effective, the United Independent Front will be ratified and beyond their reach. The Paleans and everybody else will have to deal with us on equal terms then."

"Why are you telling me all this?" Terr asked softly.

"That must be obvious," the Resident said.

Obvious, all right, Terr mused wryly. They wanted to re-cruit him to risk everything for another cause—again.

"Mr. Resident, I took an oath to protect and defend the Constitution and the Articles of Association. Call me naïve and simple, but I will do nothing to violate that oath."

"As a Wanderer—"

"A non-consenting conscript."

The Resident looked at him thoughtfully and pursed his lips. "Perhaps I was wrong in my estimate of you, Sankri."

"I'll live with the disappointment."

"You will not help us, then?"

"That's not what you asked. You're offering me a cabal whose role is not much different from this AUP Provisional Committee you're talking about. You cloak your pitch with patriotism. If that's all you're offering, try the next window. I believe in the cause and the goals of the Unified Independent Front. I don't believe its birth should be spawned from the same dark purpose driving Sargon and the Paleans. I understood the Discipline demanded a higher level of integrity. Apparently not." Terr stood up. "If you will excuse me, I need some fresh air."

"Please sit down," Ronowan said sharply.

Terr was about to tell them all to shove it, when he caught Dhar giving him a minute shake of his head. Reluctantly, he sat on the edge of his chair.

"You must excuse the Resident's rudeness and lack of polish, Sankri. Will you listen to me? As one brother to another?"

'You are all my children,' the words from the *Saftara* echoed in his mind and Terr relented. He would give them that much.

"I will listen."

"Thank you." Ronowan clasped his hands in his lap and leaned forward. "After the next general elections, the Unified Independent Front will make a petition to Captal for formal recognition as a political block. It is a formality and we anticipate the General Assembly will pass the motion without opposition. Until then, we're vulnerable, from everyone. Another seat held by the nonaligned independents is not something the major blocks view with relish, even Sofam, who nominally support us. The Paleans made a clumsy gambit to stifle us by trying to eliminate the delegates. The next attempt may be more professional and executed with a degree of finesse. There are many ways through which the UIF can still die. The Anar'on government is determined this will not happen.

"Keep in mind the Unified Independent Front is more than mere political opportunism to exert influence on the Executive Council. In a self-serving environment, one must develop defenses in order to stave off annihilation. The UIF is a defense mechanism for Kaleen, Orgomy and the surrounding independents against the predators who would absorb us. Admittedly the threat is only a political one, but freedom is a precious commodity even though the cage might be gilded. With the Discipline, no one could stand before us. That course, however, would lead us all to an even more terrible end, and an ultimate betrayal of everything we are.

"The Resident's attempt to sway you clumsy as it was crude. For that, I apologize. We all recognize you're a serving Fleet officer with new obligations and loyalties to the Diplomatic Branch. You are also a Saddish-aa Wanderer walking in the shadow of the god of Death, with the *Saftara* and the Discipline to guide your footsteps. No one is asking you to do anything, and you are answerable to yourself only. What I do ask is that you consider extending your loyalty to include our cause. Whatever you decide, your action will be respected. You must know not everyone shares our passion. This is true of Anar'on and others in the Kaleen worlds. If the UIF is to achieve recognition, it must be through voluntary participation and sharing of a common belief. Anything else will be hypocrisy."

Terr allowed the silence to linger between them, then shook his head and grinned ruefully.

"You make an eloquent and persuasive case for your cause, Mr. Ronowan, while boxing me into an emotional and guilt-ridden corner."

"I assure you—"

"Please, I wasn't criticizing. but admiring. Allow me to clear up a couple of points. Calling me a Saddish-aa Wanderer is a gracious gesture, but I fear inaccurate. Although I walk in Death's shadow, I meant it when I said I was a conscript. You attribute to me a lifetime of teaching and a depth of understanding of the Discipline I simply don't have. I'm still struggling to come to terms with what I have become. That path is already painful enough. I cannot walk another, not now."

Ronowan glanced at Monsaratt and the Resident, and nodded.

"I fear, Sankri, we may have been swept up in the moment and saw you as a valuable commodity, thus forgetting your needs and the needs of your spirit. In that, we have transgressed and I beg your forgiveness."

"If I have offended…" the Resident began.

"You have," Terr told him bluntly, then looked hard at Ronowan. "I don't resent your attempt to recruit me. On the contrary, I am flattered. What I resent is your automatic assumption that I share your singular needs. I suggest Anar'on may be committing the same transgression."

Ronowan's eyes widened and he jerked as if stung. "A disturbing thought, Sankri," he murmured slowly. "Disturbing indeed."

"And unlikely," the Resident said forcefully. "Nevertheless, it is an insightful observation."

Ronowan smiled and the Resident nodded, his eyes fixed on Terr.

"Perhaps one day, Sankri, you will choose to walk with us," Ronowan said. "And perhaps Director Anabb will come to regret his decision to draft you. Anyway, let's get you connected and see what he has to say."

* * *

Against a star-filled backdrop, Italan a gray, cratered crescent. The massive dark prow of an M-9 warship slowly swallowed the stars and obscured the asteroid. The scene shifted and expanded. Two colossal M-9s led a formation of four M-6s. Although similar in appearance and design—long elegant flattened ovals—the M-9s dwarfed their charges. Almost fifteen hundred katalans long the two ships did not mount projector domes. Along their centerline ran two parallel grooves that mounted the shield wave-guides and projector coils. The ships could fire multiple bursts in any direction from any point along the centerline. Unleashed, that power was irresistible.

As if on cue, both M-9s sent four lances of pale blue ionization at Italan. Each beam discharged 352 TeV of energy that instantly vaporized rock, metal, ices, and everything else into plasma, breaking down the atomic structure itself. Jets of yellow and orange ejecta plumed into space. The violent reaction released enormous nuclear binding energy as atoms split and reconstituted. Massive explosions tore jagged chunks from the asteroid, hurling them tumbling into space. After four minutes of continuous bombardment, only an expanding cloud of debris remained of Italan.

The ponderous starships faded, replaced by the anchorman's long grave features.

"That was two days ago and the mighty warships are now deep in Palean space, but it will take them another seven days to reach Palea. A similar force is on its way to Sargon's capital world Hakran, the Captal spokesman saying the clearest possible message must to be sent to Sargon and the Paleans. The government will not tolerate incidents such as Lemos and Italan blatantly ignore the Constitution. The show of force, the spokesman said, is meant to demonstrate Serrll's will to rise up against all who threaten its security.

"As we learned less than an hour ago, the executive government of the Palean Union has resigned and the Speaker of the Congress has formed a caretaker body. To discuss this dramatic development we have three prominent—"

Ed-Kani Takao tapped a pad on the inlaid console in his desk and stood as the Wall faded into a pool of merging colors.

"Pits and damnation!" he hissed and slammed his fist against the desk. He didn't need a dissection. He knew what the repercussions were better than anyone.

The fool had done it! Despite all the warnings from the Committee, Ti Inai could not stop himself from pursuing his singular agenda and ruined everything. *May he rot an eternity in slime!* Billions spent on Lemos, all wasted. Billions spent on Italan, all wasted. Years of planning and manpower used, also wasted. Worse, their strategy now exposed and Sargon's reputation tarnished, perhaps irretrievably. The Serrll populace had long memories and wouldn't forget easily.

If he had his way, Sargon would move in and simply annex the Palean Union. They would be getting rid of a fickle partner while consummating their merger, however forcibly. With the Fleet on the prowl, though, now impossible. They should have done it two millennia ago when the opportunity first presented itself. Now, of course, such tactics were unthinkable. Pity. It would have solved so many problems.

To the pits with Ti Inai and all Paleans.

The comms alert beeped.

"Yes?"

"They are here, sir," his assistant warned him.

Ed-Kani snapped his jaws. He got up and walked briskly into his private antechamber. The subdued conversation died and eight faces turned to look at him. Two women and five men, each a powerful figure whose words shaped Sargon and Palean destinies. One chair stood empty—Ti Inai's, recalled to Palea to help sort out the mess in their Congress. Perhaps better that way.

He appraised them, evaluating their strengths and weaknesses. Recent events have all too clearly magnified the Committee's weaknesses. Something would have to be done about that.

He walked to the long table and placed his hands on the back of his formchair. He nodded to the old Palean at the other end of the table.

"With your permission, Mr. Chairman?"

"You have the floor, Mr. Director," the elderly man piped and bobbed his head.

"Thank you," Ed-Kani said and looked at the faces around him. "We are in a crisis of identity," he began, speaking softly and evenly. "Once the current fallout dies down, some of us may no longer be here. So be it. What's important, we must refocus on our objectives and formulate strategies and tactics to see them achieved. We have revealed ourselves and the predators will be hunting. This is what I propose.

"First of all, damage control. The loss of Lemos and Italan has exposed a number of vital intelligence networks on Palea, Captal, and Hakran. These must be shut down and swept clean. It remains to be seen what damage has been done by capturing Kai Tanard, but I don't doubt it will be considerable. We can be certain the Unified Independent Front and others will make full use of any information he will supply. His links must be sanitized.

"That brings me to another and graver matter," he murmured and looked up. "The loss of Lemos an unfortunate culmination of incidents. However, there was nothing unfortunate about Italan. What Ti Inai did betrayed what we stand for, supported by his two accomplices who among us. Mr. Chairman?" The old man nodded. Ed-Kani tapped a pad on the inlaid console pad. The door panels hissed open and four hooded figures strode in, needlers held ready. Ed-Kani pointed at two startled individuals who suddenly sprang out of their seats.

"Don't move, gentlemen. Congressman Sid Kara and Pro-Consul Ke-Ravi, by order of the Chairman, for treasonous acts committed against the AUP Provisional Committee and the cause, you are hereby outcast and have no faces." The remaining members turned their backs. Ed-Kani nodded to the security types. Still in shock, the two men were escorted out. When the doors closed, Ed-Kani slowly looked around the chamber. He argued that Ti Inai should have been the one led away, but the Committee overruled him. The Palean scum simply too senior within the Committee, Captal, and the Palean Congress to be eliminated without serious political consequences. Ed-Kani picked Sid Kara to take Ti Inai's place as sacrifice. As for Ke-Ravi, the Pro-Consul had known of Ti Inai's plans and failed to alert the Committee. Ed-Kani didn't tolerate incompetence, promising himself, he and Ti Inai would meet another time to settle the score.

"Now that we've dealt with this minor unpleasantness, we need to address our next course of action. With your permission, Mr. Chairman, I open the floor to general discussion."

Epilogue

Limp and tired the long peelath branches overhead hardly moved in the furtive breeze. The air swam and shimmered above the dunes, dragging itself wearily beneath the pitiless glare of an amber sky. A dust devil swirled sand and debris around the yard and children ran shrieking chasing the vortex. The adults smiled and nodded indulgently. Tall muscular youths were making the long tables ready for the evening meal. Unpaired maidens flirted with them, their red headbands proclaiming their single status. The sandpits were dug up and the food containers, wrapped in peelath mats and leaves, were dusted off. Pleasant odors drifted in the air as the containers were opened and children crowded around the women hoping for a tasty morsel.

Still hot, the air had lost some of its heaviness, and the white sun now fat and red, and no longer burned as it hung suspended above the dunes. The last of the oark were herded into the corrals and poultry pecked through heaps of dried dung, clucking contentedly.

Terr took in the smells and the sounds around him and the memories of times gone crowded him. He tried to empty his mind, to forget, but peace eluded him. He brought with him the taint of outworlder life and he could not let go and abandon himself to the desert. He desperately yearned to be free. He yearned for release, to still the forces that stirred within him. He wanted to lose himself in the compelling simplicity of the Wanderer's lives, purely content to greet each day as it dawned. The fates were cruel and mocked him after playing him with largesse.

Restless, he wrapped his cloak about him and walked toward the setting sun.

Dhar felt helpless as he watched the retreating figure. He could hardly imagine what his brother must be feeling. Torn between the heritage of his old life and the way of the Discipline, Terr's thoughts in turmoil, he struggled to reach an equilibrium that would allow him to accept what he had become, and to glory in the gift from the god. Dhar had not thought Terr's inner torment would last this long or be such a painful one, and that torment seemed to manifest itself more strongly whenever he touched foot on Anar'on. Dhar may have given his brother life, but the price Terr seemed to be paying appeared inordinately heavy.

"Sankri is troubled, my son," a deep voice said beside him and Dhar looked at Sidhara.

"He has recently gone through much, master."

"As have you."

"Being here, I have found renewal. Sankri is unable to find that peace."

"A burden he carries, but he is also a Saddish-aa warrior and must rise to the challenge. It is only through conflict the spirit grows."

"That I could tread the path of thorns he now walks," Dhar murmured.

"We all cast our own shadow, and this, he must resolve himself, but you can comfort him."

"What am I to say that will not sound hollow or patronizing?"

"Say nothing. Your presence will be enough."

Sidhara's face hard and lined, his eyes were kindly. A lifetime of wisdom shone from those eyes. In a flash of insight, Dhar realized his master had never been off Anar'on. Wise he might be, but he acquired that wisdom in an environment that bore little resemblance to the life he and Terr led. He checked the thought and chided himself for his presumption. Surely as a Rahtir, one of the elders, his master must know all that.

He covered his eyes with his right hand in respect, turned quickly, and followed in Terr's tracks.

Dusk settled fast. Sand hissed beneath his footfalls. The

sun already sinking, left behind a purple sky. Terr sat on the crest of a dune, gazing into the desert. Dhar approached slowly. He stood beside the silent figure of his brother, then sat at his side. Terr made no move to acknowledge his presence. Breathing deeply, Dhar felt his tension drain and his spirit expanded to take in the growing darkness. Aware of his brother, yet not intruding, content to wait for the moment when Sankri wanted to share.

A hesitant breeze tugged at Terr's cape and the sands whispered to him. The desert still hot from the day's sun, but the heat cradled and didn't burn. The air rich with the oily scent of peelath, freshly cut tarad grass, of rock and sand, and the musty oark. They were smells of life and of the village behind him.

He tilted back his head and allowed his eyes to wander among the winking lights that made up the constellation of Amulran the Damned. Kneeling, holding up the bridge of the gods, the load grew heavier as more stars crowded the darkening sky. Terr pondered what it would feel like having to carry that burden for all eternity, hoping for relief when the arrow from his enemy pierced his heart. He turned his head slightly. The Stalker held his bow, already bent, ready to loose the arrow of doom that would end time.

Legend said, Amulran and the Stalker were brothers in blood and walked with other gods in the escarpment of Athal Than. A happy time and the Wanderers, children of the Saffal, were still innocent and not aware of the shadow of the god of Death beneath which they walked. Brothers they be, but a day came and Amulran wronged his brother, betraying his friendship with the Stalker. Enraged, the Stalker demanded his anger could only be slaked by the blood of his brother. As the world was young, death of either one would shatter reality and the gods were not predisposed to start over from the great nothingness. The Stalker knew what his demand meant, but he would not be swayed. He had a right.

The gods made a difficult choice. They hurled Amulran into the sky, his punishment to hold up the bridge of the gods. Should he fall, the heavens would topple into nothingness and eternity would end. So the gods froze him so he could not move. They gave the Stalker a bow and one arrow, and allowed him to kill his estranged brother. He could have his revenge, but it would also be the end of everything. If he could find it in his heart to stay his hand and forgive the wrong done to him, Amulran would be freed. Both would be freed.

Watching the bright stars with the Stalker still poised to loose his arrow, Terr wondered what the god must be thinking, seeing his enemy bent before him. He faced a cruel choice either way.

A nice story, but the Stalker was only a pattern of stars. A gust of hot wind stirred his hair and the sands whispered to him. Only a hint of purple remained in the west and night drew on her cloak.

"You did not wait for the evening meal," Dhar ventured beside him, his voice grave.

"I hungered for other food."

"And are you satisfied now?"

"I still hunger."

Dhar picked up a handful of warm sand and allowed it to trickle between his fingers. He noted the restlessness and coiled tension in his brother as Terr's foot stirred the sand.

"I feel the struggle within you, Sankri. What is troubling you?"

Terr chuckled. "What is troubling me? Having Death at my command is troubling me. The temptation to unleash it is a growing force inside me. I thought I became reconciled walking in Death's shadow, but now, I don't know if I can resist letting loose the lightnings. Would it be so wrong if I did use them?"

It would have been easy for Dhar to utter the dusty words

from the *Saftara*, but they did not seem to fit this moment. What Sankri sought was more than Dhar felt himself capable of giving, or knowing how to give.

"You alone can judge the right and the wrong of it—"

"That helps a lot."

Dhar winced and felt a growing helplessness and frustration. "Have you spoken to our master?"

"My son," Terr mimicked Sidhara's heavy, ponderous voice, "the exercise of power is a magnification of character, its littlest flaws and its greatest strengths."

"Do not mock the Discipline—"

"It mocks *me*!" Terr snarled, shrugged, and Death rode in his hands. He leveled his arms and blue lightnings flickered between them. A rumble of low thunder rolled across the dunes. "I don't want it!" he cried into the night and dropped his arms. The dunes echoed his anguish and Dhar searched for the right words to say.

"We add complexity to our lives and we remove it, my brother. Much of what we perceive as problems are merely products of our imagination, possibilities that might never eventuate. The Saffal is a demanding master and exacts a terrible tribute from those who fail to understand its ways. The Wanderers have learned to live in harmony with the desert by accepting its harshness and by taking a small measure of satisfaction and contentment from the tranquility and beauty it offers."

"And that's my problem, Nightwings. There are no sands in the deeps of Serrll space. Out there, there are moments of clarity where I can accept the fact that Death rides in my hand. Here, surrounded as I am by the desert, the gods crowd me and I fear to lose myself if I let go."

"You should embrace what you have been given."

"I cannot. It will devour me if I do. I'm being carried inexorably toward a destiny I cannot control. No matter what I do, I seem to be powerless to influence the course chosen for me by the gods. There is no free will."

"At the Center, Sankri, you said no to the Resident."

Terr grinned into the darkness. "So I did. In the greater scheme of things, did that decision, that exercise of free will, make a difference?"

"Do not mistake destiny for fatalism. Every journey has a destination, and life is the most challenging journey we face. At its end, we may be confronted by an even greater challenge. What is important is not what we bring with us, but how we gather and used it. It is the texture and density of our experiences that enriches the spirit—or not. In that, the choice is ours to make."

"That's the *Saftara* talking. What are *your* words?"

"My words? They *are* my words. I have lived my life with the words of the *Saftara* and the teachings of the Discipline. They speak truth to me."

Terr turned and searched the shadows that wrapped Dhar's face in darkness. He appreciated what his brother tried to do, but as a native Wanderer, Dhar could not truly comprehend Terr's inner struggle. For all his experience in the Fleet, away from Anar'on, Dhar remained trapped in a mindset that ruled the Wanderers.

"A parable for you then, my brother of the night," Terr said softly. "Have I made a fateful decision by joining the Diplomatic Branch?"

Oark stomped in the corral behind them and the breeze whispered to the sands.

"I cannot say, Sankri, no one can," Dhar said at length. "For me, life is very much like the shifting of the Saffal sands. The sands flow and the dunes move, but the desert remains the same. We live with the illusion that we shape our destinies, and in a sense we do, but at most what we leave behind are simply lines in the sand while the dunes carry us inexorably to whatever awaits us at our journey's end."

"Like Sargon and the Paleans, blindly playing out a dark

comedy."

"What do you mean?"

"Sargon is a concept, not an individual, and does not shape its own destiny. Sargon's populace works and dies to achieve their individual fates. Yet no matter what they do, they're powerless to influence the course chosen for them by this AUP Provisional Committee."

"Your point being?"

"As children of the gods, the Wanderers also seem free to shape their destiny," Terr said and waited. Dhar stared at him.

"An equally futile gesture, is that it? Are you saying the Unified Independent Front is carrying us toward a destiny that is not of our choosing?"

"What I'm saying, Nightwings, in the Resident, I have seen one face of the Rahtir Council and I didn't like it. Striving for power is always a dangerous thing, but not as dangerous as actually achieving it, regardless of the righteousness that underpinned the struggle."

"My brother, I would not judge the Council too harshly based on the actions of one individual."

"That's a lot of worm crap and you know it. An individual's actions are defined by the policies of the system that controls him. The Resident obviously felt the Council's policies gave him the latitude to bulldoze others to his cause."

"Perhaps, but if you note, Ronowan wasn't very impressed."

"Yeah." Terr hugged his knees. Low on his right, Aribus rose as a slender white crescent. Above them, the stars cut a thick swathe across the heavens.

Dhar picked up a handful of warm sand and allowed it to trickle between his fingers. Sankri was clearly troubled by the incident with the Resident. Could his brother be right? Had the Rahtir Council lost the link with its roots as the Unified Independent Front marched ponderously to sweep away all those who stood in its way? Dhar knew instinctively the power of inertia. Living within the shadow of Death demanded a never-ending exercise in restraint. Could that restraint be possibly slipping away from the Council? He could not believe it. No one questioned the wisdom of the Rahtir. What then? An individual rash action by the Resident?

The dunes carry everyone inexorably to whatever awaits them at the journey's end. Was Sankri talking about inertia?

"My brother, when you underwent your trial, the gods saw fit to bestow on you their gift. You cannot change what you have become. Torturing yourself will not make the gift go away."

"A gift is meant to be used, Nightwings. At Banard, if I were able, I would have blasted Tanard's ship out of space. I had the power. He meant nothing to me and it would have prevented the deaths and the pain. Shan would have his hands. Osinara and the others would have lived. Mati would have lived. The fact that I couldn't reach him without destroying myself and *Ramora* didn't diminish my desire to blot him out. Next time, my brother, I might not be able to stay my hand. That's the fear that tortures my days and haunts my nights. Tell me Nightwings, the shadow who walks at night. Should I embrace Death that walks inside me?"

Terr stood up and raised his arms.

"Do you hear me? I don't want to be a god!" he howled in despair, dropped his arms, and walked into darkness.

About the author

Stefan Vučak has written twenty-one novels, which include eight SF books in the Shadow Gods Saga. His *Cry of Eagles* won the coveted Readers' Favorite silver medal award, and his *All the Evils* was the prestigious Eric Hoffer contest finalist and Readers' Favorite silver medal winner. *Strike for Honor* won the gold medal.

Stefan leveraged a successful career in the Information Technology industry, which took him to the Middle East working on cellphone systems. Writing has been a road of discovery, helping him broaden his horizons. He also spends time as an editor and book reviewer. Stefan lives in Melbourne, Australia.

To learn more about Stefan Vučak, visit his:
Website: www.stefanvucak.com
Facebook: www.facebook.com/StefanVucakAuthor
Twitter: @stefanvucak

More Books by Stefan Vučak

https://www.stefanvucak.com/Books/

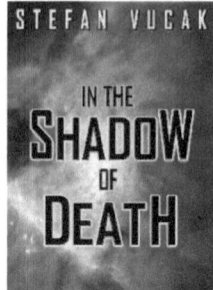